SWORD ART ONLINE GIRLS' OPS 003

ART: NEKO NEKOBYOU

ORIGINAL STORY: REKI KAWAHARA

CHARACTER DESIGN: abec

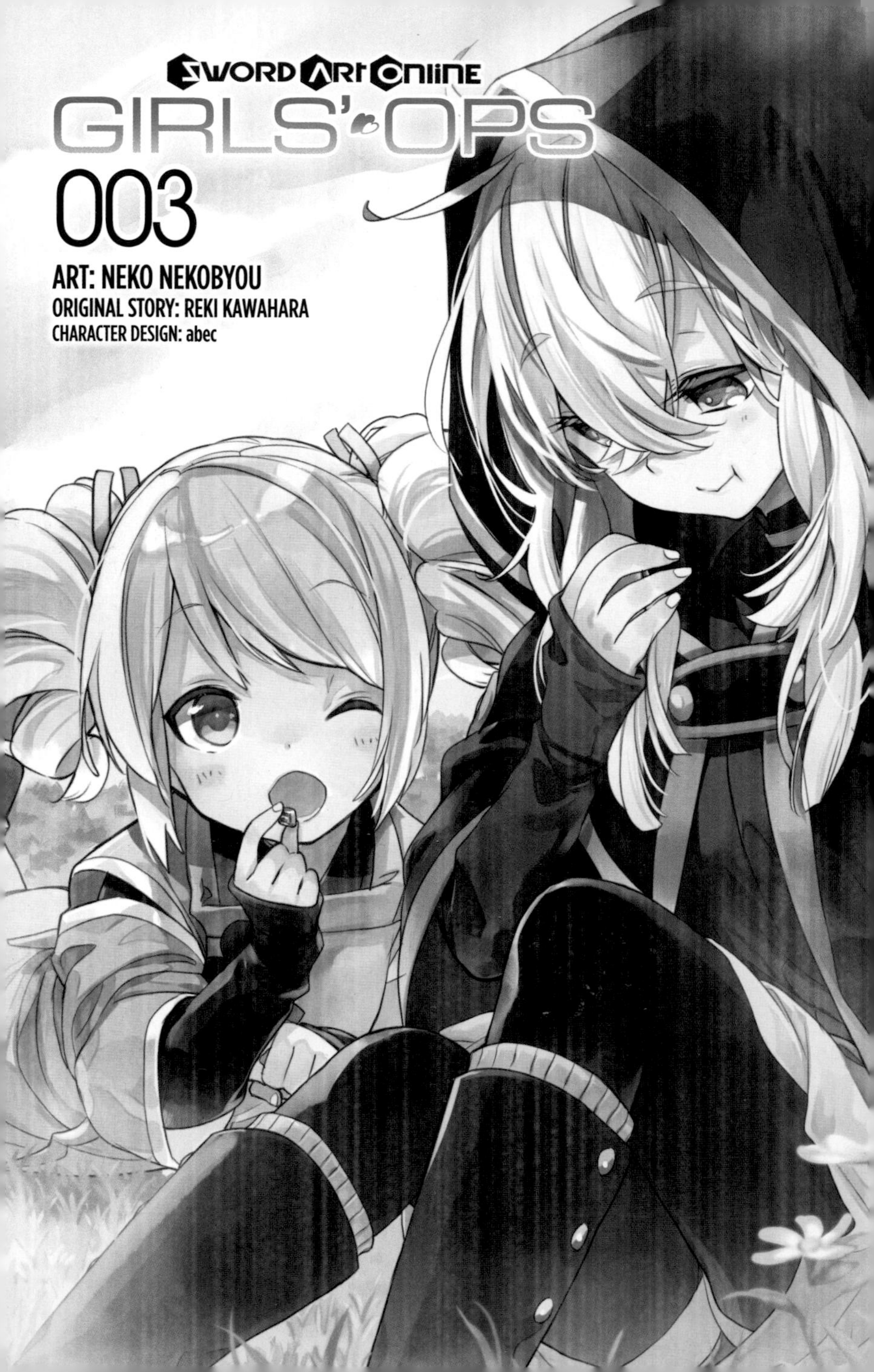

003

SWORD ART ONLINE
GIRLS' OPERATIONS

art: Neko Nekobyou
original story: Reki Kawahara
character design: abec

Contents

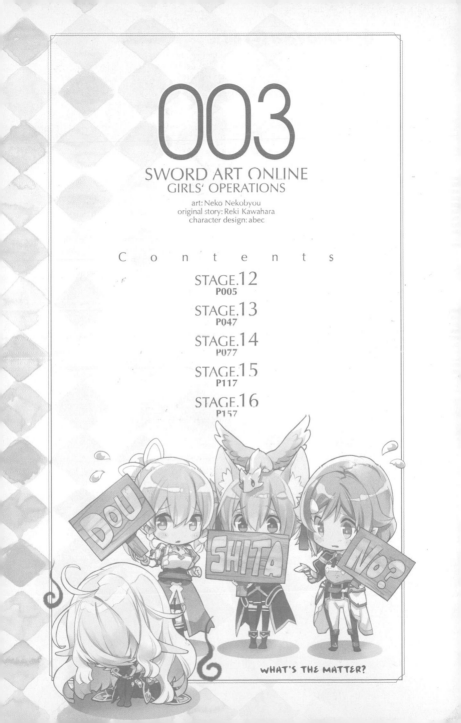

DOU

SHITA

NO?

WHAT'S THE MATTER?

SWORD ART ONLINE
GIRLS' OPS 003

SWORD ART ONLINE
GIRLS' OPERATIONS

ART: NEKO NEKOBYOU
ORIGINAL STORY: REKI KAWAHARA
CHARACTER DESIGN: abec

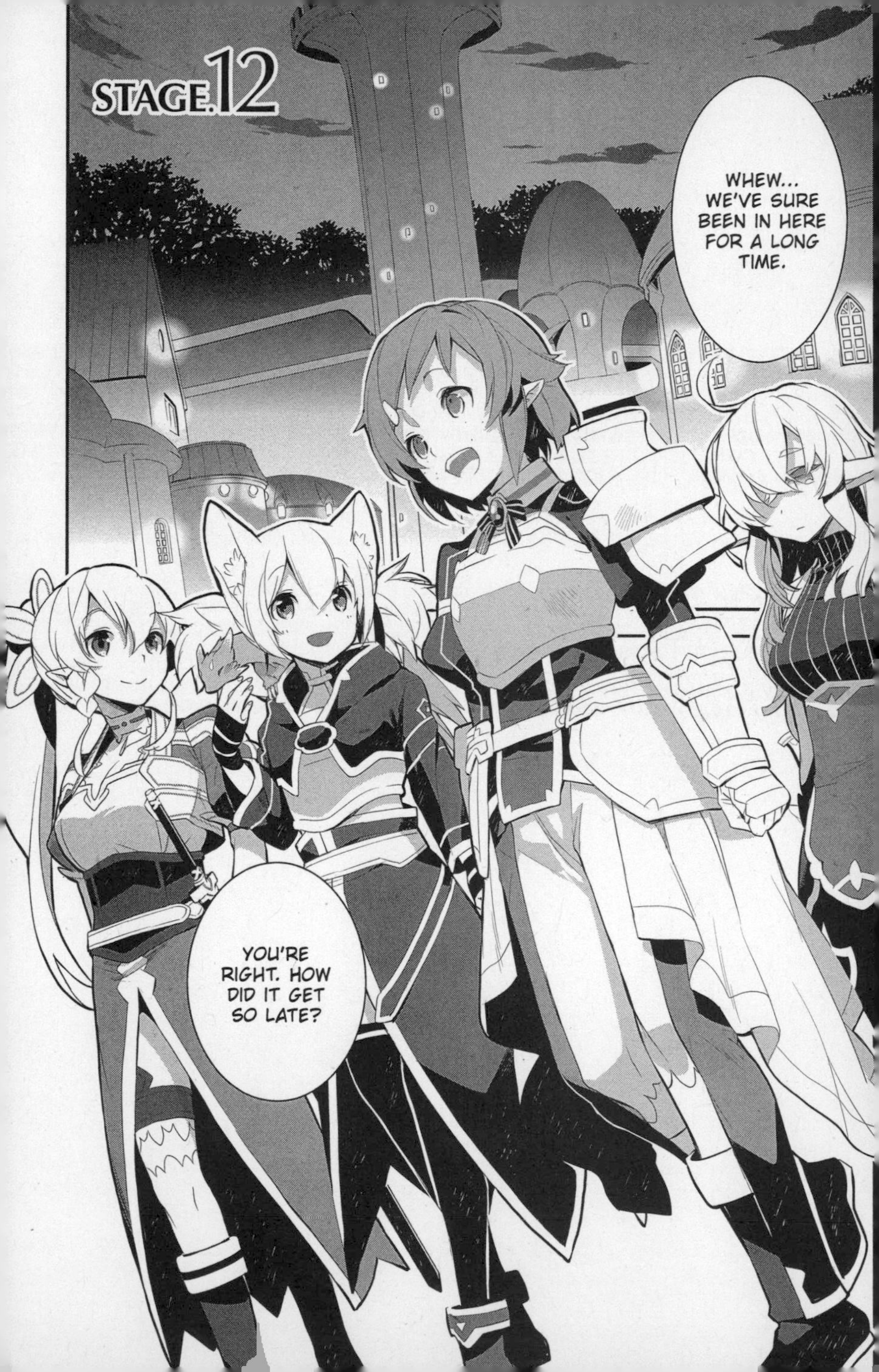
STAGE.12
WHEW... WE'VE SURE BEEN IN HERE FOR A LONG TIME.
YOU'RE RIGHT. HOW DID IT GET SO LATE?

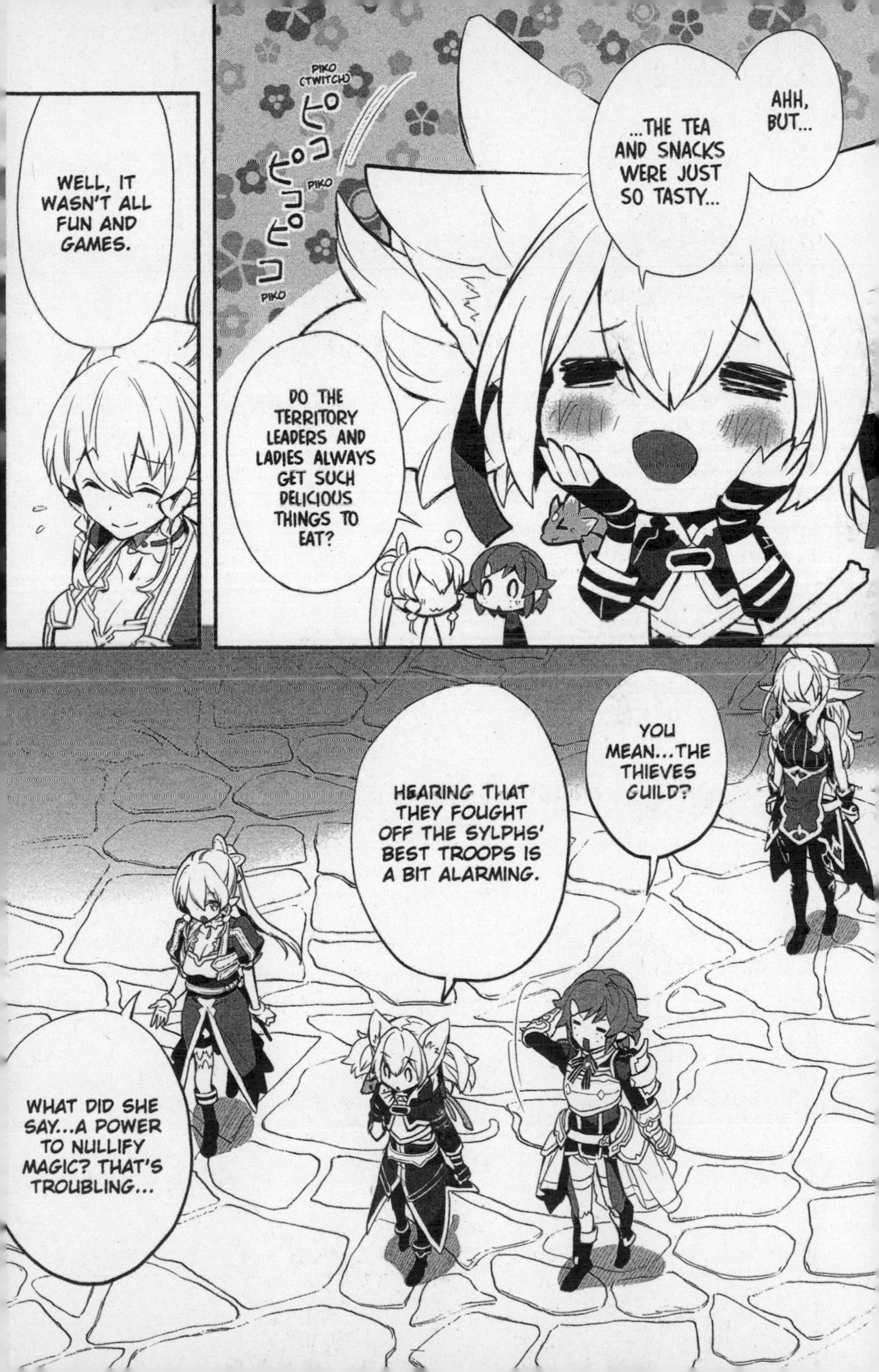
AHH, BUT...
...THE TEA AND SNACKS WERE JUST SO TASTY...
ピコピコピコ
PIKO (TWITCH)
PIKO
PIKO
DO THE TERRITORY LEADERS AND LADIES ALWAYS GET SUCH DELICIOUS THINGS TO EAT?
WELL, IT WASN'T ALL FUN AND GAMES.
YOU MEAN...THE THIEVES GUILD?
HEARING THAT THEY FOUGHT OFF THE SYLPHS' BEST TROOPS IS A BIT ALARMING.
WHAT DID SHE SAY...A POWER TO NULLIFY MAGIC? THAT'S TROUBLING...

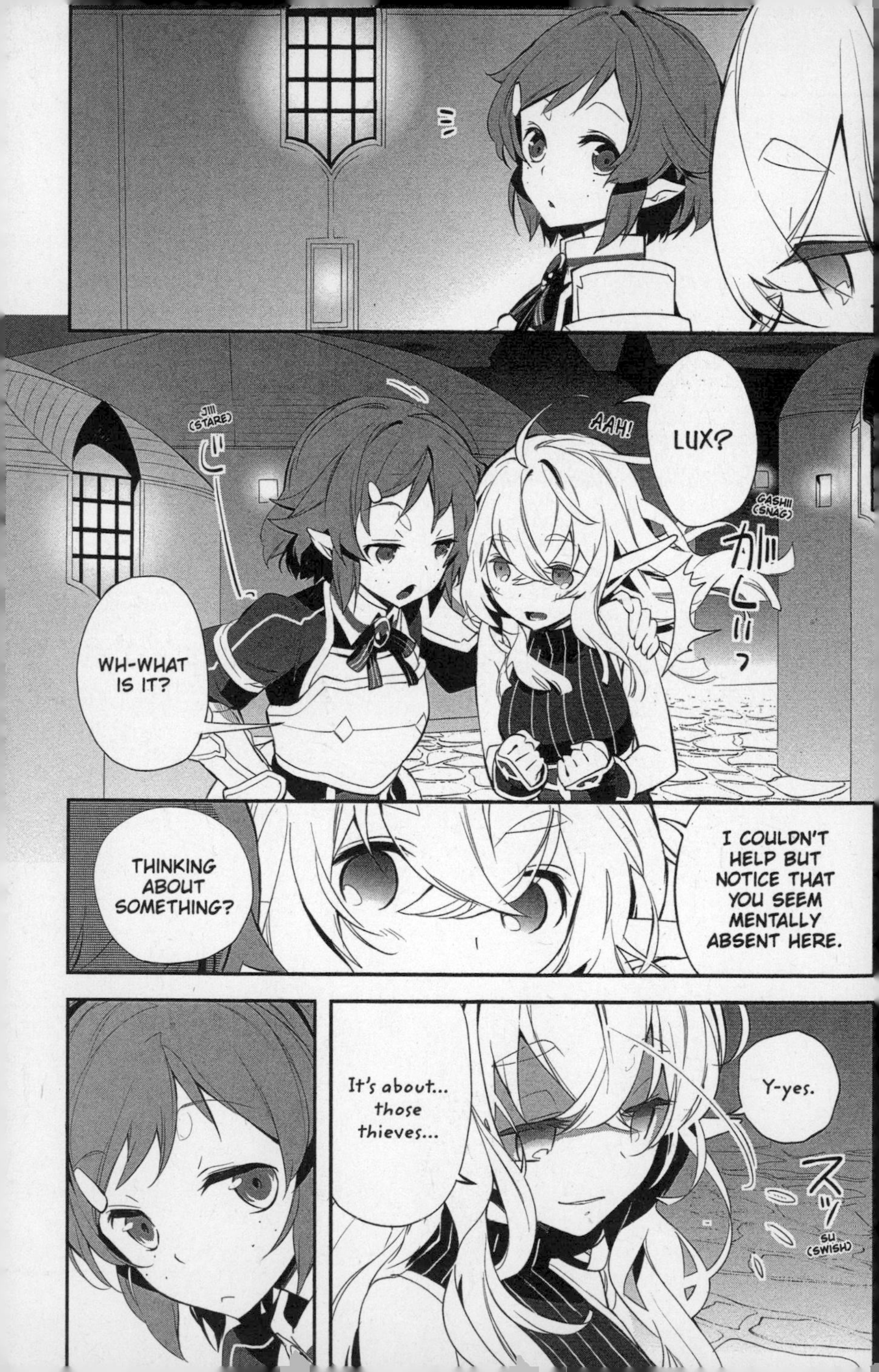
LUX?
AAH!
GASHII (SNAG)
ガシッ
JIII (STARE)
じー
WH-WHAT IS IT?
I COULDN'T HELP BUT NOTICE THAT YOU SEEM MENTALLY ABSENT HERE.
THINKING ABOUT SOMETHING?
Y-yes.
スッ
SU (SWISH)
It's about... those thieves...

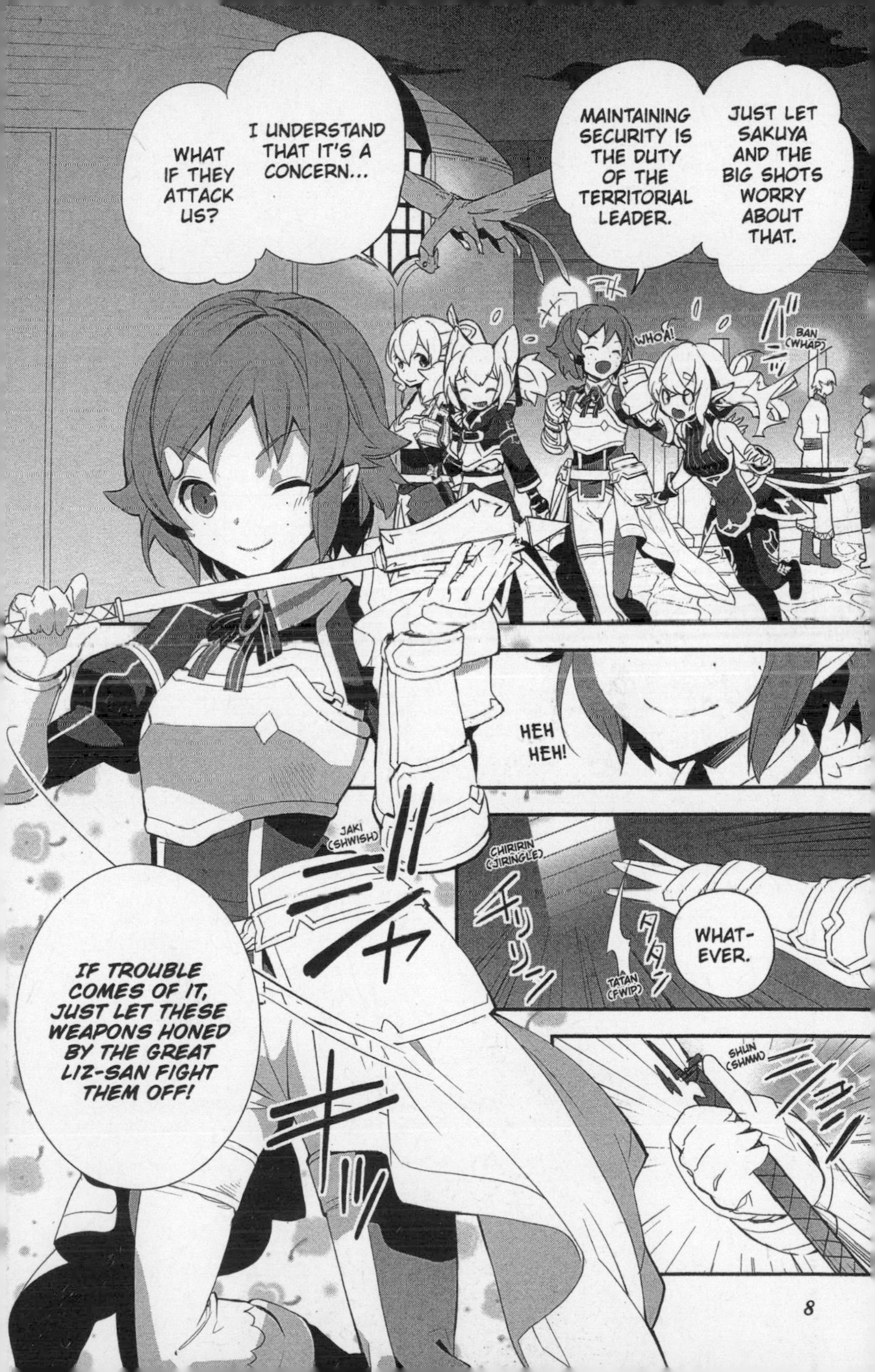
JUST LET SAKUYA AND THE BIG SHOTS WORRY ABOUT THAT.
MAINTAINING SECURITY IS THE DUTY OF THE TERRITORIAL LEADER.
BAN (WHAP)
WHOA!
I UNDERSTAND THAT IT'S A CONCERN...
WHAT IF THEY ATTACK US?
HEH HEH!
WHAT-EVER.
CHIRIRIN (JIRINGLE)
TATAN (FWIP)
SHUN (SHWM)
JAKI (SHWISH)
IF TROUBLE COMES OF IT, JUST LET THESE WEAPONS HONED BY THE GREAT LIZ-SAN FIGHT THEM OFF!

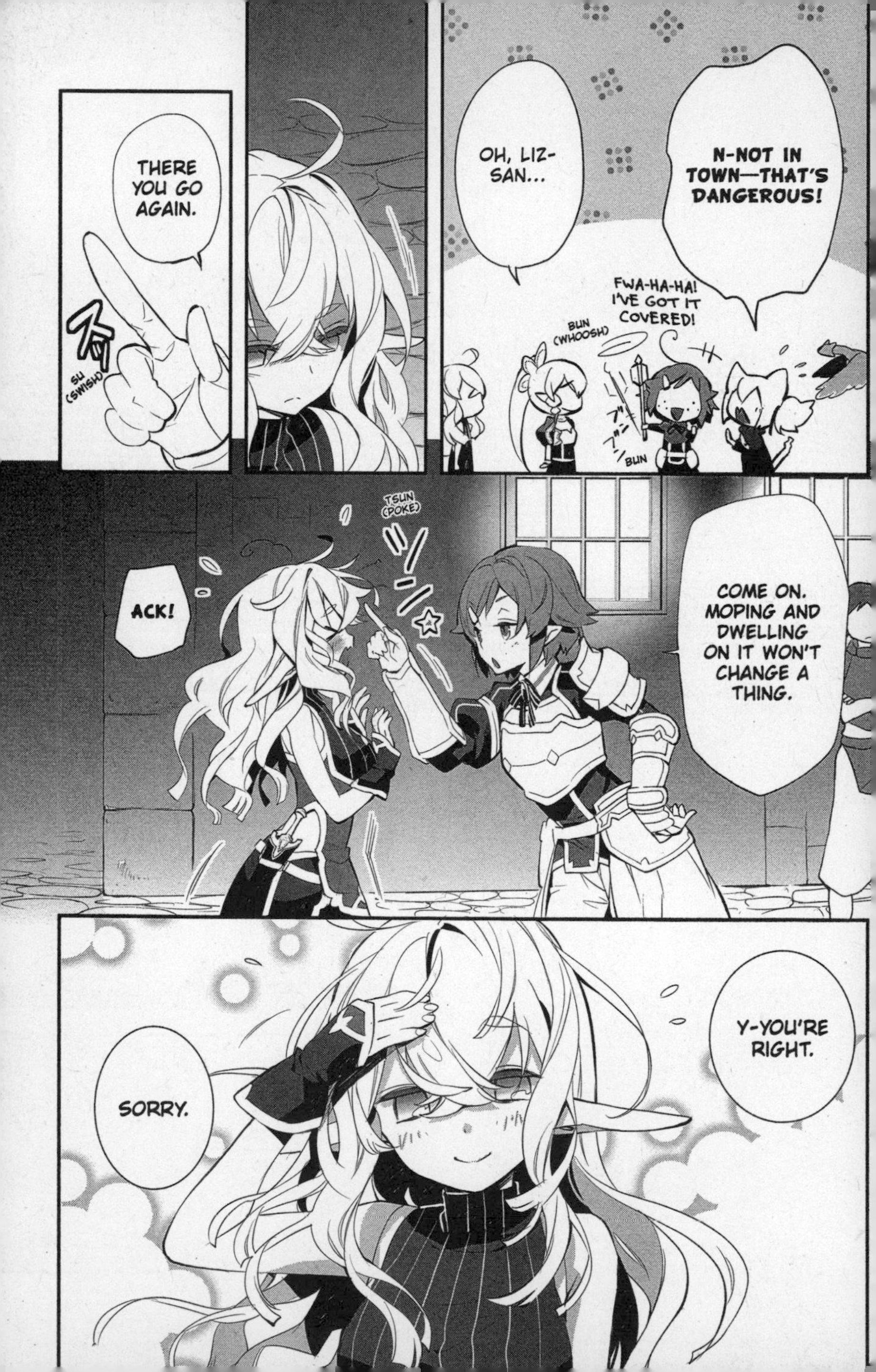
N-NOT IN TOWN—THAT'S DANGEROUS!
OH, LIZ-SAN...
FWA-HA-HA! I'VE GOT IT COVERED!
BUN (WHOOSH)
BUN
THERE YOU GO AGAIN.
SU (SWISH)
COME ON. MOPING AND DWELLING ON IT WON'T CHANGE A THING.
TSUN (POKE)
ACK!
Y-YOU'RE RIGHT.
SORRY.

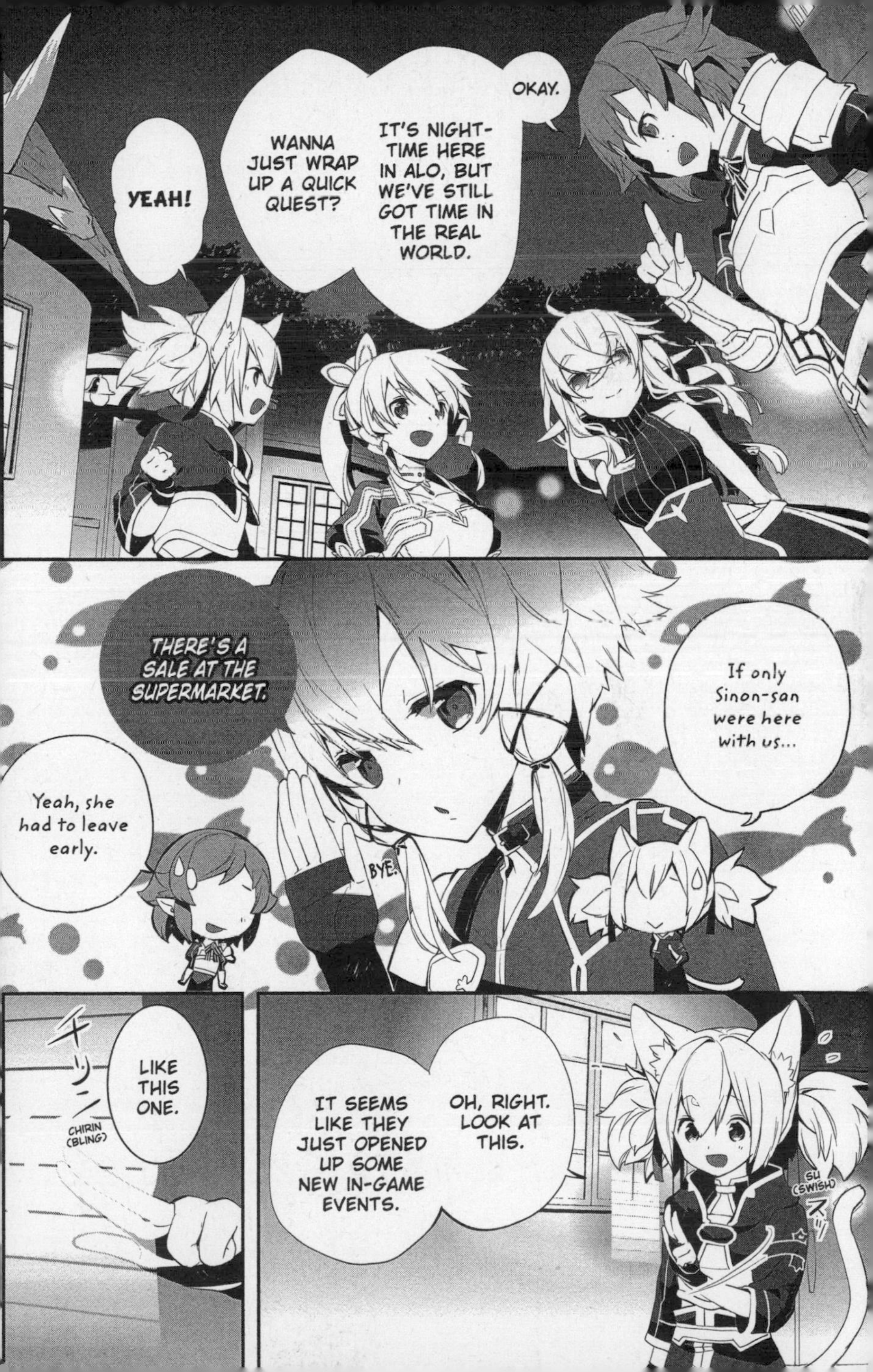
OKAY.
IT'S NIGHT-TIME HERE IN ALO, BUT WE'VE STILL GOT TIME IN THE REAL WORLD.
WANNA JUST WRAP UP A QUICK QUEST?
YEAH!
If only Sinon-san were here with us...
THERE'S A SALE AT THE SUPERMARKET.
BYE.
Yeah, she had to leave early.
OH, RIGHT. LOOK AT THIS.
IT SEEMS LIKE THEY JUST OPENED UP SOME NEW IN-GAME EVENTS.
スッ
SU (SWISH)
LIKE THIS ONE.
チリン
CHIRIN (BLING)

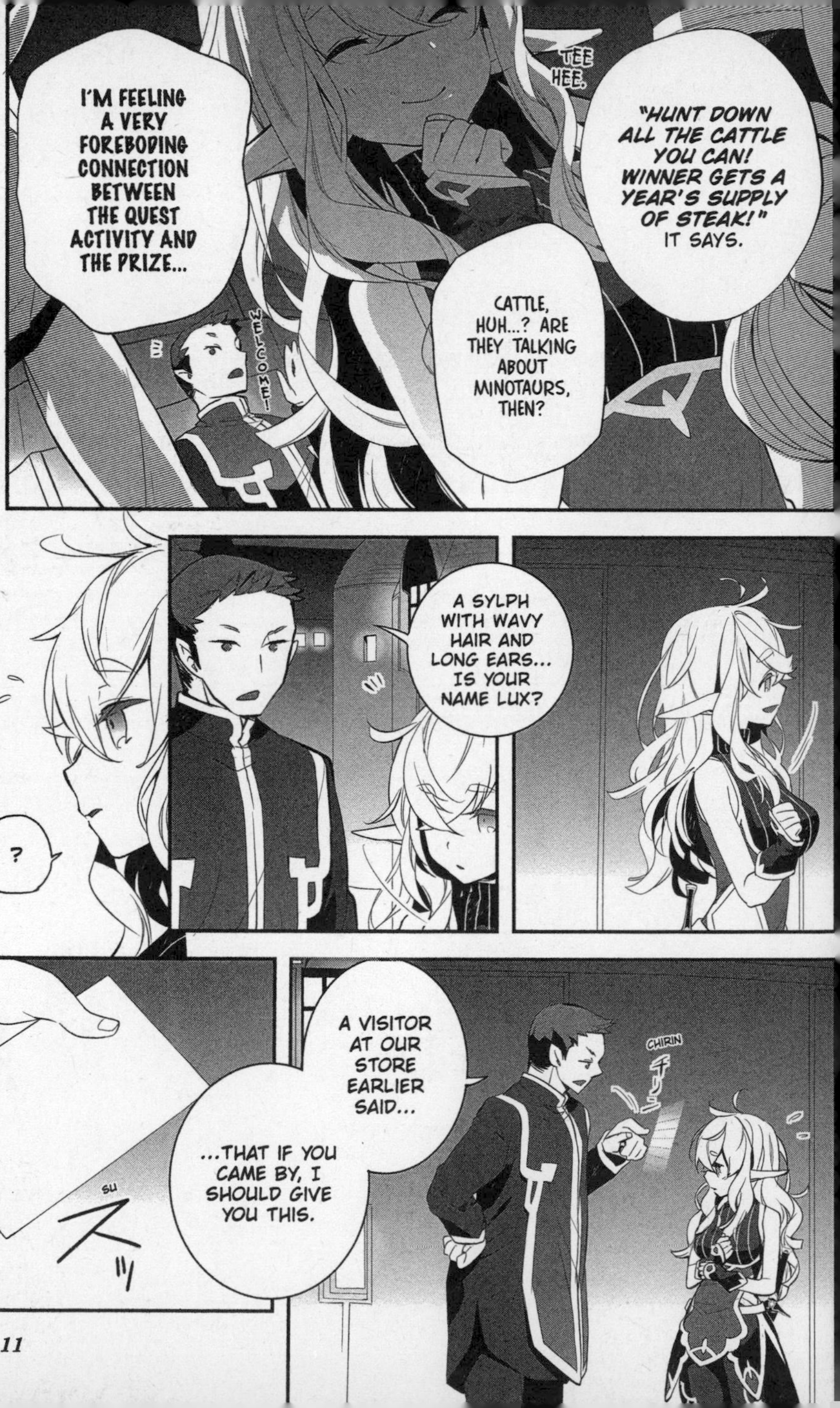
"HUNT DOWN ALL THE CATTLE YOU CAN! WINNER GETS A YEAR'S SUPPLY OF STEAK!" IT SAYS.
TEE HEE.
CATTLE, HUH...? ARE THEY TALKING ABOUT MINOTAURS, THEN?
I'M FEELING A VERY FOREBODING CONNECTION BETWEEN THE QUEST ACTIVITY AND THE PRIZE...
WELCOME!
A SYLPH WITH WAVY HAIR AND LONG EARS... IS YOUR NAME LUX?
?
CHIRIN
A VISITOR AT OUR STORE EARLIER SAID...
...THAT IF YOU CAME BY, I SHOULD GIVE YOU THIS.
SU

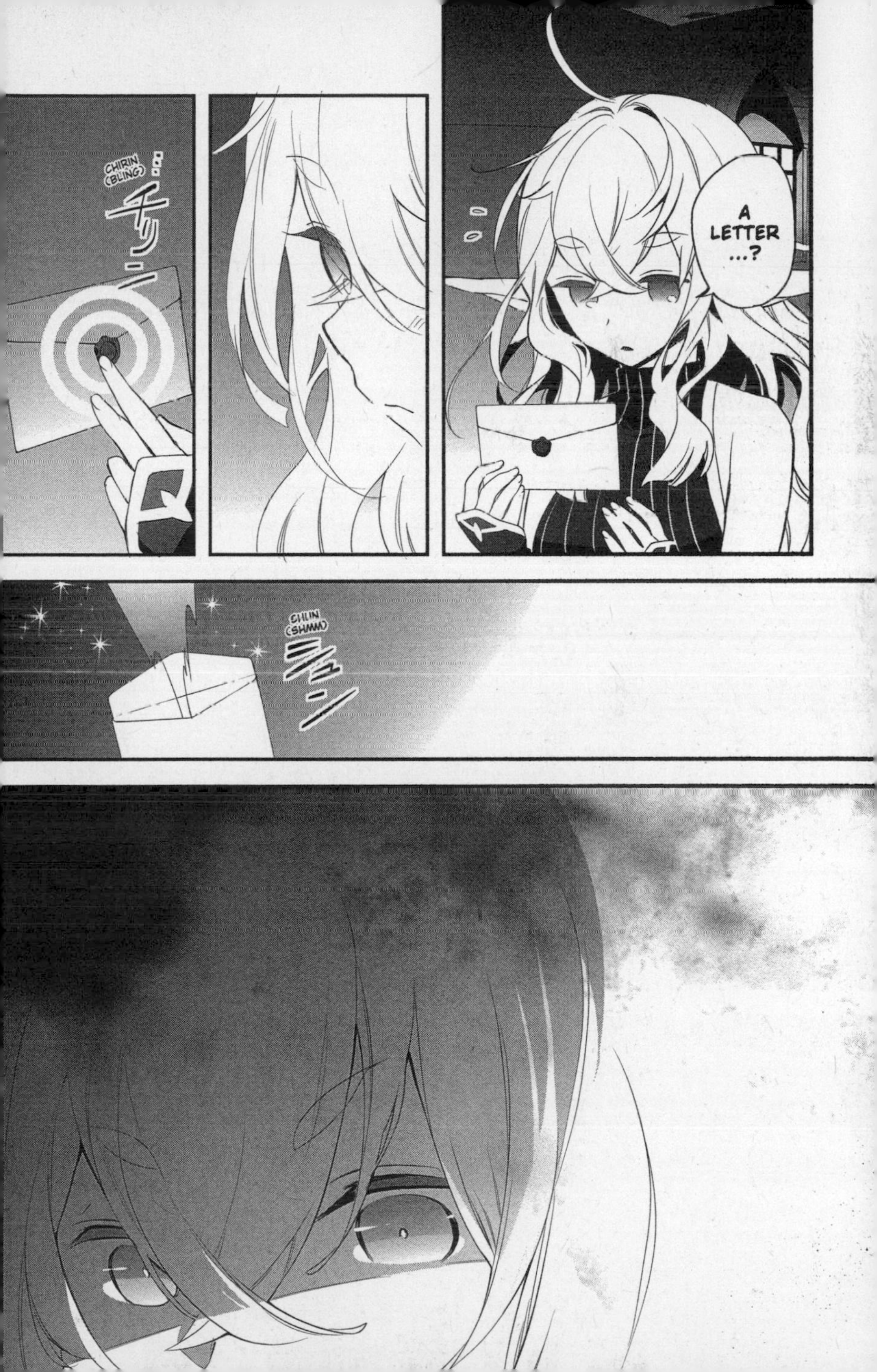
A LETTER ...?
CHIRIN (BLING)
CHLIN (SHMM)

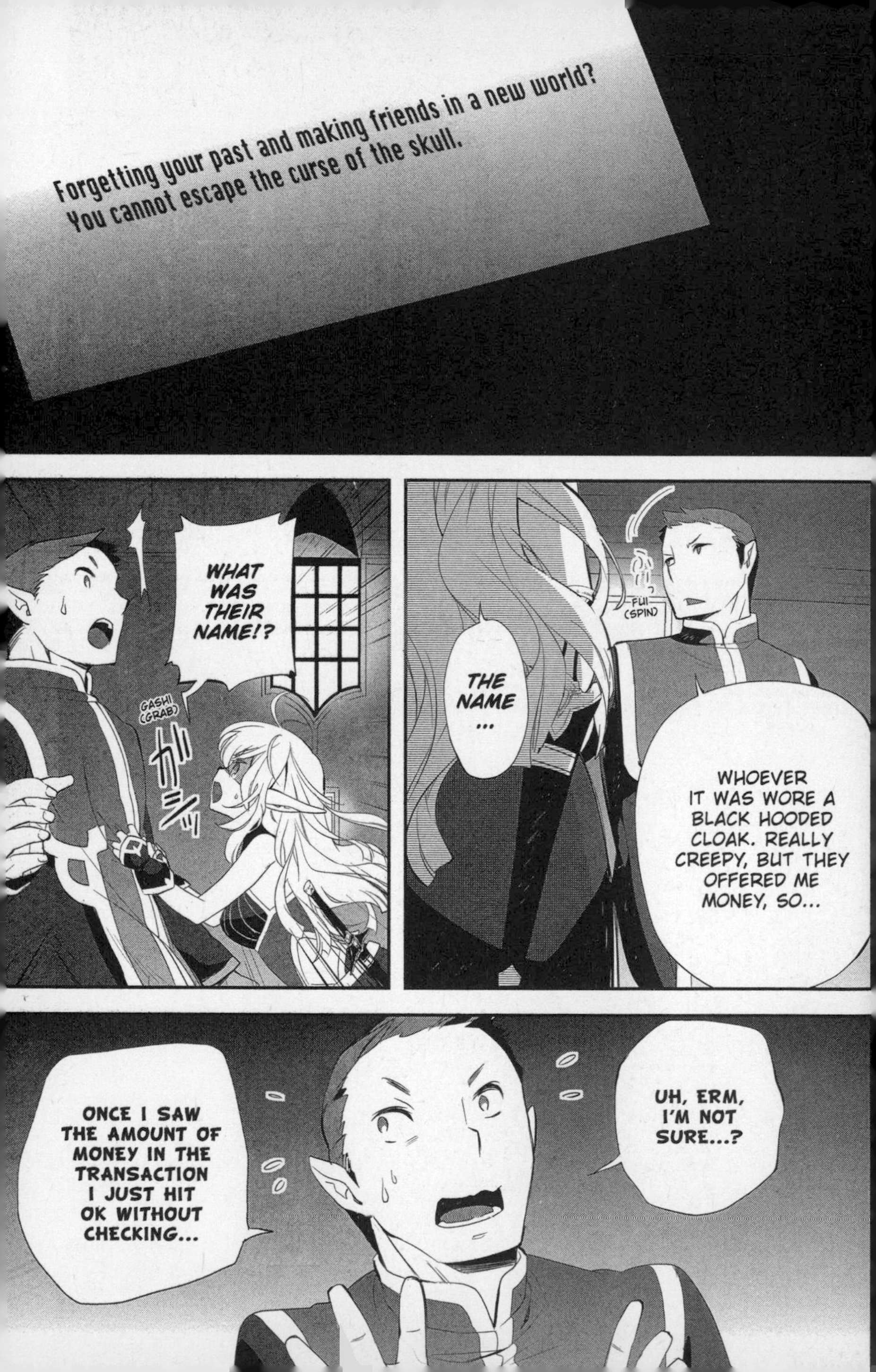
Forgetting your past and making friends in a new world?
You cannot escape the curse of the skull.
FUI (SPIN)
THE NAME...
WHOEVER IT WAS WORE A BLACK HOODED CLOAK. REALLY CREEPY, BUT THEY OFFERED ME MONEY, SO...
WHAT WAS THEIR NAME!?
GASHI (GRAB)
UH, ERM, I'M NOT SURE...?
ONCE I SAW THE AMOUNT OF MONEY IN THE TRANSACTION I JUST HIT OK WITHOUT CHECKING...

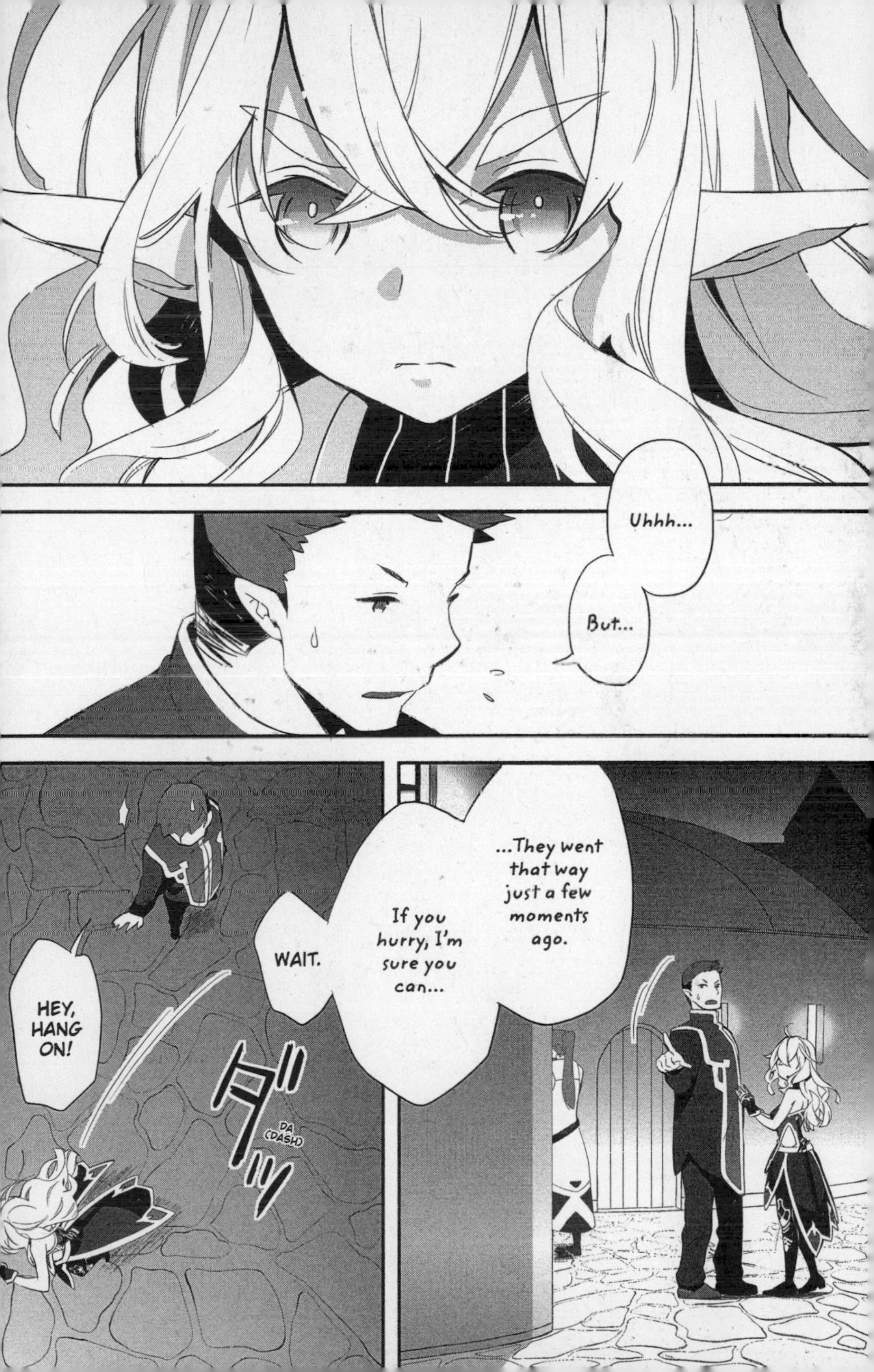
Uhhh...
But...
...They went that way just a few moments ago.
If you hurry, I'm sure you can...
WAIT.
HEY, HANG ON!
DA (DASH)

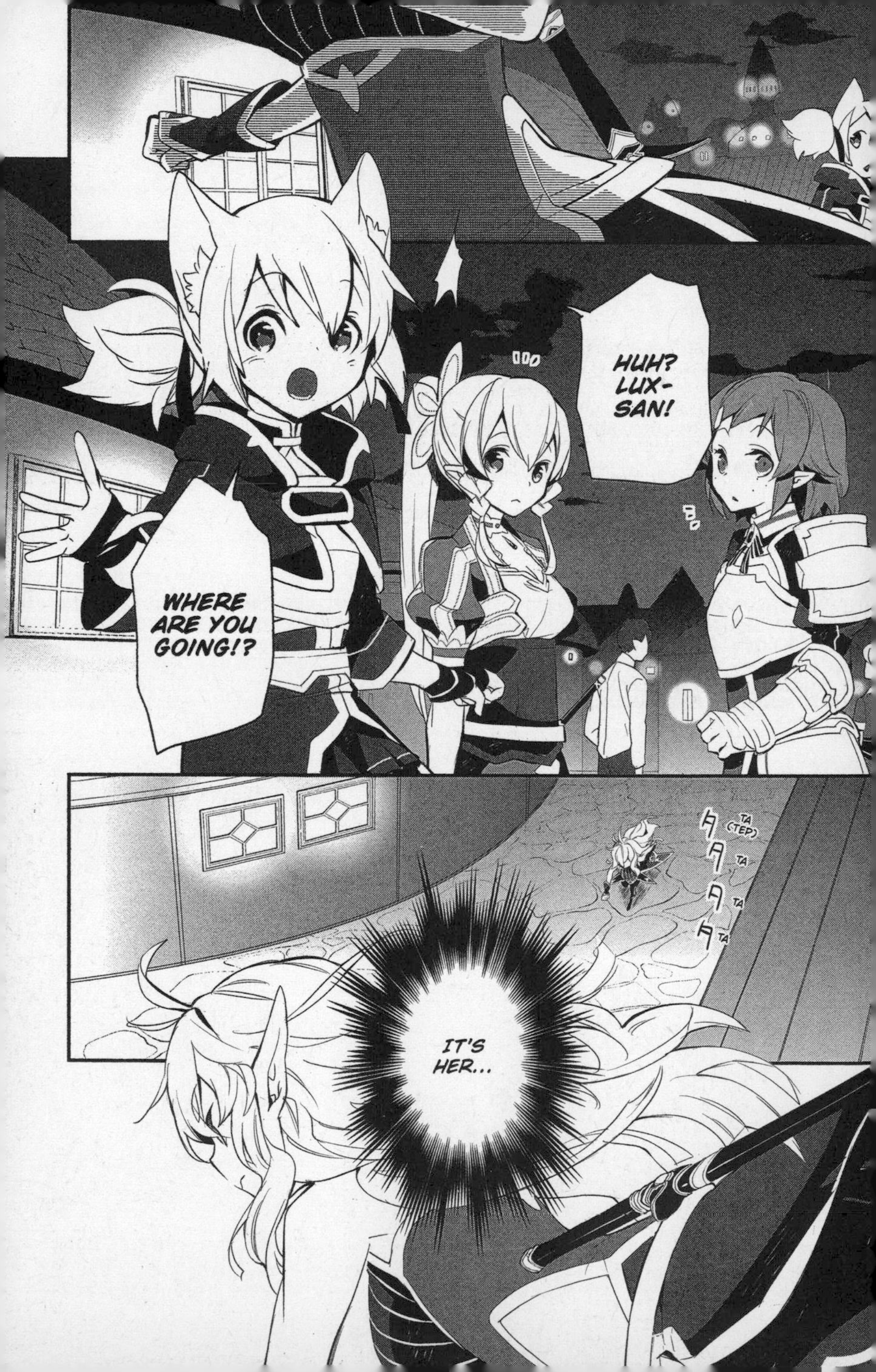
HUH? LUX-SAN!
WHERE ARE YOU GOING!?
TA (TEP)
TA
TA
TA
IT'S HER...

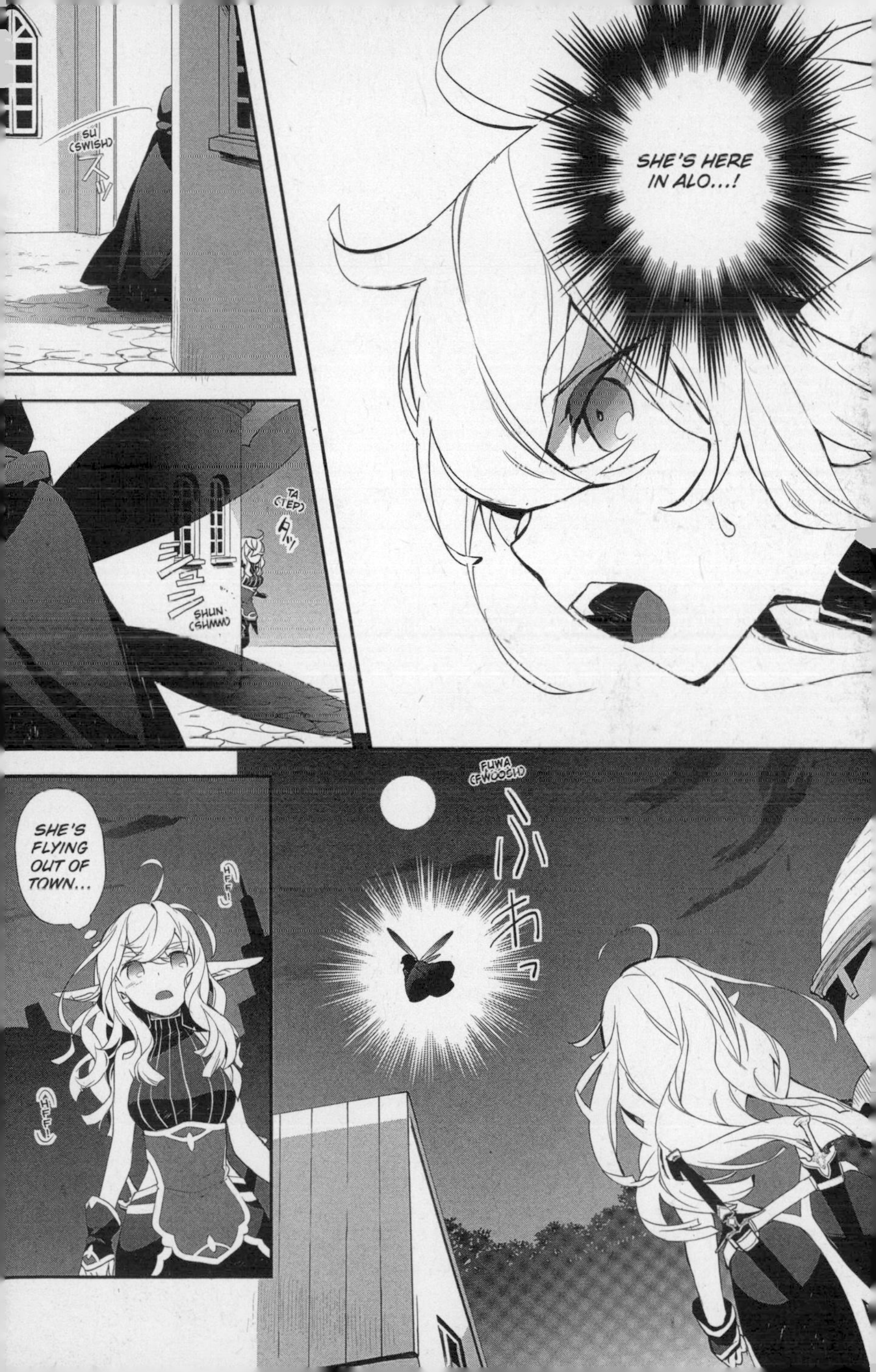
SHE'S HERE IN ALO...!
SU (SWISH)
スッ
TA (TEP)
タッ
シュン
SHUN (SHMM)
FUWA (FWOOSH)
ふわっ
SHE'S FLYING OUT OF TOWN...
HFF
HFF

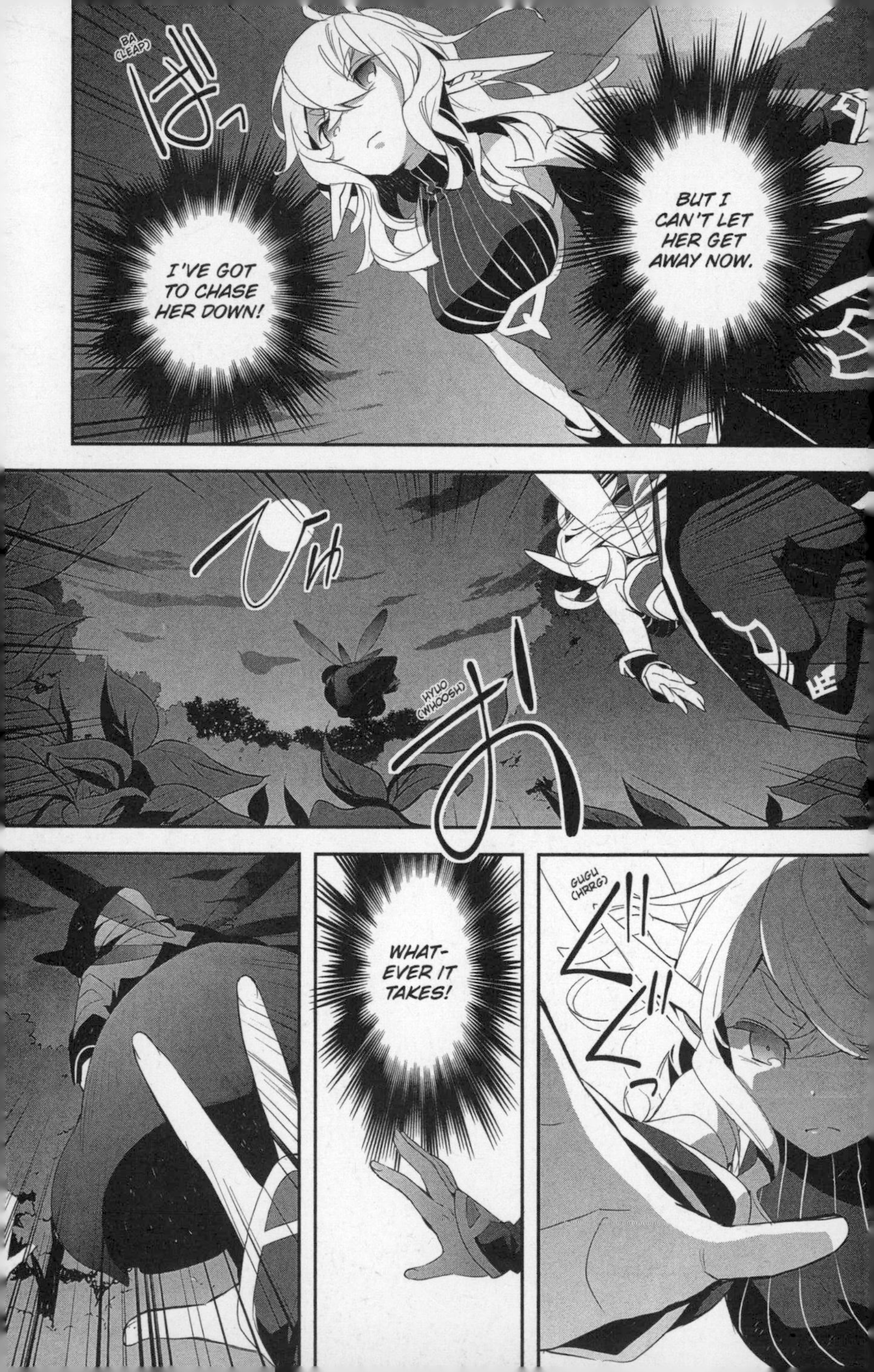
BA (LEAP)
BUT I CAN'T LET HER GET AWAY NOW.
I'VE GOT TO CHASE HER DOWN!
HYUO (WHOOSH)
GUGU (HRRG)
WHAT-EVER IT TAKES!

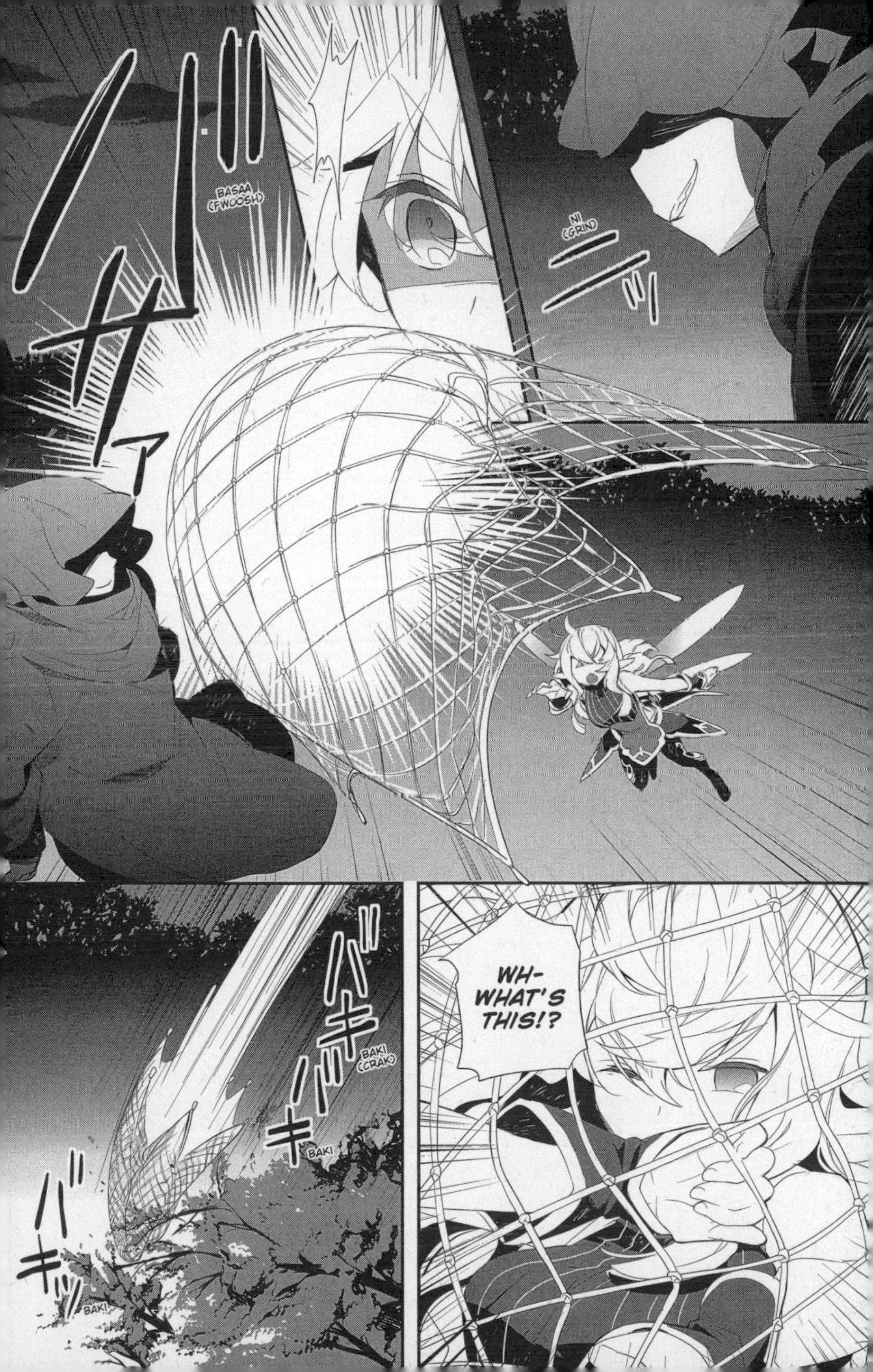
NI
(GRIN)
BASAA
(FWOOSH)
WH-
WHAT'S
THIS!?
BAKI
(CRAK)
BAKI
BAK!

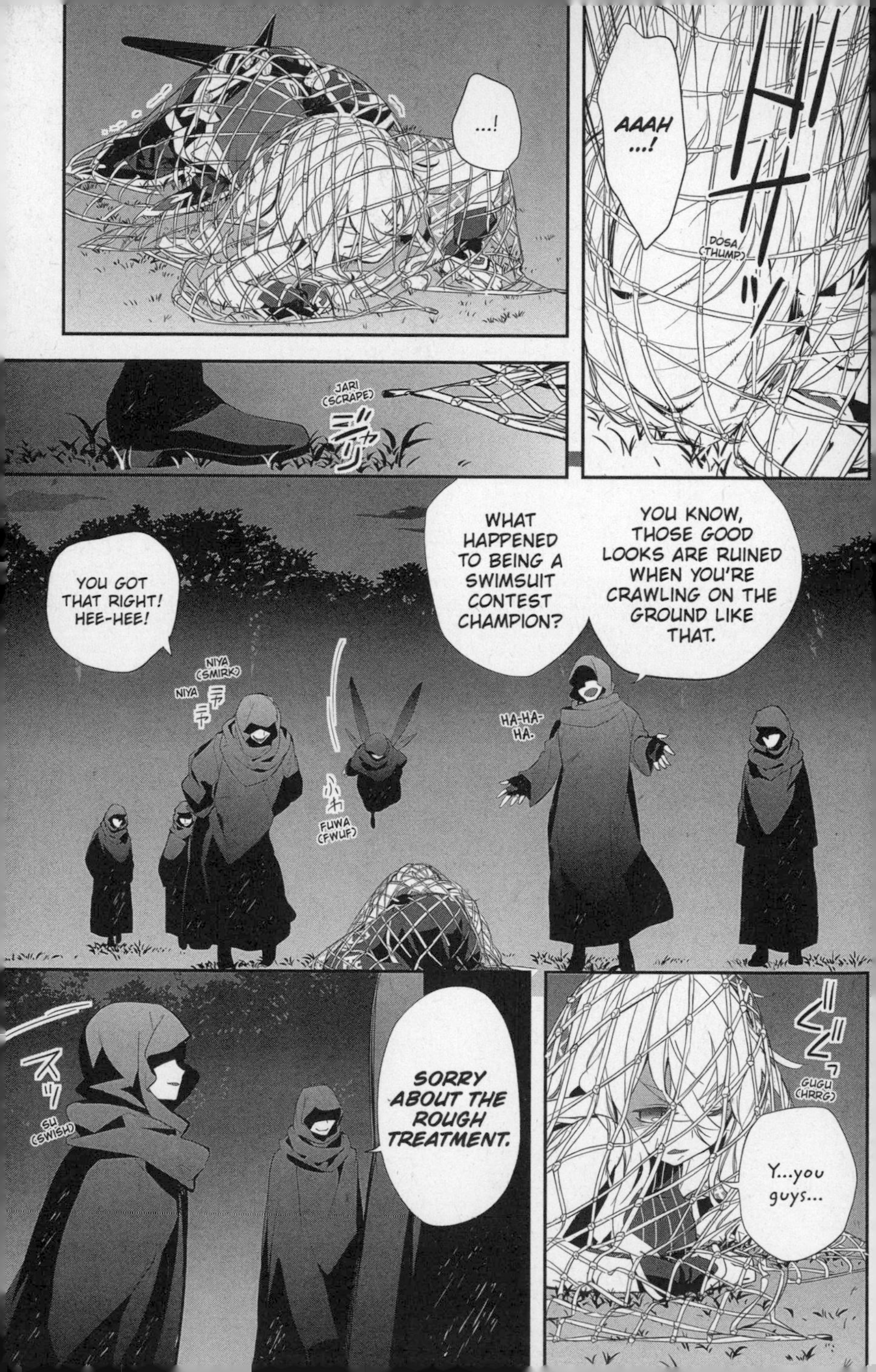

AAAH ...!
DOSA (THUMP)
...!
JARI (SCRAPE)
YOU KNOW, THOSE GOOD LOOKS ARE RUINED WHEN YOU'RE CRAWLING ON THE GROUND LIKE THAT.
WHAT HAPPENED TO BEING A SWIMSUIT CONTEST CHAMPION?
HA-HA-HA.
YOU GOT THAT RIGHT! HEE-HEE!
NIYA (SMIRK) NIYA
FUWA (FWUF)
GUGU (HRRG)
Y...you guys...
SORRY ABOUT THE ROUGH TREATMENT.
SU (SWISH)

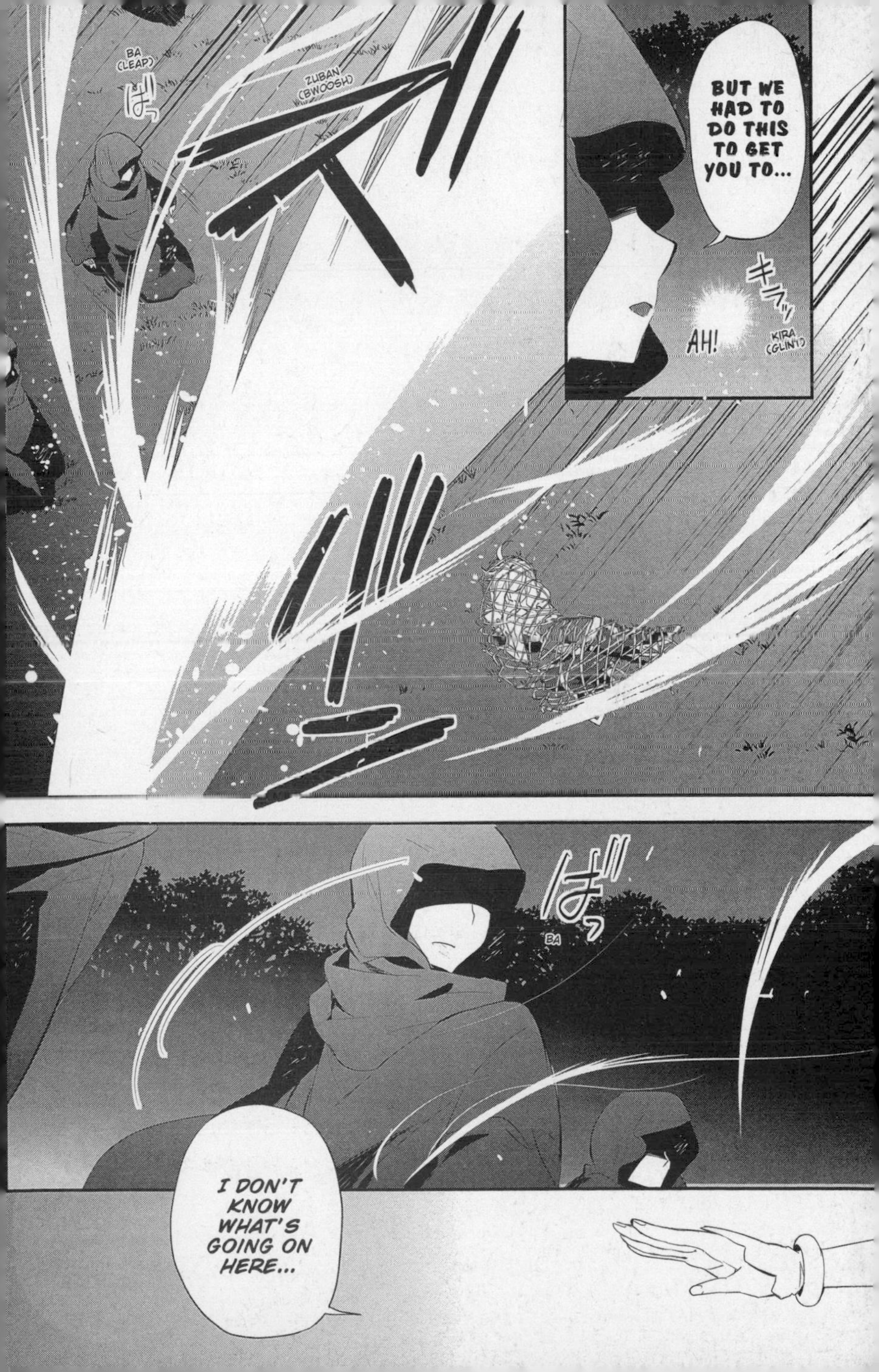
BUT WE HAD TO DO THIS TO GET YOU TO...
キラッ
KIRA (GLINT)
AH!
ばっ
BA (LEAP)
ZUBAN (BWOOSH)
ばっ
BA
I DON'T KNOW WHAT'S GOING ON HERE...

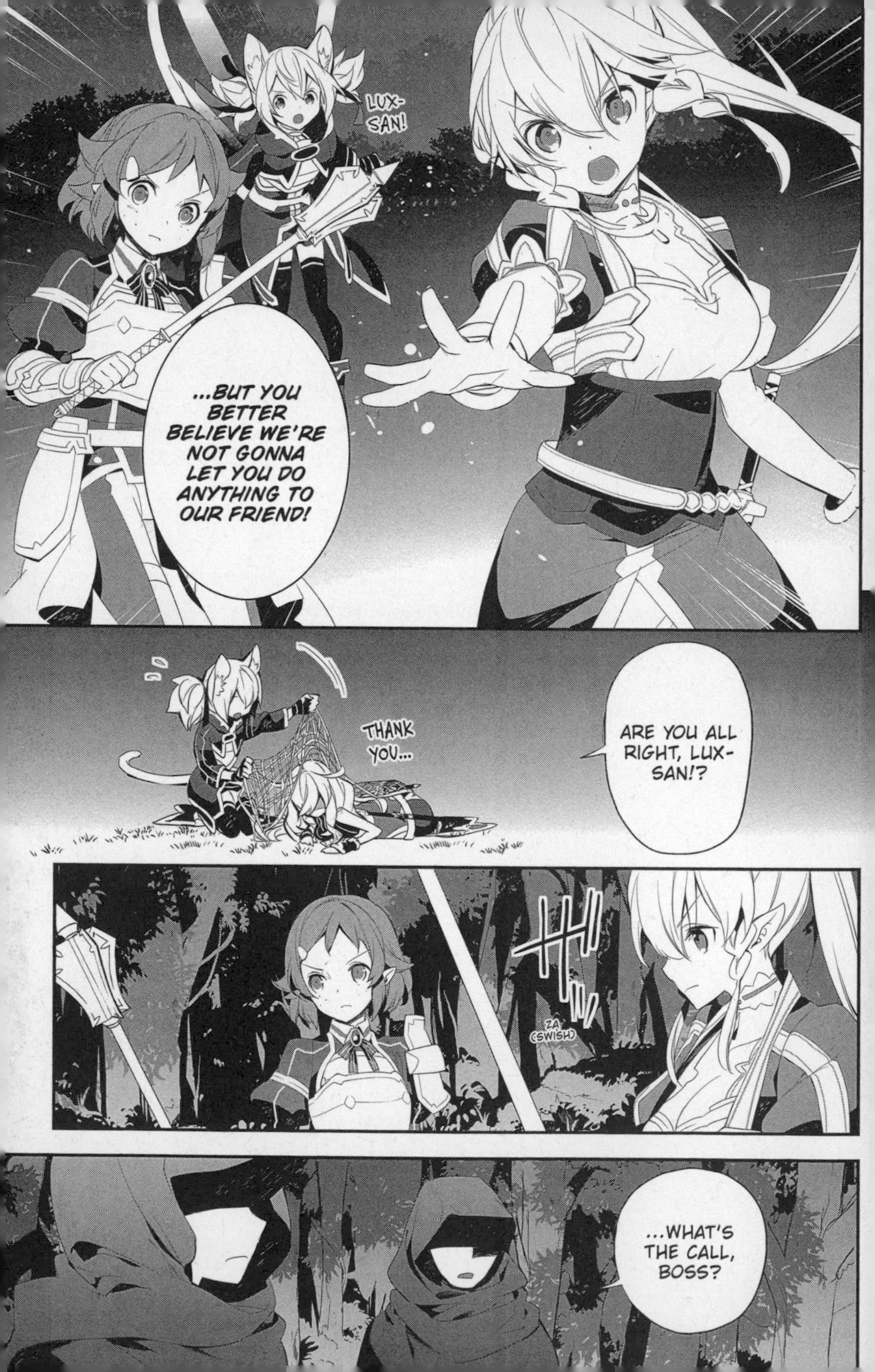
LUX-SAN!
...BUT YOU BETTER BELIEVE WE'RE NOT GONNA LET YOU DO ANYTHING TO OUR FRIEND!
ARE YOU ALL RIGHT, LUX-SAN!?
THANK YOU...
ZA (SWISH)
...WHAT'S THE CALL, BOSS?

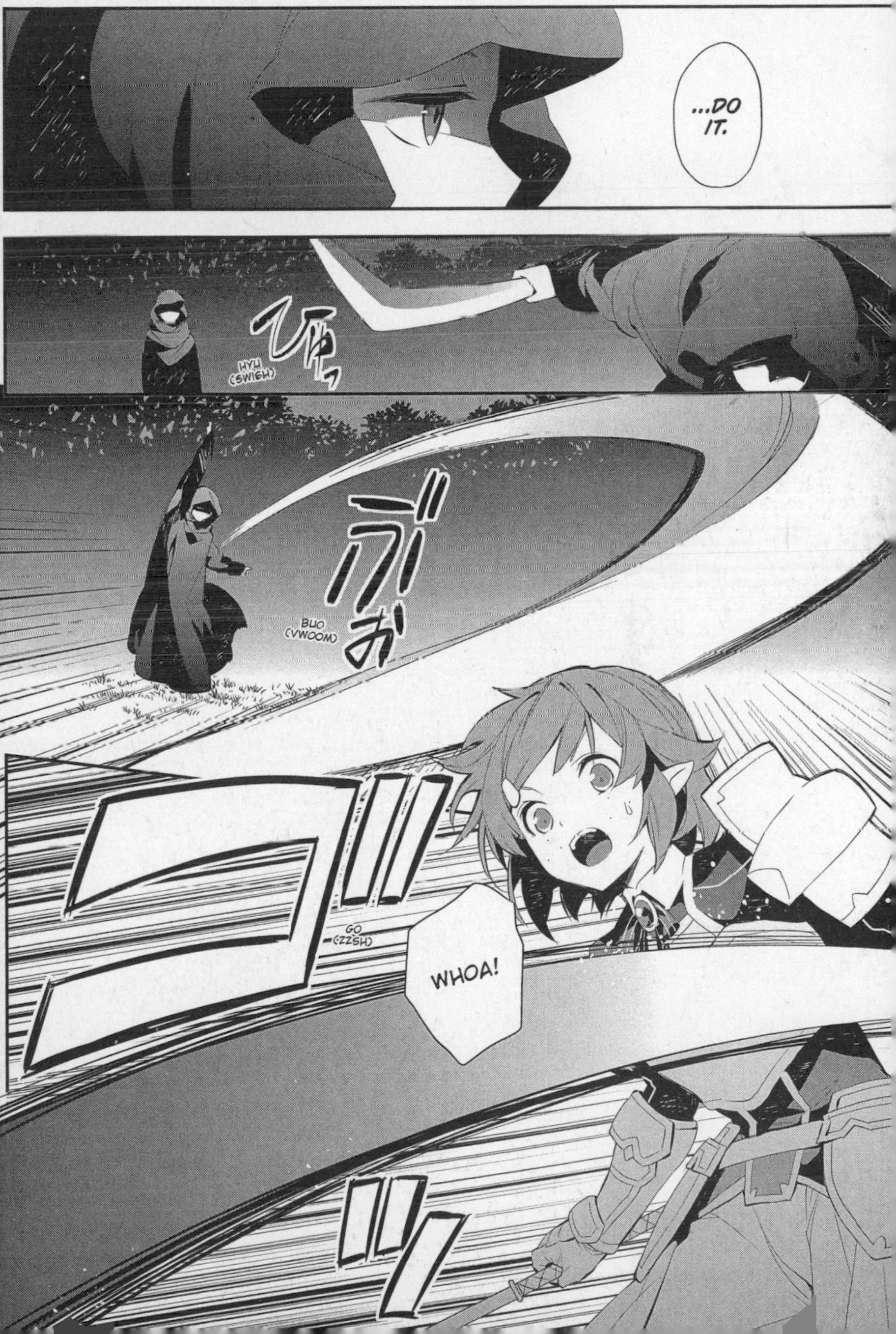
...DO IT.
HYU (SWISH)
BUO (VWOOM)
GO (ZZSH)
WHOA!

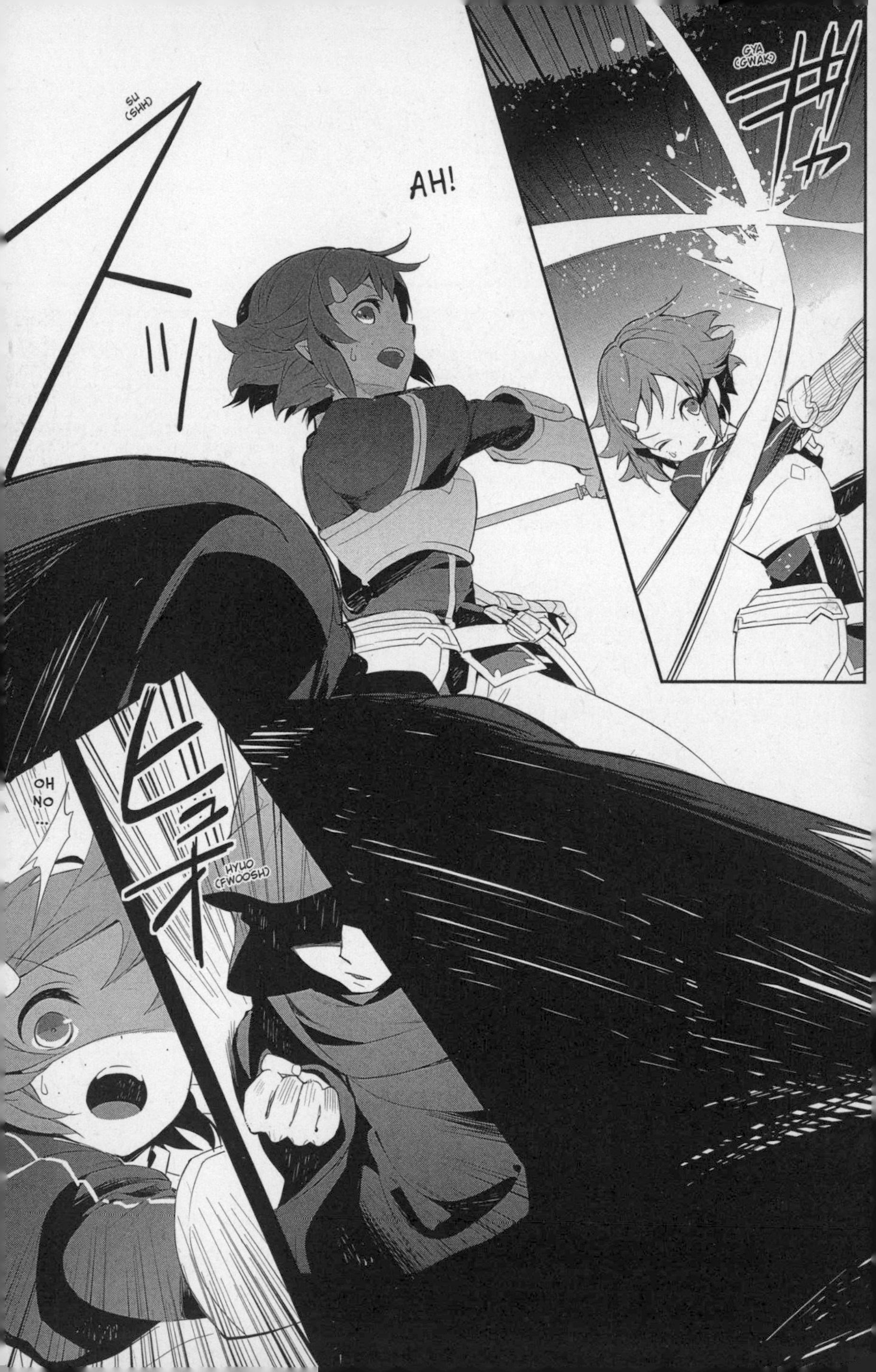
GYA (GWAK)
SU (SHH)
AH!
HYUO (FWOOSH)
OH NO ...

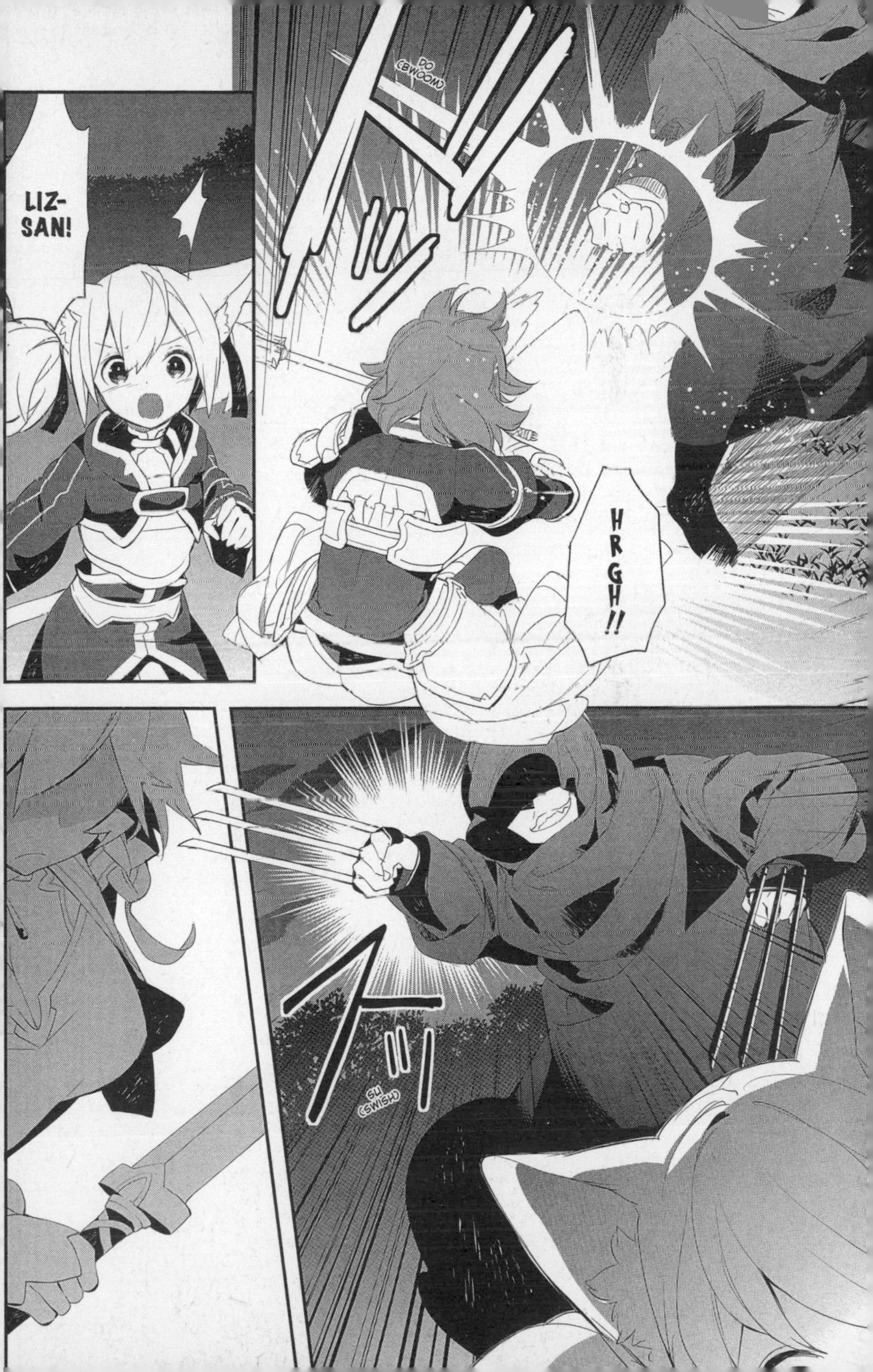
DO (BWOOM)
HRGH!!
LIZ-SAN!
SU (SWISH)

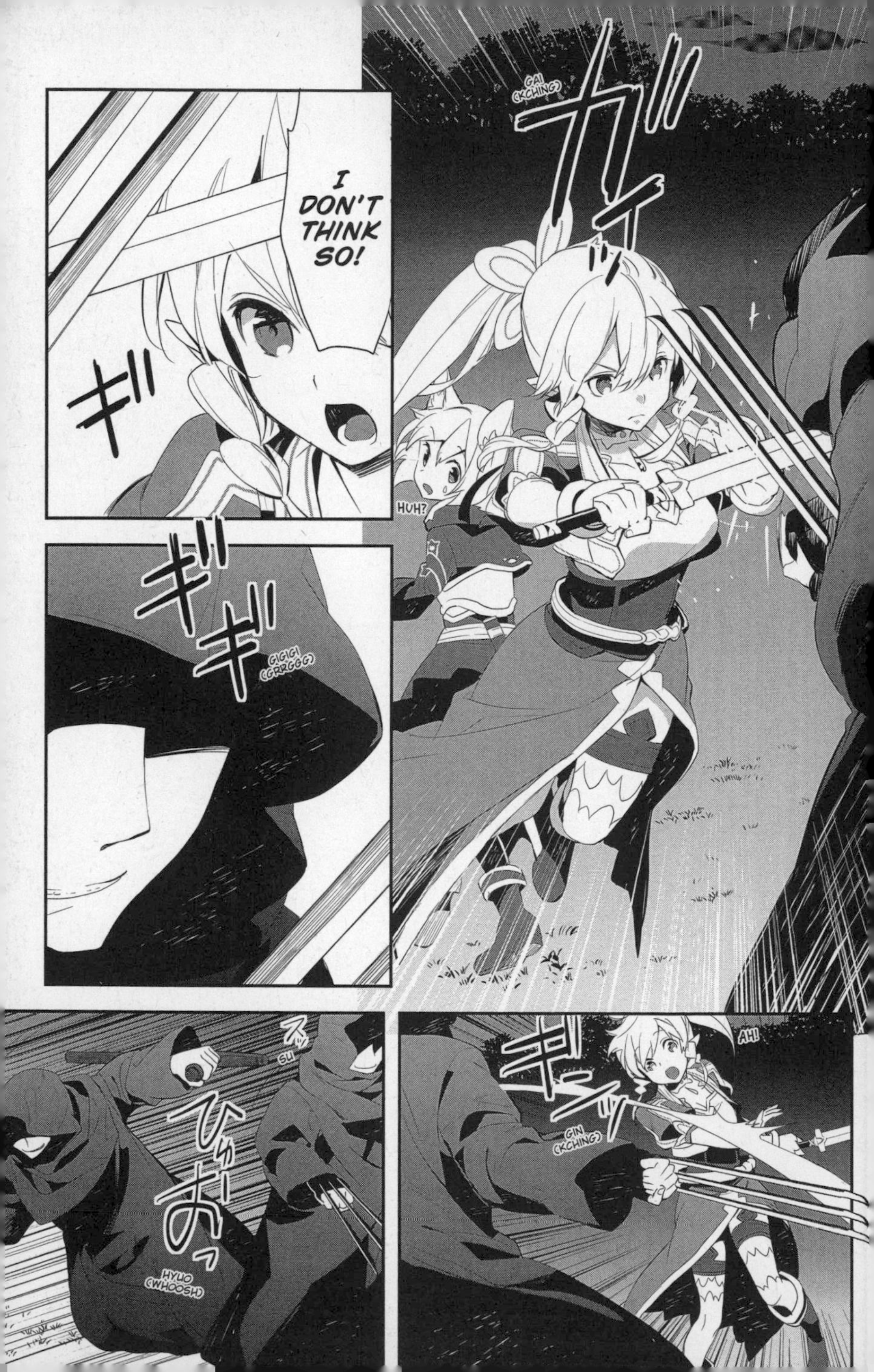
GAI (KCHING)
HUH?
I DON'T THINK SO!
GIGIGI (GRRGGG)
AH!
GIN (KCHING)
SU
HYUO (WHOOSH)

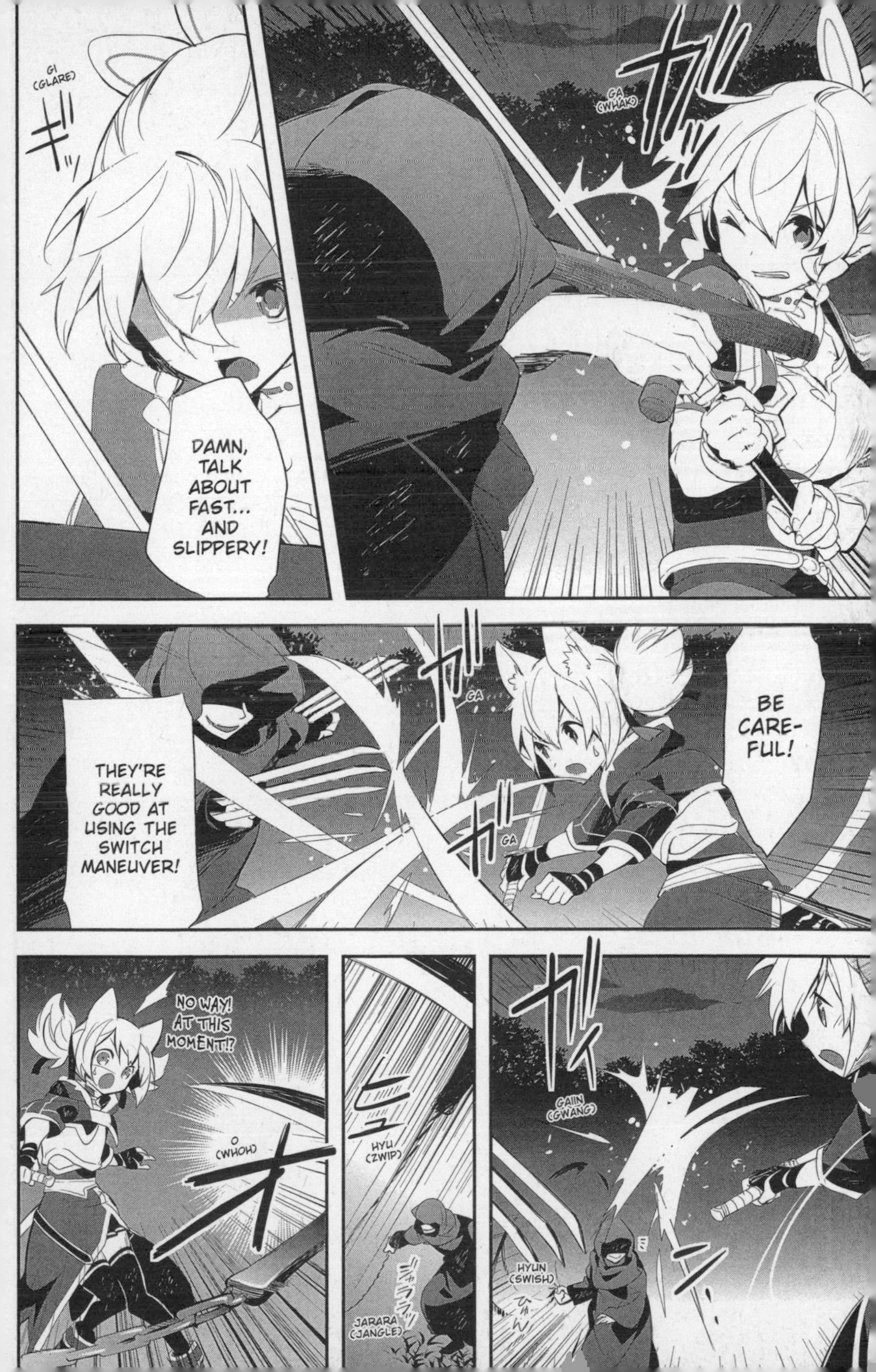
GA (WHAK)
GI (GLARE)
DAMN, TALK ABOUT FAST... AND SLIPPERY!
BE CARE-FUL!
GA
GA
THEY'RE REALLY GOOD AT USING THE SWITCH MANEUVER!
GAIIN (GWANG)
HYUN (SWISH)
HYU (ZWIP)
JARARA (JANGLE)
NO WAY! AT THIS MOMENT!?
O (WHOH)

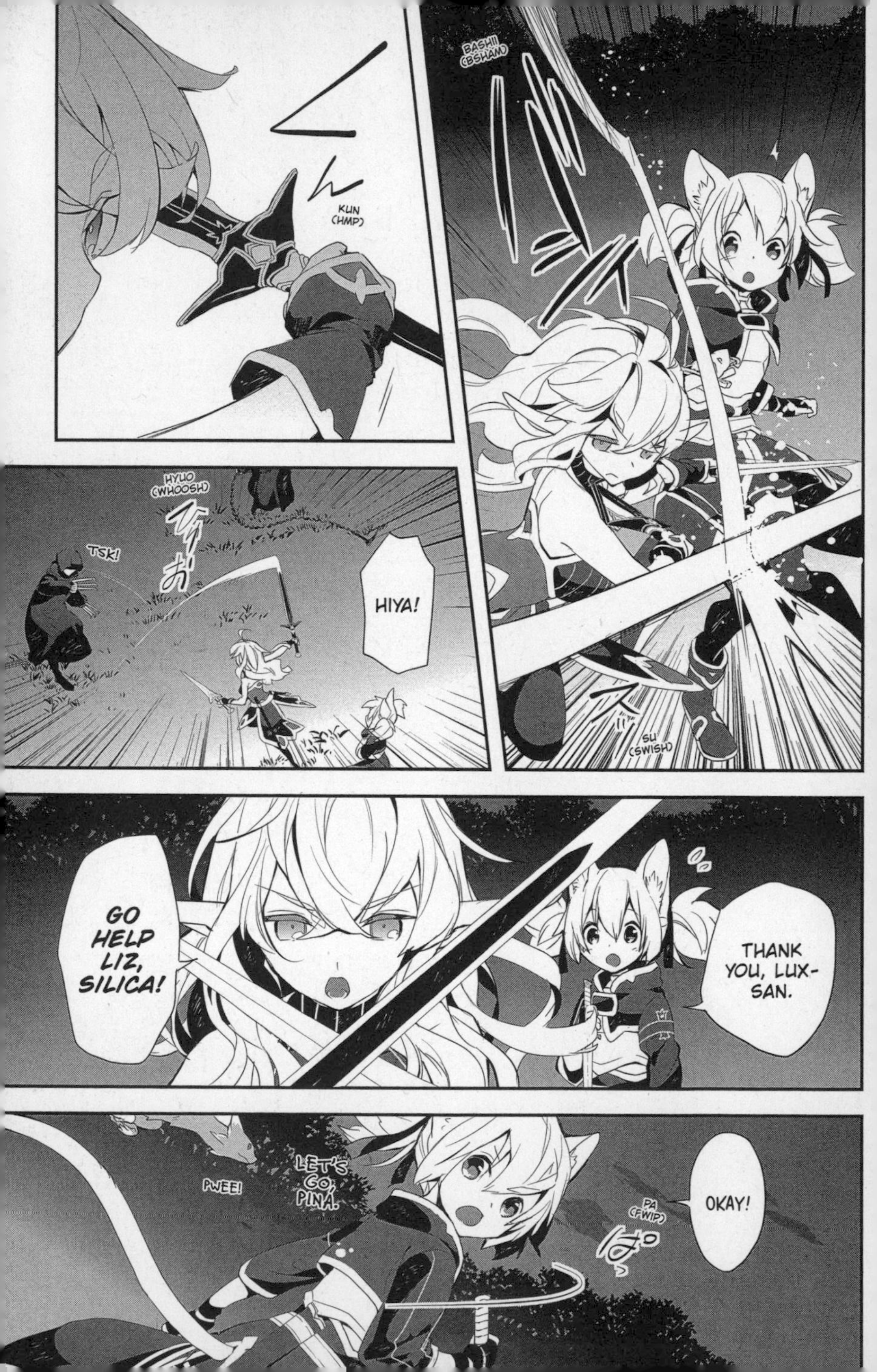
BASHI! (BSHAM)
SU (SWISH)
KUN (HMP)
HYUO (WHOOSH)
TSK!
HIYA!
GO HELP LIZ, SILICA!
THANK YOU, LUX-SAN.
OKAY!
PA (FWIP)
LET'S GO, PINA.
PWEE!

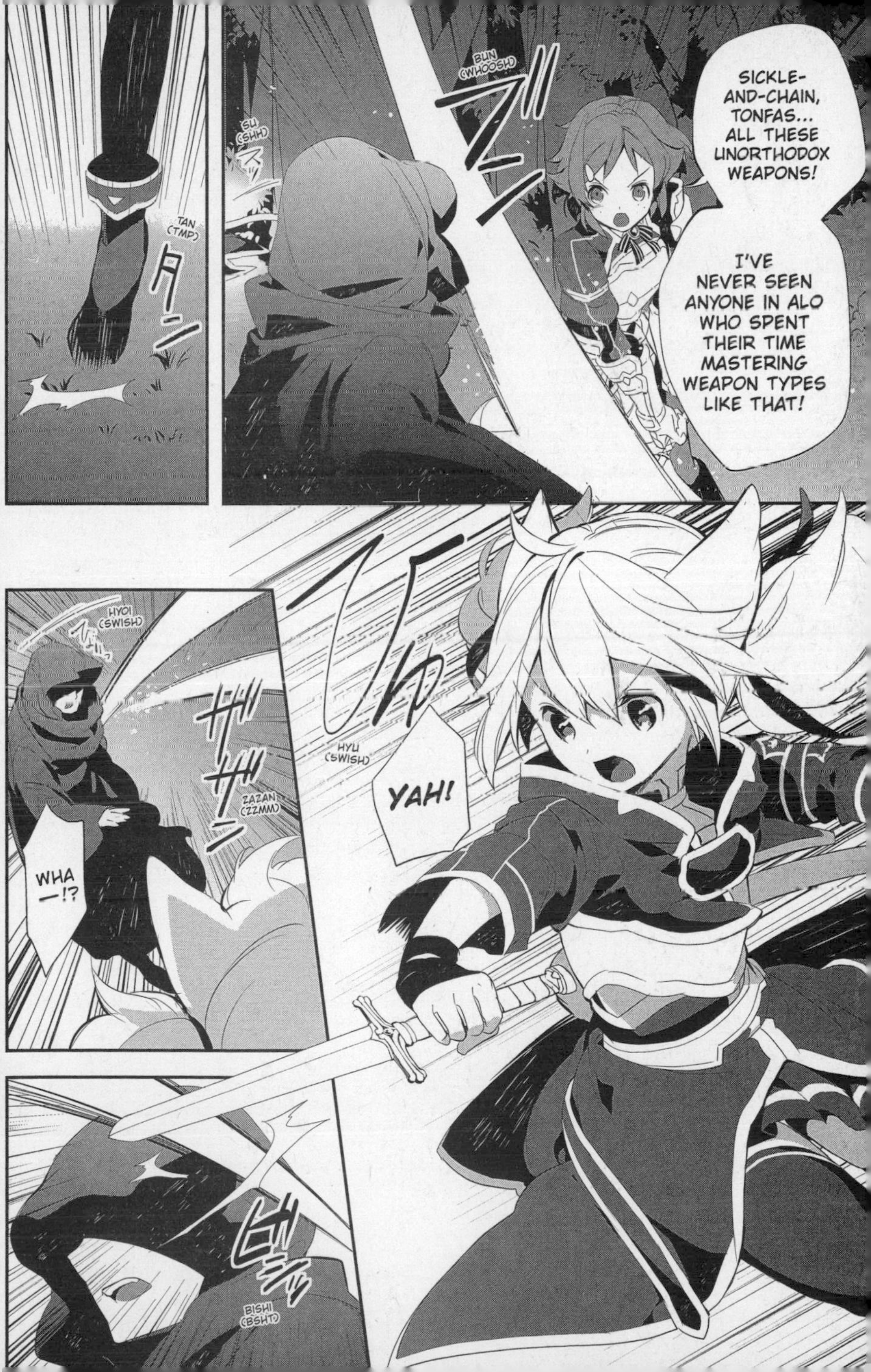
SICKLE-AND-CHAIN, TONFAS... ALL THESE UNORTHODOX WEAPONS!
I'VE NEVER SEEN ANYONE IN ALO WHO SPENT THEIR TIME MASTERING WEAPON TYPES LIKE THAT!
BUN (WHOOSH)
SU (SHH)
TAN (TMP)
HYU (SWISH)
YAH!
HYOI (SWISH)
ZAZAN (ZZMM)
WHA—!?
BISHI (BSHT)

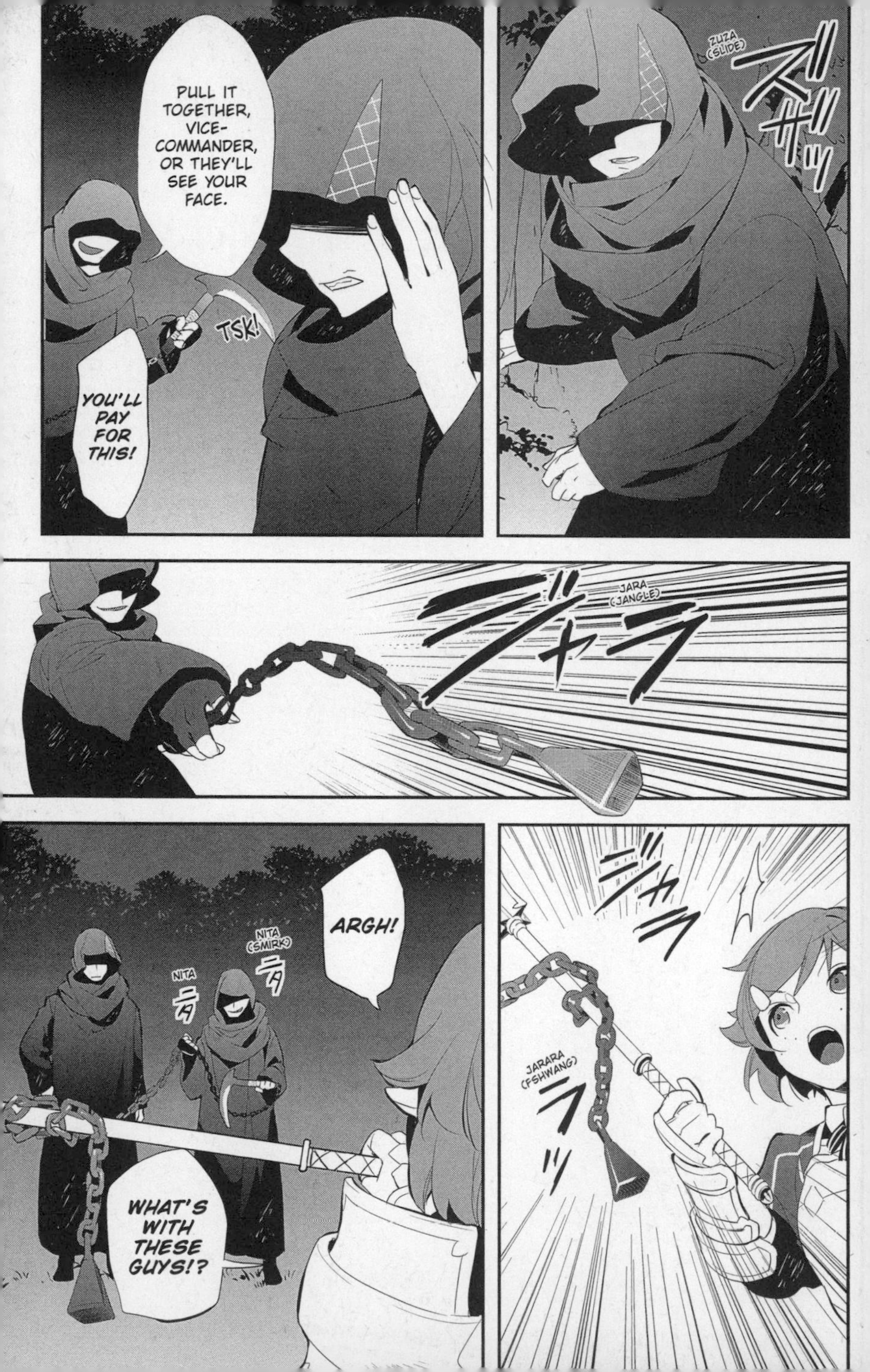
ZUZA (SLIDE)
PULL IT TOGETHER, VICE-COMMANDER, OR THEY'LL SEE YOUR FACE.
TSK!
YOU'LL PAY FOR THIS!
JARA (JANGLE)
JARARA (FSHWANG)
ARGH!
NITA (SMIRK)
NITA
WHAT'S WITH THESE GUYS!?

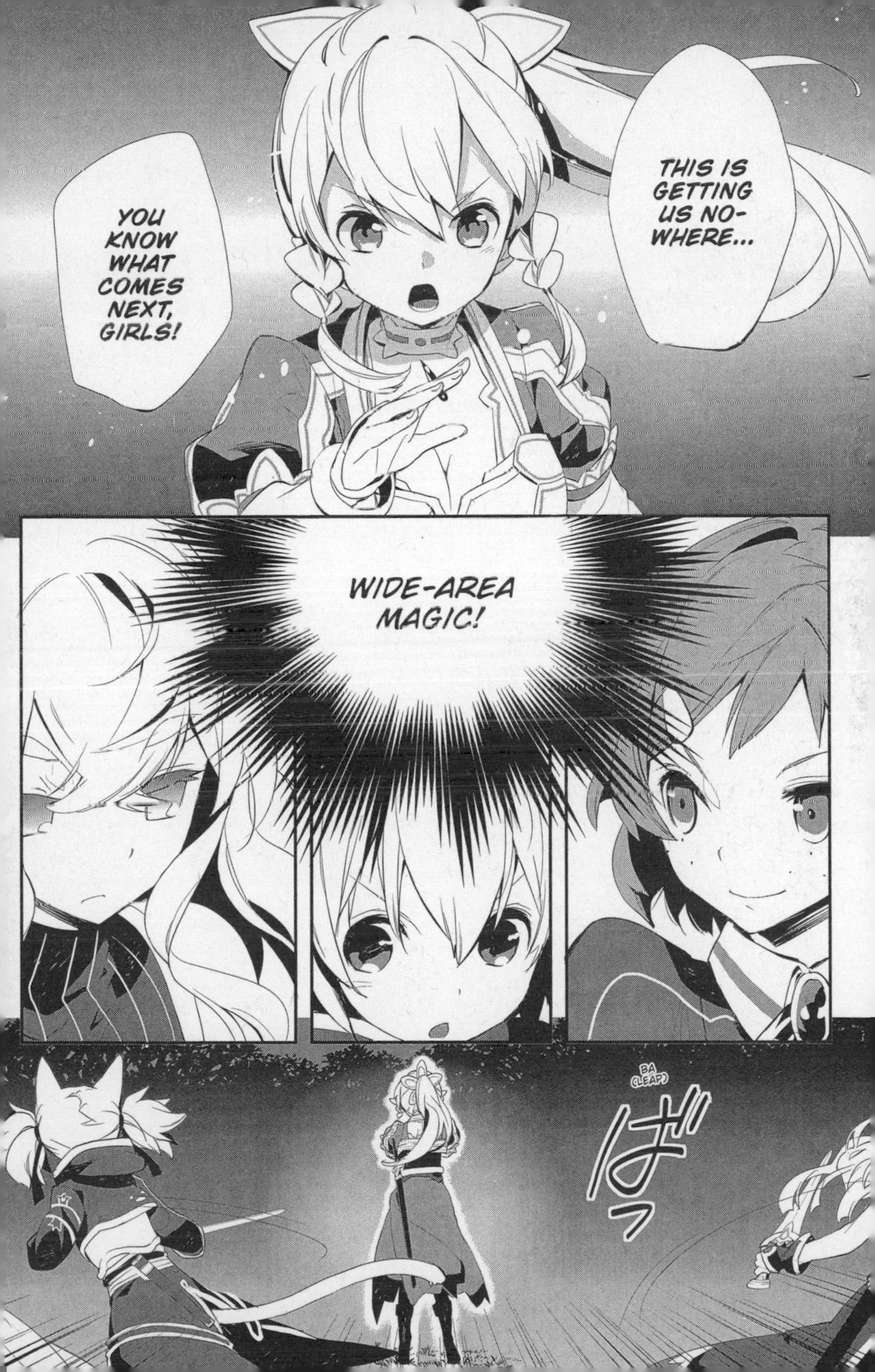
THIS IS GETTING US NO-WHERE...
YOU KNOW WHAT COMES NEXT, GIRLS!
WIDE-AREA MAGIC!
BA (LEAP)
ばっ

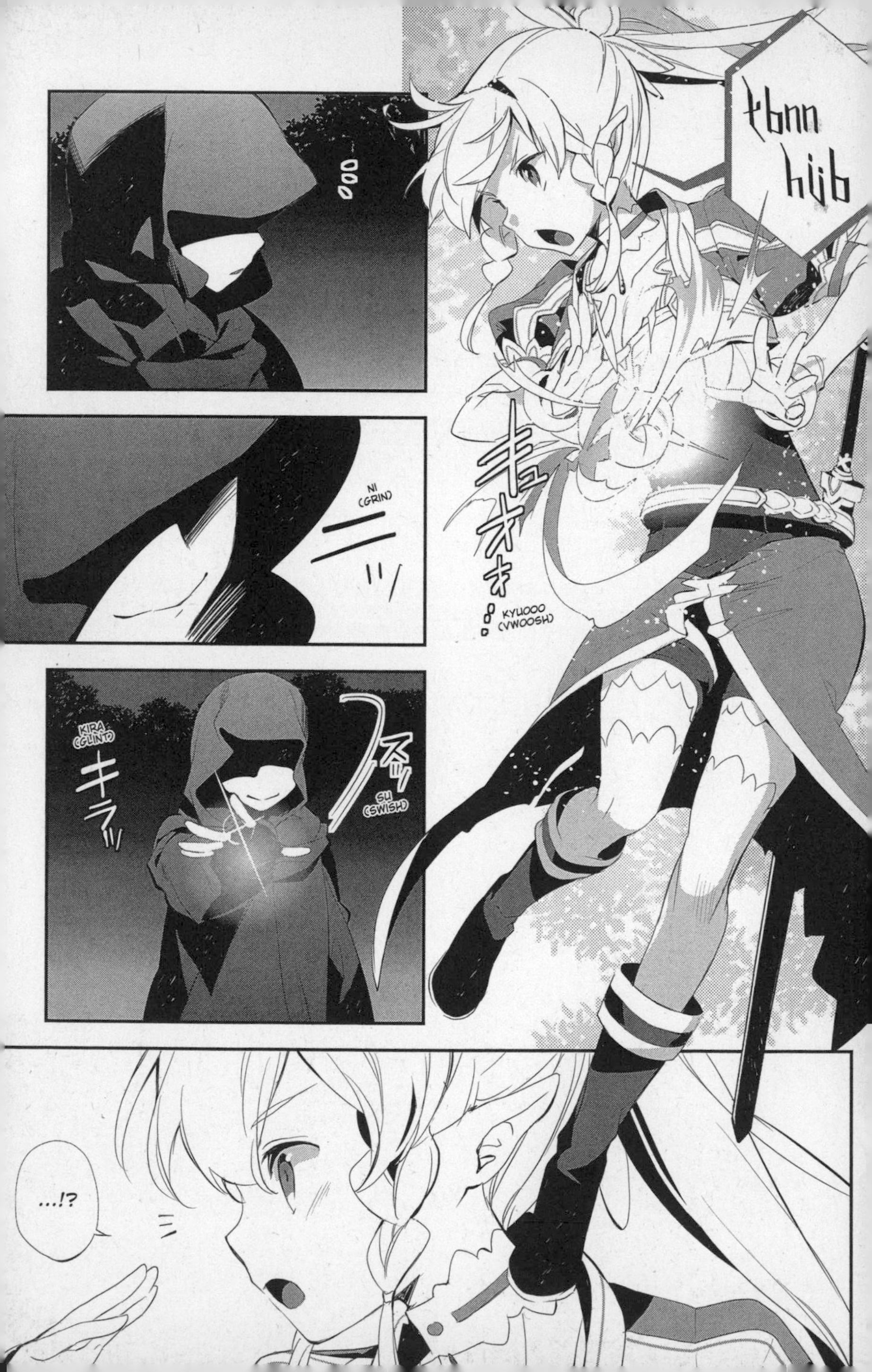

キュオォ
KYUOOO (VWOOSH)
...
ニッ
NI (GRIN)
スッ
SU (SWISH)
キラッ
KIRA (GLINT)
...!?

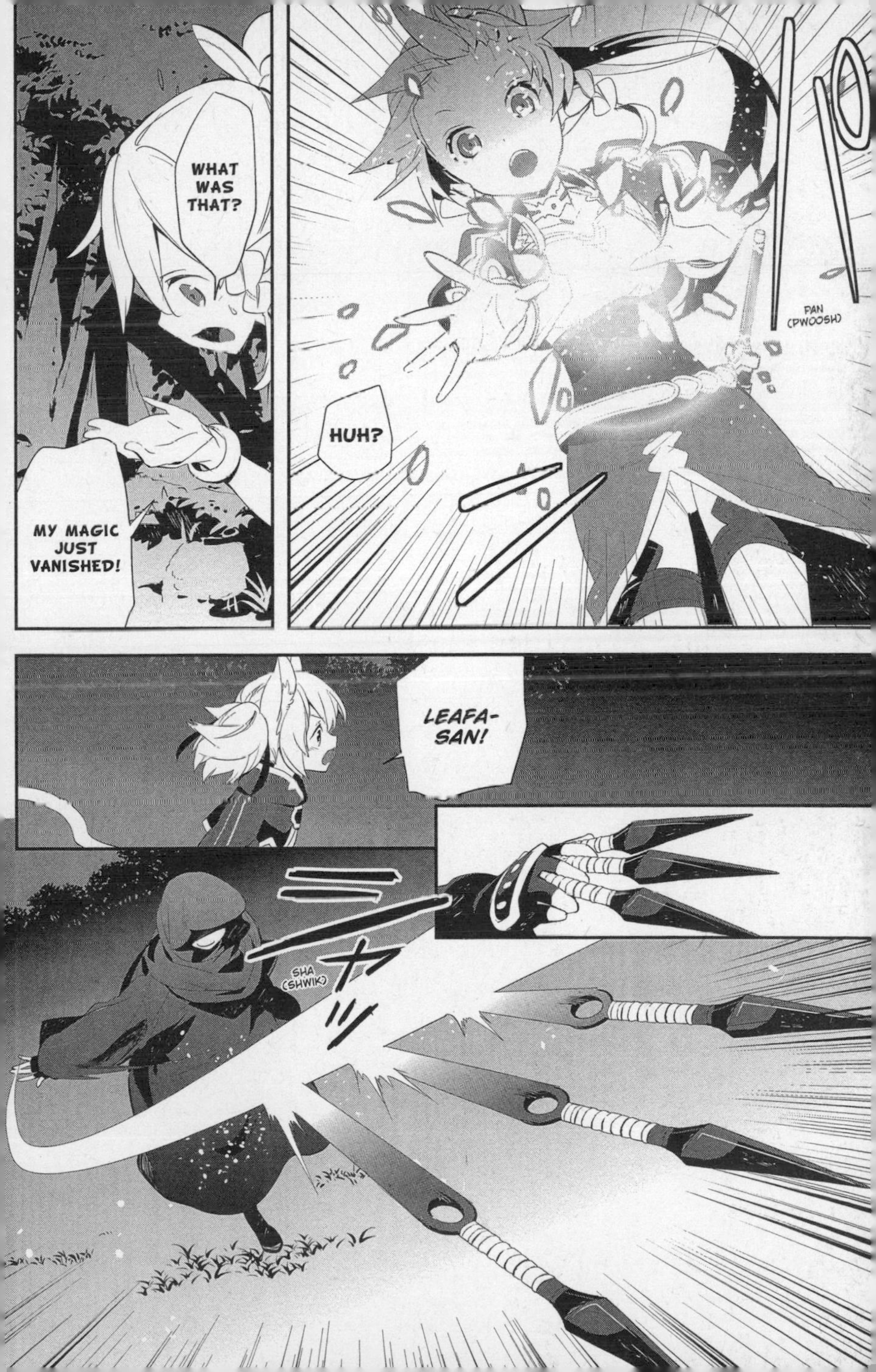
PAN
(PWOOSH)
HUH?
WHAT WAS THAT?
MY MAGIC JUST VANISHED!
LEAFA-SAN!
SHA
(SHWIK)

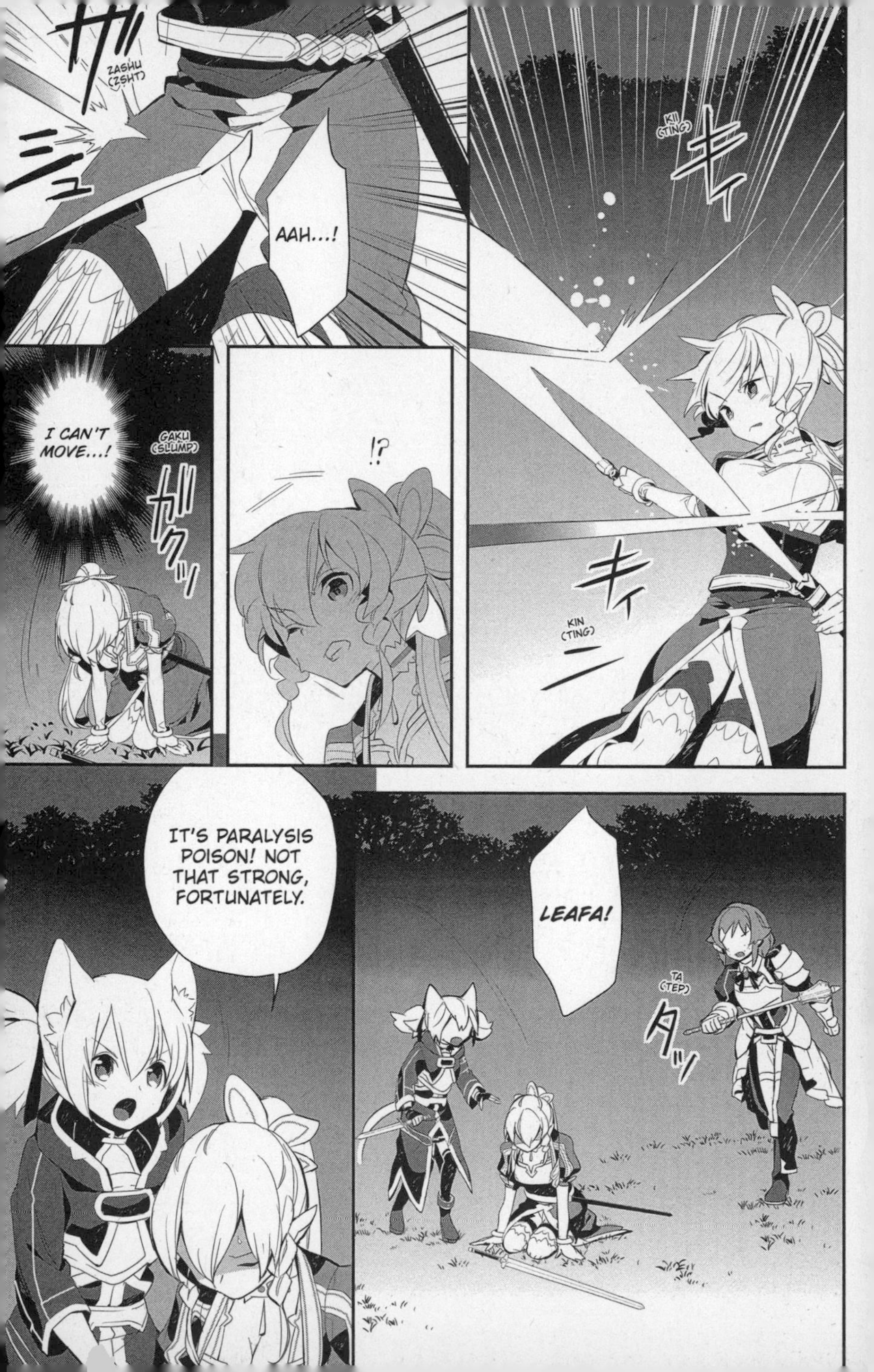
KII (TING)
KIN (TING)
ZASHU (ZSHT)
AAH...!
!?
I CAN'T MOVE...!
GAKU (SLUMP)
LEAFA!
TA (TEP)
IT'S PARALYSIS POISON! NOT THAT STRONG, FORTUNATELY.

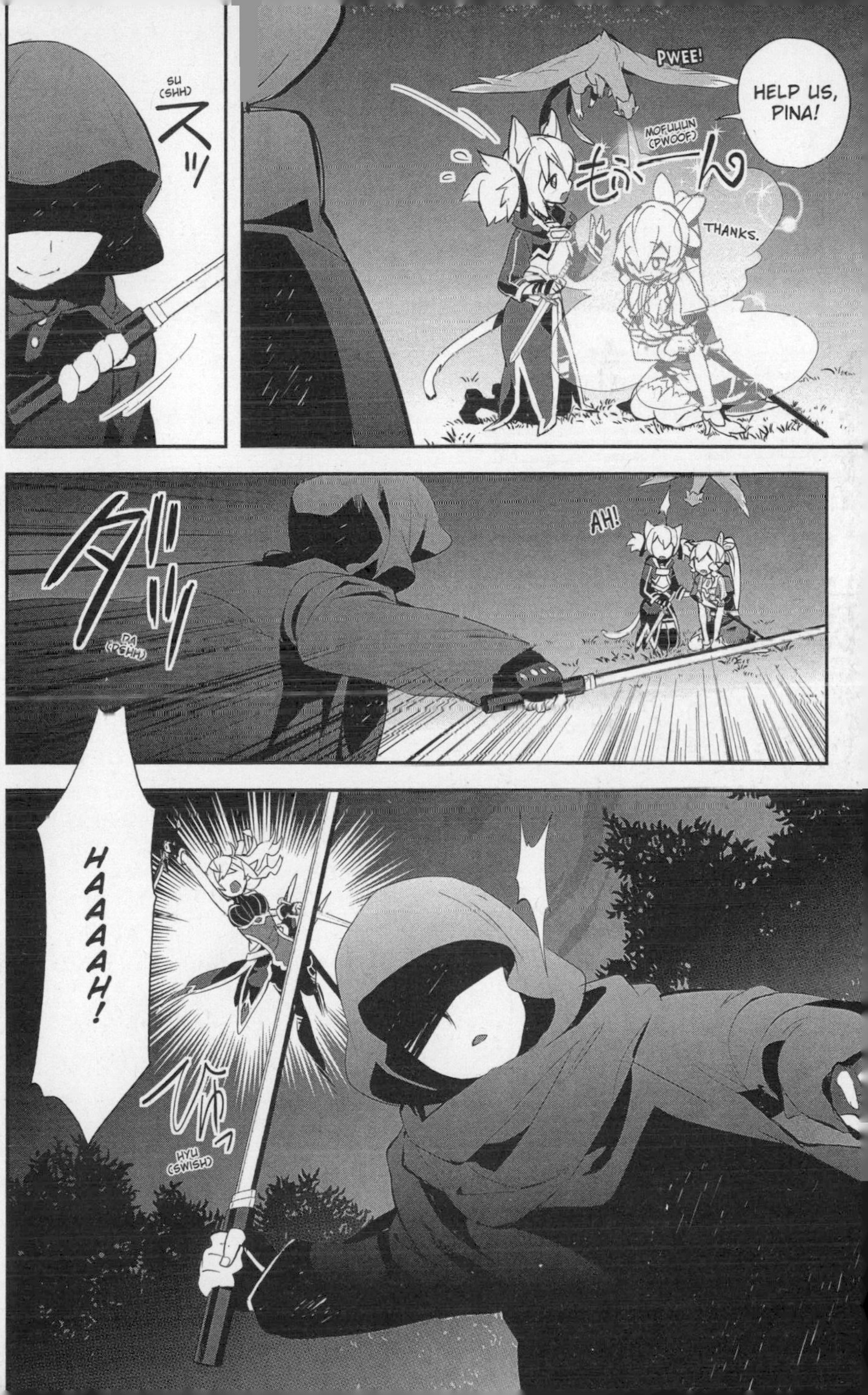
HELP US, PINA!
PWEE!
MOFUUUN (PWOOF)
もふーん
THANKS.
SU (SHH)
スッ
AH!
ダッ
DA (PSHH)
HAAAAAH!
ひゅっ
HYU (SWISH)

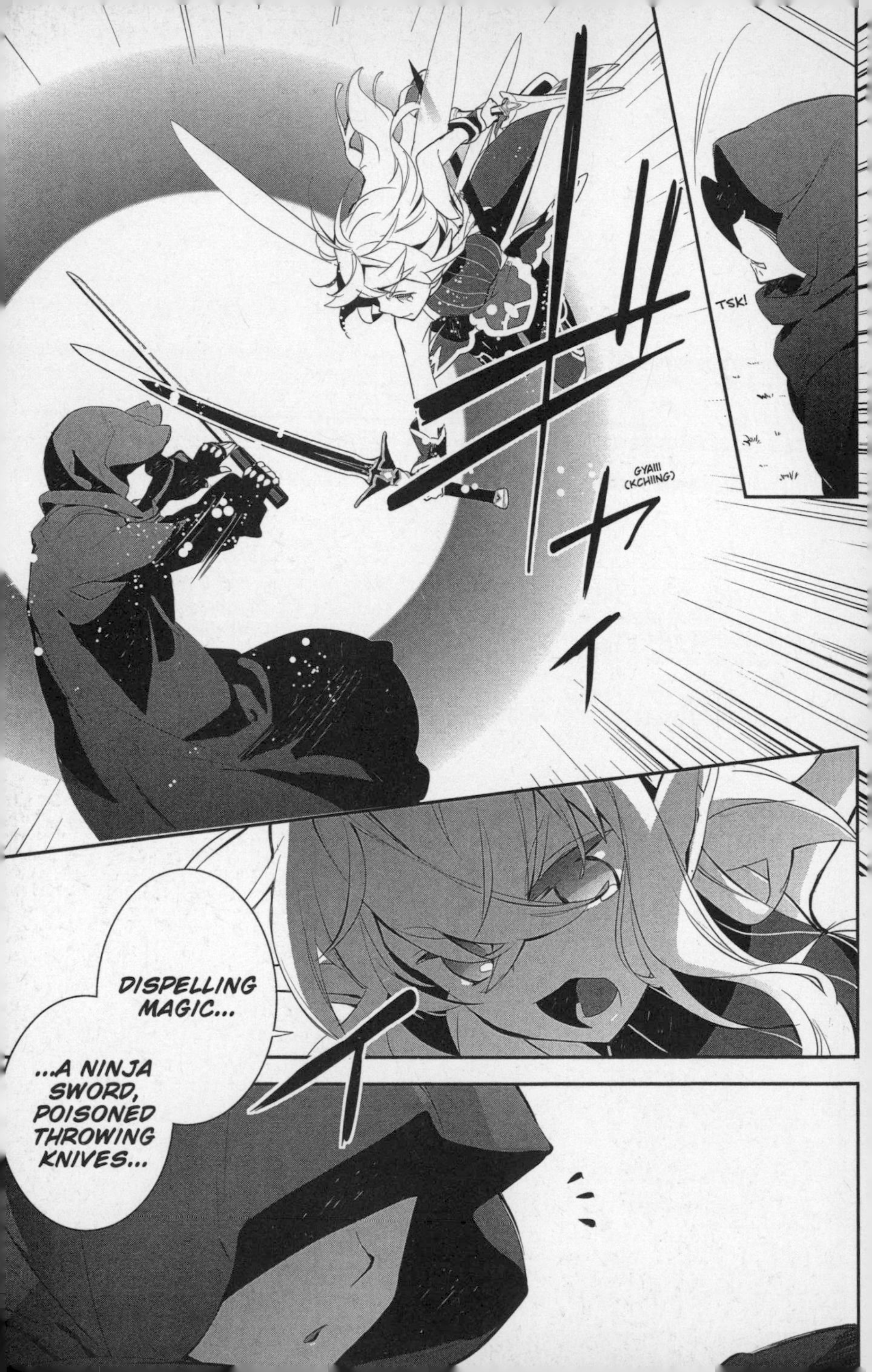
TSK!
GYAIII (KCHIING)
DISPELLING MAGIC...
...A NINJA SWORD, POISONED THROWING KNIVES...

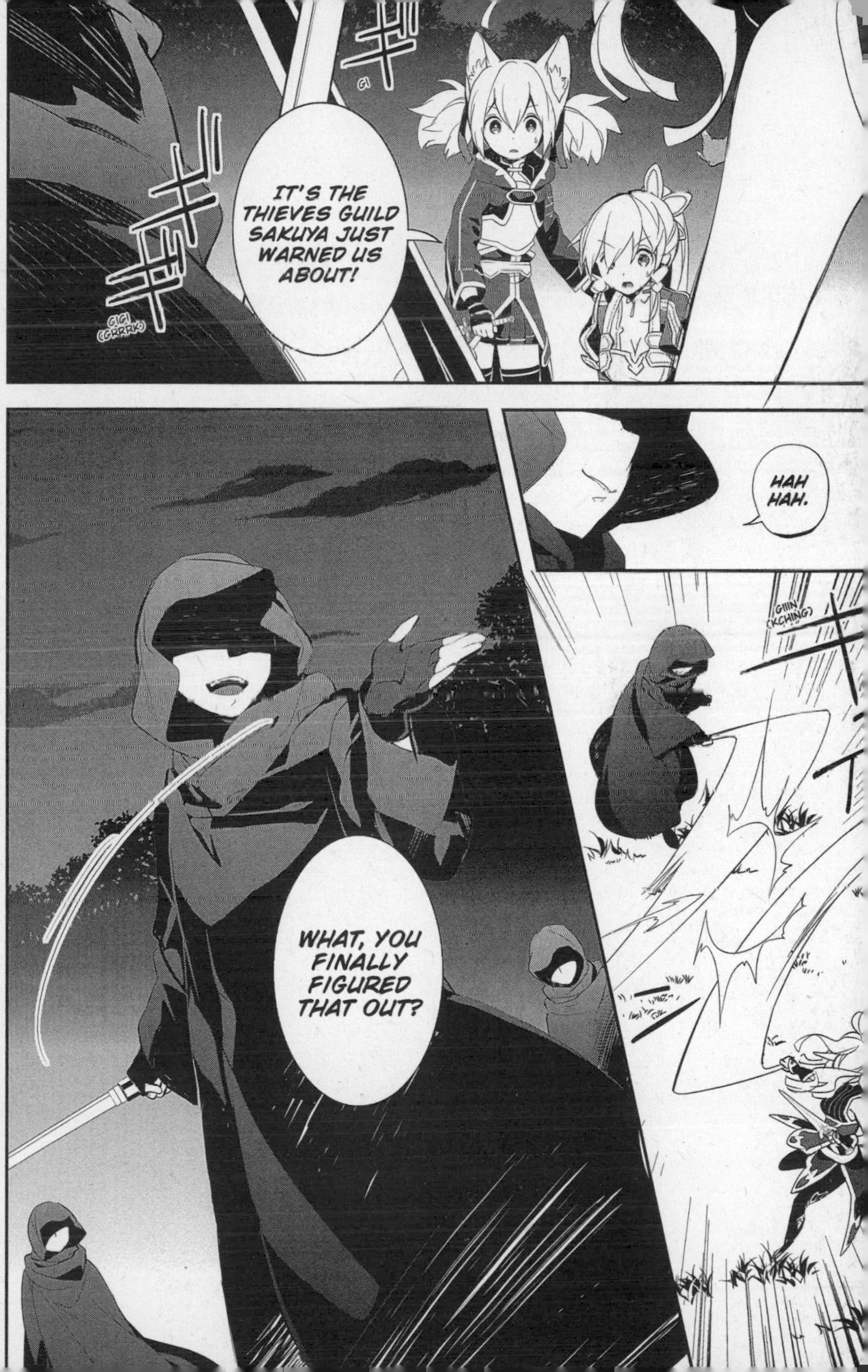
GI
IT'S THE THIEVES GUILD SAKUYA JUST WARNED US ABOUT!
GIGI (GRRRK)
HAH HAH.
GIIIN (KCHING)
WHAT, YOU FINALLY FIGURED THAT OUT?

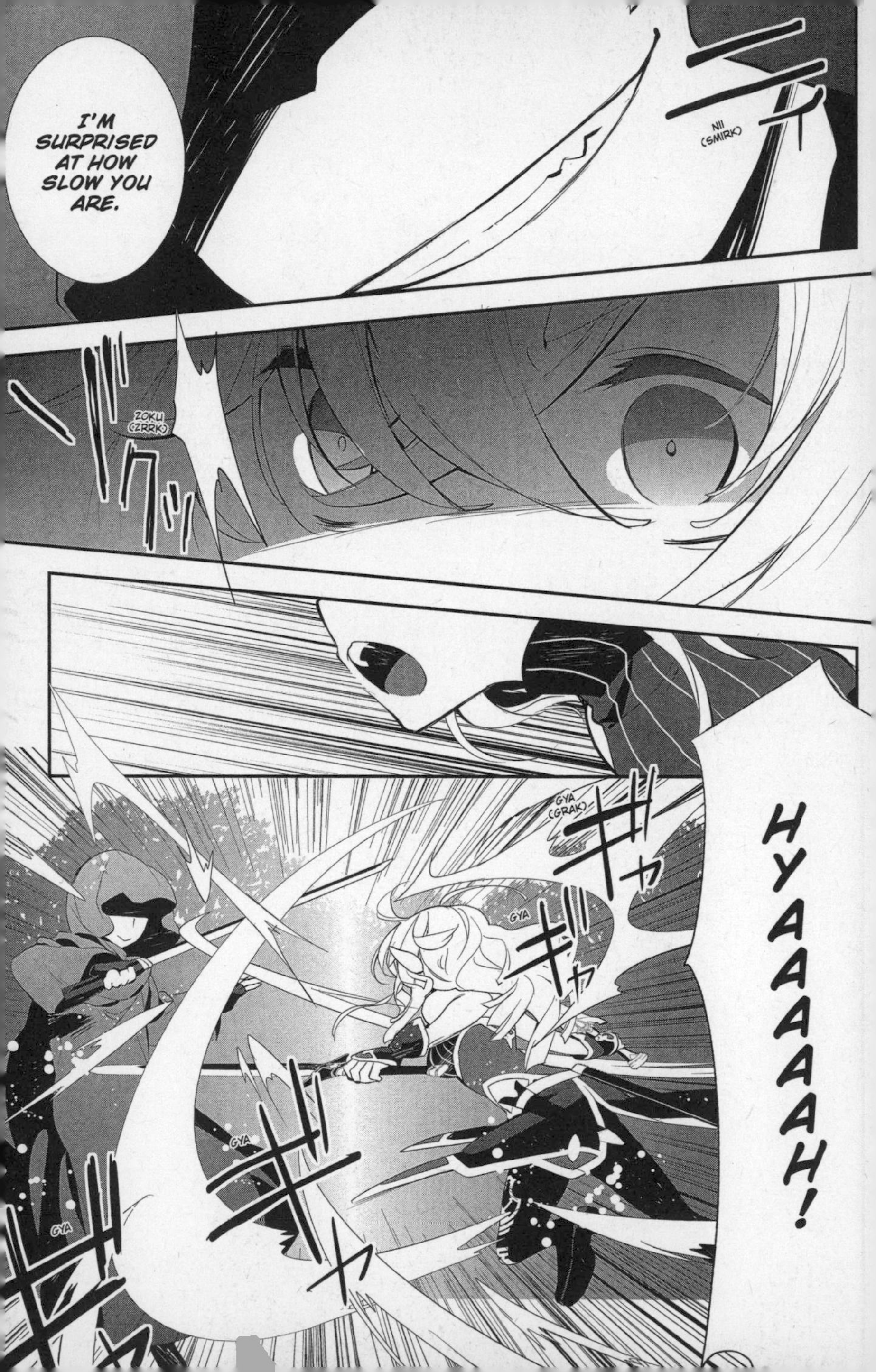
NII (SMIRK)
I'M SURPRISED AT HOW SLOW YOU ARE.
ZOKU (ZRRK)
GYA (GRAK)
HYAAAAAAH!
GYA
GYA
GYA

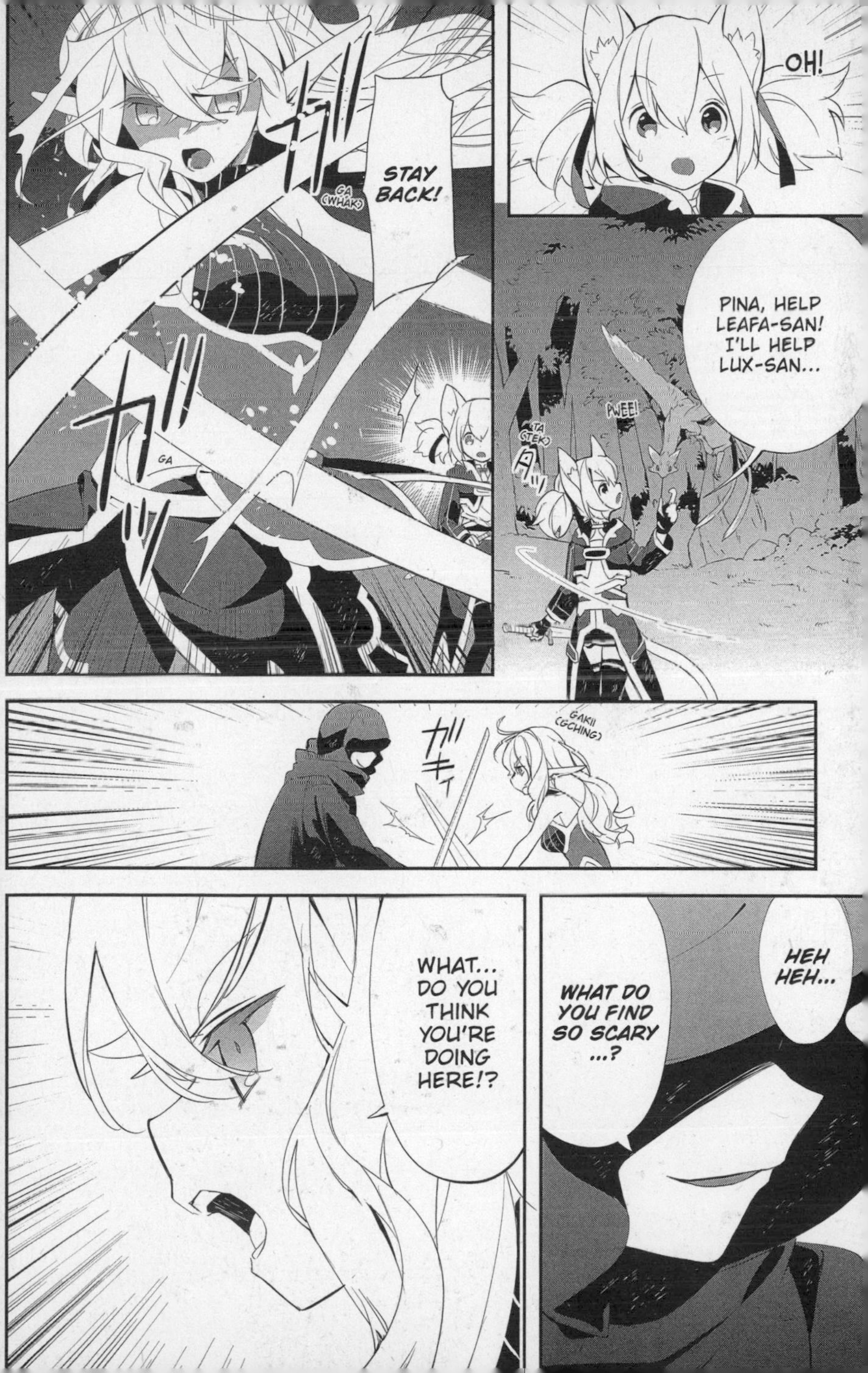
OH!
PINA, HELP LEAFA-SAN! I'LL HELP LUX-SAN...
PWEE!
TA (TEK)
STAY BACK!
GA (WHAK)
GA
GAKII (GCHING)
HEH HEH...
WHAT DO YOU FIND SO SCARY ...?
WHAT... DO YOU THINK YOU'RE DOING HERE!?

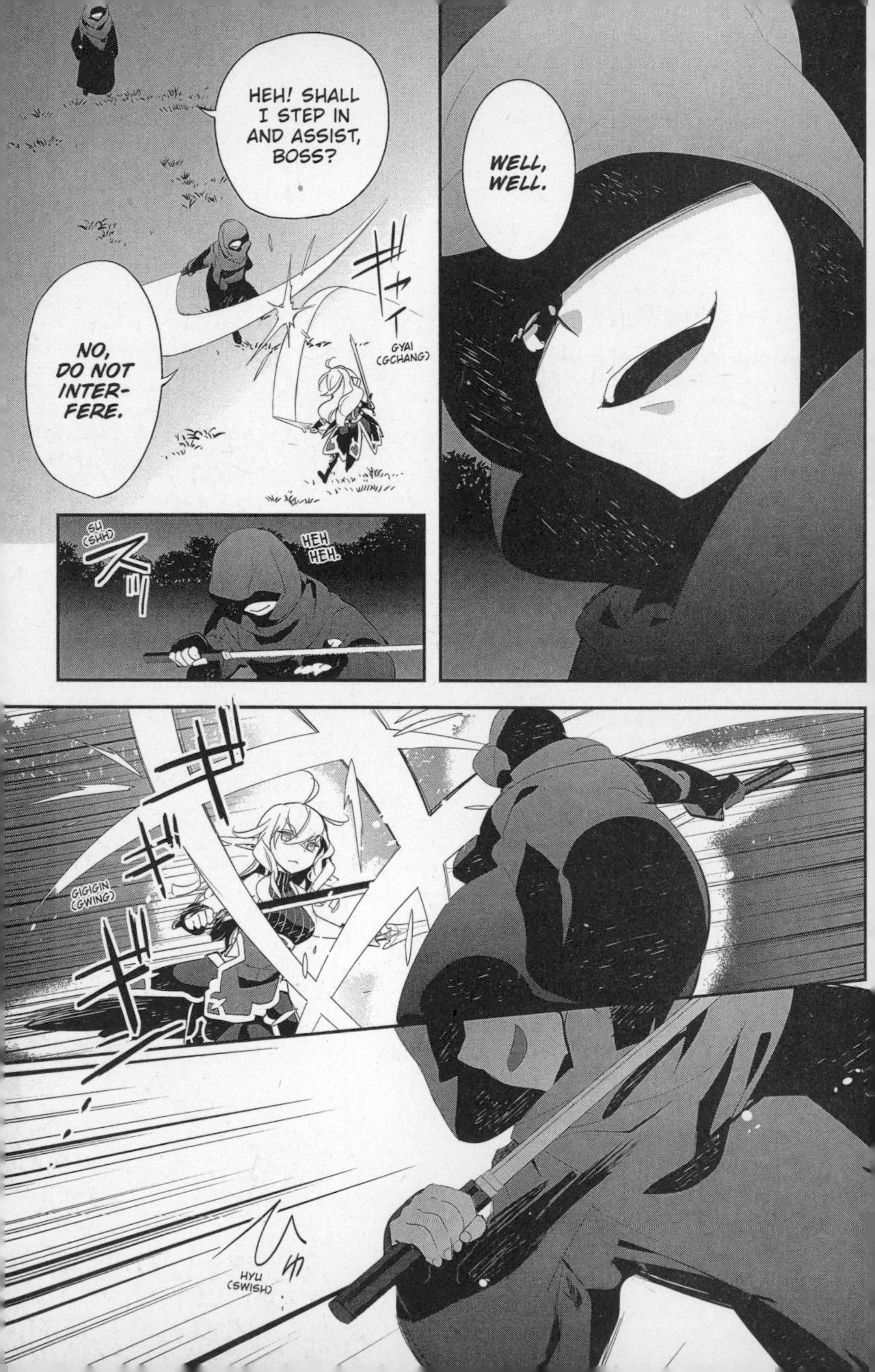
WELL, WELL.
HEH! SHALL I STEP IN AND ASSIST, BOSS?
ギャイ
GYAI (GCHANG)
NO, DO NOT INTERFERE.
SU (SHH)
スッ
HEH HEH.
ギギギン
GIGIGIN (GWING)
ひゅ
HYU (SWISH)

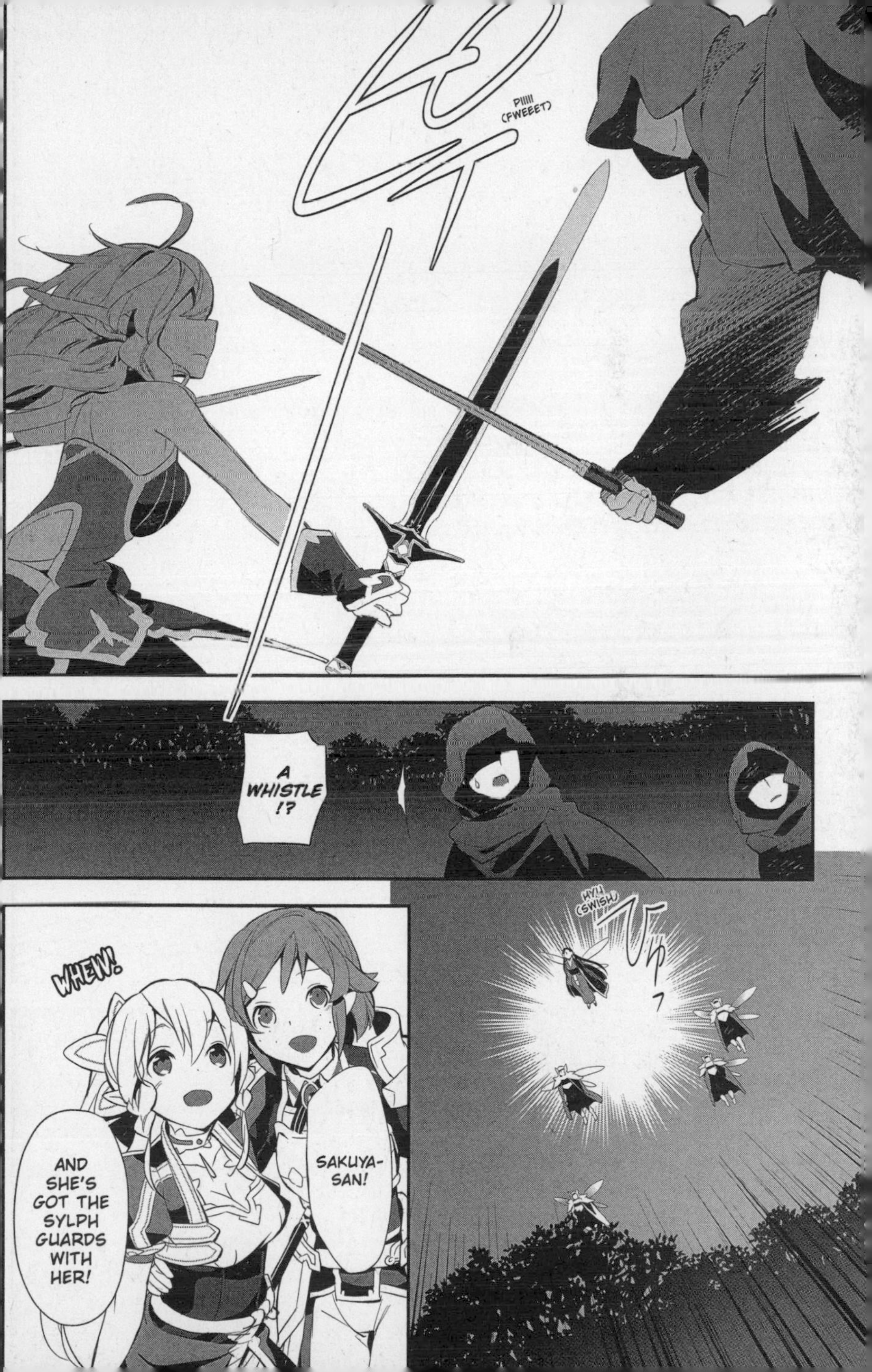
PIIIII
(FWEEET)
A WHISTLE !?
HYU
(SWISH)
WHEW!
SAKUYA-SAN!
AND SHE'S GOT THE SYLPH GUARDS WITH HER!

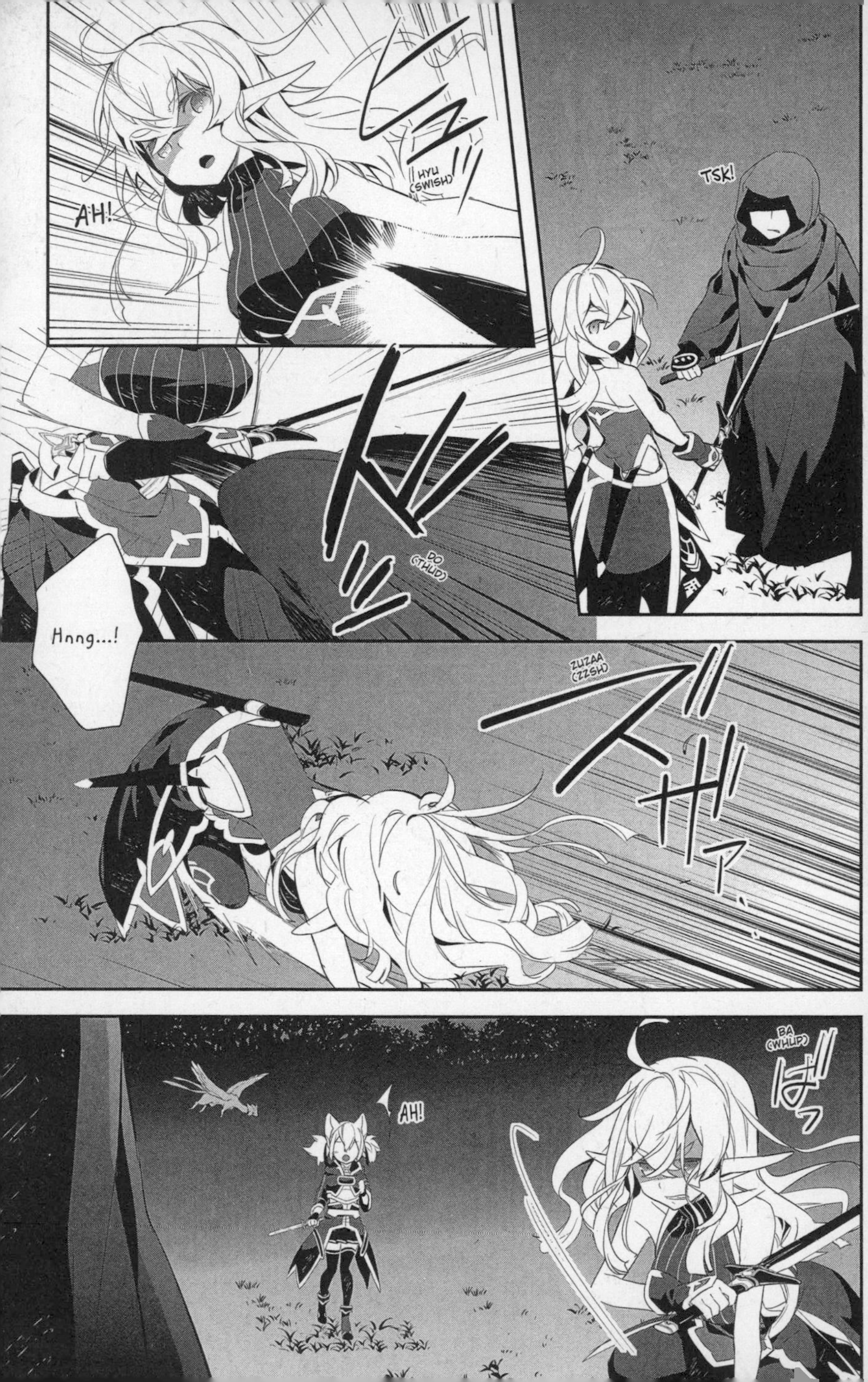
TSK!
HYU (SWISH)
AH!
DO (THUD)
Hnng...!
ZUZAA (ZZSH)
BA (WHUP)
AH!

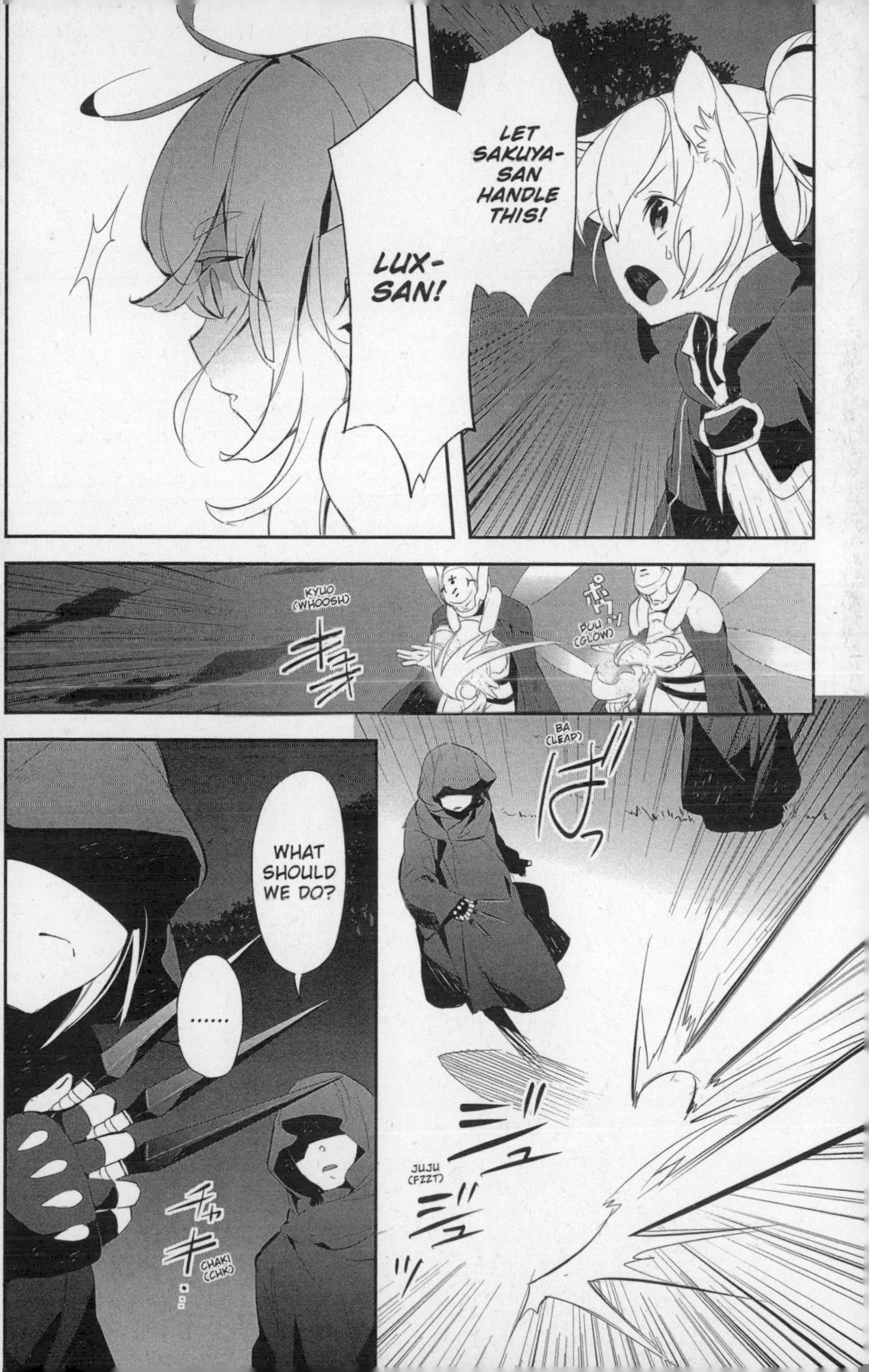
LET SAKUYA-SAN HANDLE THIS!
LUX-SAN!
PUU (GLOW)
KYUO (WHOOSH)
BA (LEAP)
JUJU (FZZT)
WHAT SHOULD WE DO?
......
CHAKI (CHK)

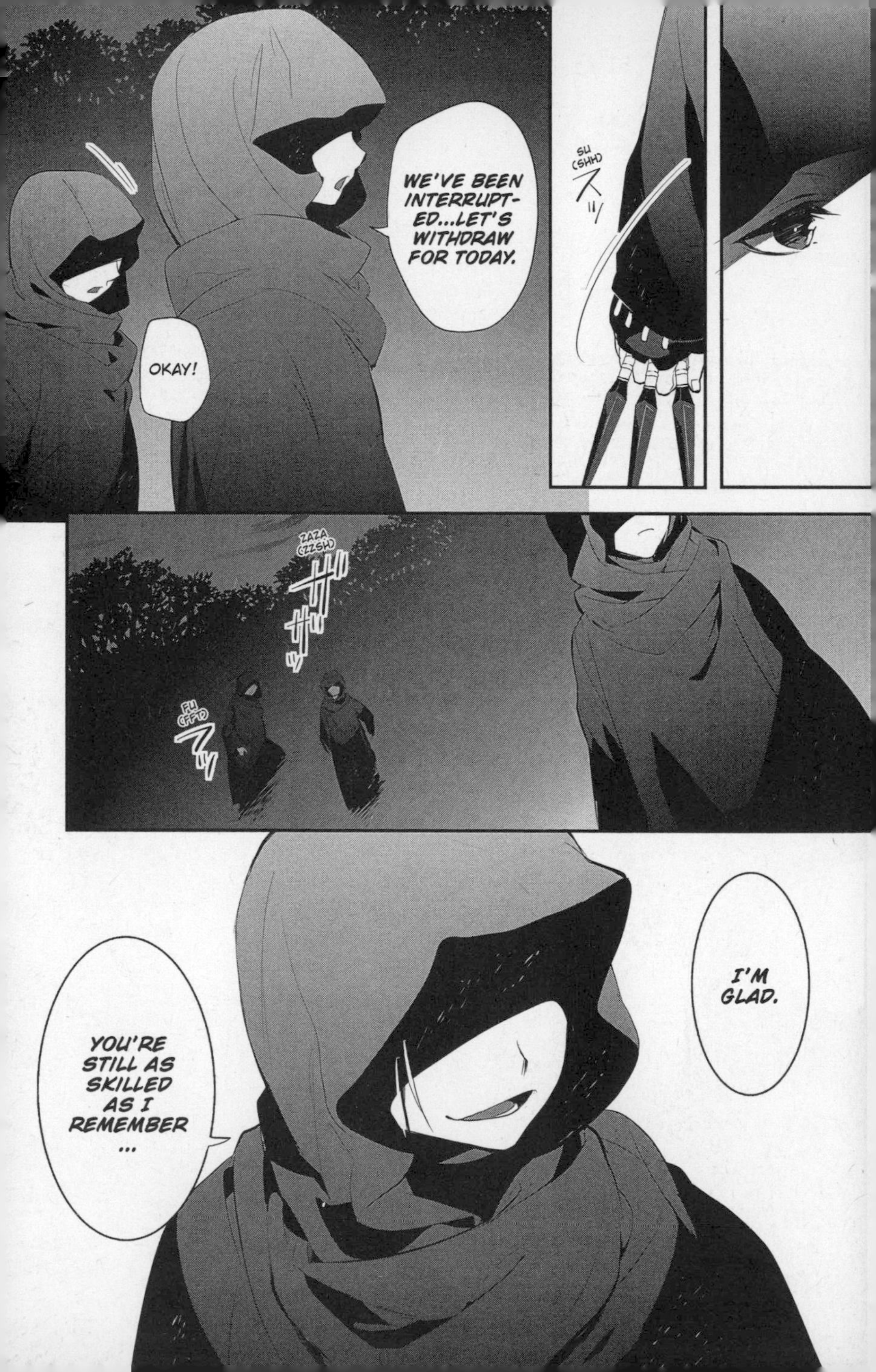
SU (SHH)
スッ
WE'VE BEEN INTERRUPTED...LET'S WITHDRAW FOR TODAY.
OKAY!
ZAZA (ZZSH)
ザザッ
FU (FFT)
フッ
I'M GLAD.
YOU'RE STILL AS SKILLED AS I REMEMBER...

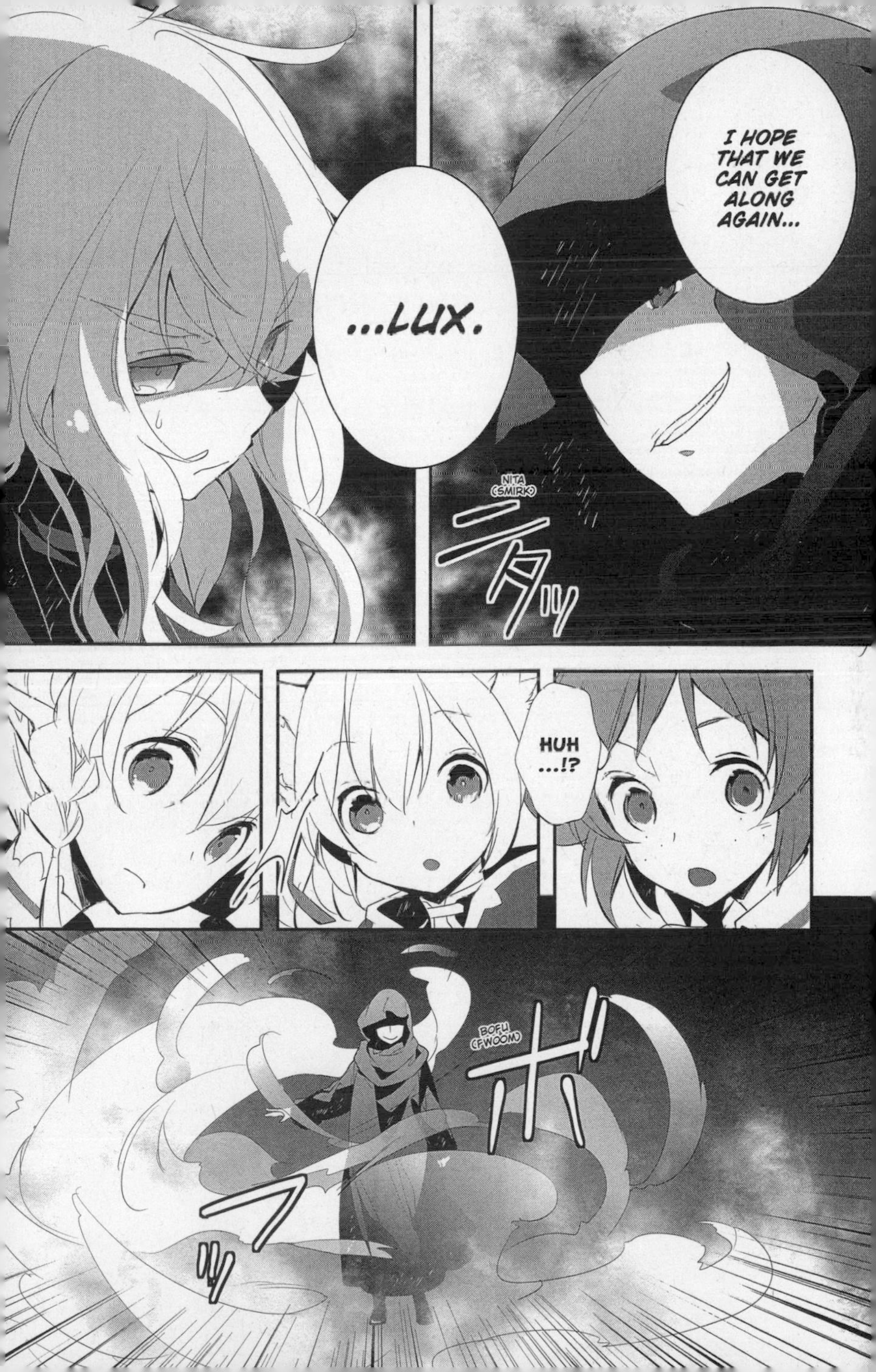
I HOPE THAT WE CAN GET ALONG AGAIN...
NITA (SMIRK)
ニタッ
...LUX.
HUH ...!?
BOFU (FWOOM)
ボフッ

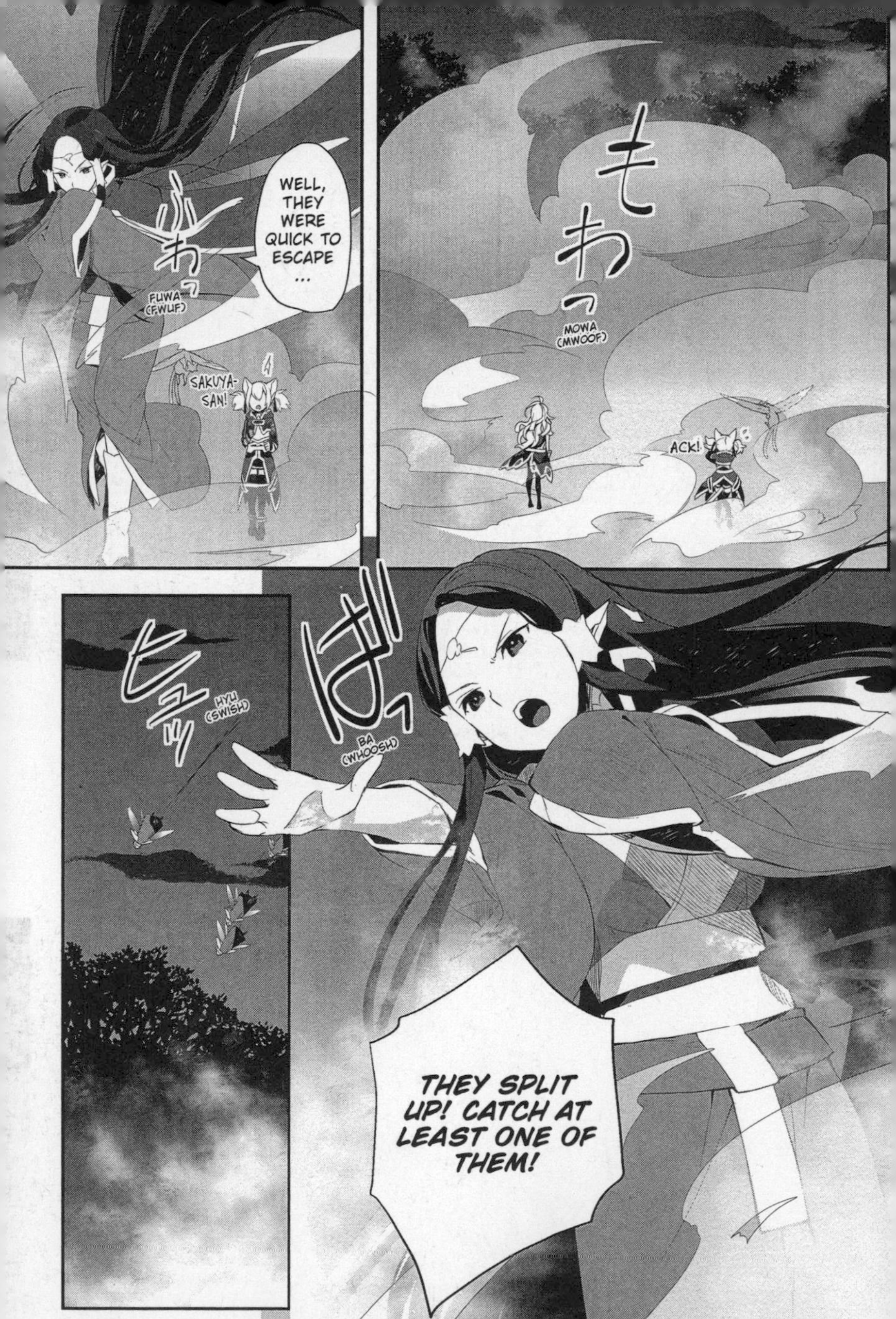
もわっ
MOWA (MWOOF)
ACK!
ふわっ
FUWA (FWUF)
WELL, THEY WERE QUICK TO ESCAPE ...
SAKUYA-SAN!
ばっ
BA (WHOOSH)
THEY SPLIT UP! CATCH AT LEAST ONE OF THEM!
ヒュッ
HYU (SWISH)

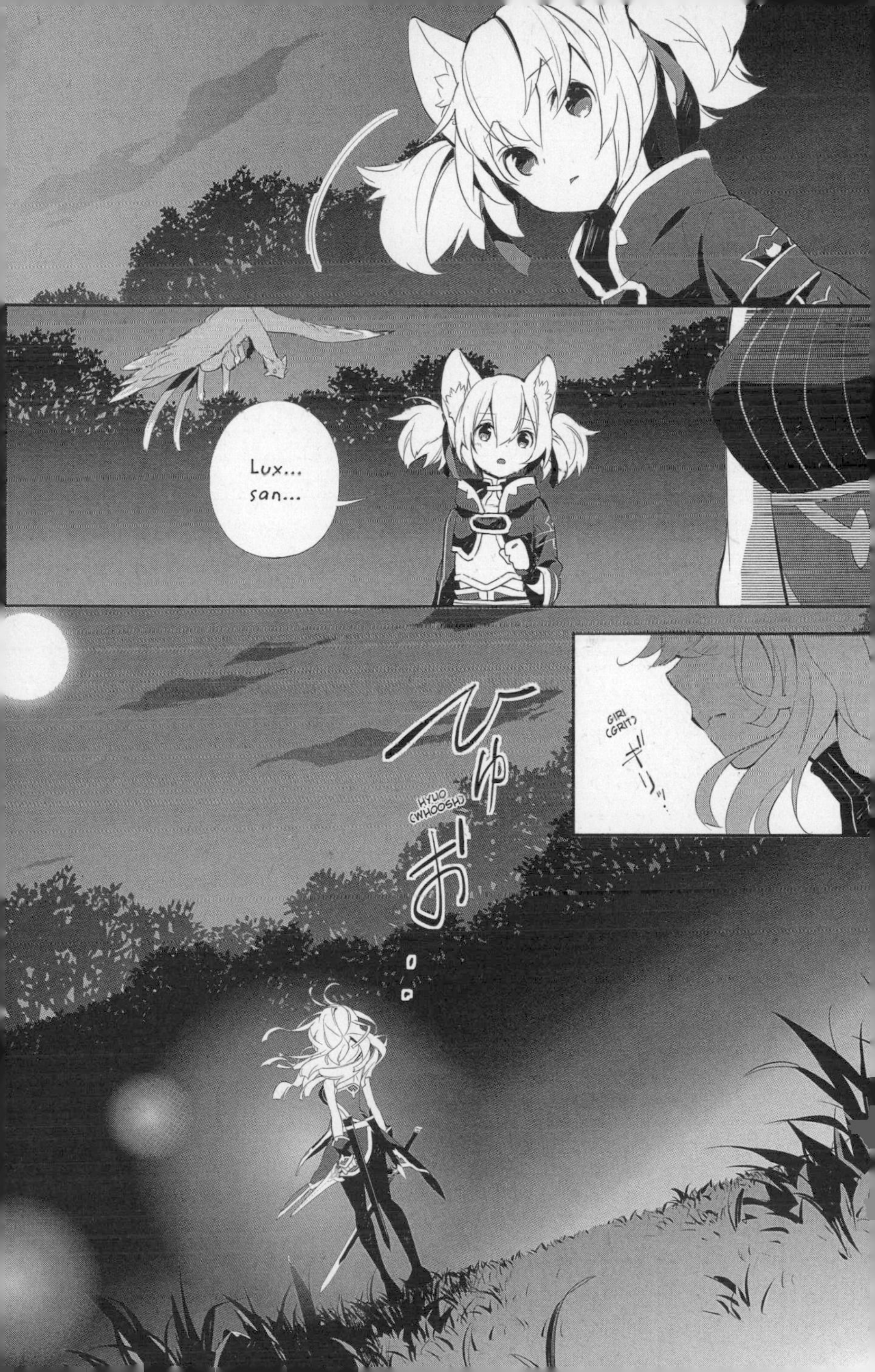
Lux... san...
GIRI (GRIT)
ギリッ
ひゅお
HYUO (WHOOSH)

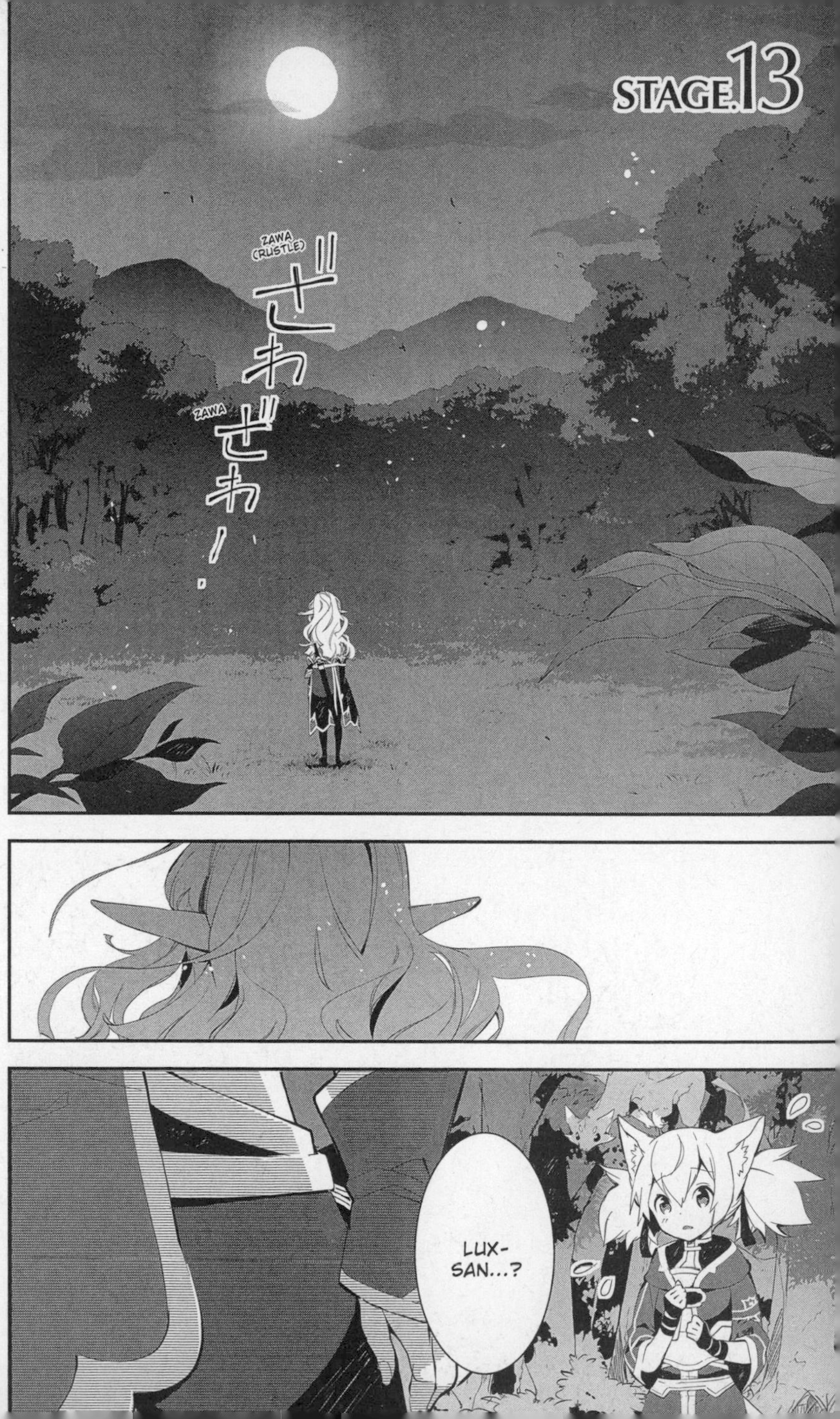
STAGE.13
ZAWA (RUSTLE)
ざわ
ZAWA
ざわ…
LUX-SAN…?

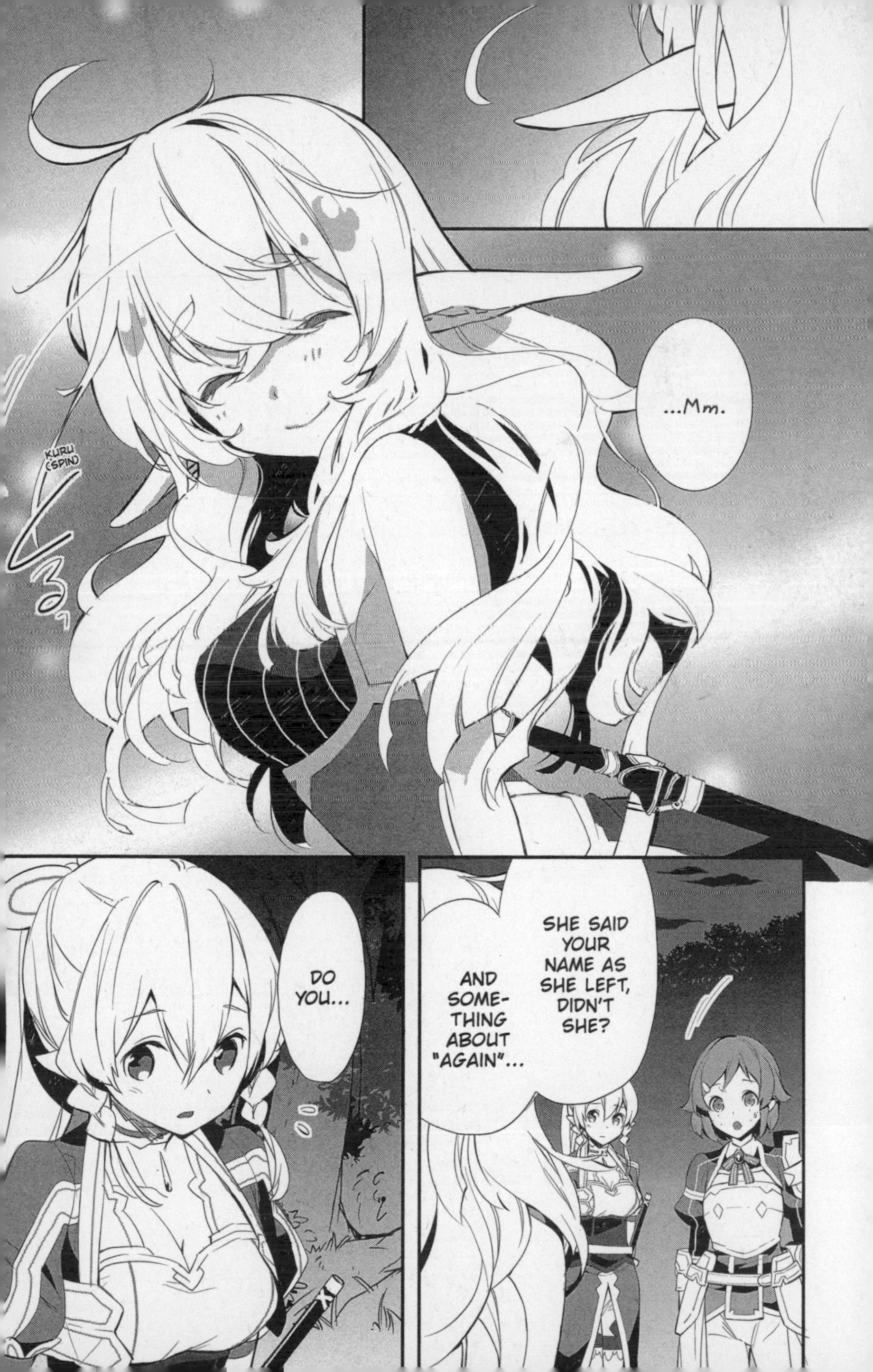
...Mm.
KURU (SPIN)
SHE SAID YOUR NAME AS SHE LEFT, DIDN'T SHE?
AND SOME-THING ABOUT "AGAIN"...
DO YOU...

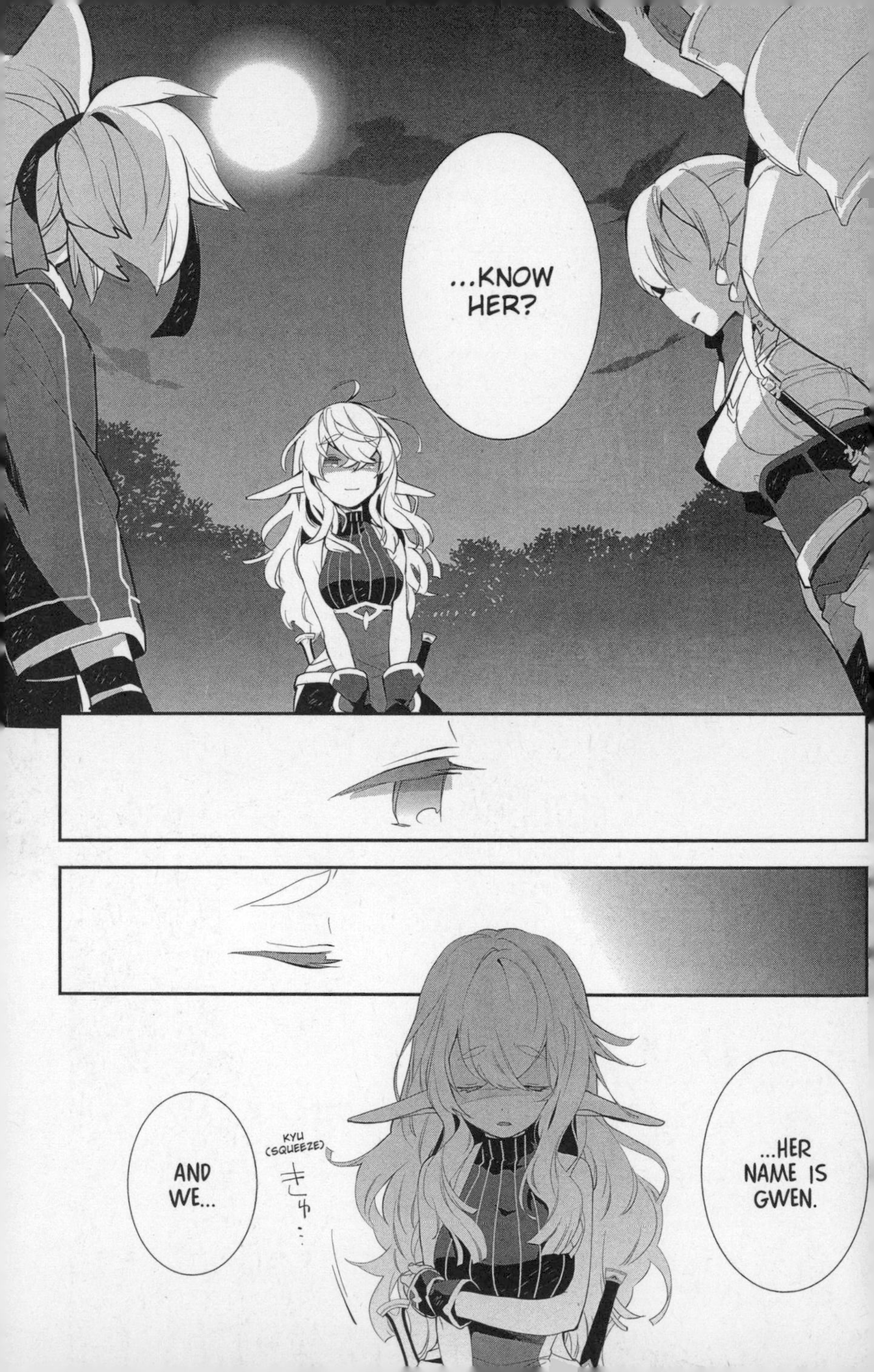
...KNOW HER?
...HER NAME IS GWEN.
KYU (SQUEEZE)
きゅ
AND WE...

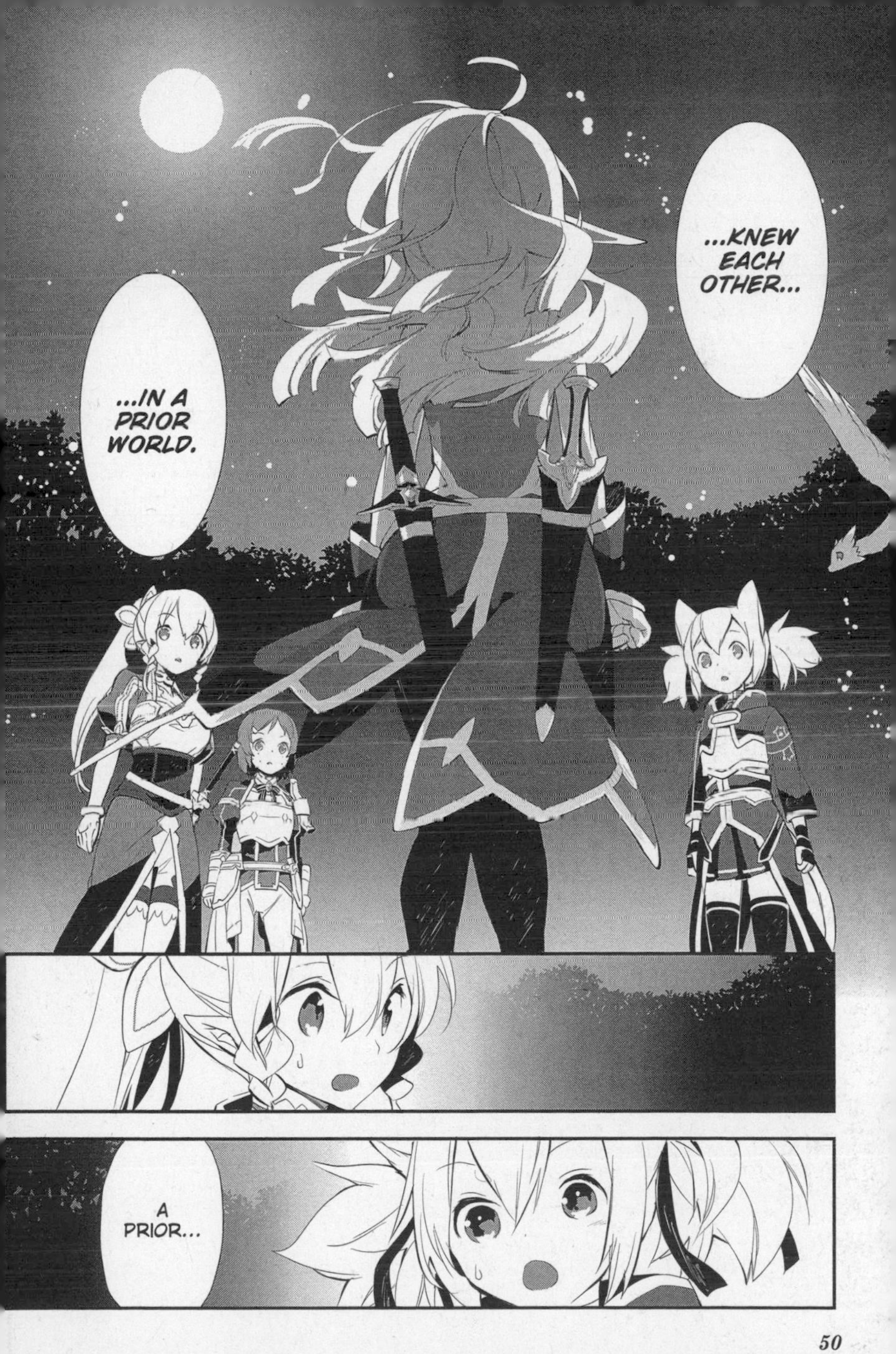
...KNEW EACH OTHER...
...IN A PRIOR WORLD.
A PRIOR...

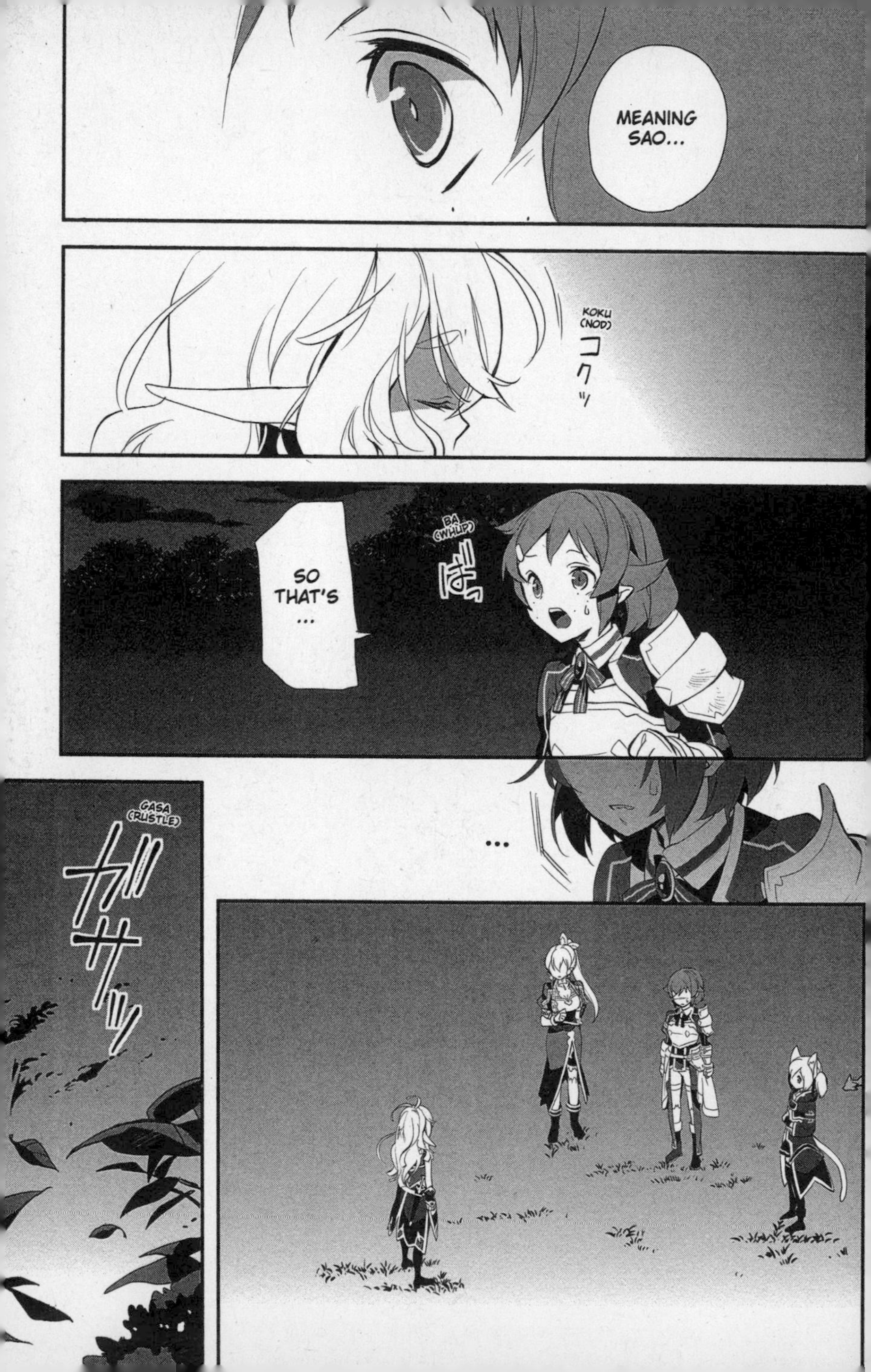
MEANING SAO...
KOKU (NOD)
コクッ
BA (WHUP)
ばっ
SO THAT'S ...
...
GASA (RUSTLE)
ガサッ

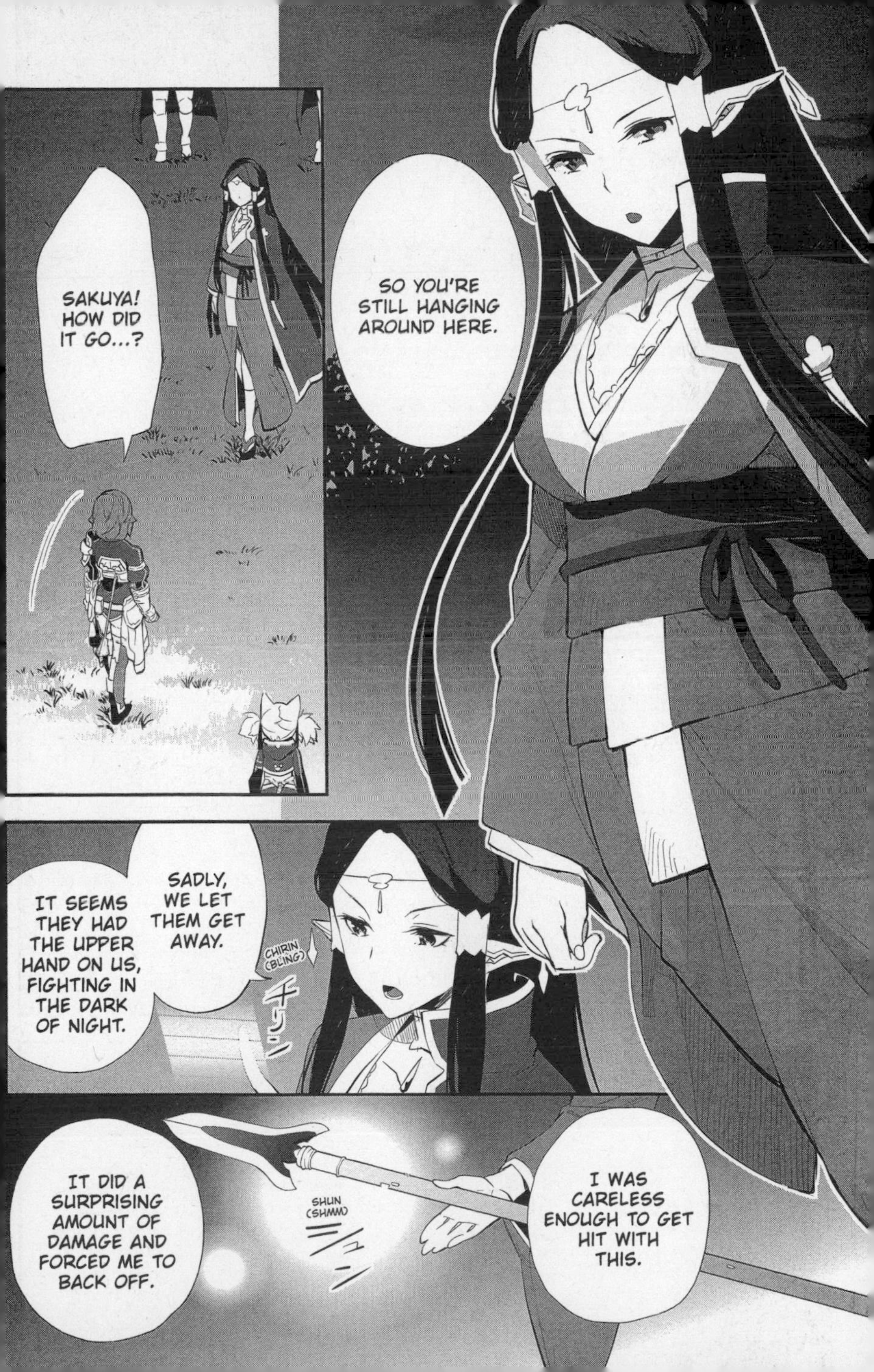
SO YOU'RE STILL HANGING AROUND HERE.
SAKUYA! HOW DID IT GO...?
SADLY, WE LET THEM GET AWAY.
IT SEEMS THEY HAD THE UPPER HAND ON US, FIGHTING IN THE DARK OF NIGHT.
CHIRIN (BLING)
I WAS CARELESS ENOUGH TO GET HIT WITH THIS.
SHUN (SHMM)
IT DID A SURPRISING AMOUNT OF DAMAGE AND FORCED ME TO BACK OFF.

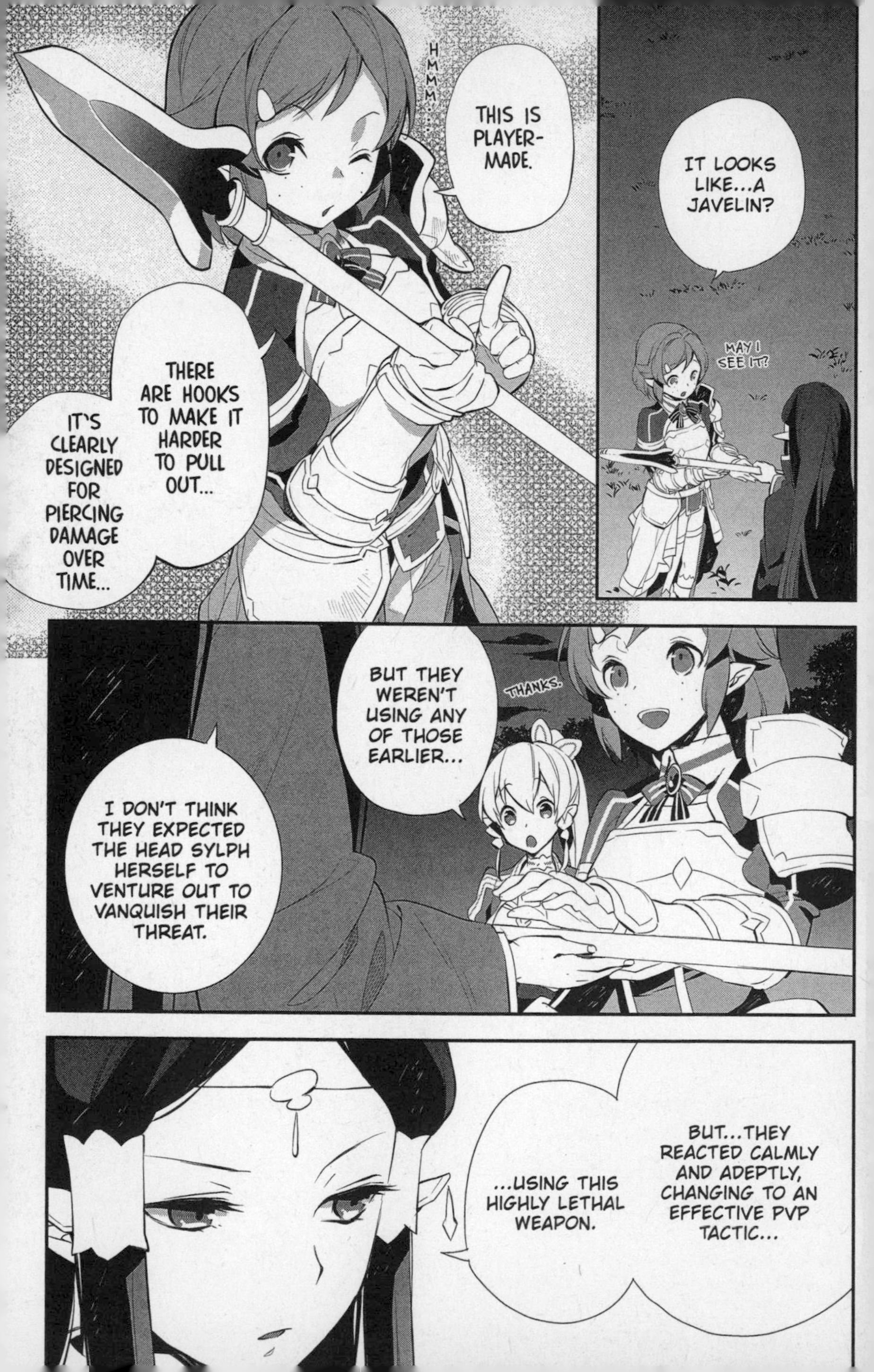
IT LOOKS LIKE...A JAVELIN?
MAY I SEE IT?
HMMM...
THIS IS PLAYER-MADE.
THERE ARE HOOKS TO MAKE IT HARDER TO PULL OUT...
IT'S CLEARLY DESIGNED FOR PIERCING DAMAGE OVER TIME...
THANKS.
BUT THEY WEREN'T USING ANY OF THOSE EARLIER...
I DON'T THINK THEY EXPECTED THE HEAD SYLPH HERSELF TO VENTURE OUT TO VANQUISH THEIR THREAT.
BUT...THEY REACTED CALMLY AND ADEPTLY, CHANGING TO AN EFFECTIVE PVP TACTIC...
...USING THIS HIGHLY LETHAL WEAPON.

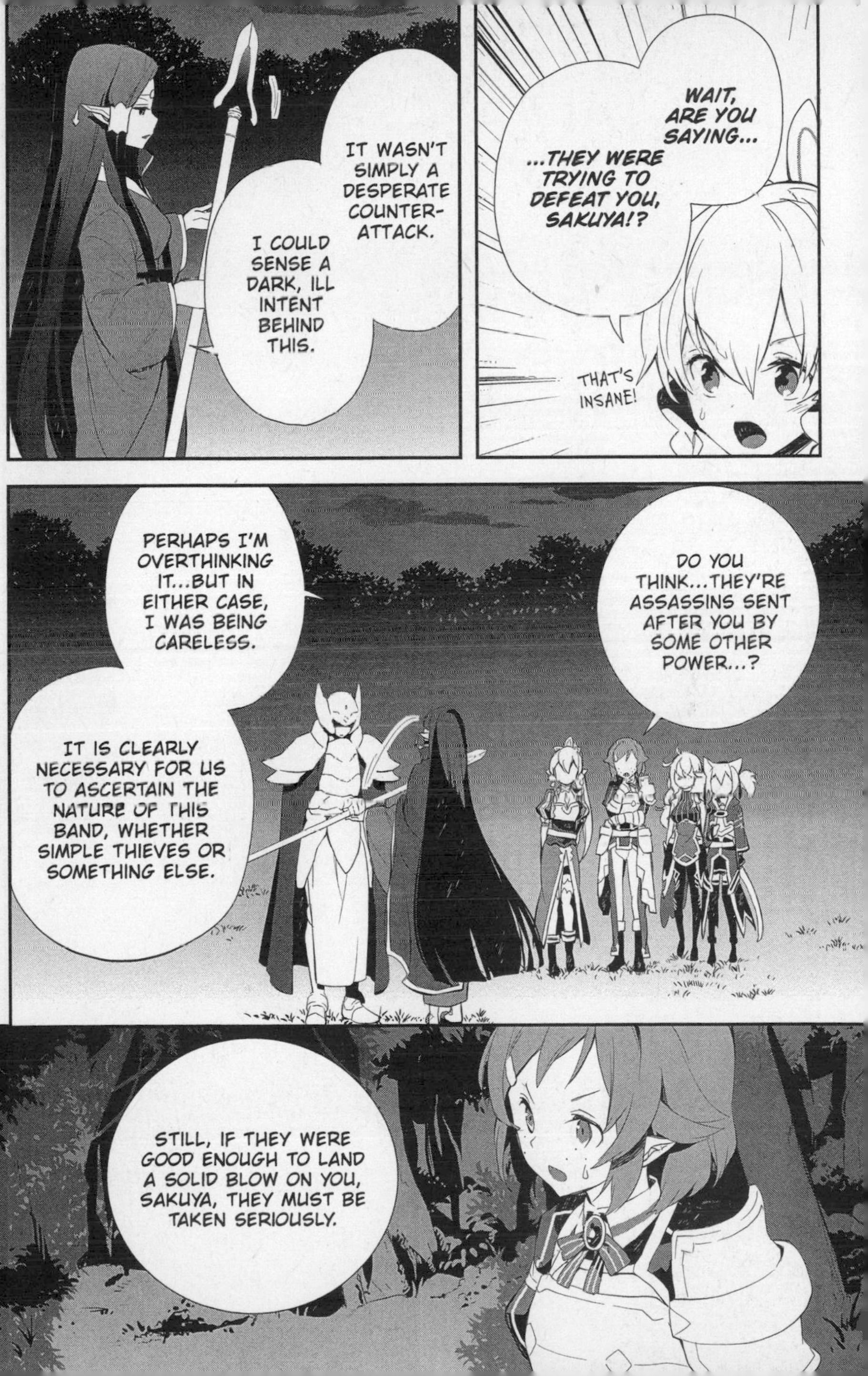
WAIT, ARE YOU SAYING...
...THEY WERE TRYING TO DEFEAT YOU, SAKUYA!?
THAT'S INSANE!
IT WASN'T SIMPLY A DESPERATE COUNTER-ATTACK.
I COULD SENSE A DARK, ILL INTENT BEHIND THIS.
DO YOU THINK...THEY'RE ASSASSINS SENT AFTER YOU BY SOME OTHER POWER...?
PERHAPS I'M OVERTHINKING IT...BUT IN EITHER CASE, I WAS BEING CARELESS.
IT IS CLEARLY NECESSARY FOR US TO ASCERTAIN THE NATURE OF THIS BAND, WHETHER SIMPLE THIEVES OR SOMETHING ELSE.
STILL, IF THEY WERE GOOD ENOUGH TO LAND A SOLID BLOW ON YOU, SAKUYA, THEY MUST BE TAKEN SERIOUSLY.

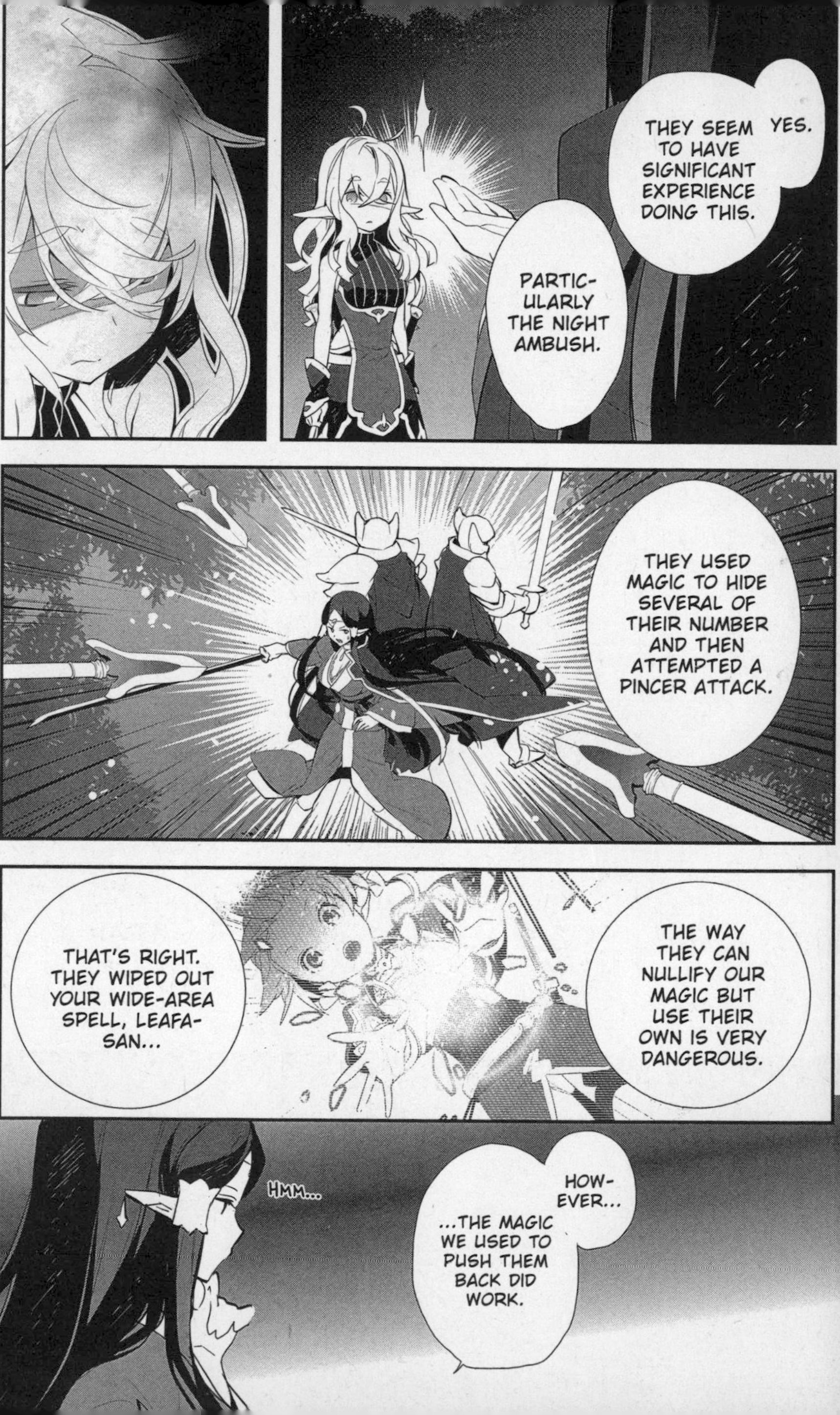
YES.
THEY SEEM TO HAVE SIGNIFICANT EXPERIENCE DOING THIS.
PARTIC-ULARLY THE NIGHT AMBUSH.
THEY USED MAGIC TO HIDE SEVERAL OF THEIR NUMBER AND THEN ATTEMPTED A PINCER ATTACK.
THE WAY THEY CAN NULLIFY OUR MAGIC BUT USE THEIR OWN IS VERY DANGEROUS.
THAT'S RIGHT. THEY WIPED OUT YOUR WIDE-AREA SPELL, LEAFA-SAN...
HOW-EVER...
...THE MAGIC WE USED TO PUSH THEM BACK DID WORK.
HMM...

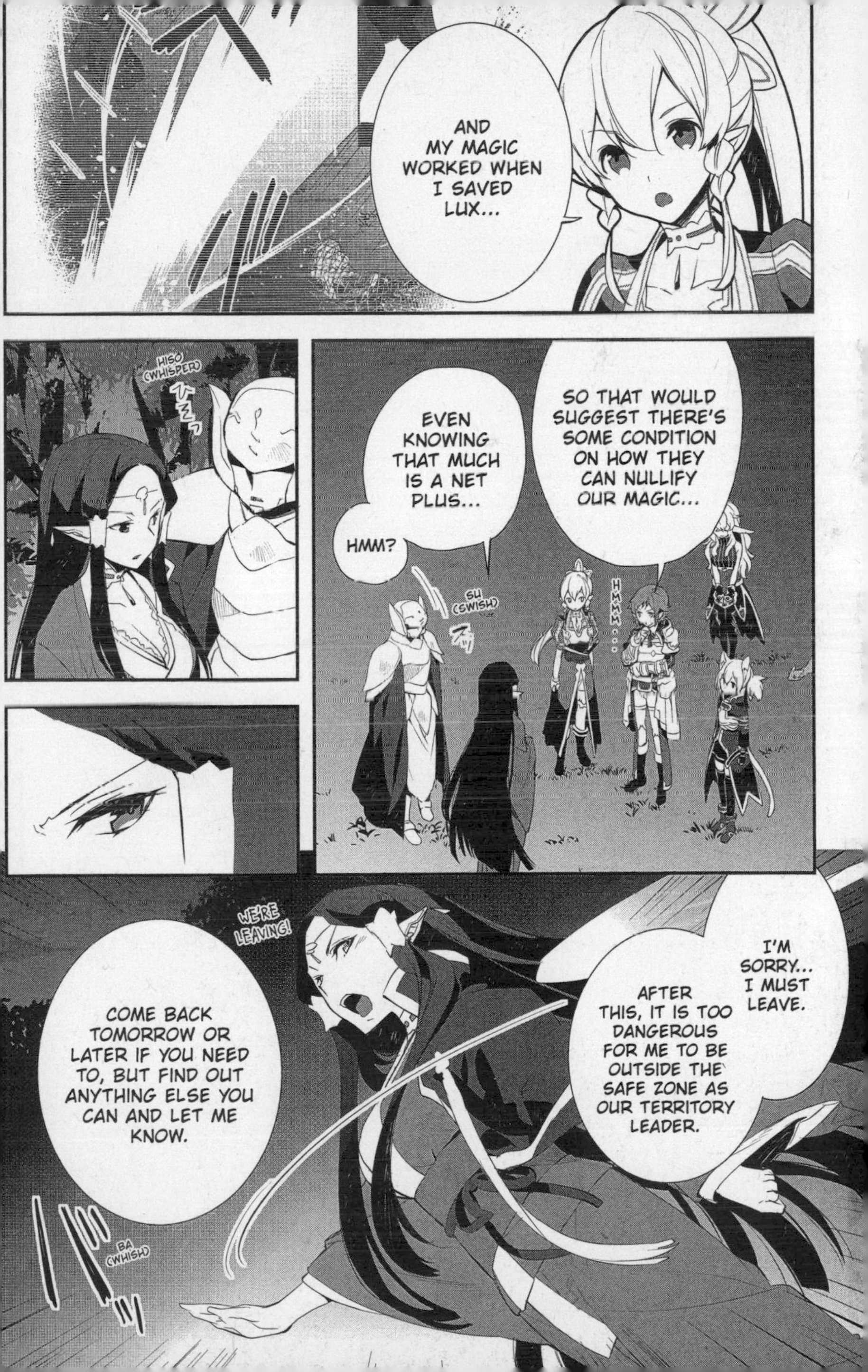
AND MY MAGIC WORKED WHEN I SAVED LUX...
SO THAT WOULD SUGGEST THERE'S SOME CONDITION ON HOW THEY CAN NULLIFY OUR MAGIC...
HMMM...
EVEN KNOWING THAT MUCH IS A NET PLUS...
HMM?
SU (SWISH)
HISO (WHISPER)
I'M SORRY... I MUST LEAVE.
AFTER THIS, IT IS TOO DANGEROUS FOR ME TO BE OUTSIDE THE SAFE ZONE AS OUR TERRITORY LEADER.
WE'RE LEAVING!
COME BACK TOMORROW OR LATER IF YOU NEED TO, BUT FIND OUT ANYTHING ELSE YOU CAN AND LET ME KNOW.
BA (WHISH)

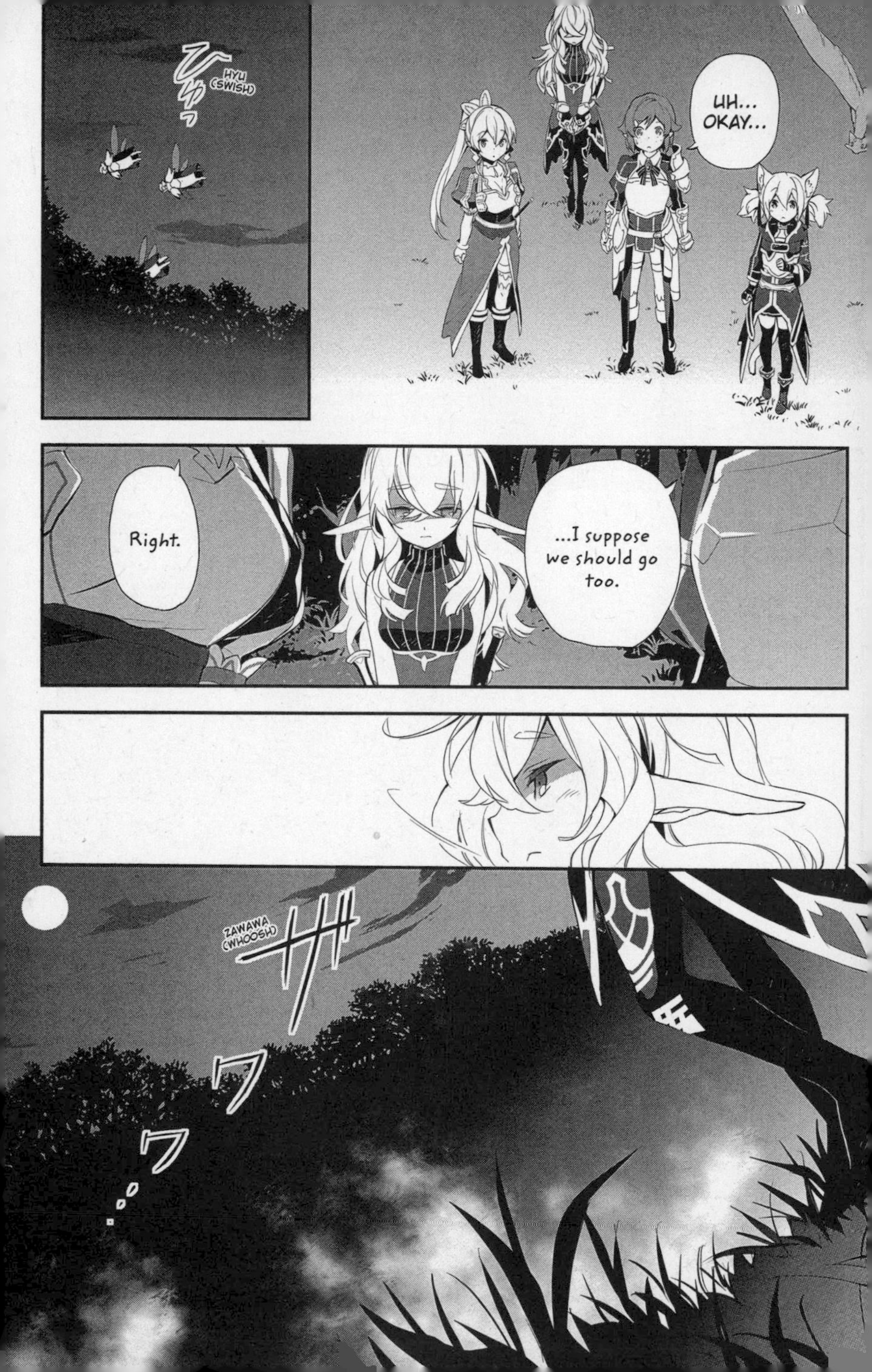
UH... OKAY...
ひゅっ
HYU (SWISH)
...I suppose we should go too.
Right.
ザワワ
ZAWAWA (WHOOSH)

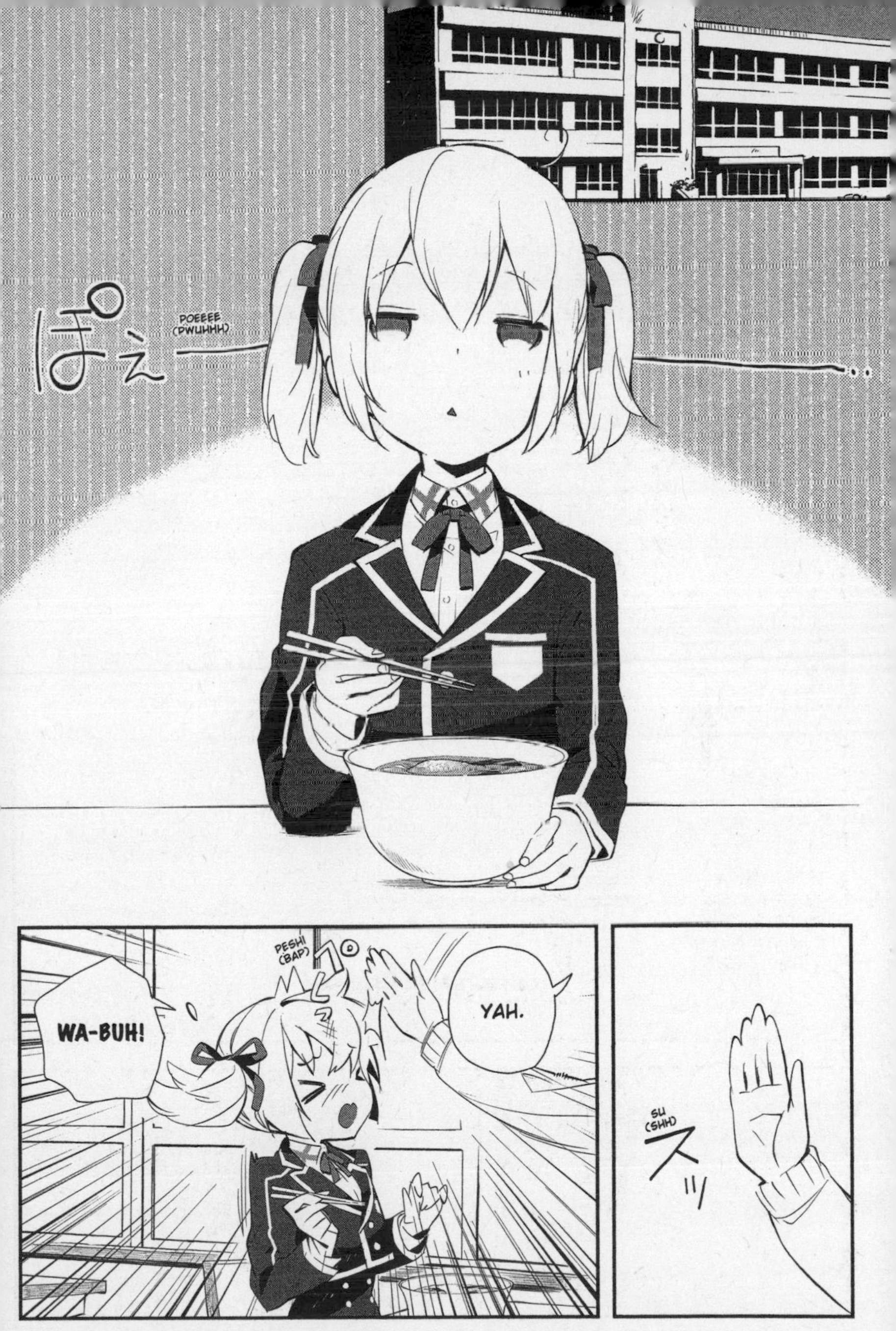
ぽえー
POEEEE (PWUHHH)
スッ
SU (SHH)
YAH.
PESHI (BAP)
WA-BUH!

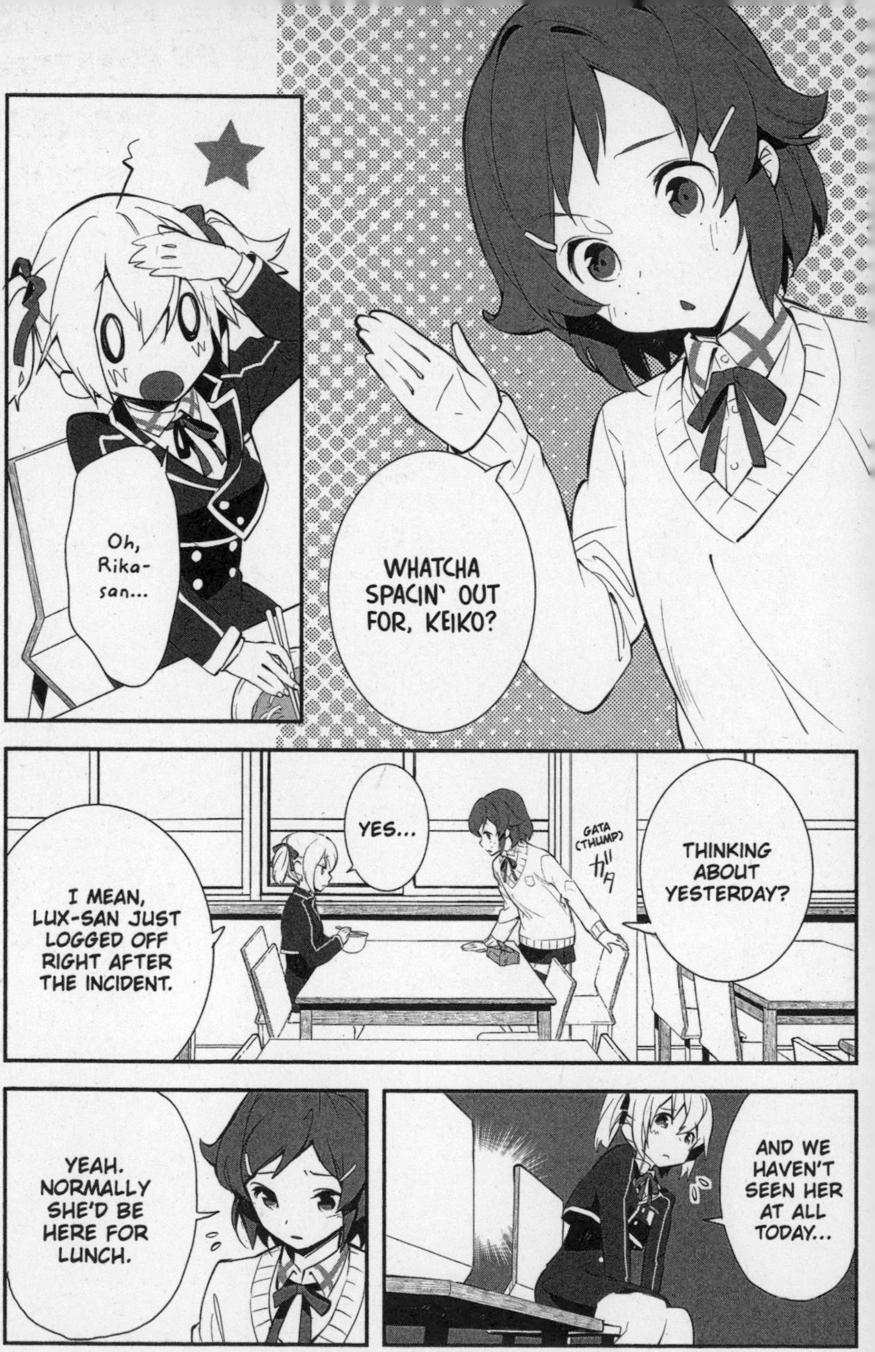
WHATCHA SPACIN' OUT FOR, KEIKO?
Oh, Rika-san...
THINKING ABOUT YESTERDAY?
GATA (THUMP)
ガタ
YES...
I MEAN, LUX-SAN JUST LOGGED OFF RIGHT AFTER THE INCIDENT.
AND WE HAVEN'T SEEN HER AT ALL TODAY...
YEAH. NORMALLY SHE'D BE HERE FOR LUNCH.

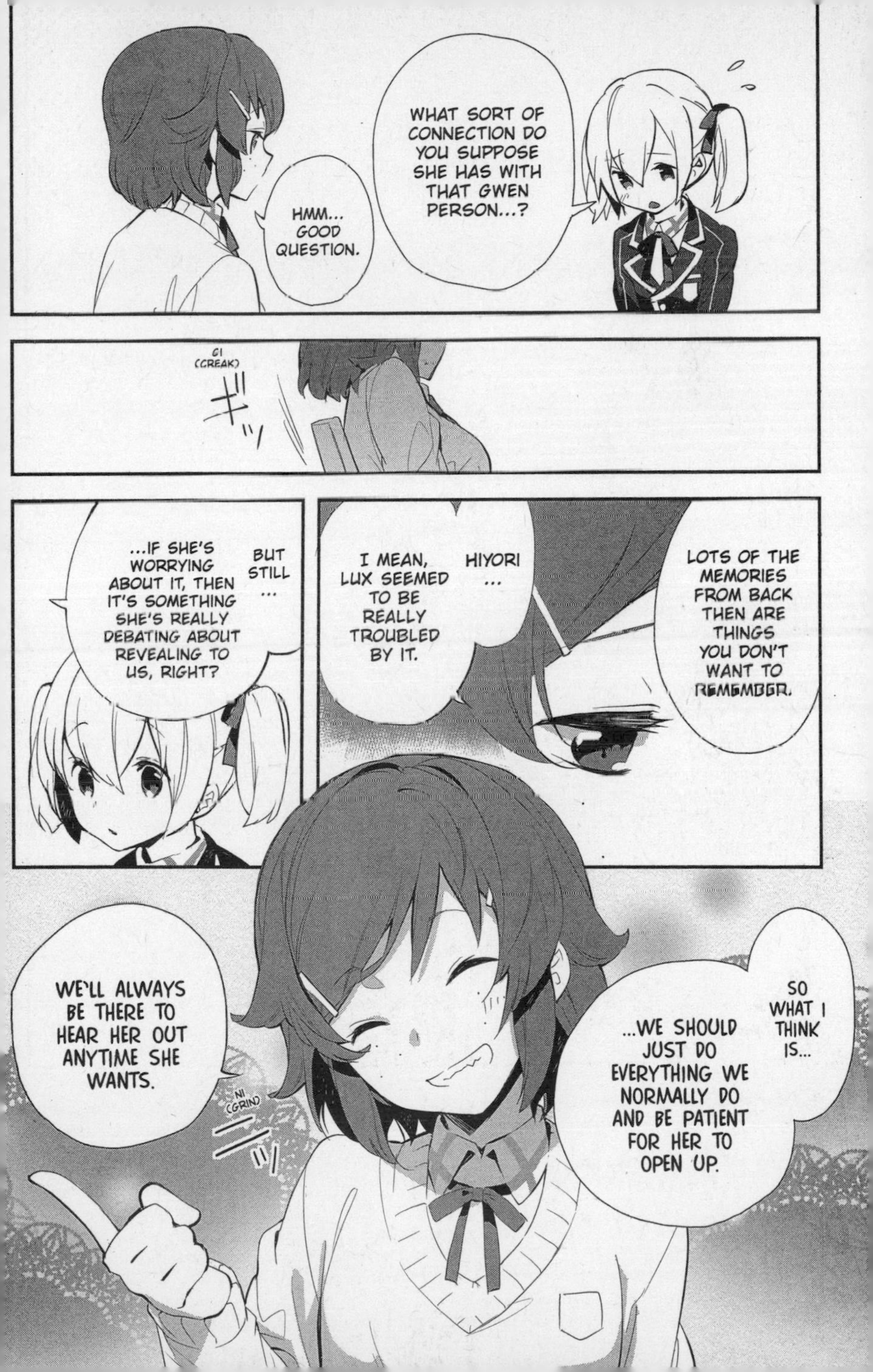
WHAT SORT OF CONNECTION DO YOU SUPPOSE SHE HAS WITH THAT GWEN PERSON...?
HMM... GOOD QUESTION.
GI (CREAK)
LOTS OF THE MEMORIES FROM BACK THEN ARE THINGS YOU DON'T WANT TO REMEMBER.
HIYORI ...
I MEAN, LUX SEEMED TO BE REALLY TROUBLED BY IT.
BUT STILL ...
...IF SHE'S WORRYING ABOUT IT, THEN IT'S SOMETHING SHE'S REALLY DEBATING ABOUT REVEALING TO US, RIGHT?
SO WHAT I THINK IS...
...WE SHOULD JUST DO EVERYTHING WE NORMALLY DO AND BE PATIENT FOR HER TO OPEN UP.
NI (GRIN)
WE'LL ALWAYS BE THERE TO HEAR HER OUT ANYTIME SHE WANTS.

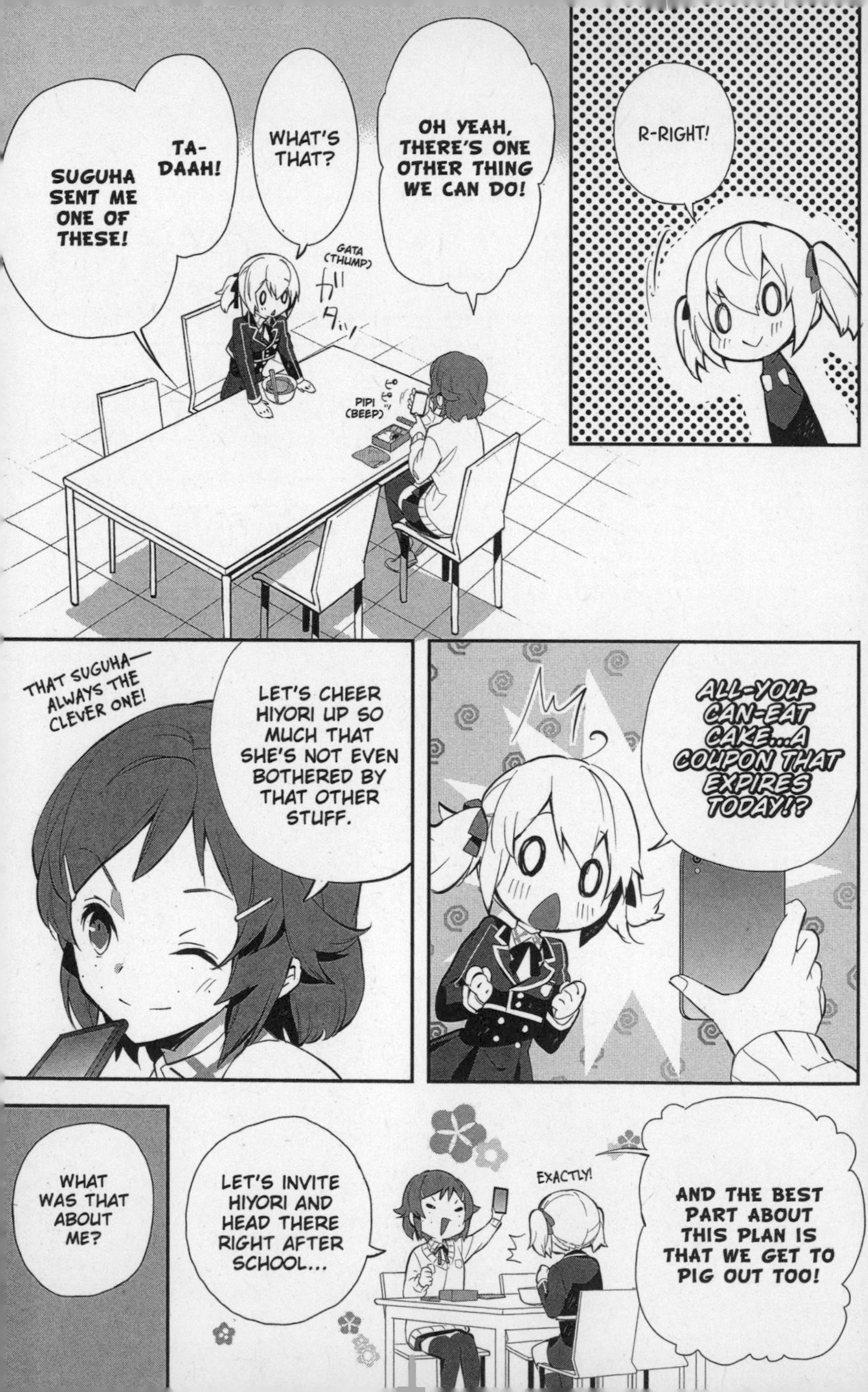
R-RIGHT!
OH YEAH, THERE'S ONE OTHER THING WE CAN DO!
GATA (THUMP)
WHAT'S THAT?
TA-DAAH!
SUGUHA SENT ME ONE OF THESE!
PIPI (BEEP)
ALL-YOU-CAN-EAT CAKE...A COUPON THAT EXPIRES TODAY!?
LET'S CHEER HIYORI UP SO MUCH THAT SHE'S NOT EVEN BOTHERED BY THAT OTHER STUFF.
THAT SUGUHA— ALWAYS THE CLEVER ONE!
AND THE BEST PART ABOUT THIS PLAN IS THAT WE GET TO PIG OUT TOO!
EXACTLY!
LET'S INVITE HIYORI AND HEAD THERE RIGHT AFTER SCHOOL...
WHAT WAS THAT ABOUT ME?

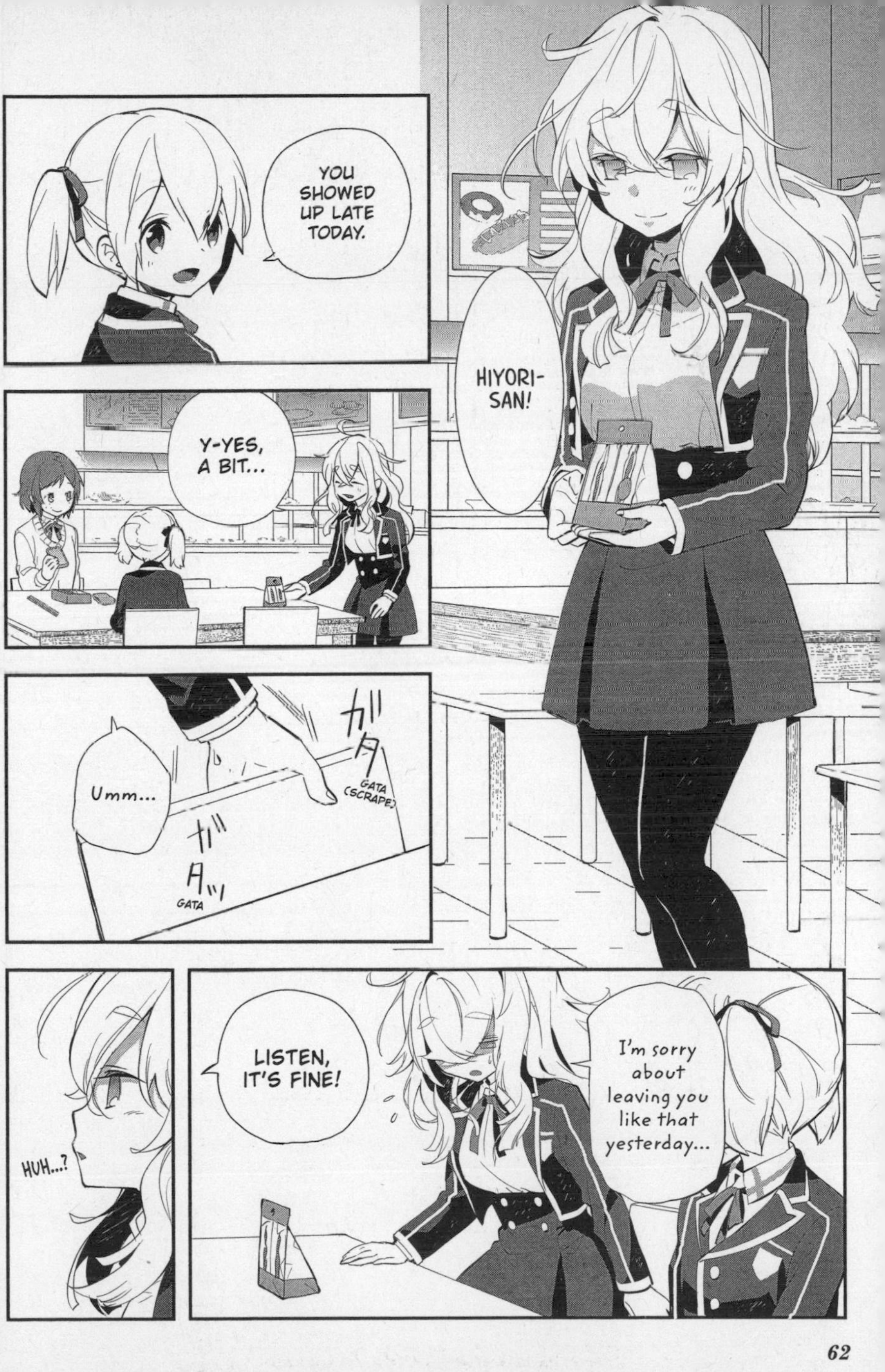
HIYORI-SAN!
YOU SHOWED UP LATE TODAY.
Y-YES, A BIT...
ガタ
GATA (SCRAPE)
Umm...
ガタッ
GATA
I'm sorry about leaving you like that yesterday...
LISTEN, IT'S FINE!
HUH...?

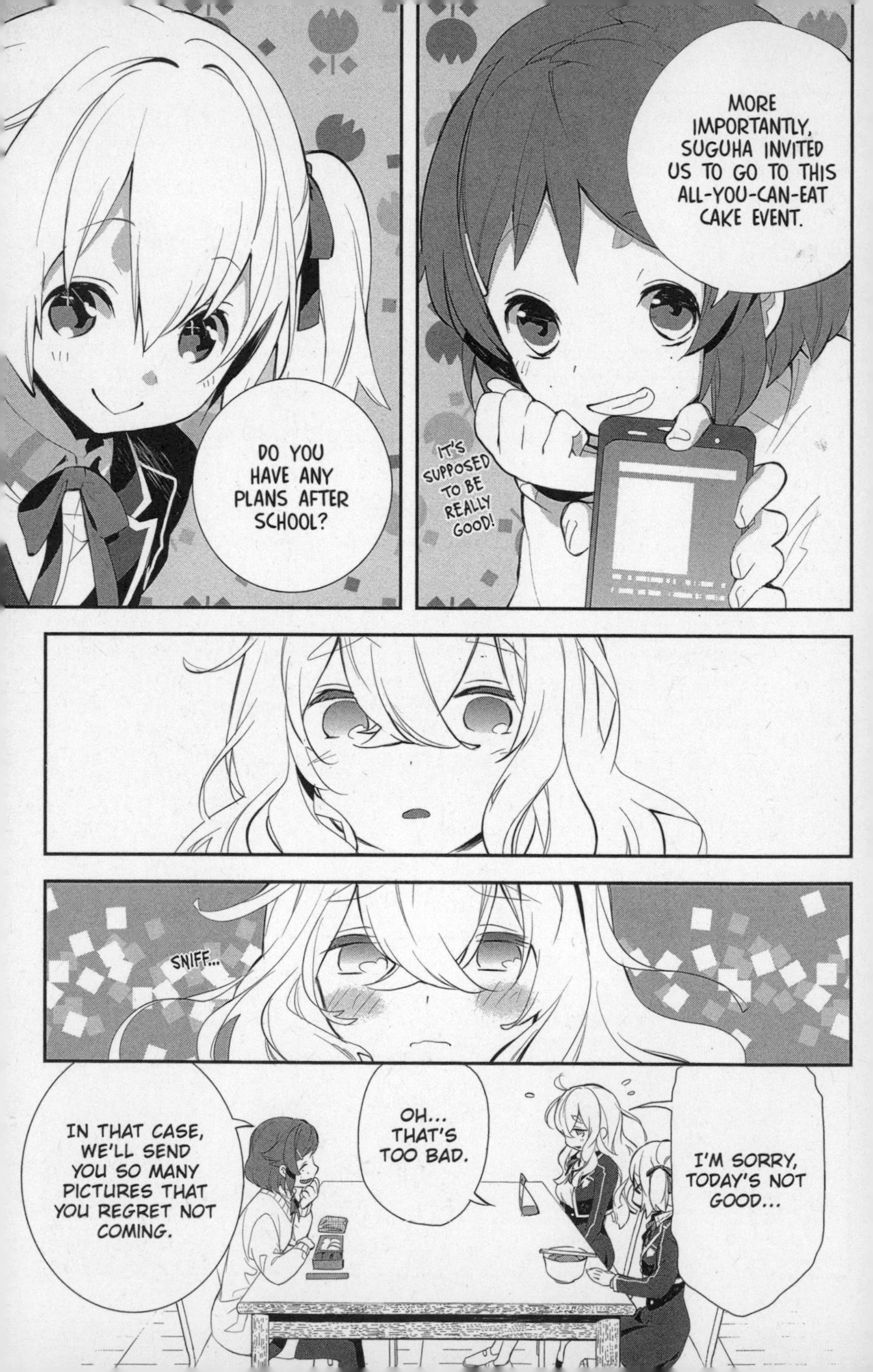
MORE IMPORTANTLY, SUGUHA INVITED US TO GO TO THIS ALL-YOU-CAN-EAT CAKE EVENT.
IT'S SUPPOSED TO BE REALLY GOOD!
DO YOU HAVE ANY PLANS AFTER SCHOOL?
SNIFF...
I'M SORRY, TODAY'S NOT GOOD...
OH... THAT'S TOO BAD.
IN THAT CASE, WE'LL SEND YOU SO MANY PICTURES THAT YOU REGRET NOT COMING.

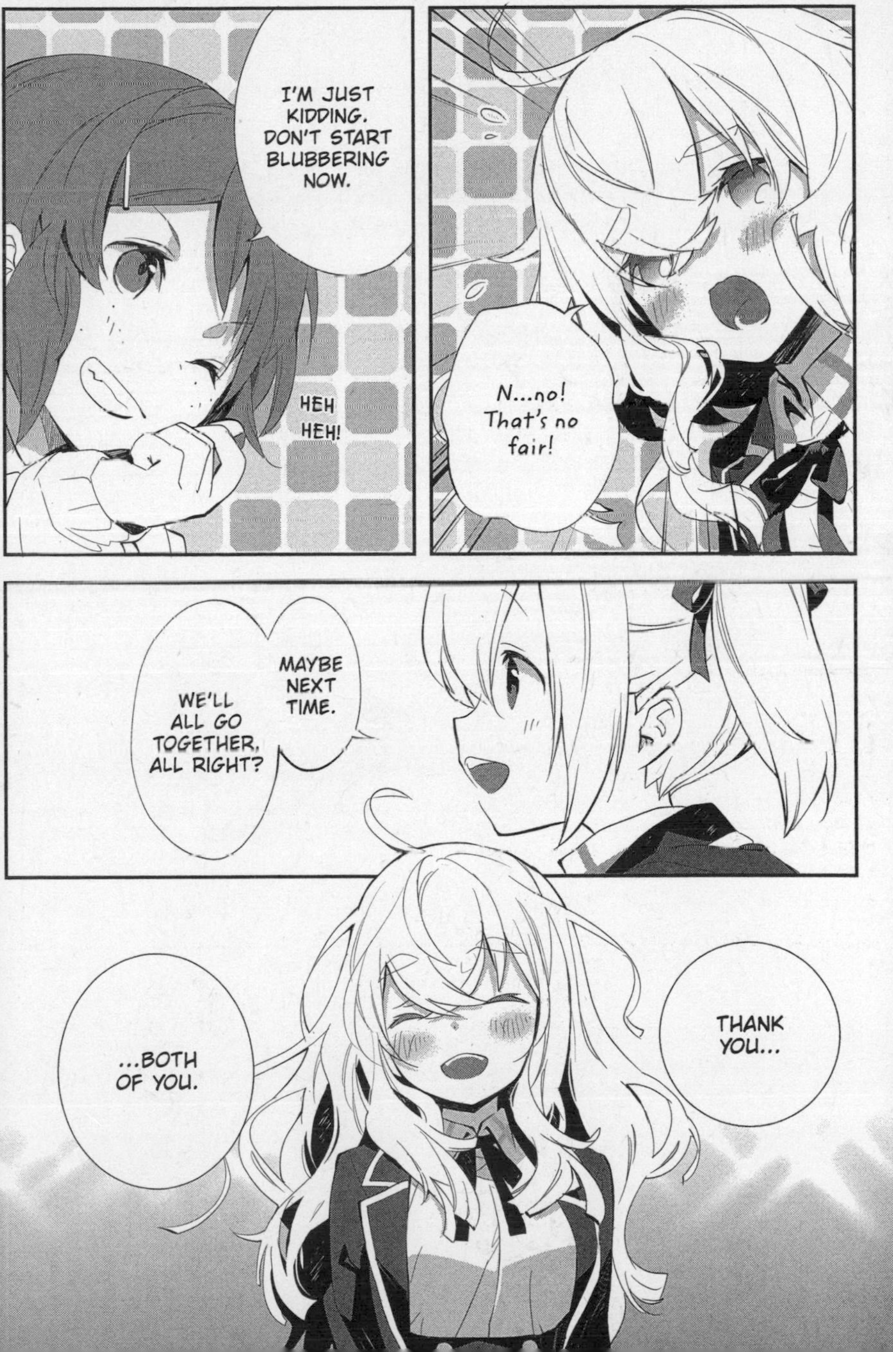
N...no! That's no fair!
I'M JUST KIDDING. DON'T START BLUBBERING NOW.
HEH HEH!
MAYBE NEXT TIME.
WE'LL ALL GO TOGETHER, ALL RIGHT?
THANK YOU...
...BOTH OF YOU.

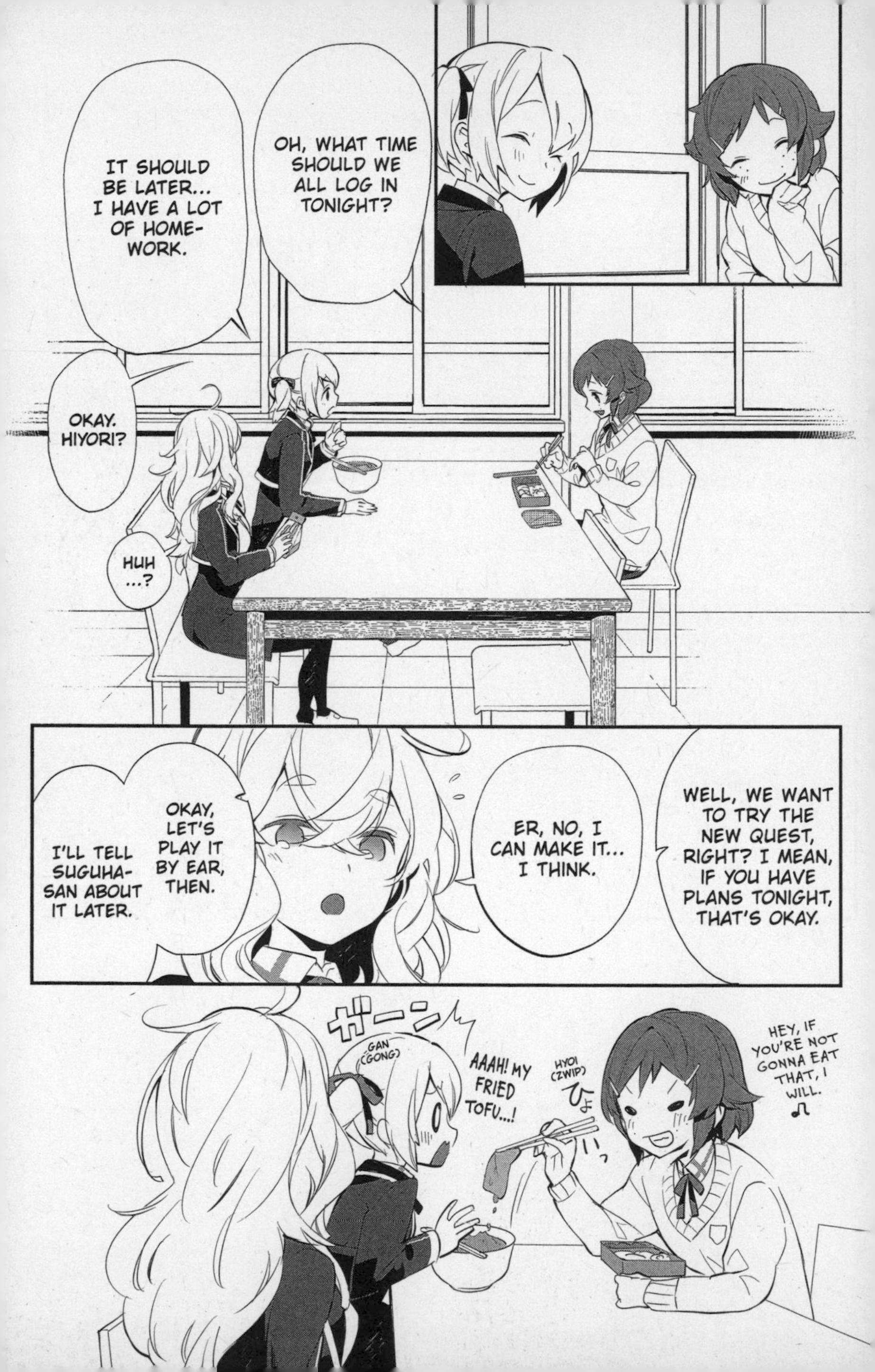
OH, WHAT TIME SHOULD WE ALL LOG IN TONIGHT?
IT SHOULD BE LATER... I HAVE A LOT OF HOME-WORK.
OKAY. HIYORI?
HUH ...?
WELL, WE WANT TO TRY THE NEW QUEST, RIGHT? I MEAN, IF YOU HAVE PLANS TONIGHT, THAT'S OKAY.
ER, NO, I CAN MAKE IT... I THINK.
OKAY, LET'S PLAY IT BY EAR, THEN.
I'LL TELL SUGUHA-SAN ABOUT IT LATER.
HEY, IF YOU'RE NOT GONNA EAT THAT, I WILL. ♫
ひょ
HYOI (ZWIP)
AAAH! MY FRIED TOFU...!
ガーン
GAN (GONG)

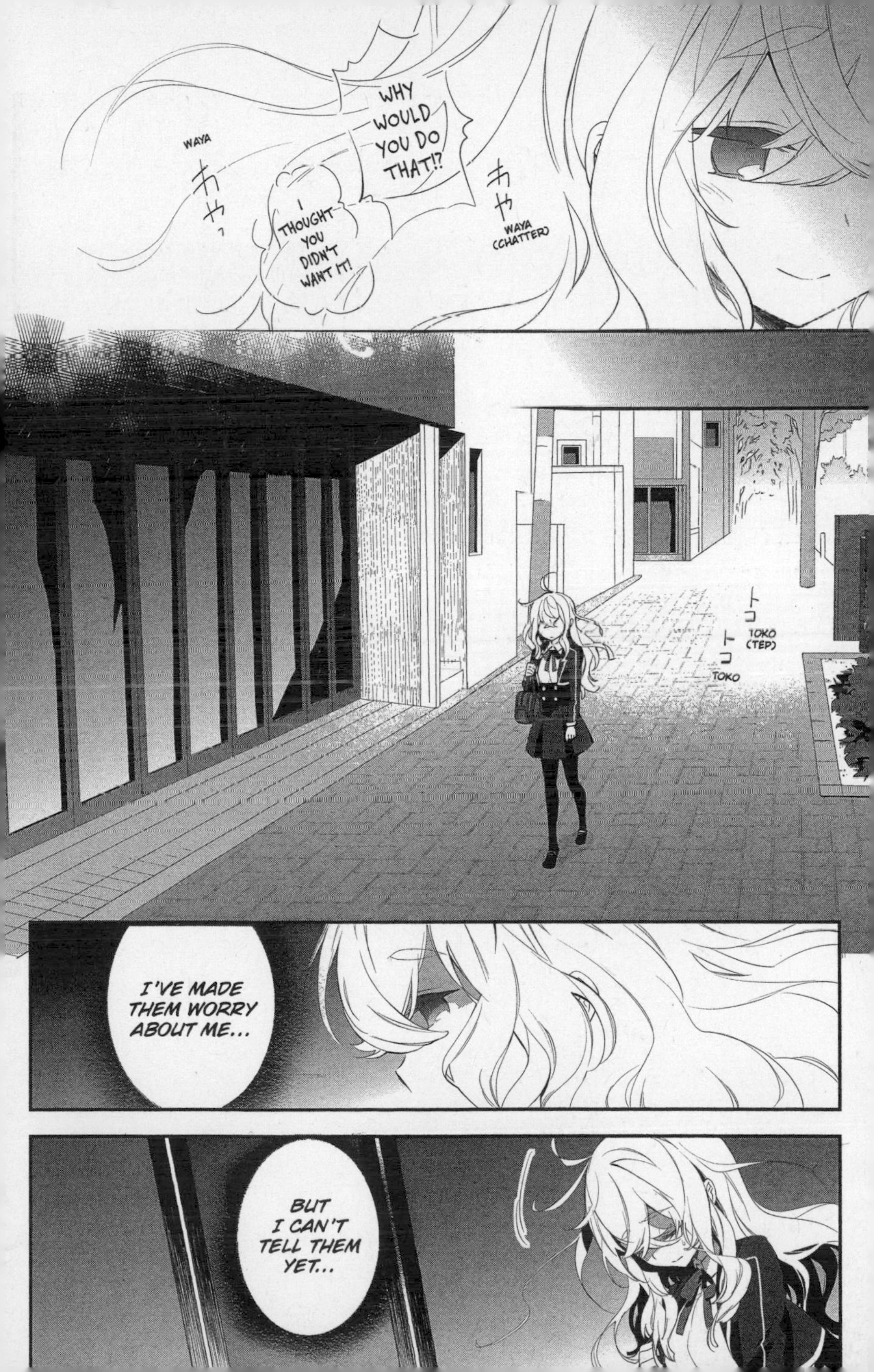
WHY WOULD YOU DO THAT!?
わや
WAYA (CHATTER)
I THOUGHT YOU DIDN'T WANT IT!
わや
WAYA
トコ
TOKO (TEP)
トコ
TOKO
I'VE MADE THEM WORRY ABOUT ME...
BUT I CAN'T TELL THEM YET...

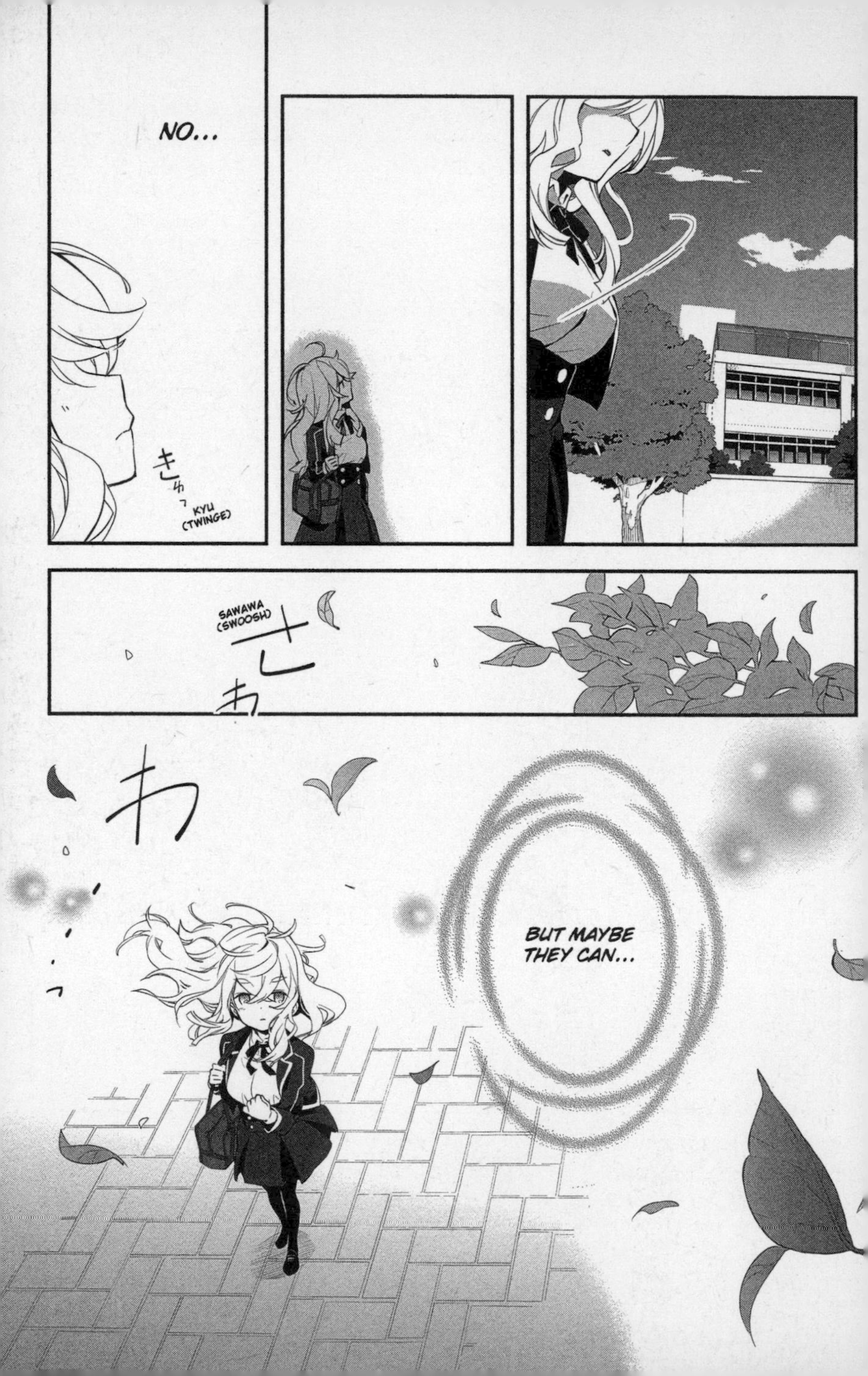
NO...
KYU (TWINGE)
SAWAWA (SWOOSH)
BUT MAYBE THEY CAN...

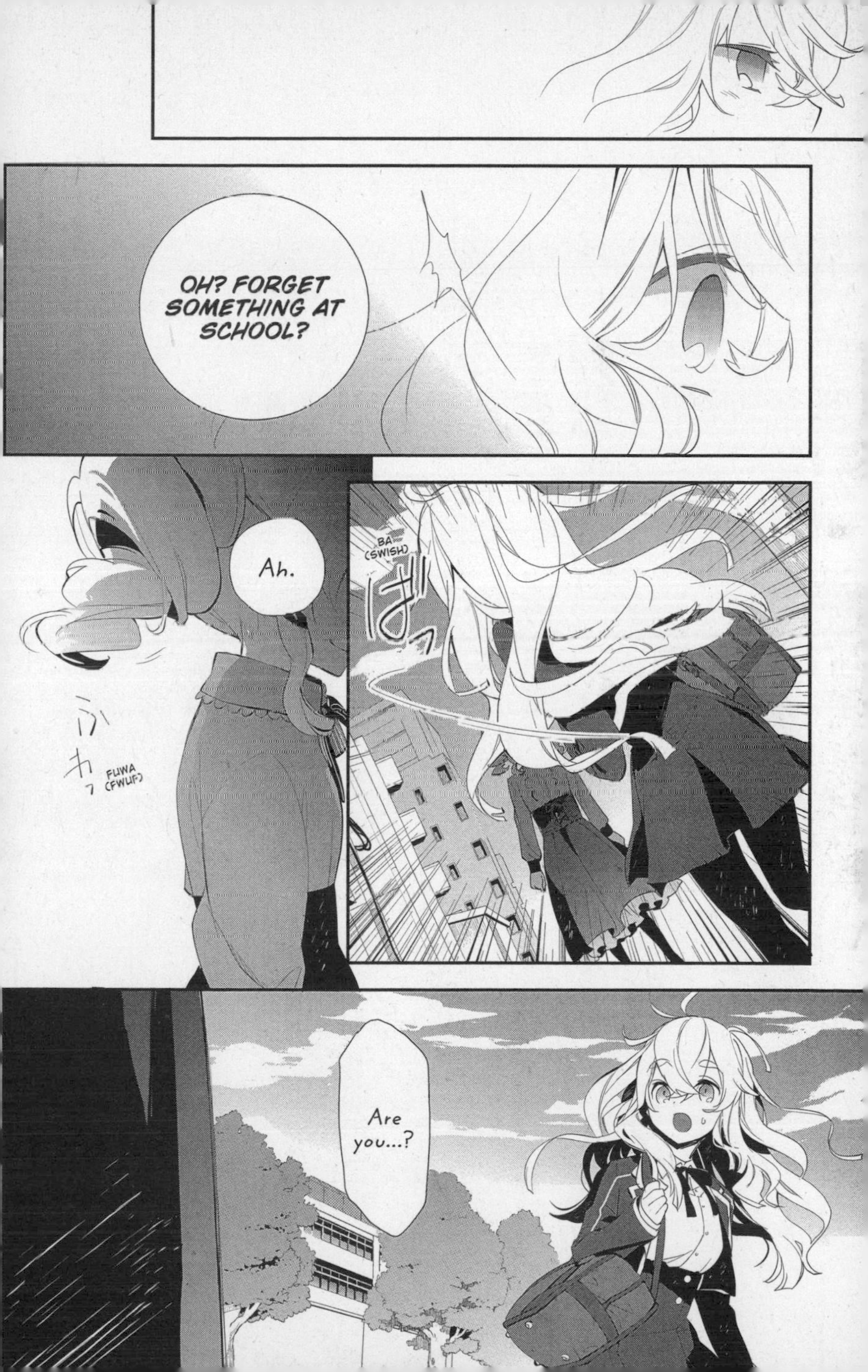
OH? FORGET SOMETHING AT SCHOOL?
ばっ
BA (SWISH)
Ah.
ふわ
FUWA (FWUF)
Are you...?

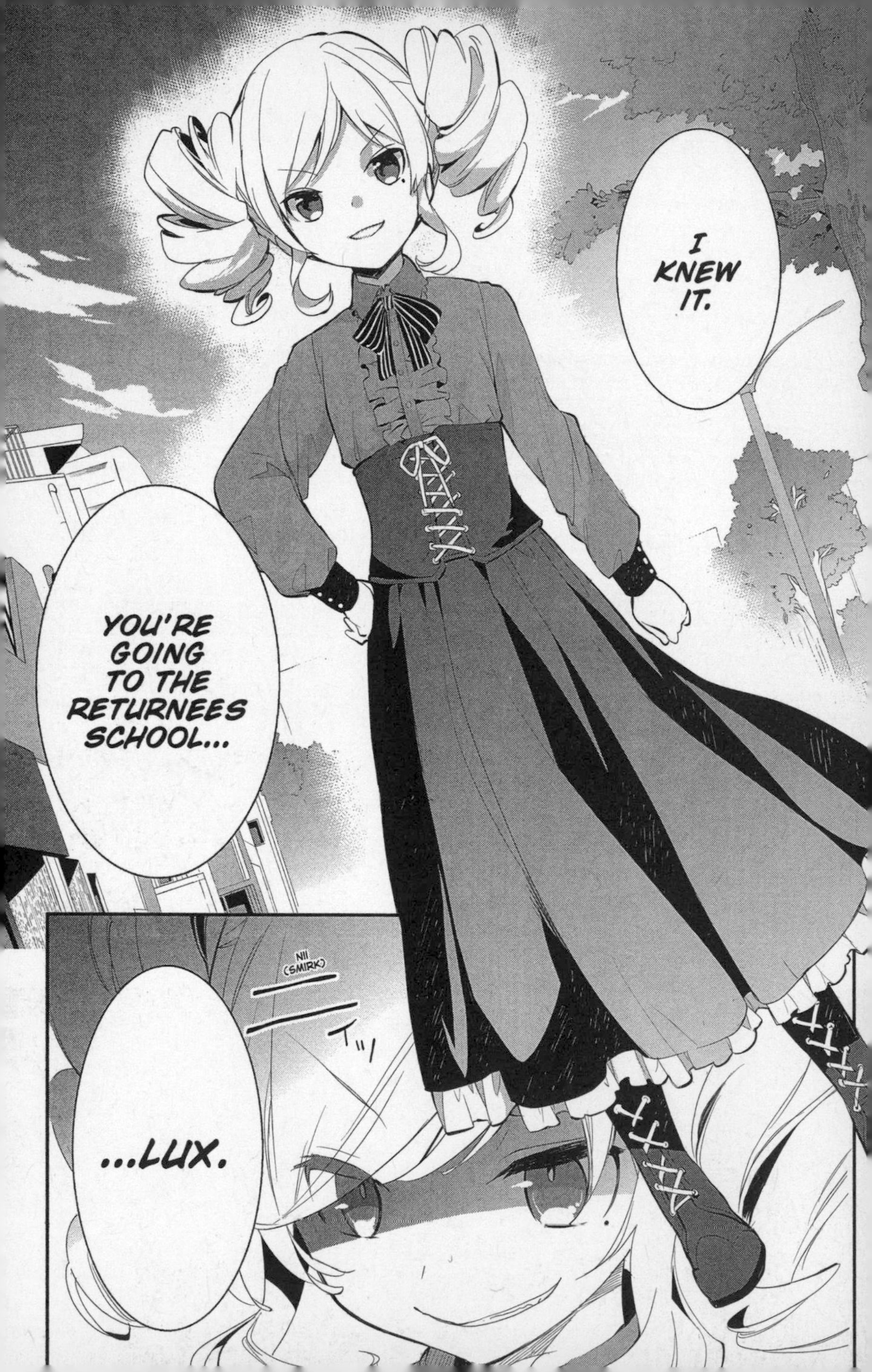
I KNEW IT.
YOU'RE GOING TO THE RETURNEES SCHOOL...
NII (SMIRK)
...LUX.

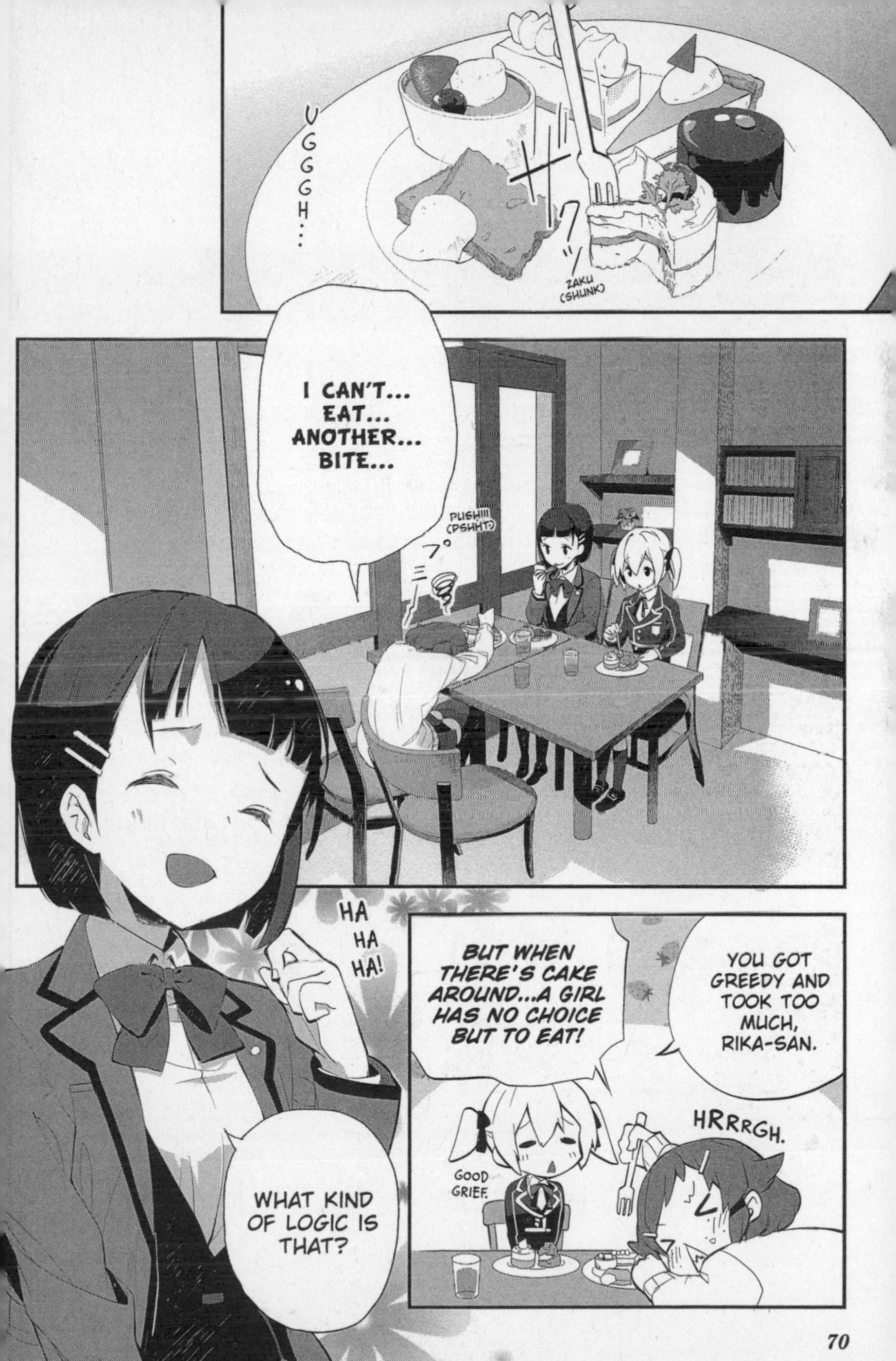
UGGGH...
ZAKU (SHUNK)
I CAN'T... EAT... ANOTHER... BITE...
PUSH!!! (PSHHT)
YOU GOT GREEDY AND TOOK TOO MUCH, RIKA-SAN.
BUT WHEN THERE'S CAKE AROUND...A GIRL HAS NO CHOICE BUT TO EAT!
HRRRGH.
GOOD GRIEF.
HA HA HA!
WHAT KIND OF LOGIC IS THAT?

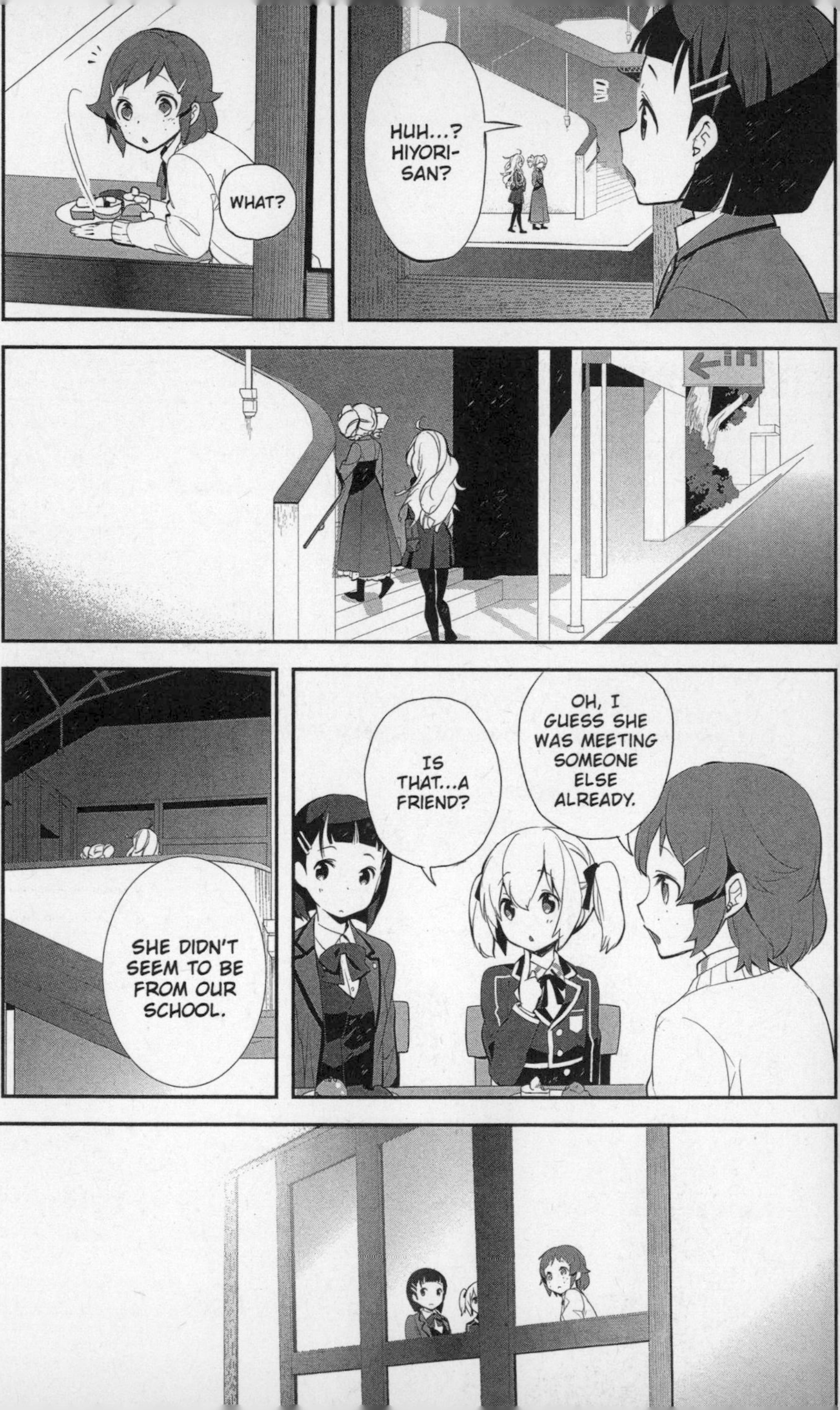
HUH...? HIYORI-SAN?
WHAT?
in
OH, I GUESS SHE WAS MEETING SOMEONE ELSE ALREADY.
IS THAT...A FRIEND?
SHE DIDN'T SEEM TO BE FROM OUR SCHOOL.

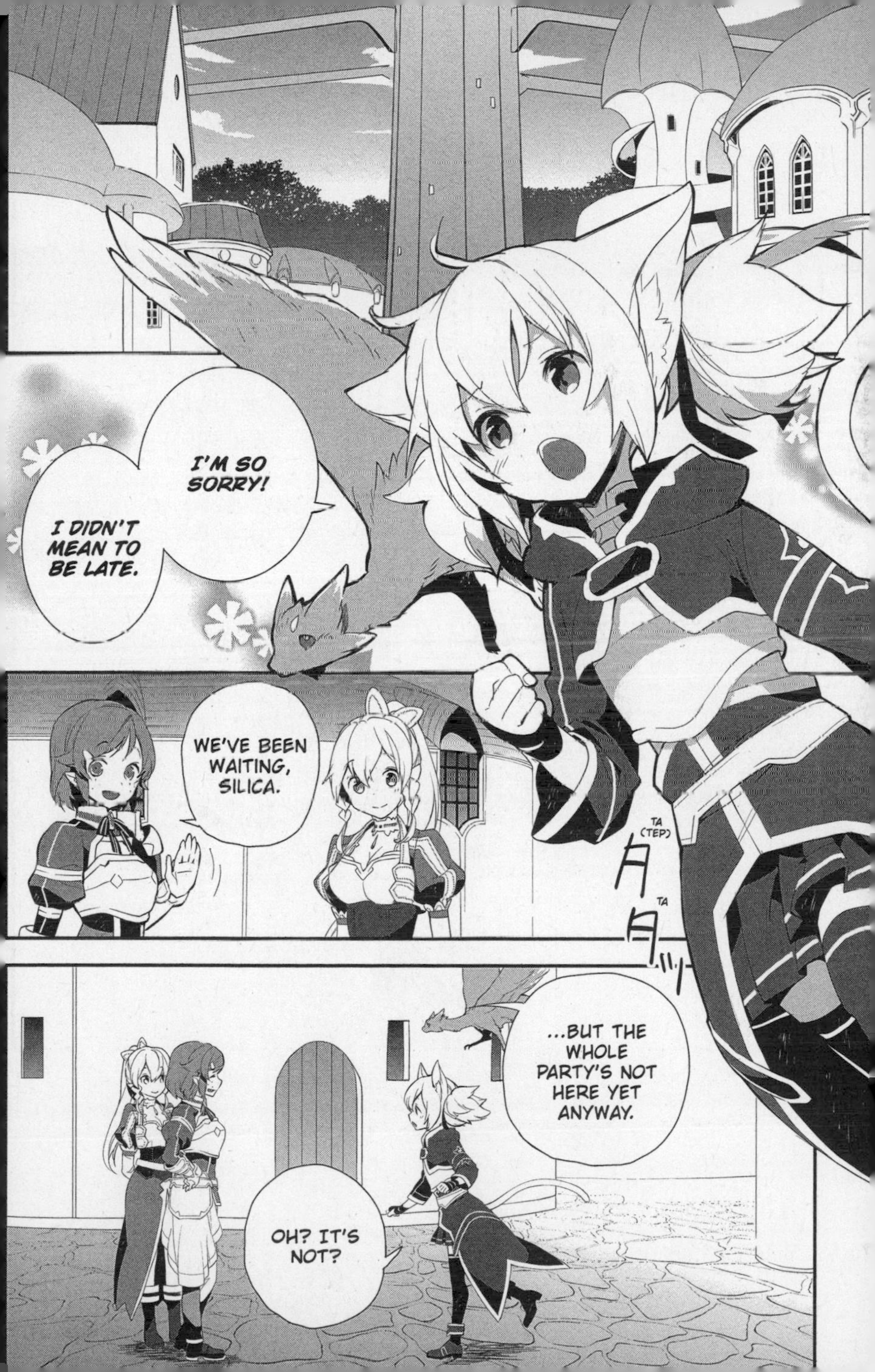
I'M SO SORRY!
I DIDN'T MEAN TO BE LATE.
TA (TEP)
TA
WE'VE BEEN WAITING, SILICA.
...BUT THE WHOLE PARTY'S NOT HERE YET ANYWAY.
OH? IT'S NOT?

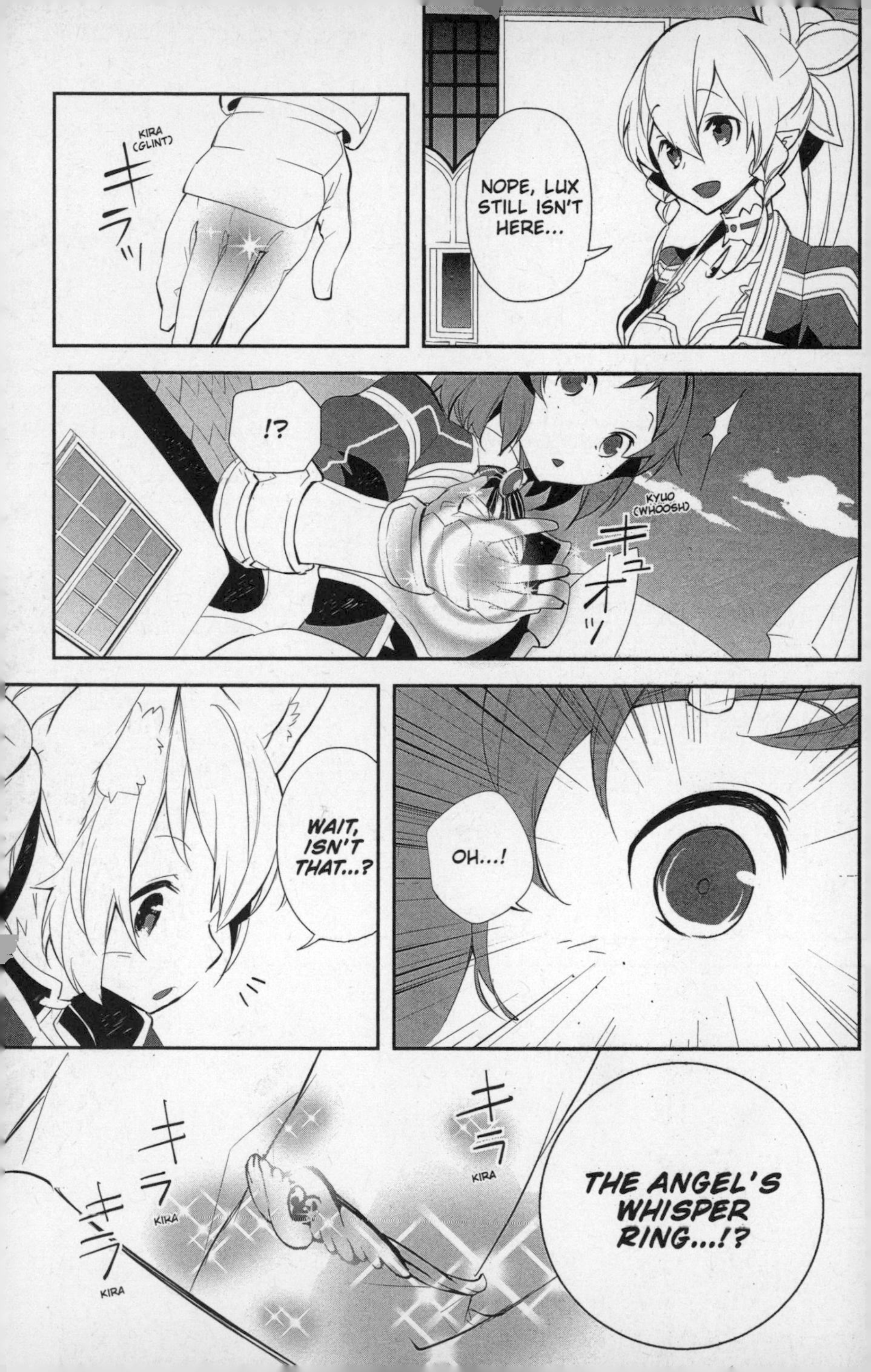
NOPE, LUX STILL ISN'T HERE...
KIRA (GLINT)
キラッ
!?
KYUO (WHOOSH)
キュオッ
OH...!
WAIT, ISN'T THAT...?
THE ANGEL'S WHISPER RING...!?
キラ
KIRA
キラ
KIRA
キラ
KIRA

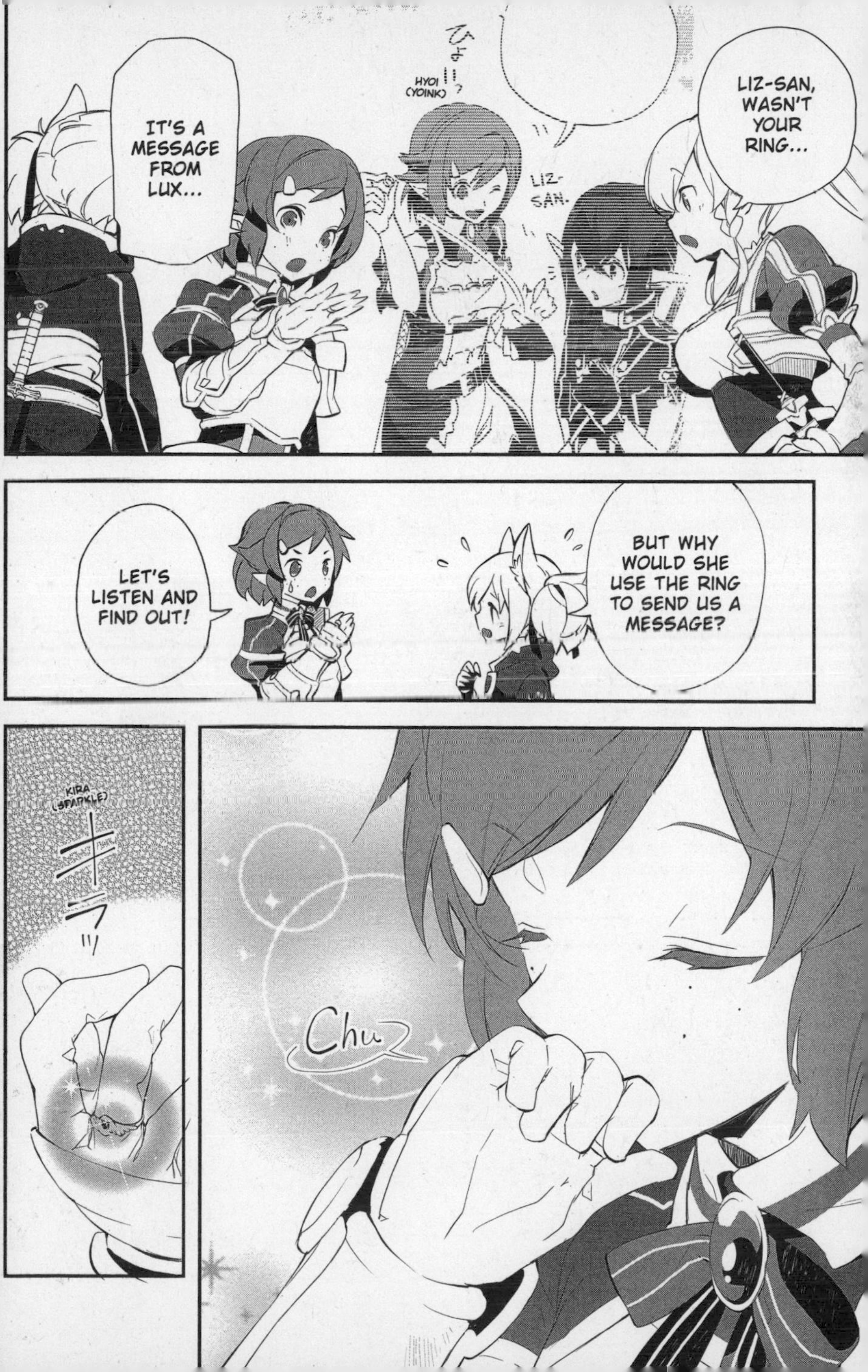
LIZ-SAN, WASN'T YOUR RING...
HYOI (YOINK)
LIZ-SAN.
IT'S A MESSAGE FROM LUX...
BUT WHY WOULD SHE USE THE RING TO SEND US A MESSAGE?
LET'S LISTEN AND FIND OUT!
Chu
KIRA (SPARKLE)

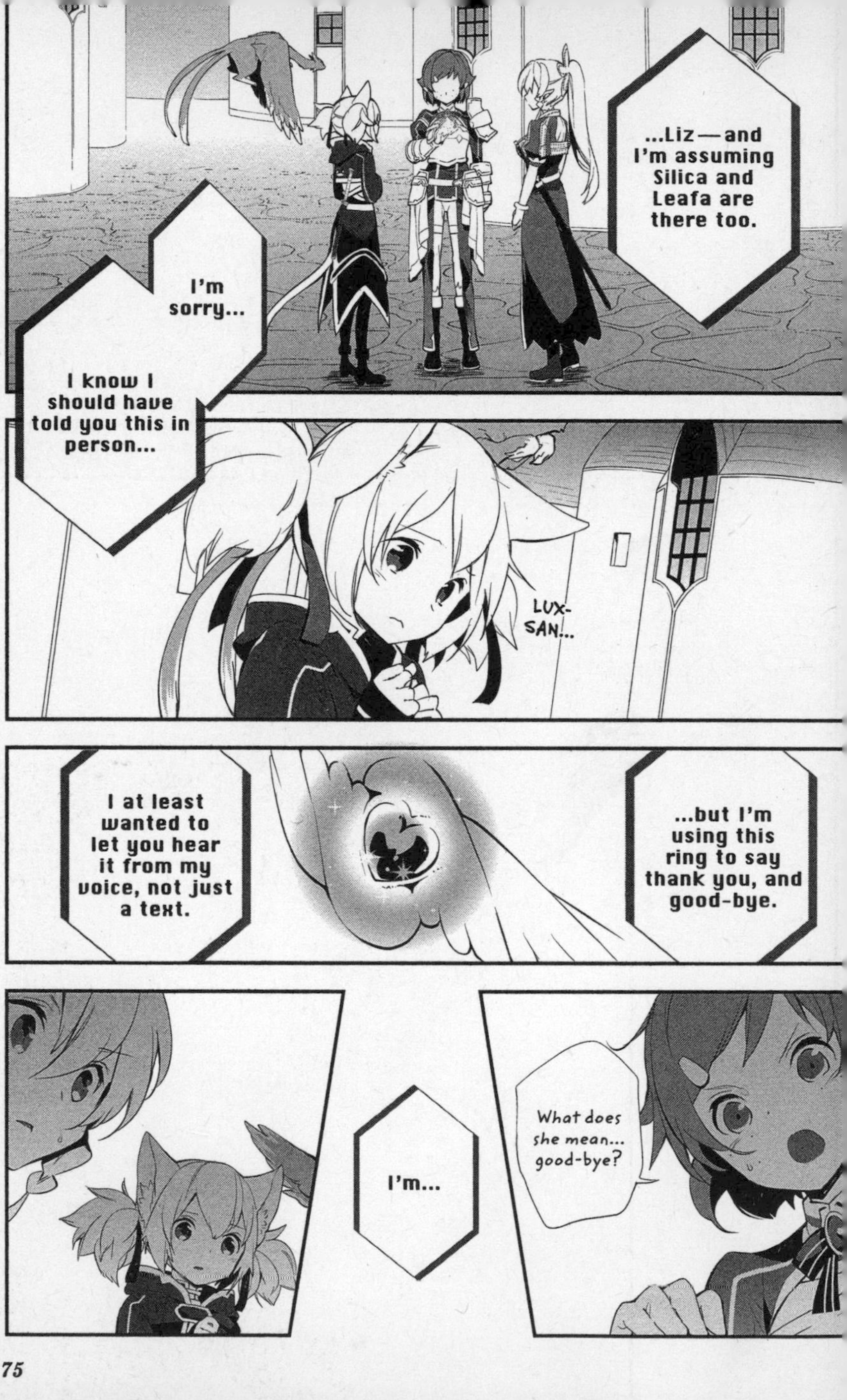
...Liz — and I'm assuming Silica and Leafa are there too.
I'm sorry...
I know I should have told you this in person...
LUX-SAN...
...but I'm using this ring to say thank you, and good-bye.
I at least wanted to let you hear it from my voice, not just a text.
What does she mean... good-bye?
I'm...

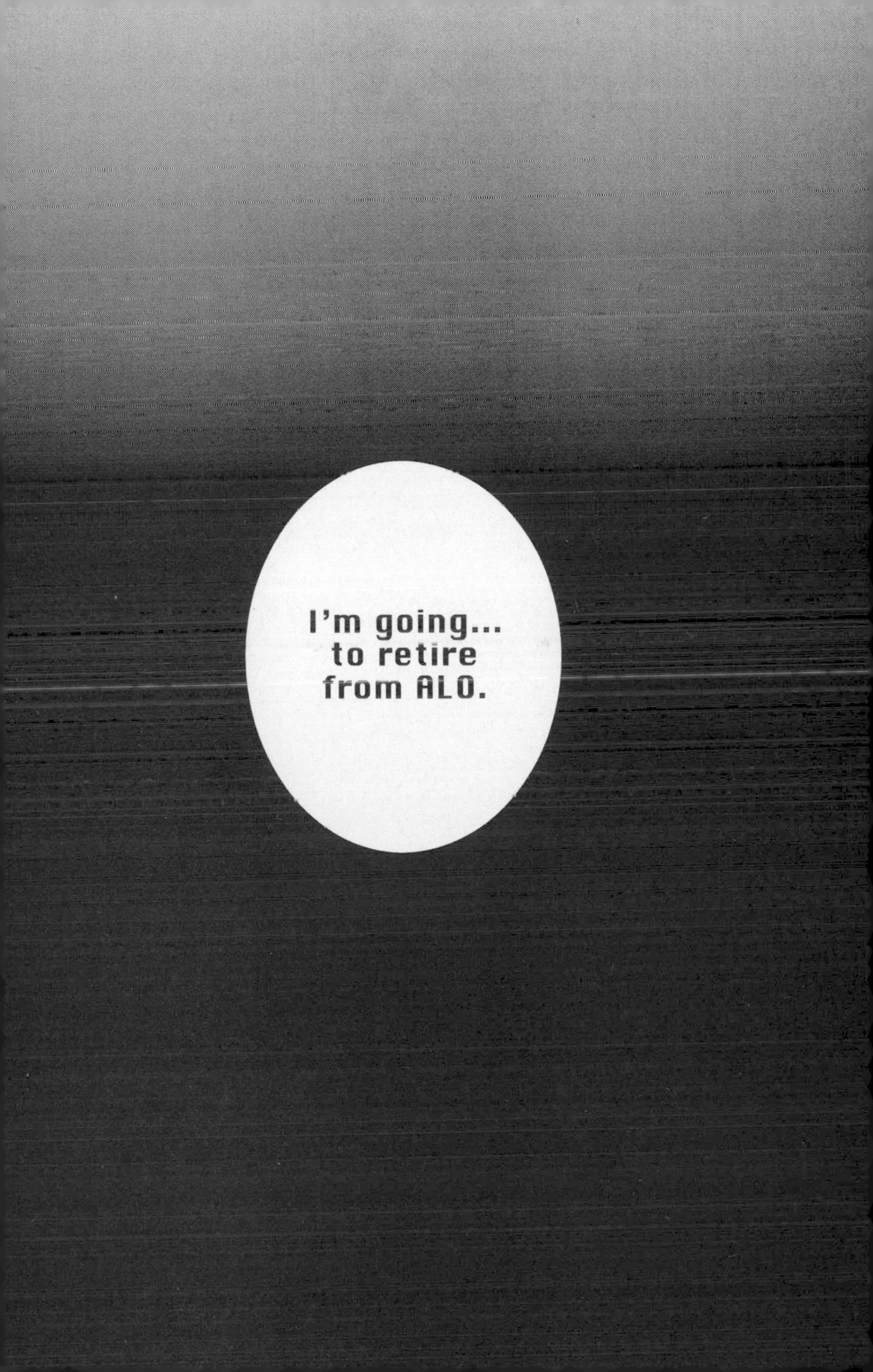
I'm going... to retire from ALO.

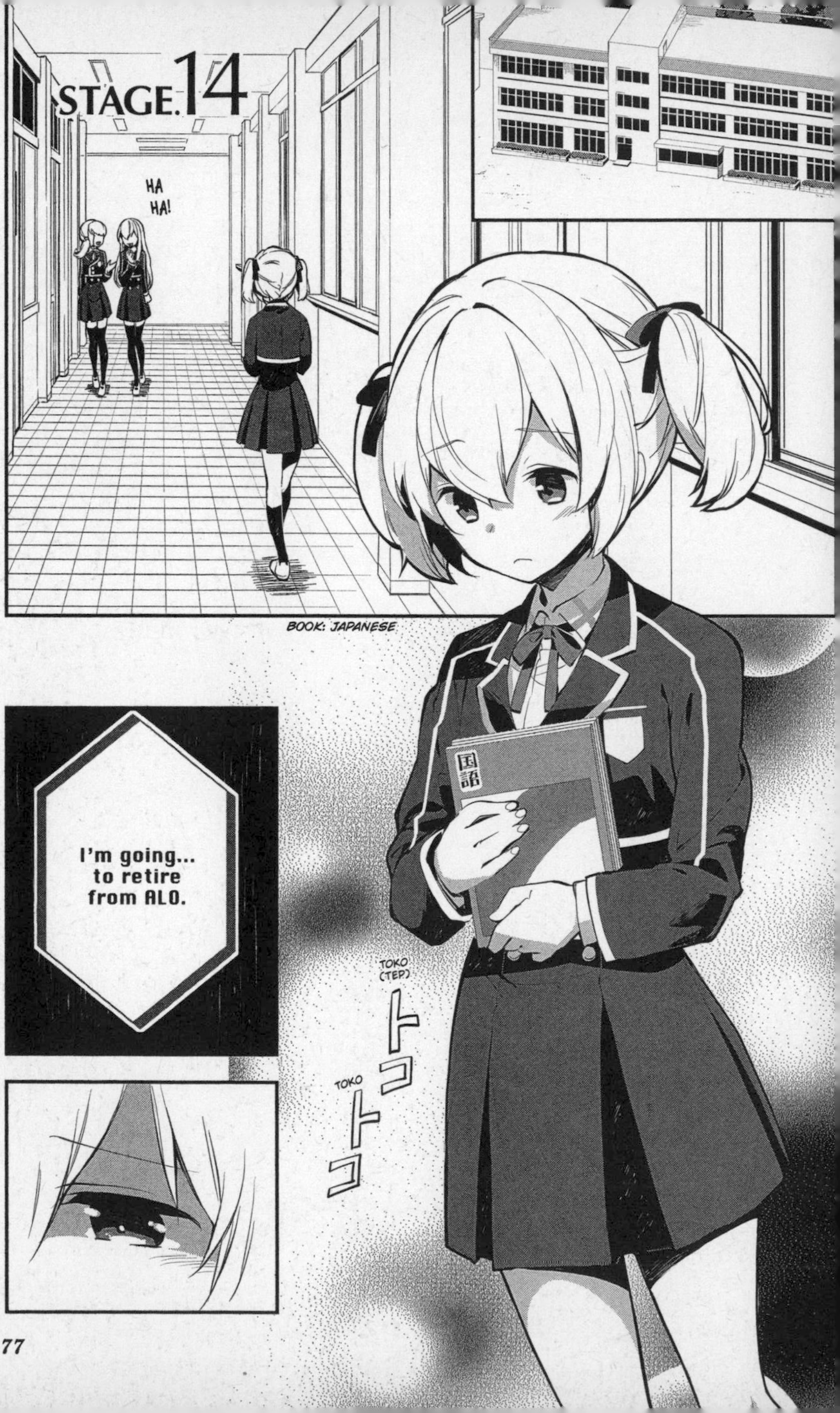
STAGE.14
HA HA!
BOOK: JAPANESE
国語
TOKO (TEP)
トコ
TOKO
トコ
I'm going... to retire from ALO.

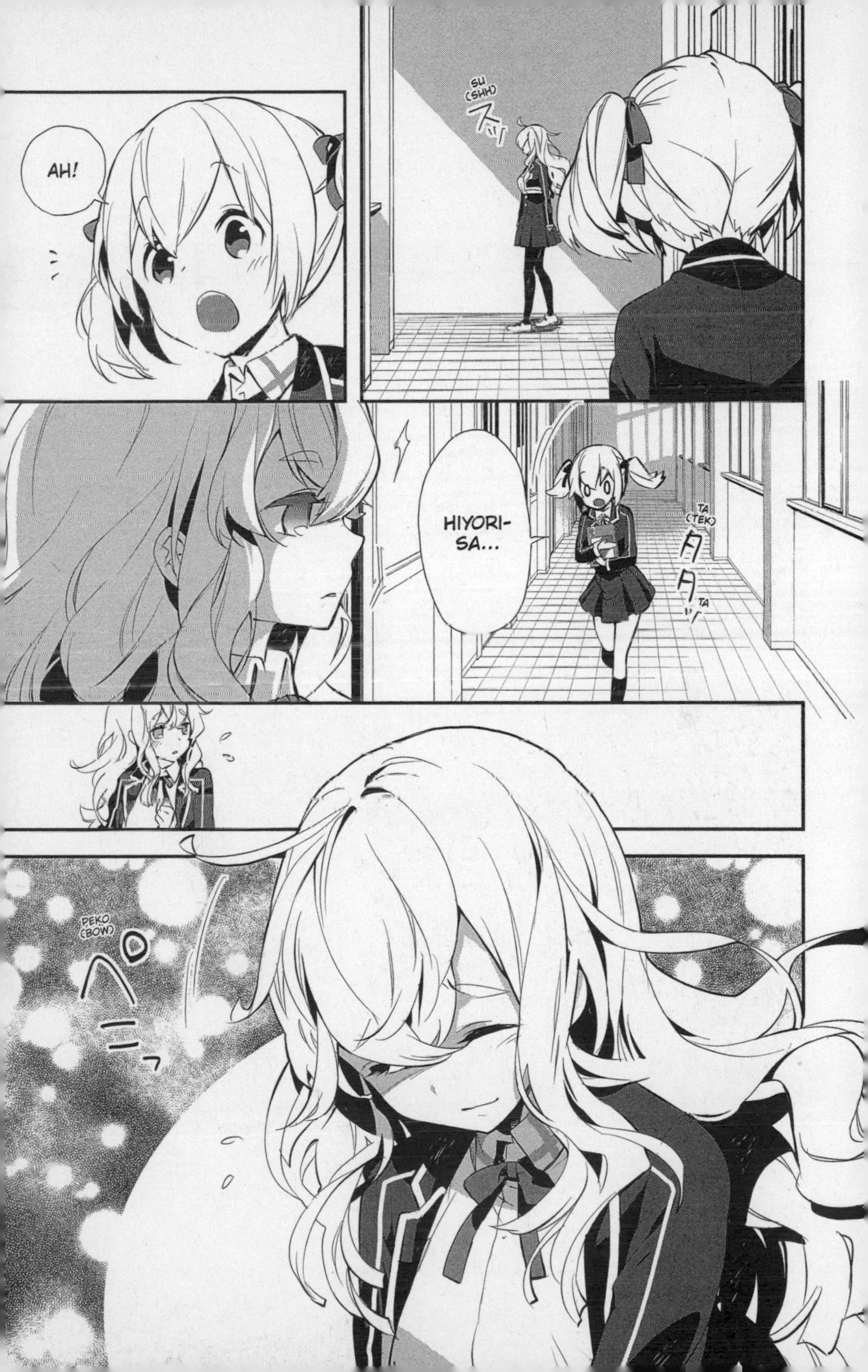
SU (SHH)
AH!
HIYORI-SA...
TA (TEK)
TA
PEKO (BOW)

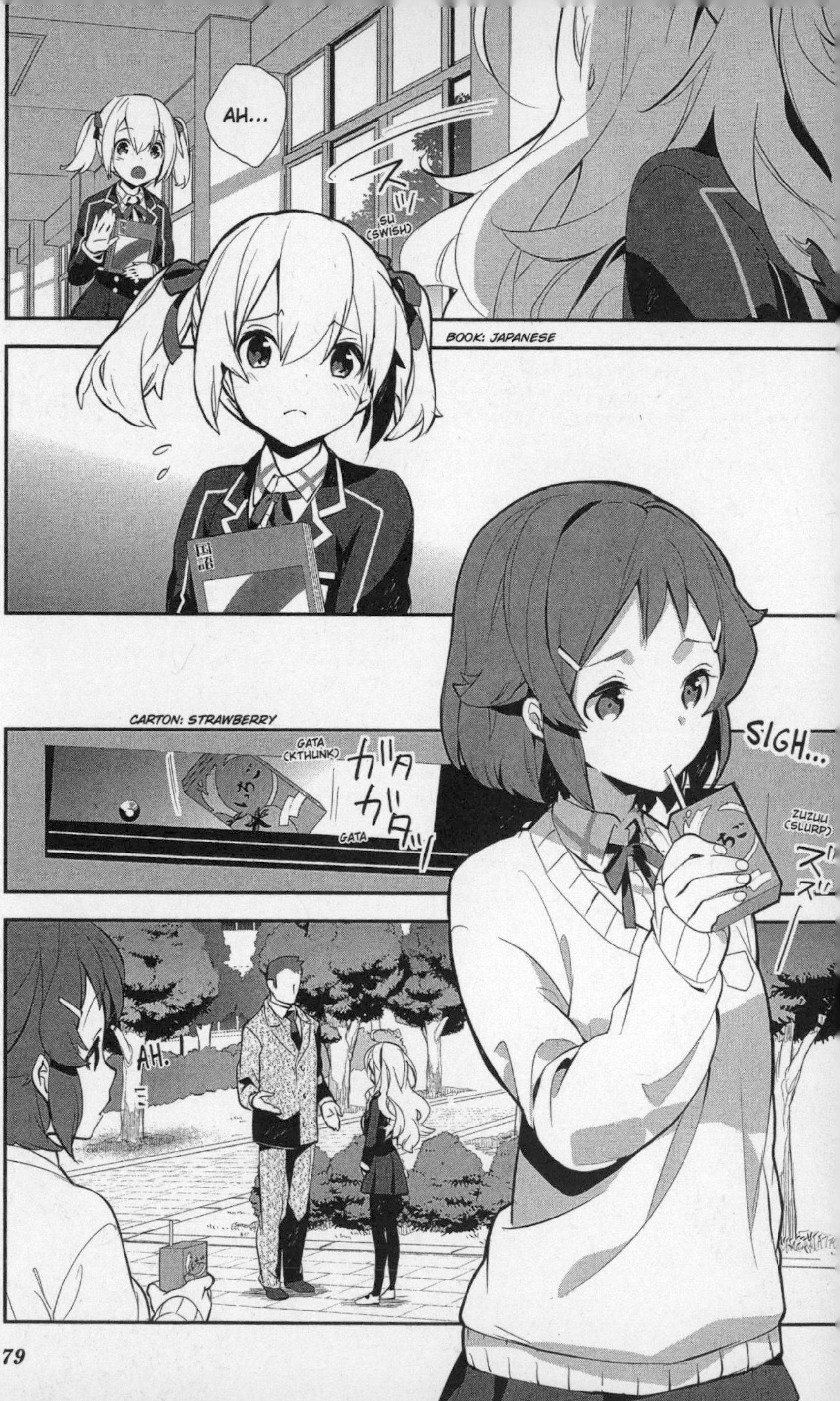

AH...
SU (SWISH)
BOOK: JAPANESE
SIGH...
ZUZUU (SLURP)
CARTON: STRAWBERRY
GATA (KTHUNK)
GATA
AH.

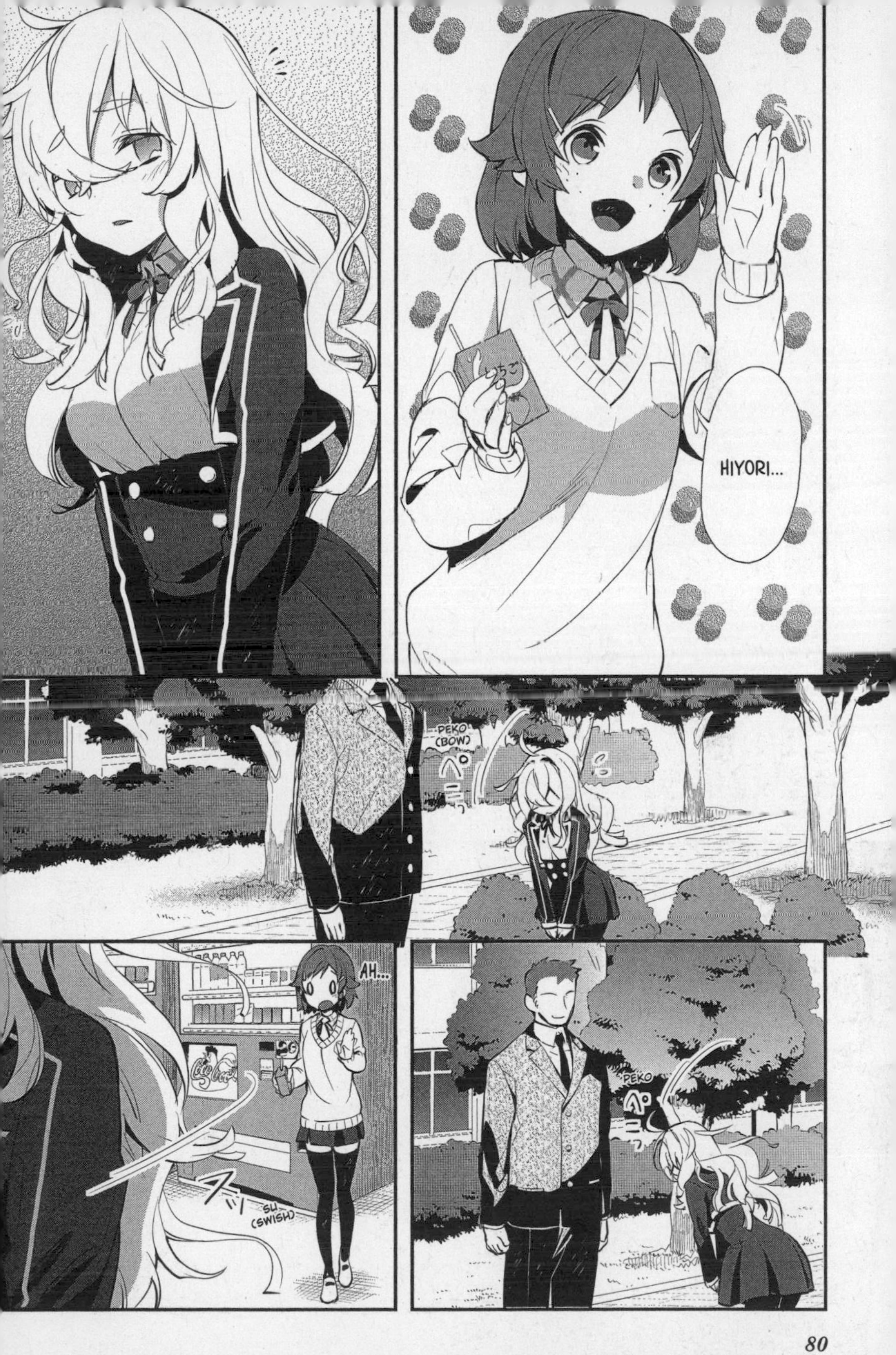
HIYORI...
PEKO (BOW)
PEKO
AH...
SU (SWISH)

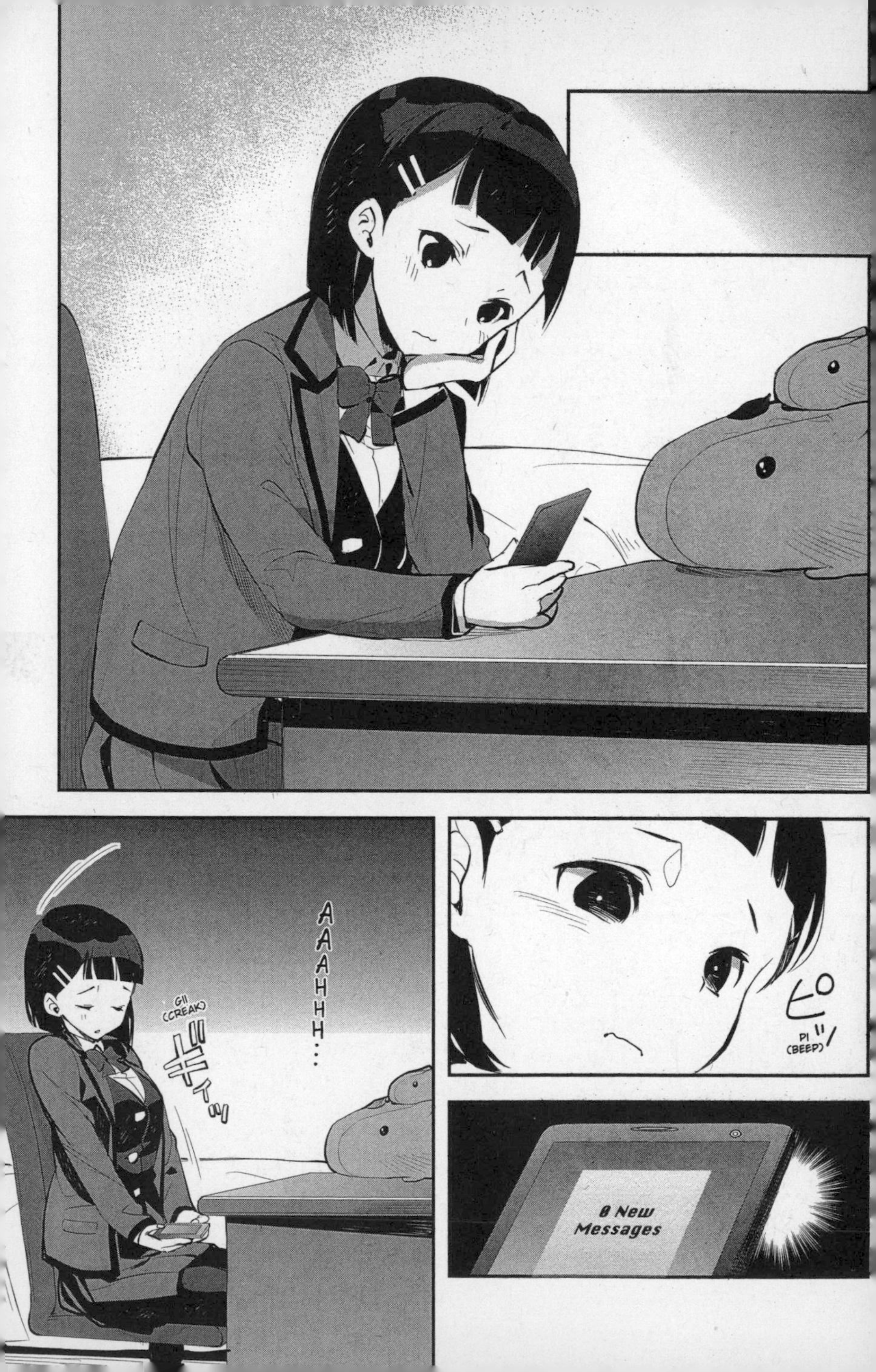
ピッ
PI (BEEP)
0 New Messages
AAAAHHH...
GII (CREAK)
ギィッ

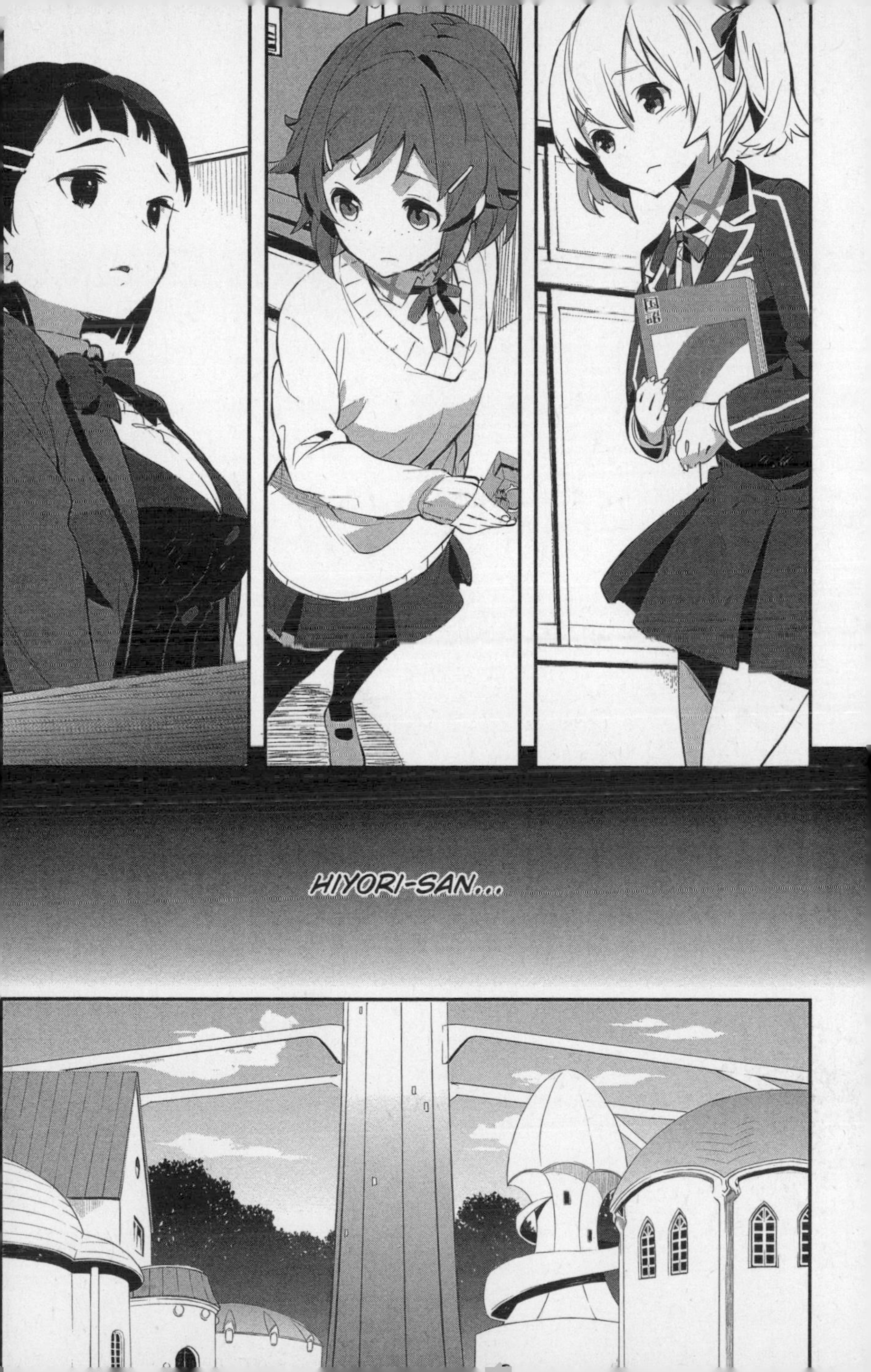
HIYORI-SAN...

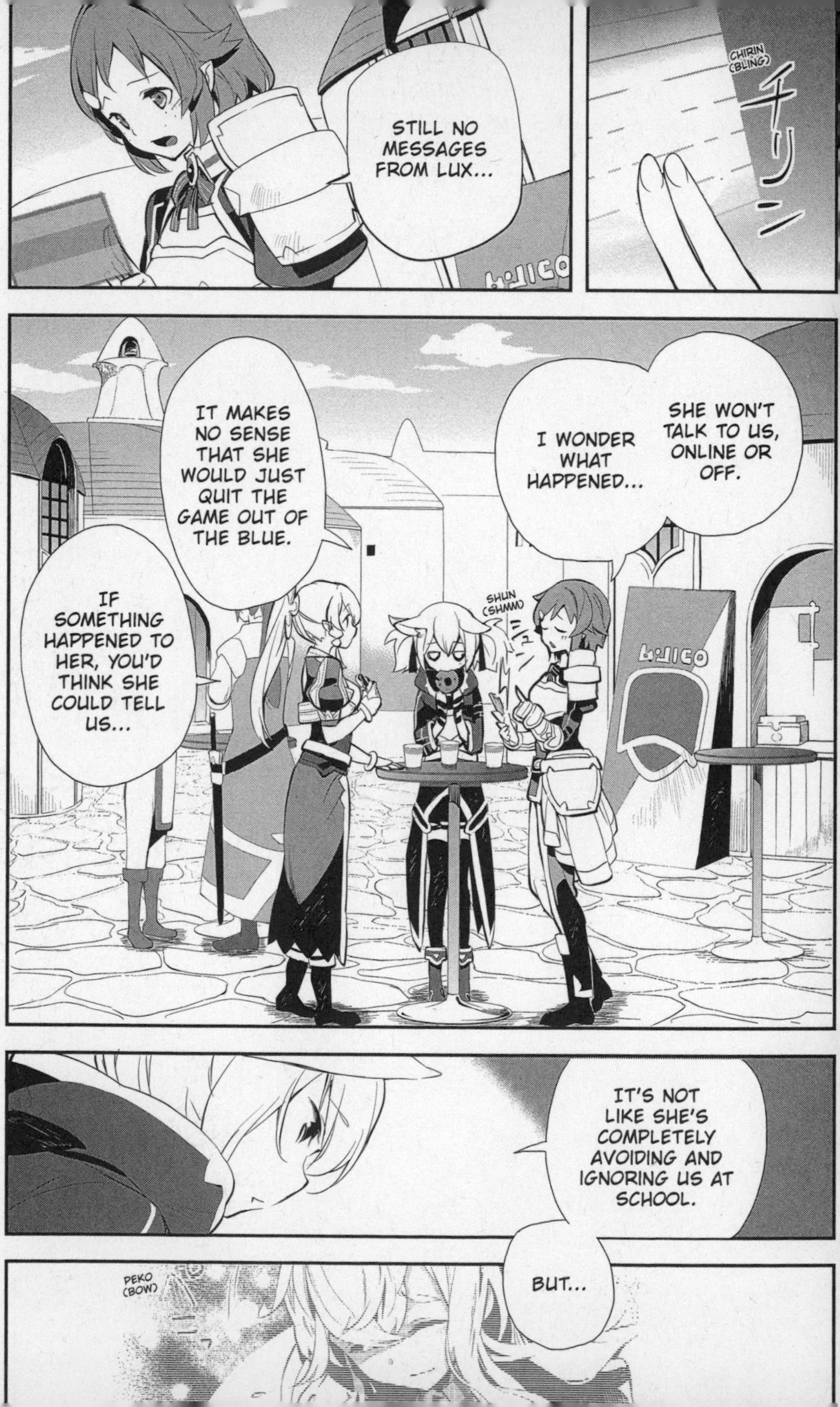
CHIRIN (BLING)
STILL NO MESSAGES FROM LUX...
SHE WON'T TALK TO US, ONLINE OR OFF.
I WONDER WHAT HAPPENED...
IT MAKES NO SENSE THAT SHE WOULD JUST QUIT THE GAME OUT OF THE BLUE.
SHUN (SHMM)
IF SOMETHING HAPPENED TO HER, YOU'D THINK SHE COULD TELL US...
IT'S NOT LIKE SHE'S COMPLETELY AVOIDING AND IGNORING US AT SCHOOL.
BUT...
PEKO (BOW)

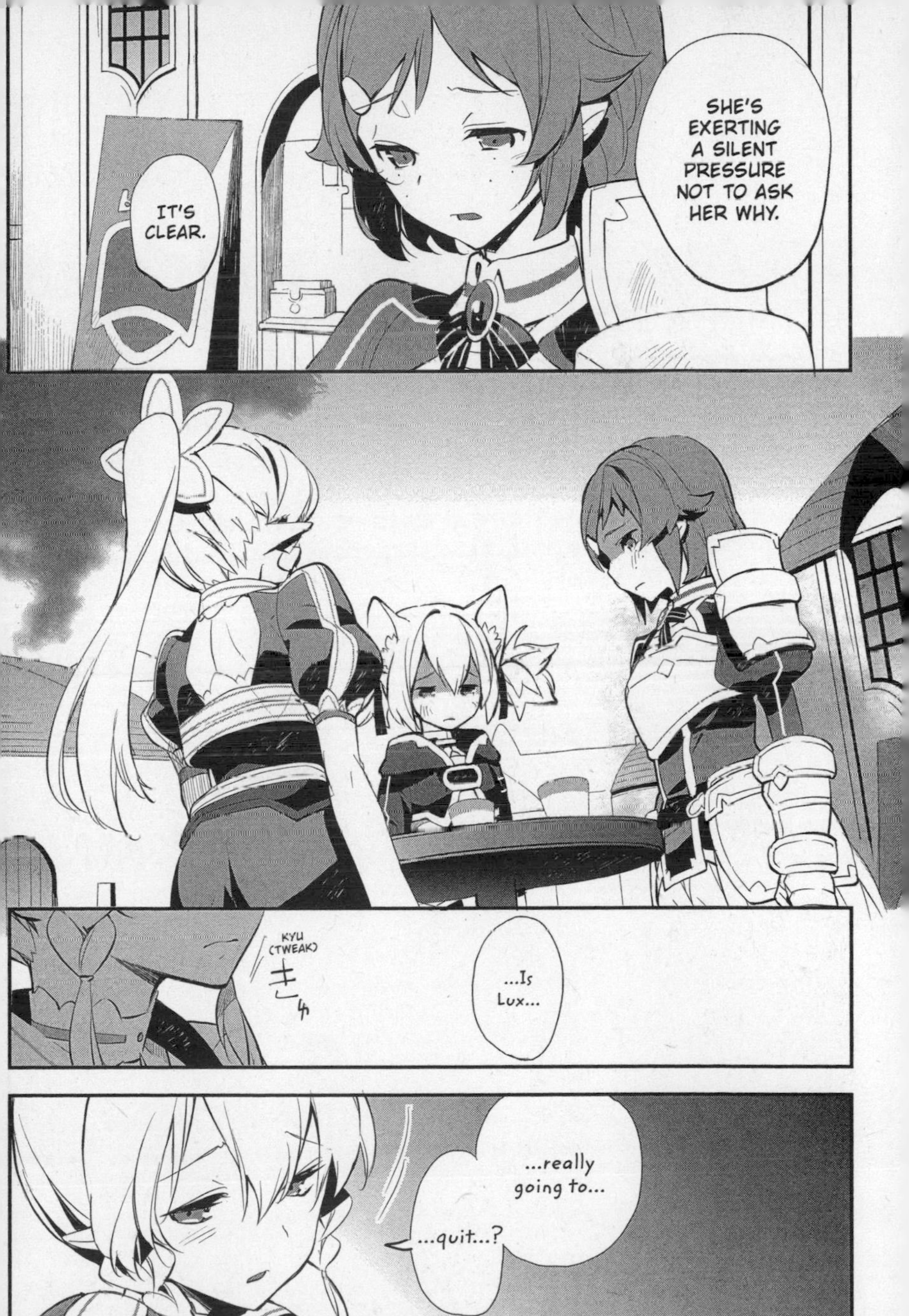
SHE'S EXERTING A SILENT PRESSURE NOT TO ASK HER WHY.
IT'S CLEAR.
...Is Lux...
KYU (TWEAK)
...really going to...
...quit...?

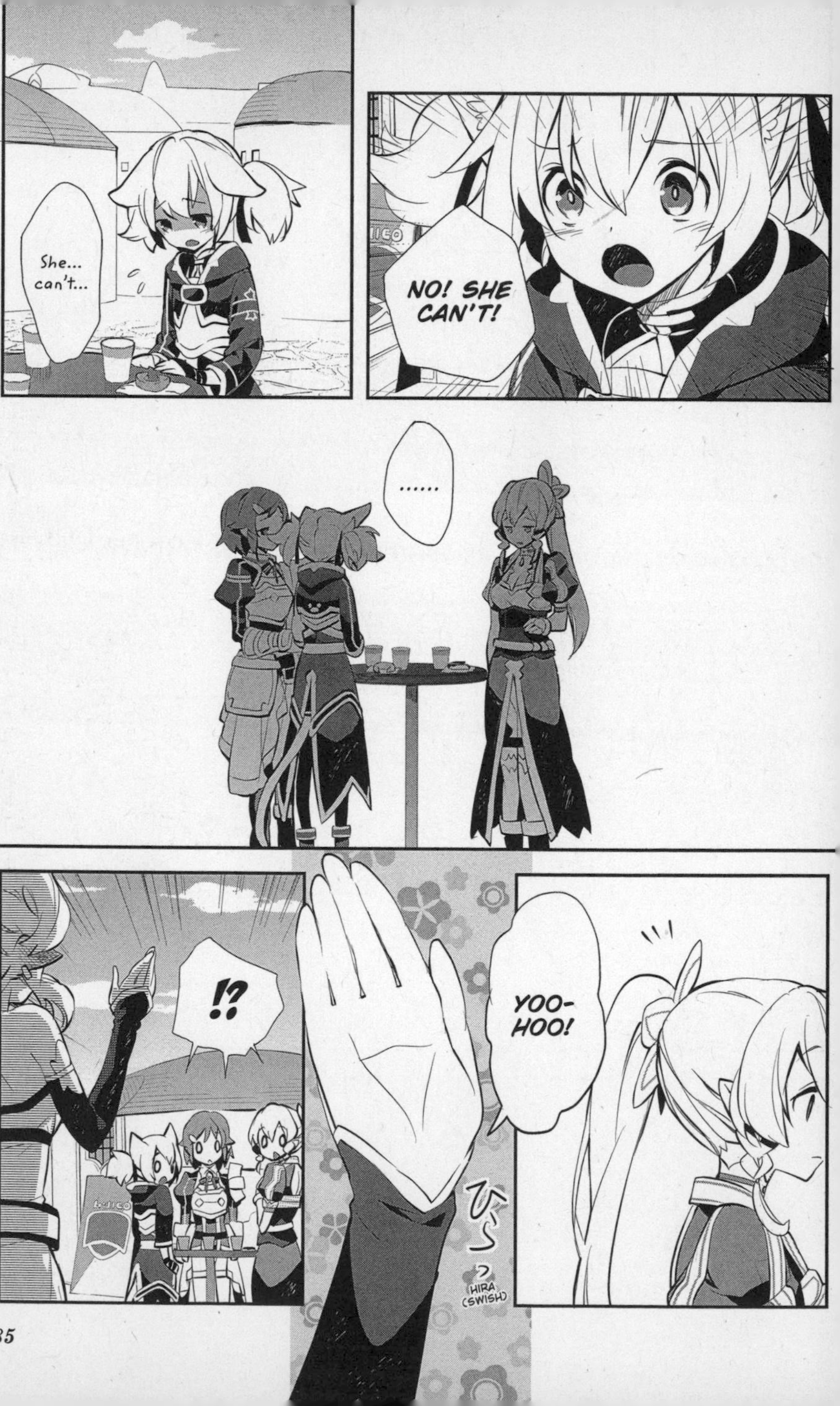
NO! SHE CAN'T!
She... can't...
......
YOO-HOO!
ひら
HIRA (SWISH)
!?

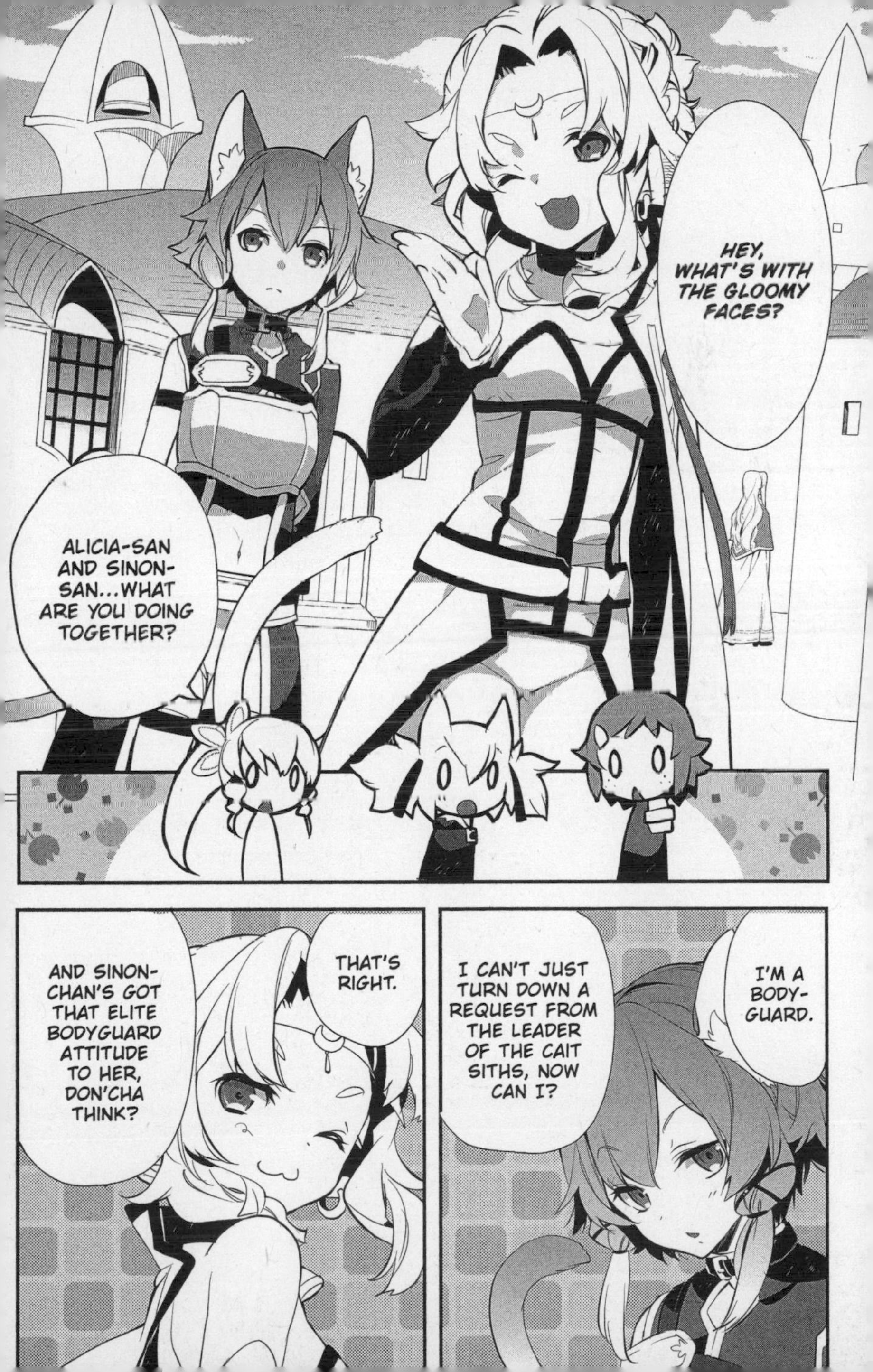
HEY, WHAT'S WITH THE GLOOMY FACES?
ALICIA-SAN AND SINON-SAN...WHAT ARE YOU DOING TOGETHER?
I'M A BODY-GUARD.
I CAN'T JUST TURN DOWN A REQUEST FROM THE LEADER OF THE CAIT SITHS, NOW CAN I?
THAT'S RIGHT.
AND SINON-CHAN'S GOT THAT ELITE BODYGUARD ATTITUDE TO HER, DON'CHA THINK?

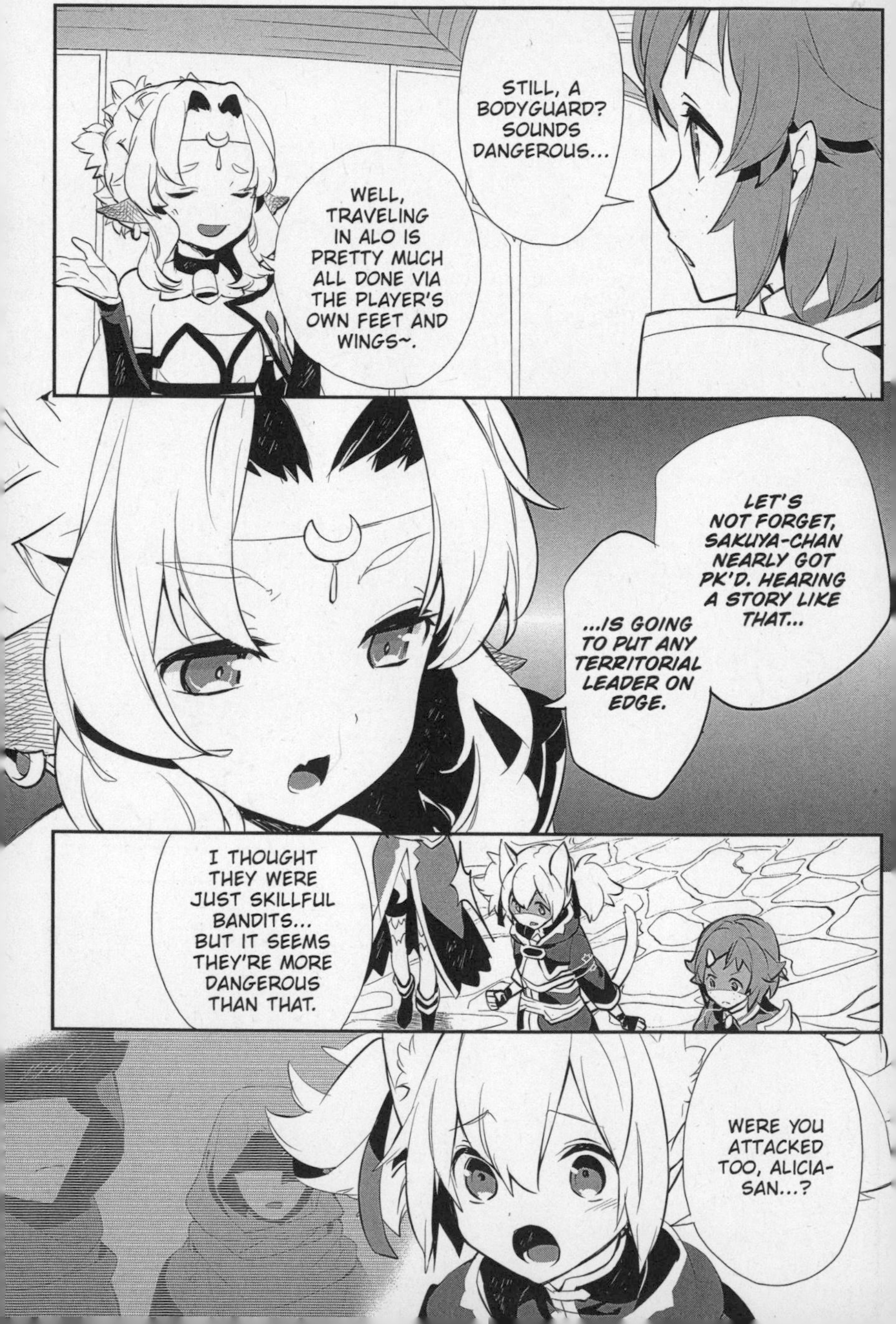
STILL, A BODYGUARD? SOUNDS DANGEROUS...
WELL, TRAVELING IN ALO IS PRETTY MUCH ALL DONE VIA THE PLAYER'S OWN FEET AND WINGS~.
LET'S NOT FORGET, SAKUYA-CHAN NEARLY GOT PK'D. HEARING A STORY LIKE THAT...
...IS GOING TO PUT ANY TERRITORIAL LEADER ON EDGE.
I THOUGHT THEY WERE JUST SKILLFUL BANDITS... BUT IT SEEMS THEY'RE MORE DANGEROUS THAN THAT.
WERE YOU ATTACKED TOO, ALICIA-SAN...?

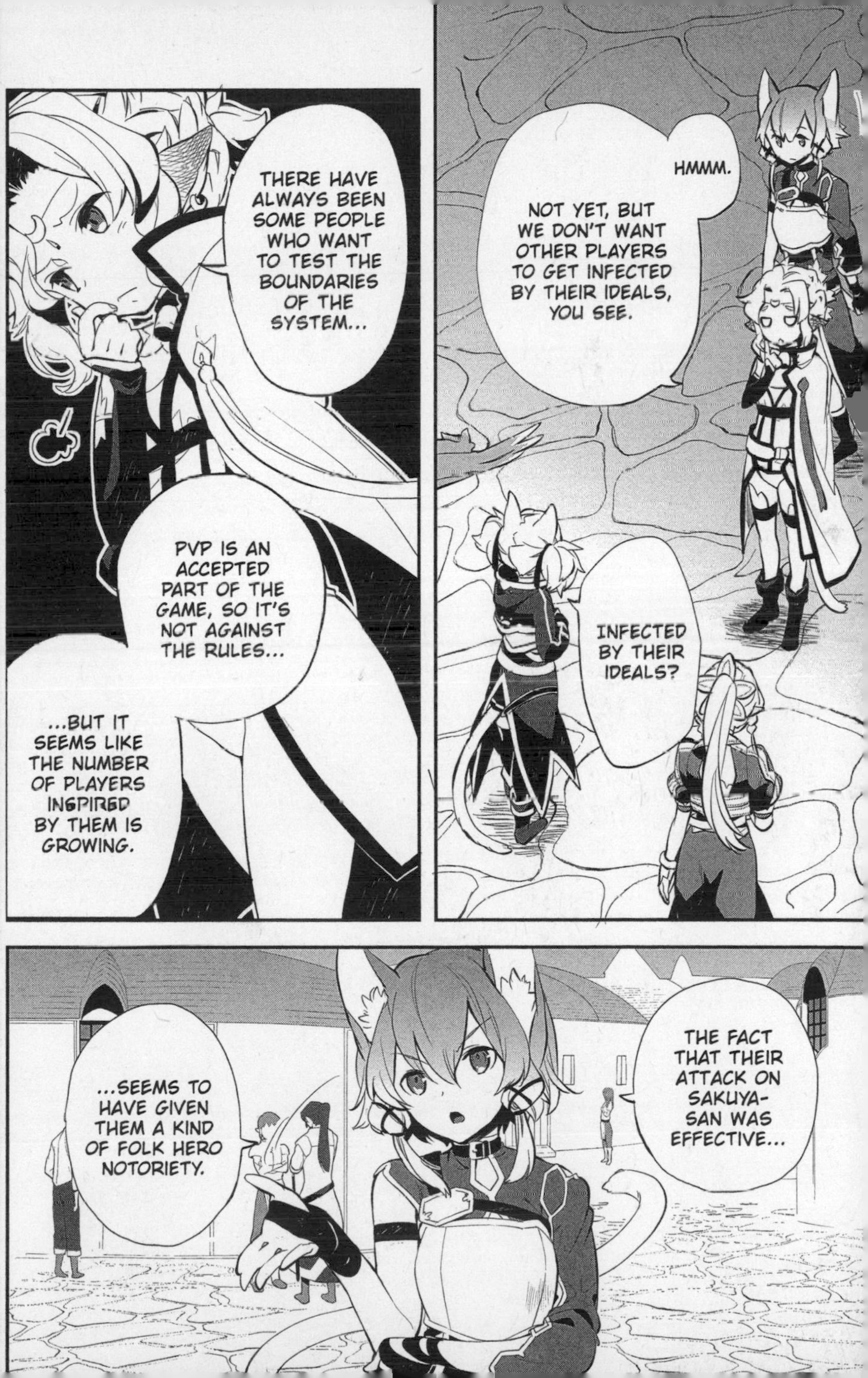
HMMM.
NOT YET, BUT WE DON'T WANT OTHER PLAYERS TO GET INFECTED BY THEIR IDEALS, YOU SEE.
INFECTED BY THEIR IDEALS?
THERE HAVE ALWAYS BEEN SOME PEOPLE WHO WANT TO TEST THE BOUNDARIES OF THE SYSTEM...
PVP IS AN ACCEPTED PART OF THE GAME, SO IT'S NOT AGAINST THE RULES...
...BUT IT SEEMS LIKE THE NUMBER OF PLAYERS INSPIRED BY THEM IS GROWING.
THE FACT THAT THEIR ATTACK ON SAKUYA-SAN WAS EFFECTIVE...
...SEEMS TO HAVE GIVEN THEM A KIND OF FOLK HERO NOTORIETY.

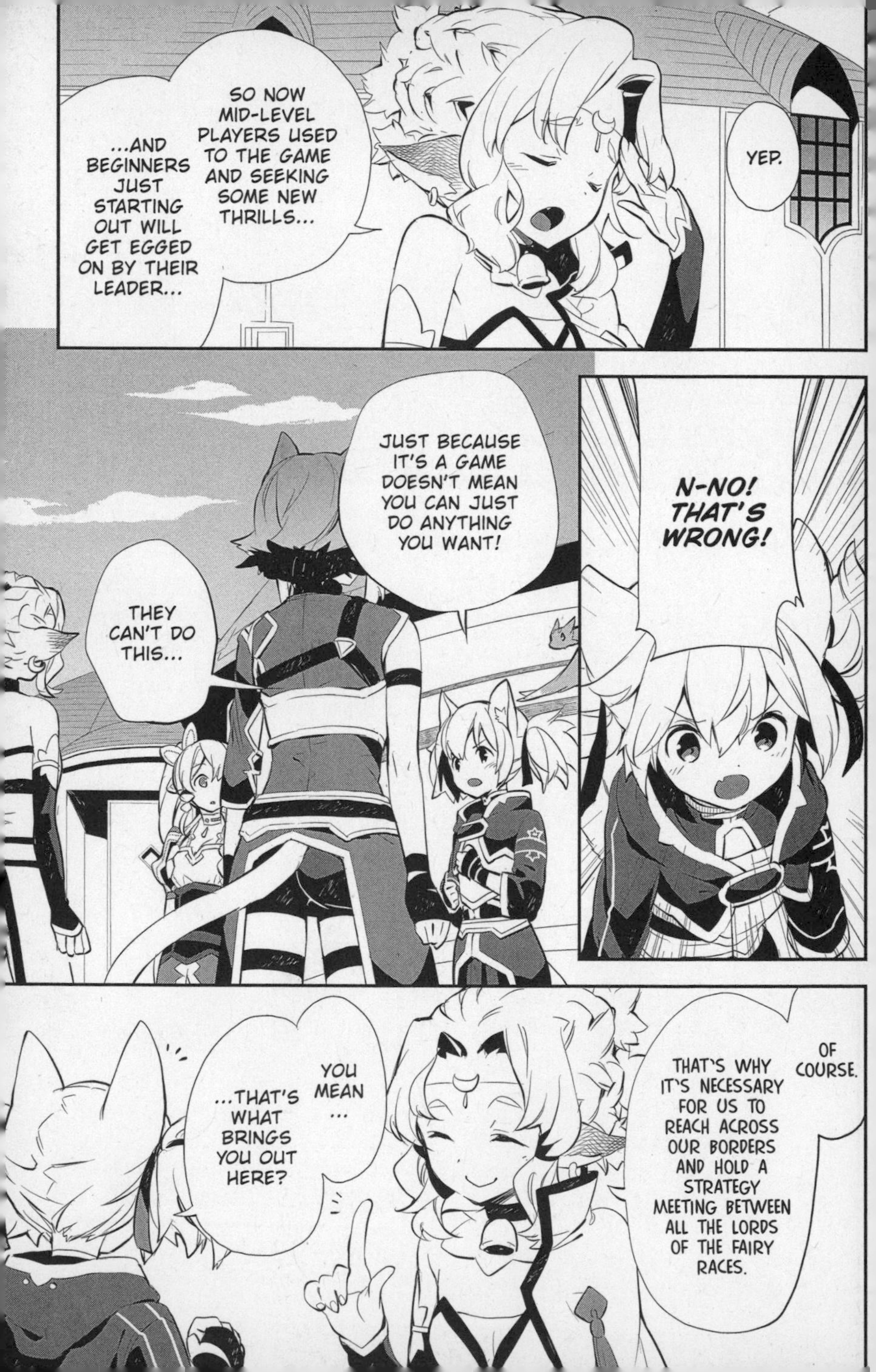
YEP.
SO NOW MID-LEVEL PLAYERS USED TO THE GAME AND SEEKING SOME NEW THRILLS...
...AND BEGINNERS JUST STARTING OUT WILL GET EGGED ON BY THEIR LEADER...
N-NO! THAT'S WRONG!
JUST BECAUSE IT'S A GAME DOESN'T MEAN YOU CAN JUST DO ANYTHING YOU WANT!
THEY CAN'T DO THIS...
OF COURSE.
THAT'S WHY IT'S NECESSARY FOR US TO REACH ACROSS OUR BORDERS AND HOLD A STRATEGY MEETING BETWEEN ALL THE LORDS OF THE FAIRY RACES.
YOU MEAN...
...THAT'S WHAT BRINGS YOU OUT HERE?

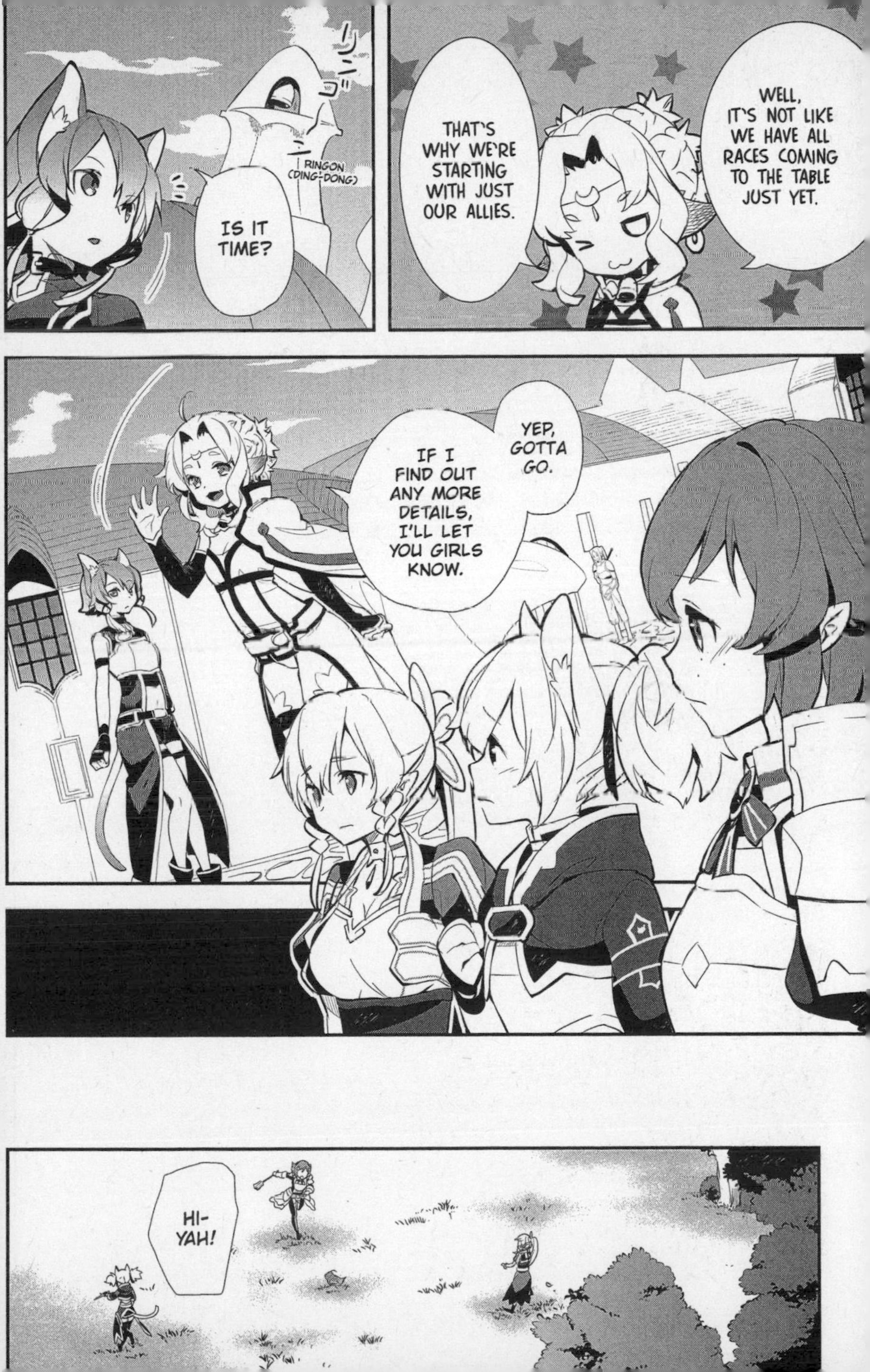
WELL, IT'S NOT LIKE WE HAVE ALL RACES COMING TO THE TABLE JUST YET.
THAT'S WHY WE'RE STARTING WITH JUST OUR ALLIES.
RINGON (DING-DONG)
IS IT TIME?
YEP, GOTTA GO.
IF I FIND OUT ANY MORE DETAILS, I'LL LET YOU GIRLS KNOW.
HI-YAH!

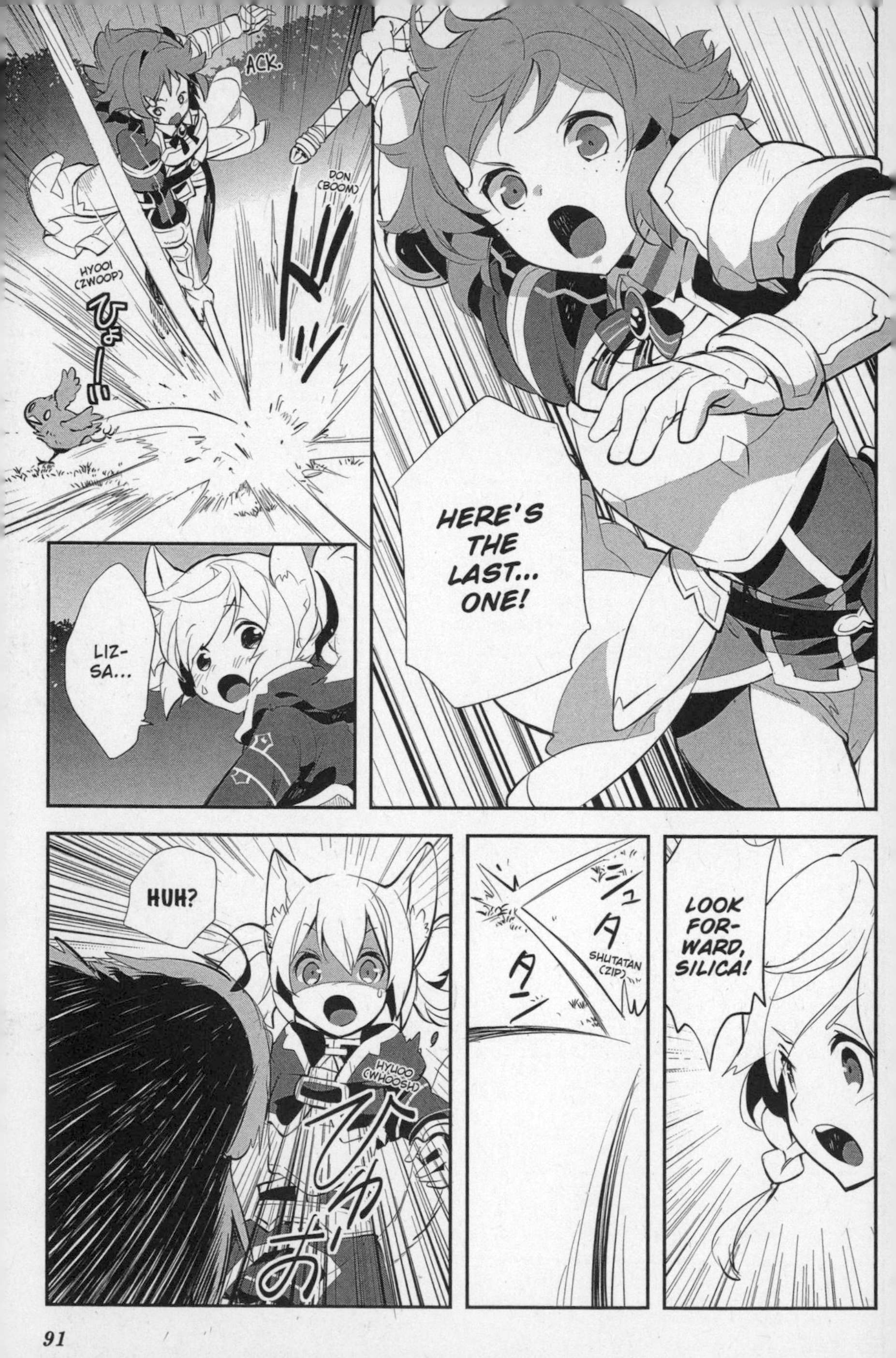
HERE'S THE LAST... ONE!
ACK.
DON (BOOM)
HYOOI (ZWOOP)
LIZ-SA...
LOOK FOR-WARD, SILICA!
SHUTATAN (ZIP)
HUH?
HYUHOO (WHOOSH)

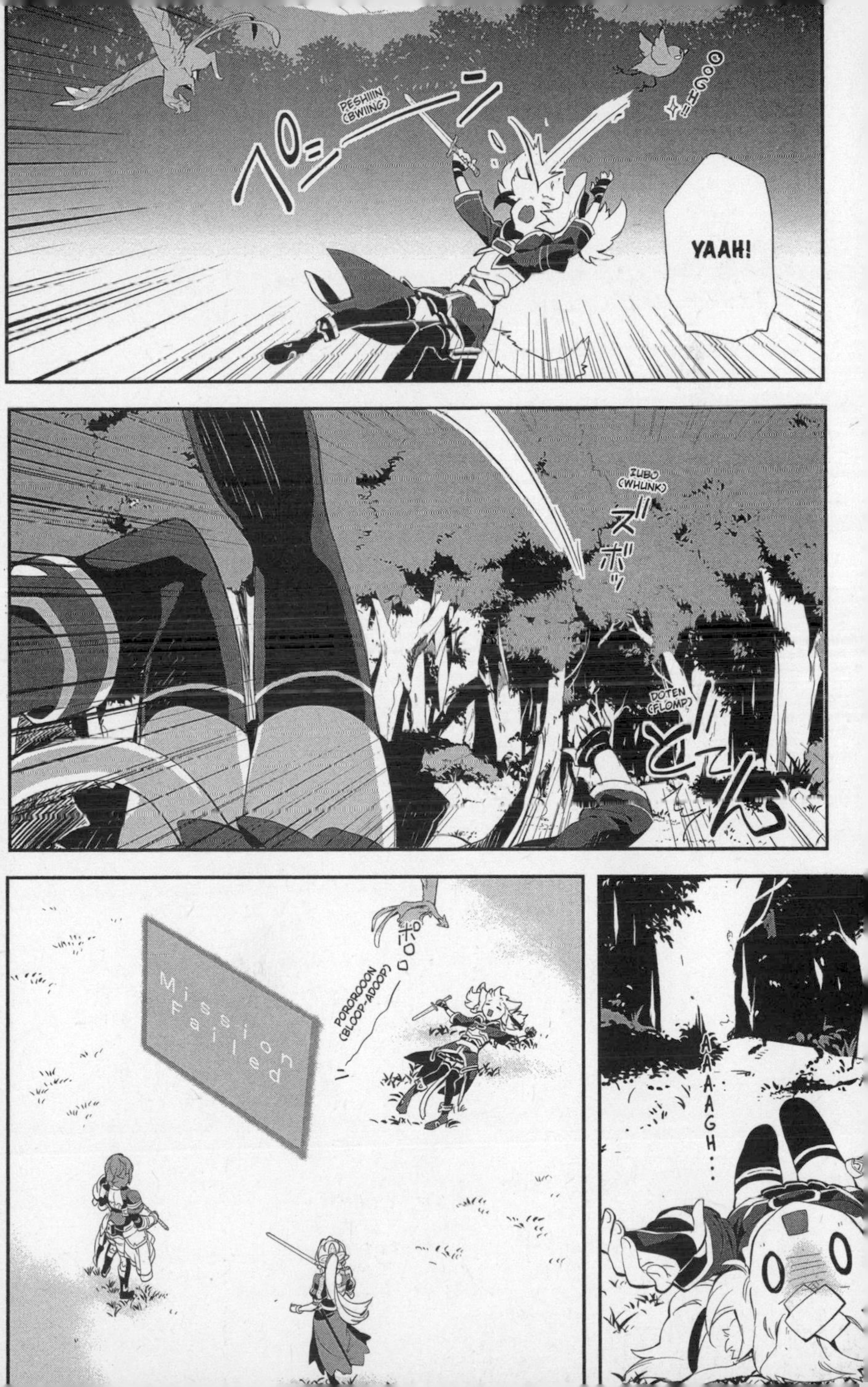
YAAH!
OOGH!!
PESHIIIN (BWIING)
ZUBO (WHUNK)
DOTEN (FLOMP)
AAAAGH...
POROROOON (BLOOP-ADOOP)
Mission Failed

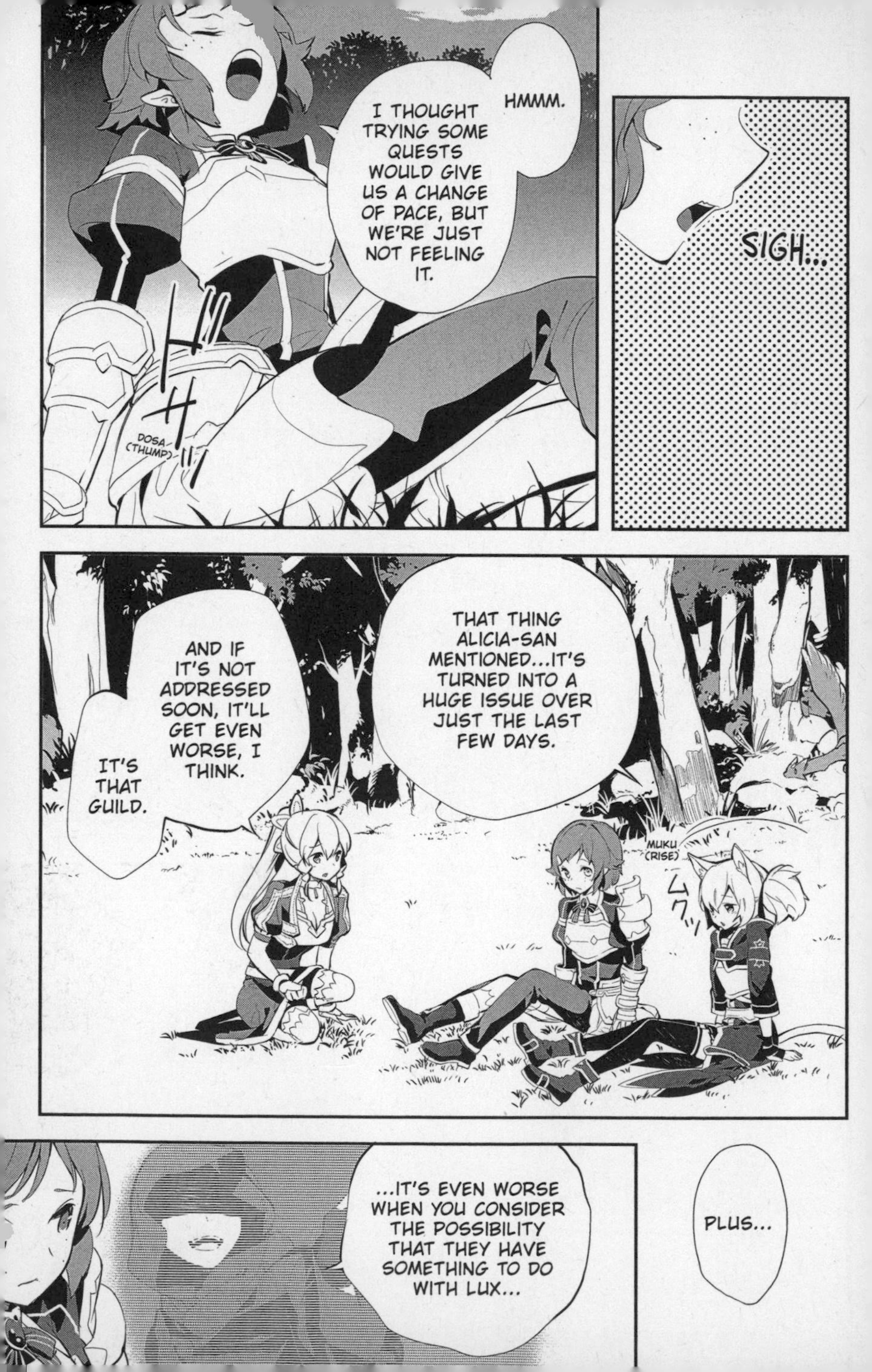
SIGH...
HMMM.
I THOUGHT TRYING SOME QUESTS WOULD GIVE US A CHANGE OF PACE, BUT WE'RE JUST NOT FEELING IT.
DOSA (THUMP)
THAT THING ALICIA-SAN MENTIONED...IT'S TURNED INTO A HUGE ISSUE OVER JUST THE LAST FEW DAYS.
IT'S THAT GUILD.
AND IF IT'S NOT ADDRESSED SOON, IT'LL GET EVEN WORSE, I THINK.
MUKU (RISE)
PLUS...
...IT'S EVEN WORSE WHEN YOU CONSIDER THE POSSIBILITY THAT THEY HAVE SOMETHING TO DO WITH LUX...

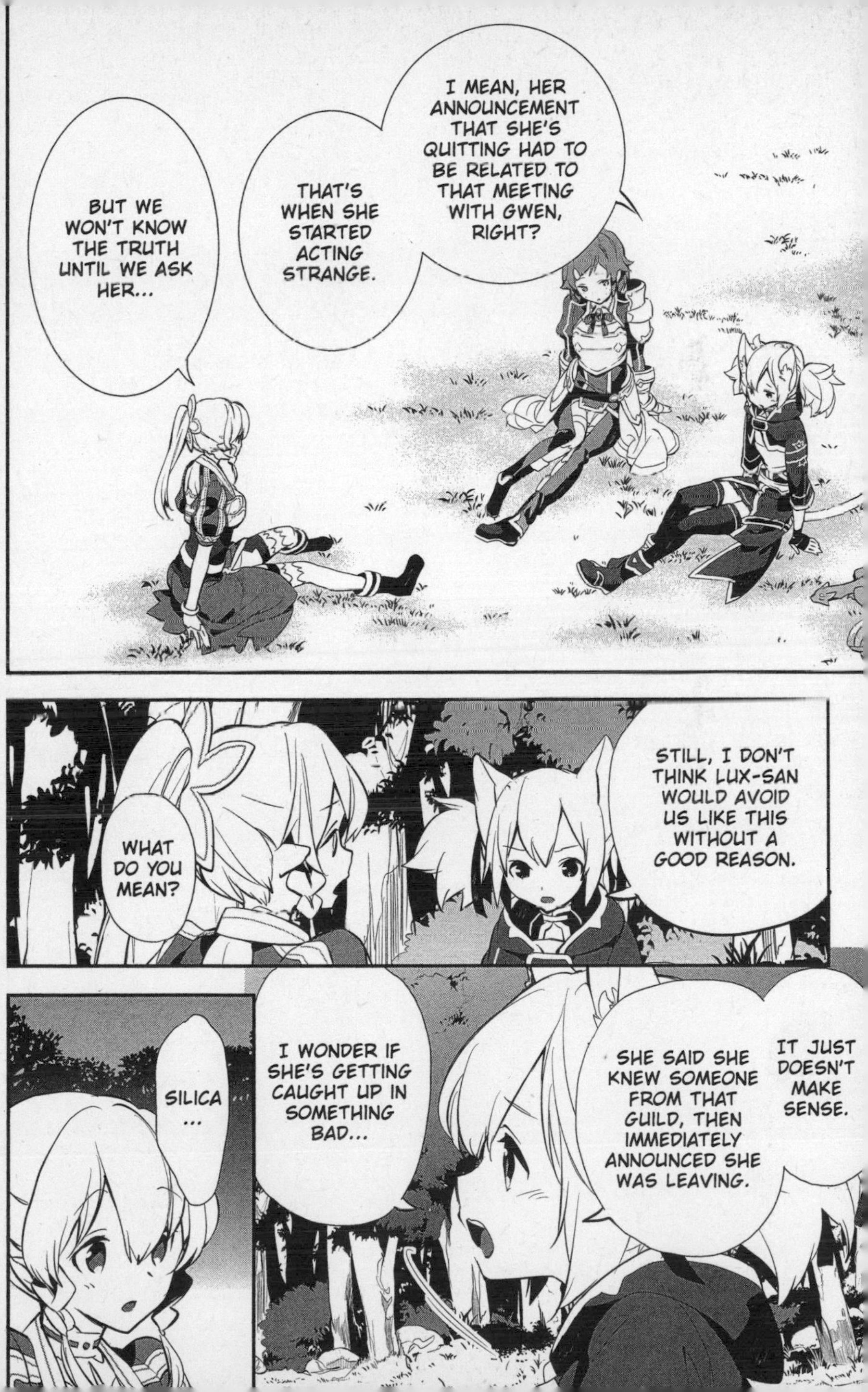
I MEAN, HER ANNOUNCEMENT THAT SHE'S QUITTING HAD TO BE RELATED TO THAT MEETING WITH GWEN, RIGHT?
THAT'S WHEN SHE STARTED ACTING STRANGE.
BUT WE WON'T KNOW THE TRUTH UNTIL WE ASK HER...
STILL, I DON'T THINK LUX-SAN WOULD AVOID US LIKE THIS WITHOUT A GOOD REASON.
WHAT DO YOU MEAN?
IT JUST DOESN'T MAKE SENSE.
SHE SAID SHE KNEW SOMEONE FROM THAT GUILD, THEN IMMEDIATELY ANNOUNCED SHE WAS LEAVING.
I WONDER IF SHE'S GETTING CAUGHT UP IN SOMETHING BAD...
SILICA ...

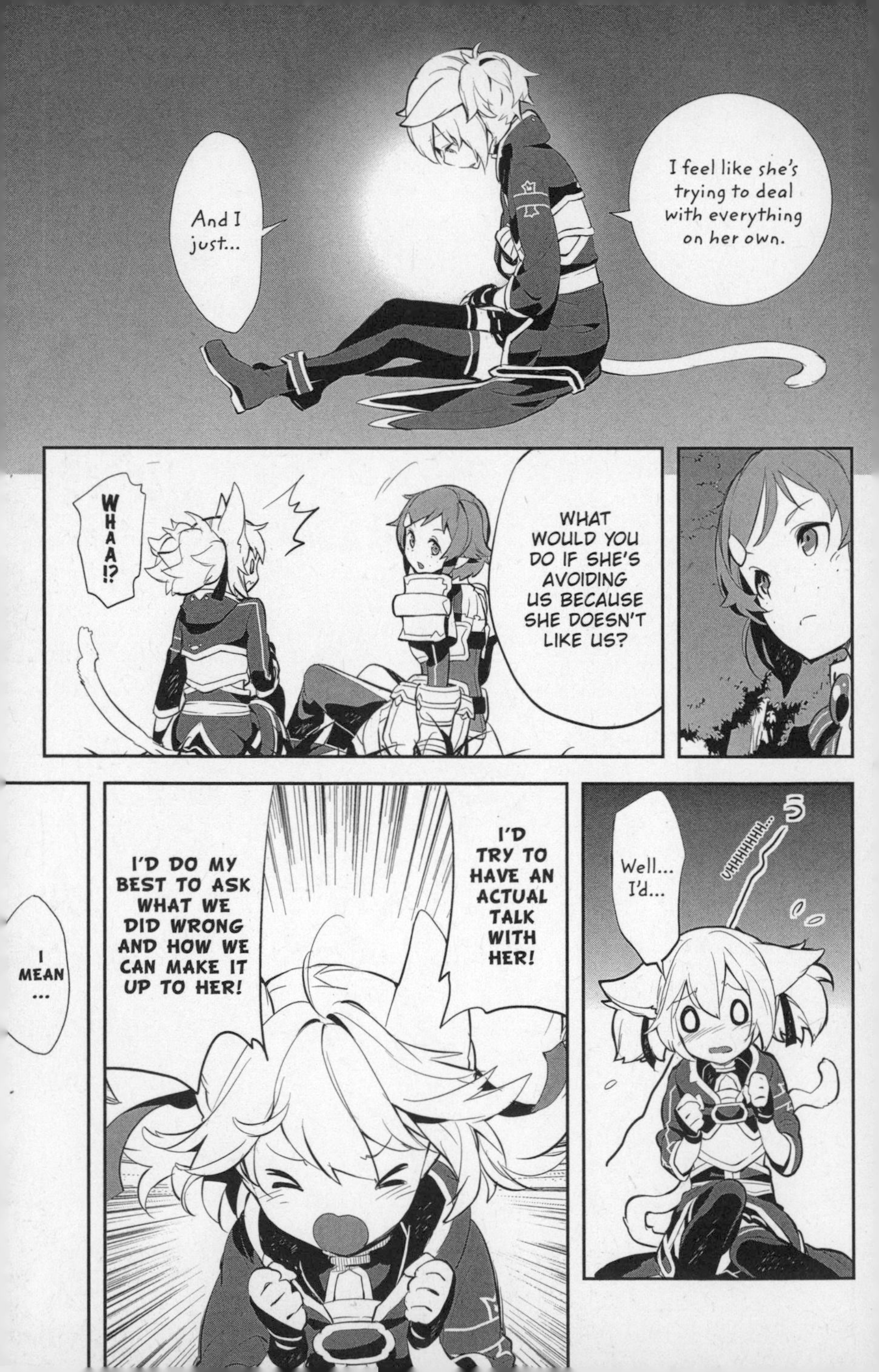
I feel like she's trying to deal with everything on her own.
And I just...
WHAT WOULD YOU DO IF SHE'S AVOIDING US BECAUSE SHE DOESN'T LIKE US?
WHAA!?
Well... I'd...
UHHHHHHH...
う
I'D TRY TO HAVE AN ACTUAL TALK WITH HER!
I'D DO MY BEST TO ASK WHAT WE DID WRONG AND HOW WE CAN MAKE IT UP TO HER!
I MEAN ...

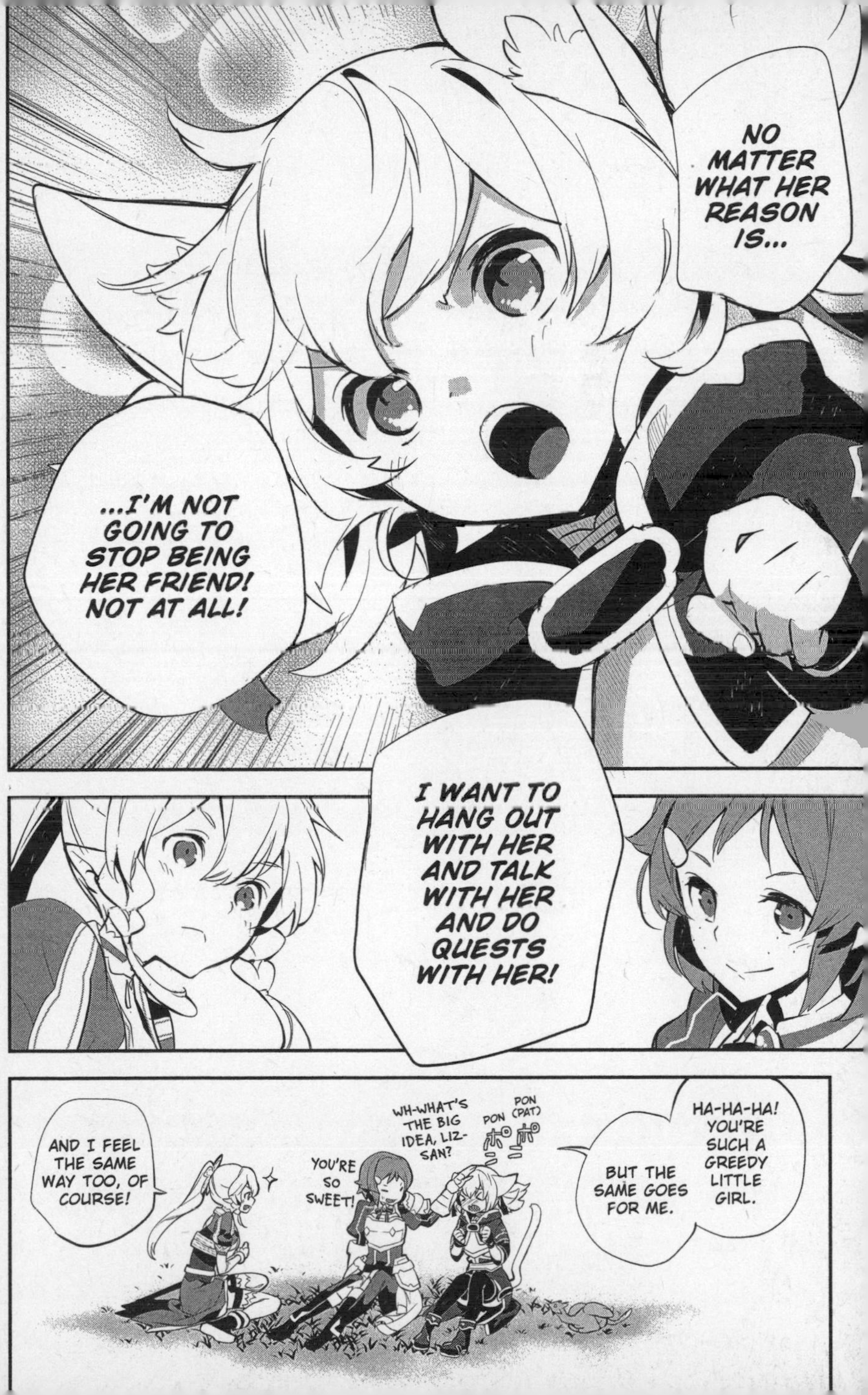
NO MATTER WHAT HER REASON IS...
...I'M NOT GOING TO STOP BEING HER FRIEND! NOT AT ALL!
I WANT TO HANG OUT WITH HER AND TALK WITH HER AND DO QUESTS WITH HER!
HA-HA-HA! YOU'RE SUCH A GREEDY LITTLE GIRL.
BUT THE SAME GOES FOR ME.
PON PON (PAT)
WH-WHAT'S THE BIG IDEA, LIZ-SAN?
YOU'RE SO SWEET!
AND I FEEL THE SAME WAY TOO, OF COURSE!

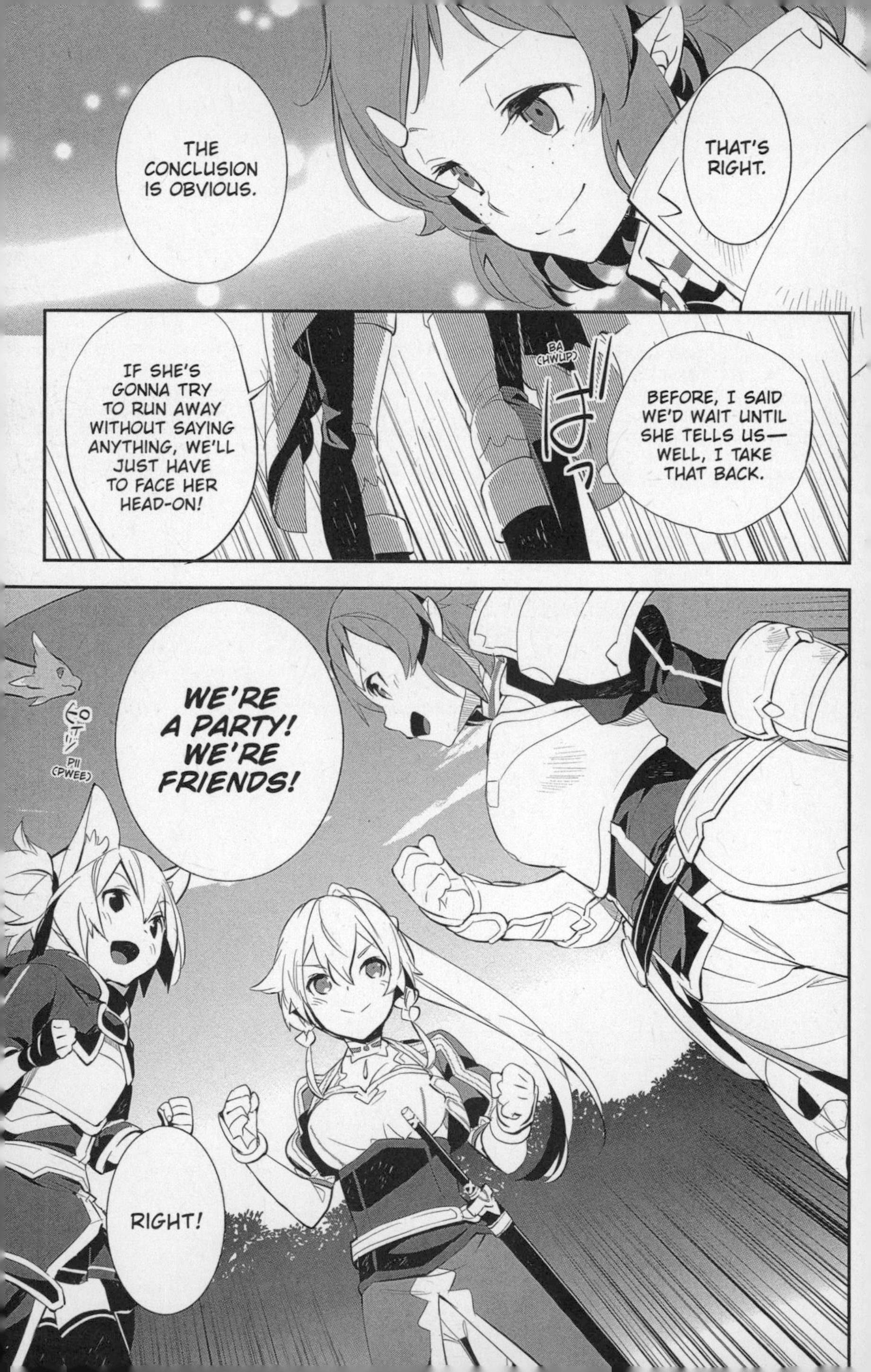
THAT'S RIGHT.
THE CONCLUSION IS OBVIOUS.
BEFORE, I SAID WE'D WAIT UNTIL SHE TELLS US— WELL, I TAKE THAT BACK.
BA (HWUP)
IF SHE'S GONNA TRY TO RUN AWAY WITHOUT SAYING ANYTHING, WE'LL JUST HAVE TO FACE HER HEAD-ON!
WE'RE A PARTY! WE'RE FRIENDS!
PII (PWEE)
RIGHT!

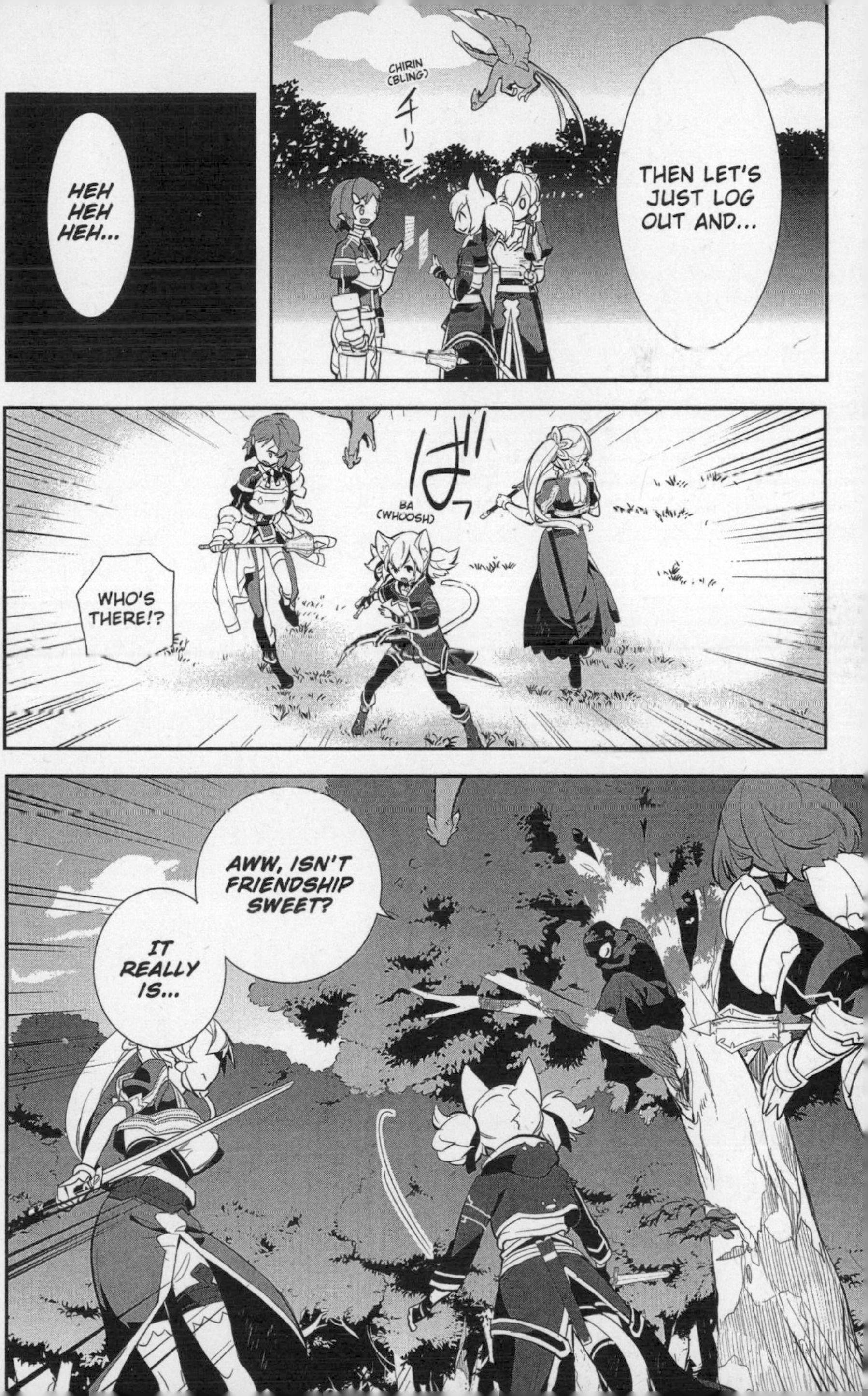
THEN LET'S JUST LOG OUT AND...
CHIRIN (BLING)
HEH HEH HEH...
ばっ
BA (WHOOSH)
WHO'S THERE!?
AWW, ISN'T FRIENDSHIP SWEET?
IT REALLY IS...

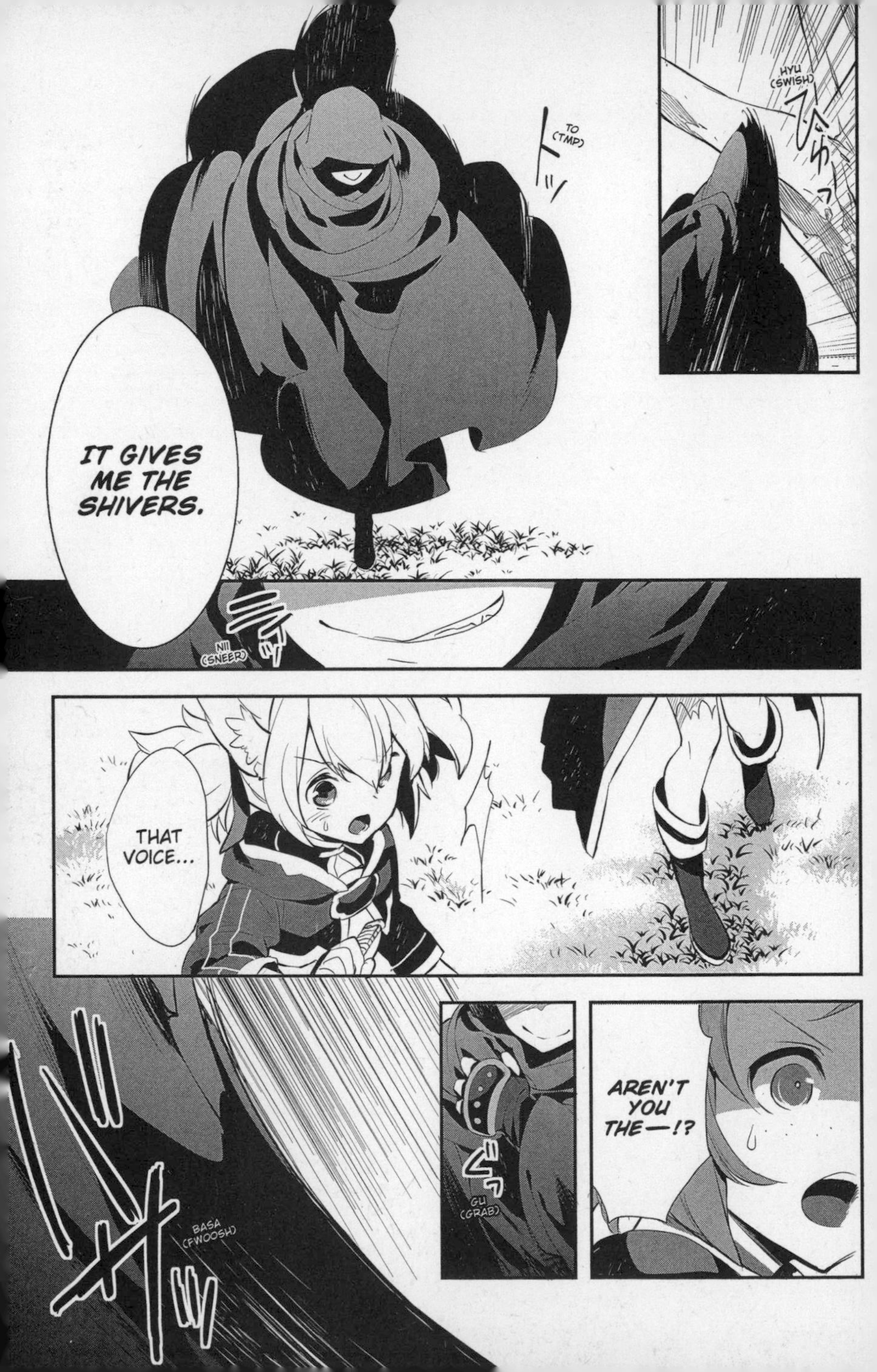
HYU (SWISH)
TO (TMP)
IT GIVES ME THE SHIVERS.
NII (SNEER)
THAT VOICE...
AREN'T YOU THE—!?
GU (GRAB)
BASA (FWOOSH)

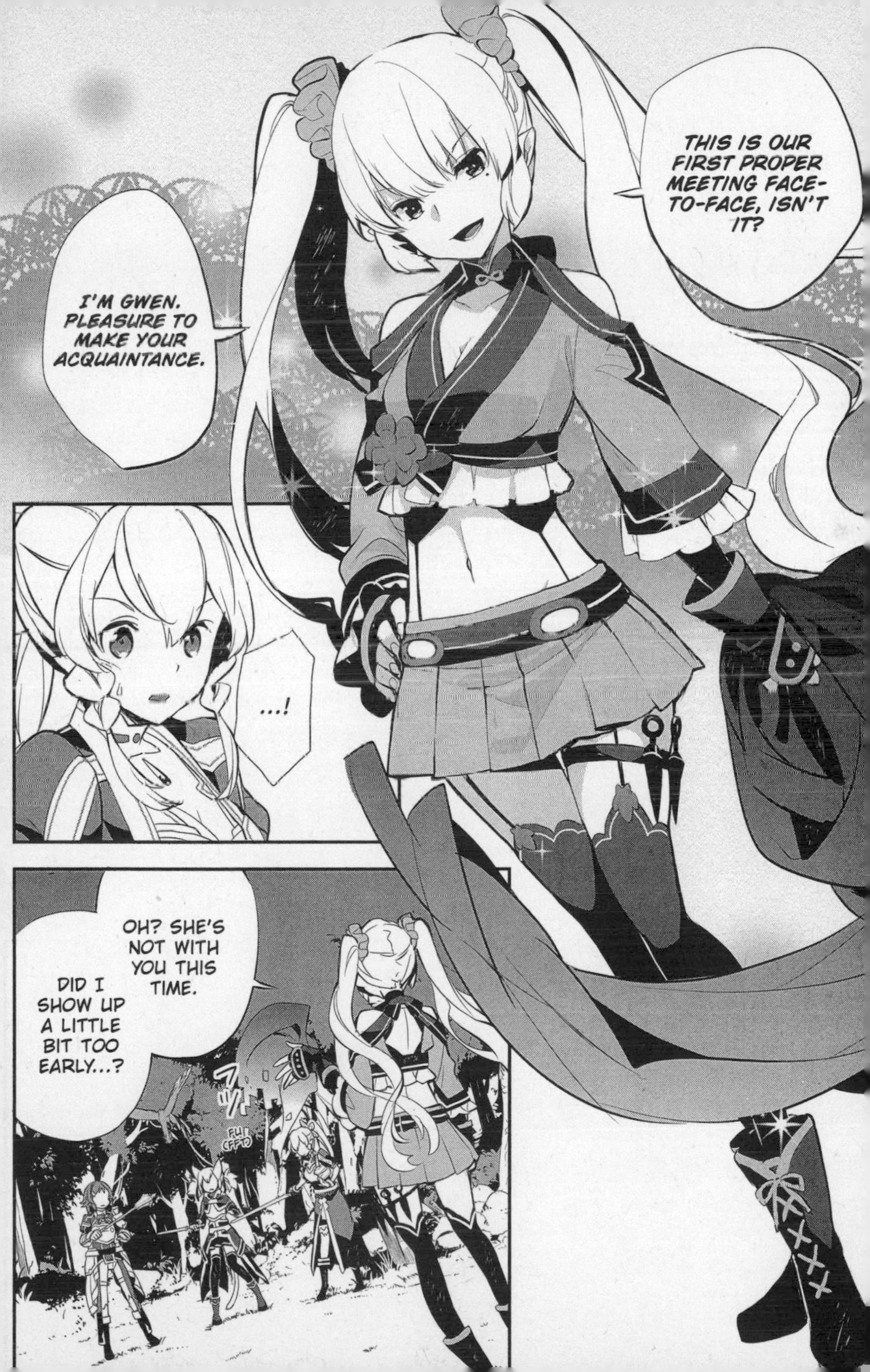
THIS IS OUR FIRST PROPER MEETING FACE-TO-FACE, ISN'T IT?
I'M GWEN. PLEASURE TO MAKE YOUR ACQUAINTANCE.
...!
OH? SHE'S NOT WITH YOU THIS TIME.
DID I SHOW UP A LITTLE BIT TOO EARLY...?
フッ
FU (FFT)

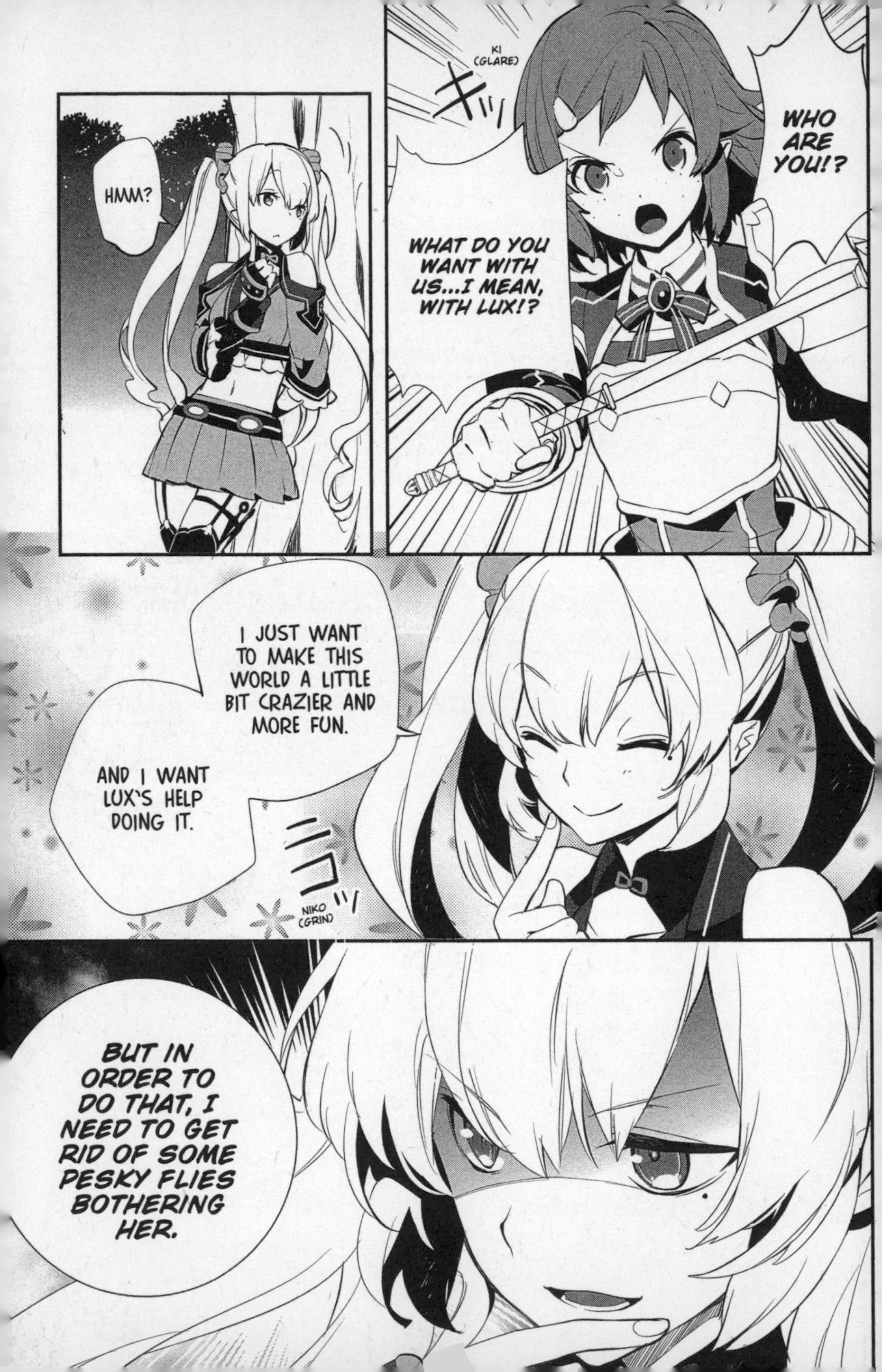
KI (GLARE)
WHO ARE YOU!?
WHAT DO YOU WANT WITH US...I MEAN, WITH LUX!?
HMM?
I JUST WANT TO MAKE THIS WORLD A LITTLE BIT CRAZIER AND MORE FUN.
AND I WANT LUX'S HELP DOING IT.
NIKO (GRIN)
BUT IN ORDER TO DO THAT, I NEED TO GET RID OF SOME PESKY FLIES BOTHERING HER.

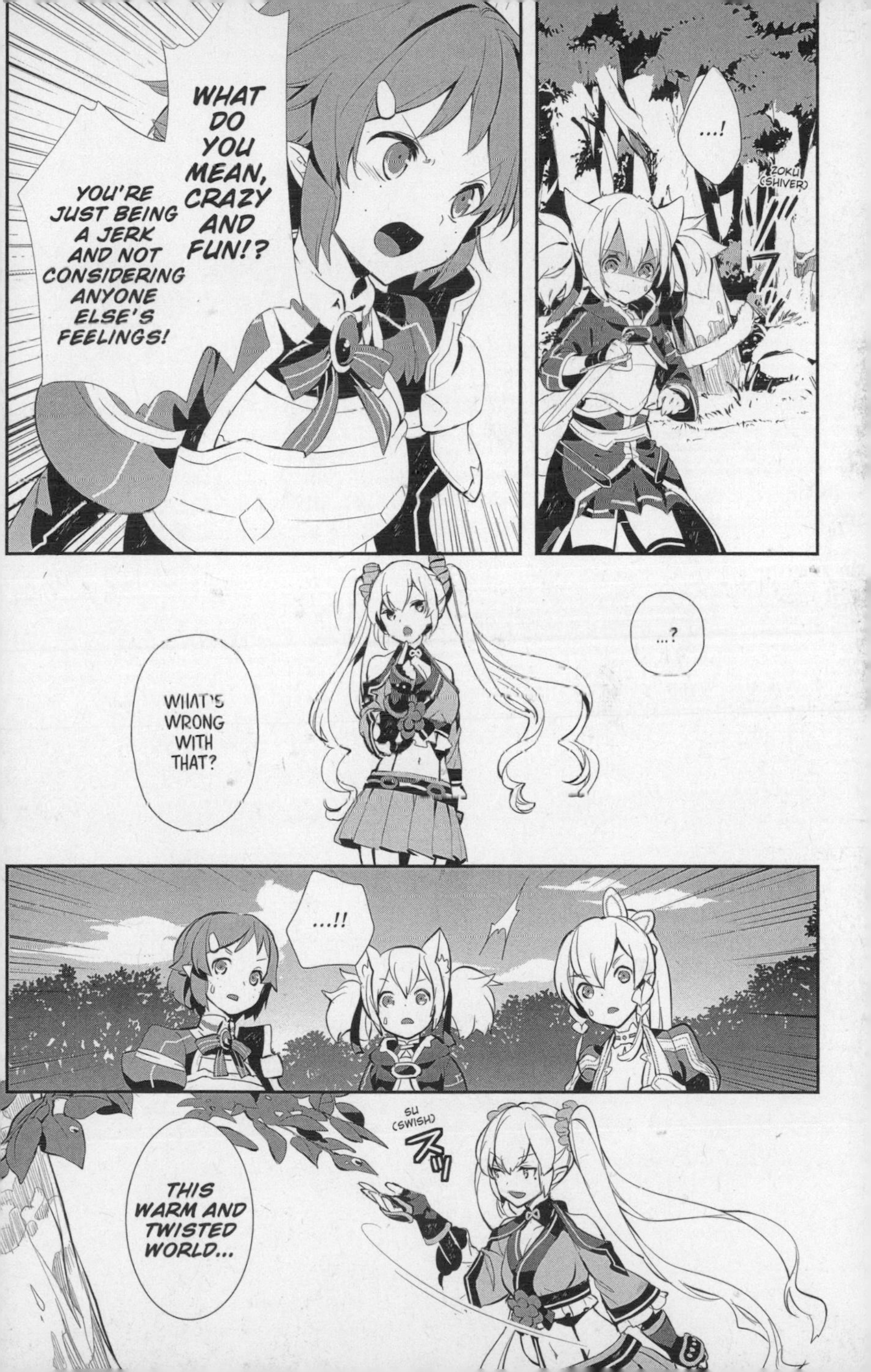
...!
ZOKU (SHIVER)
WHAT DO YOU MEAN, CRAZY AND FUN!?
YOU'RE JUST BEING A JERK AND NOT CONSIDERING ANYONE ELSE'S FEELINGS!
...?
WHAT'S WRONG WITH THAT?
...!!
SU (SWISH)
スッ
THIS WARM AND TWISTED WORLD...

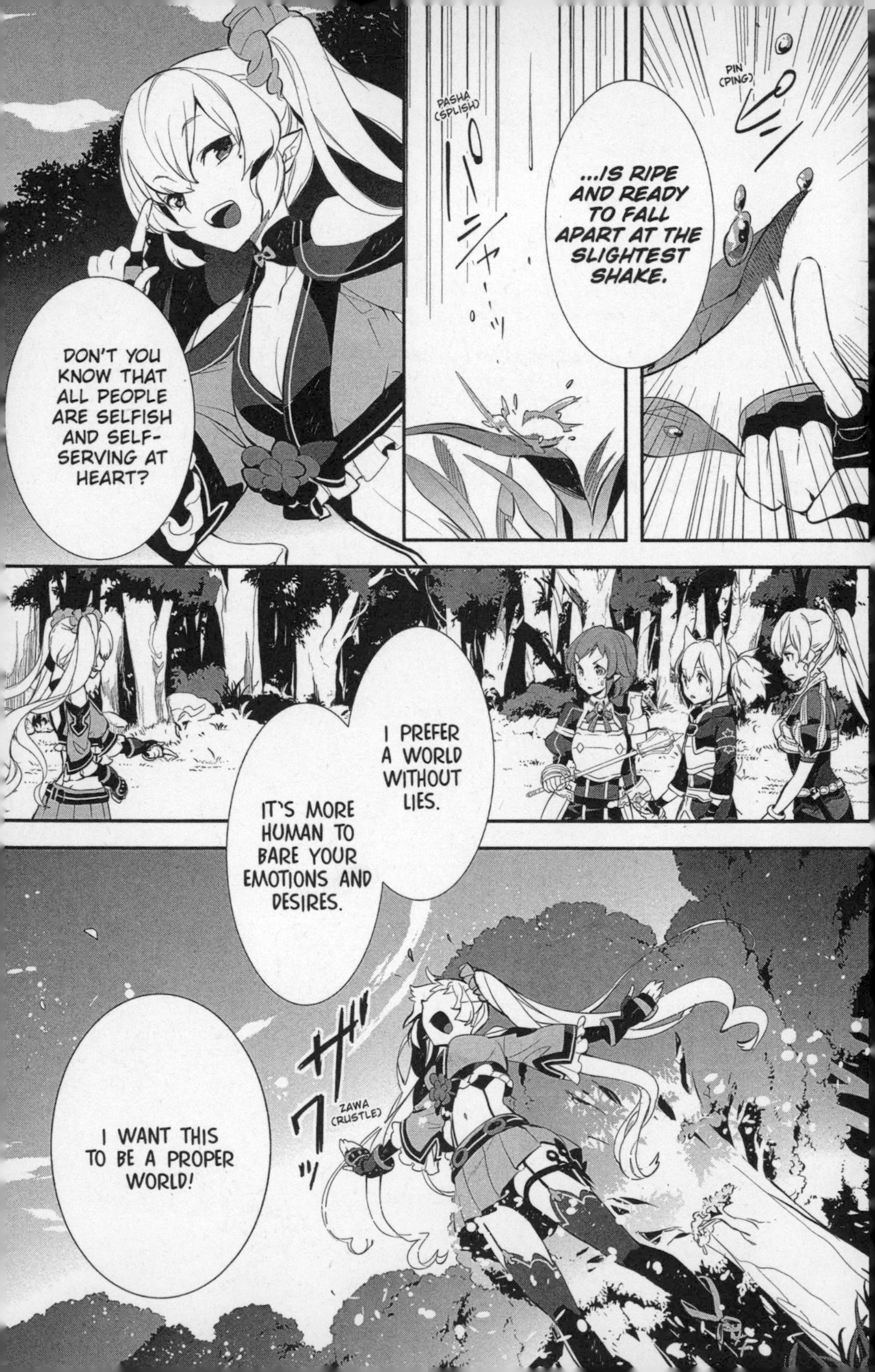
PIN (PING)
...IS RIPE AND READY TO FALL APART AT THE SLIGHTEST SHAKE.
PASHA (SPLISH)
DON'T YOU KNOW THAT ALL PEOPLE ARE SELFISH AND SELF-SERVING AT HEART?
I PREFER A WORLD WITHOUT LIES.
IT'S MORE HUMAN TO BARE YOUR EMOTIONS AND DESIRES.
ZAWA (RUSTLE)
I WANT THIS TO BE A PROPER WORLD!

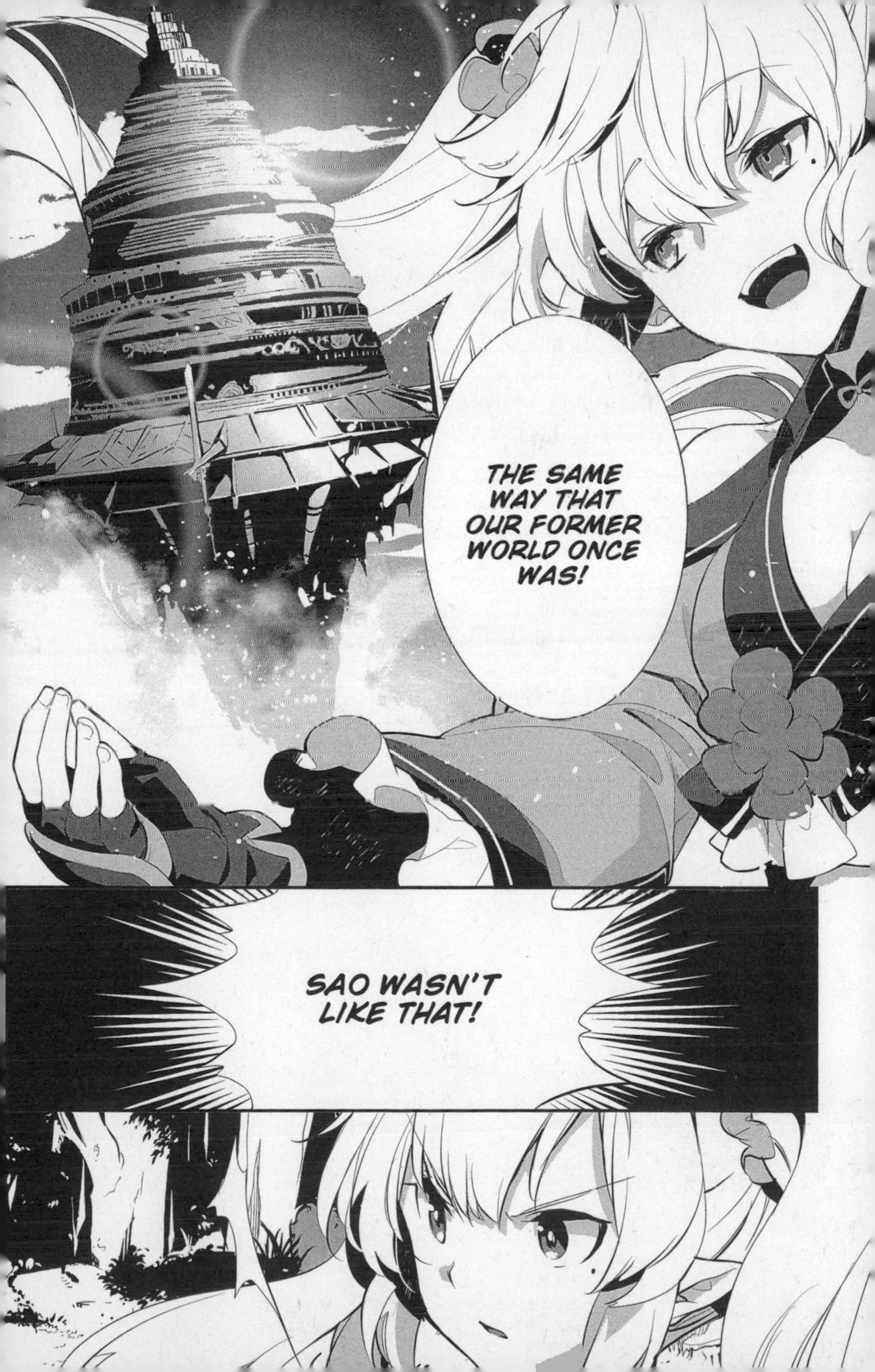
THE SAME WAY THAT OUR FORMER WORLD ONCE WAS!
SAO WASN'T LIKE THAT!

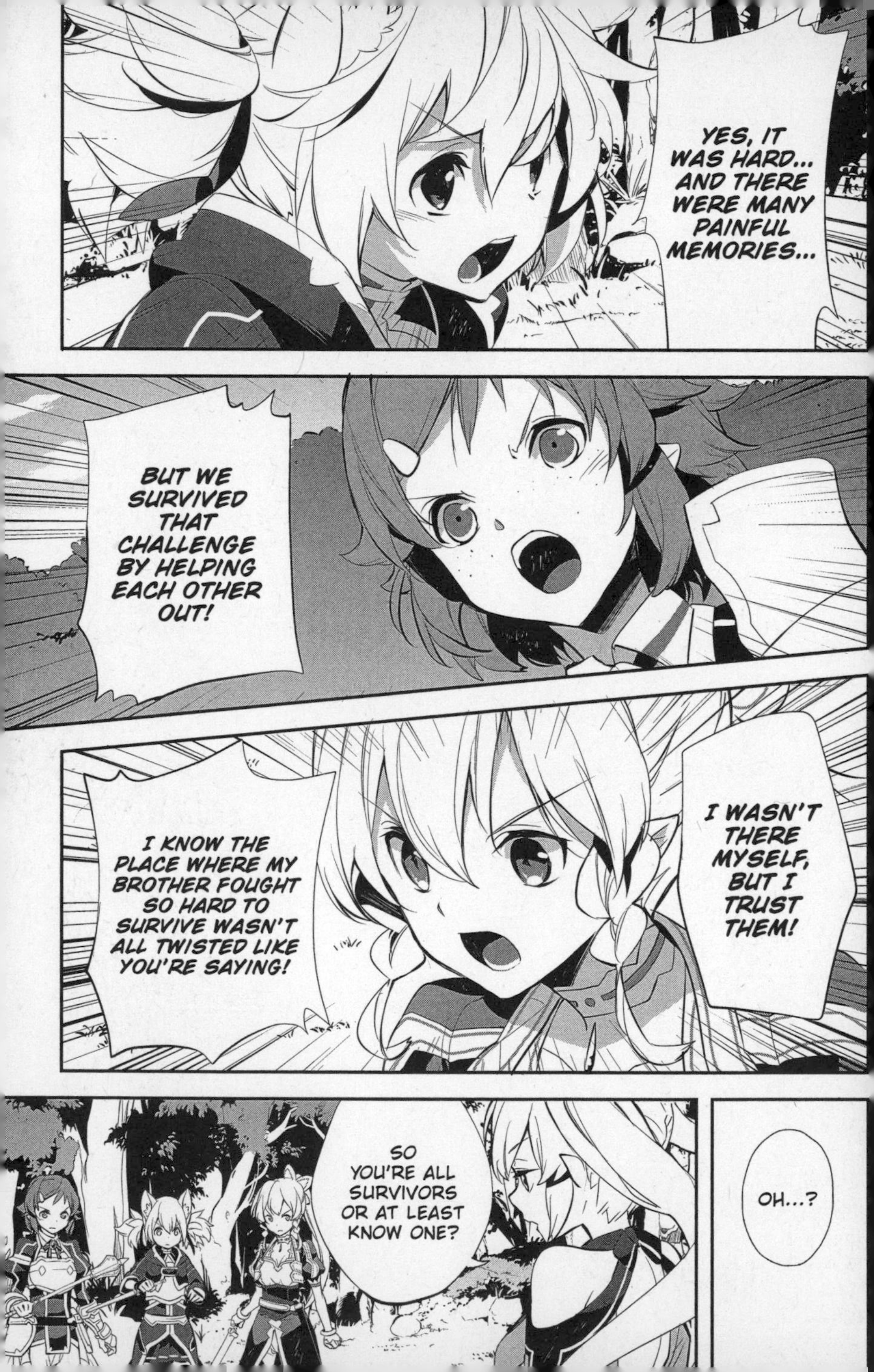
YES, IT WAS HARD... AND THERE WERE MANY PAINFUL MEMORIES...
BUT WE SURVIVED THAT CHALLENGE BY HELPING EACH OTHER OUT!
I WASN'T THERE MYSELF, BUT I TRUST THEM!
I KNOW THE PLACE WHERE MY BROTHER FOUGHT SO HARD TO SURVIVE WASN'T ALL TWISTED LIKE YOU'RE SAYING!
OH...?
SO YOU'RE ALL SURVIVORS OR AT LEAST KNOW ONE?

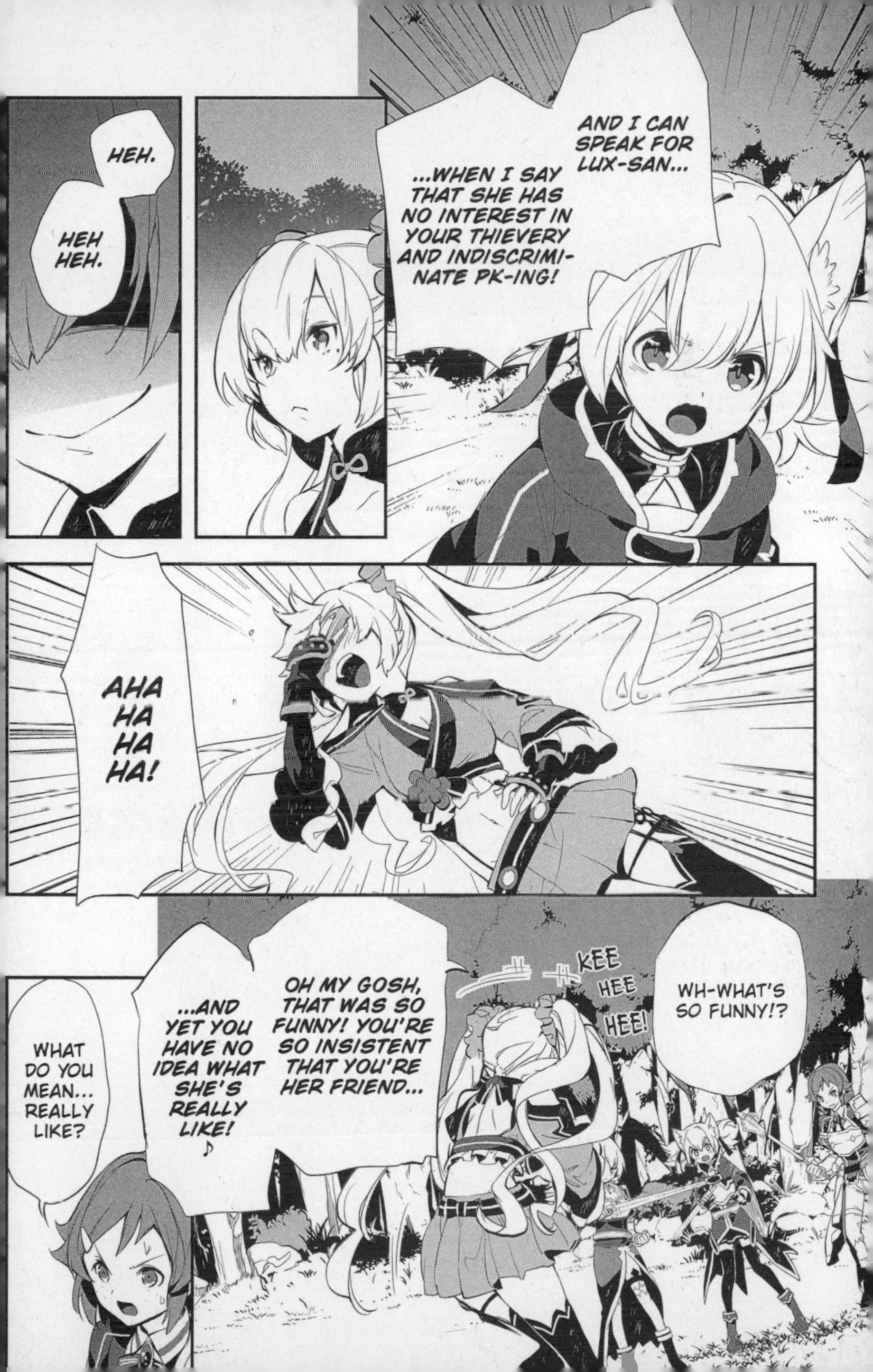
AND I CAN SPEAK FOR LUX-SAN...
...WHEN I SAY THAT SHE HAS NO INTEREST IN YOUR THIEVERY AND INDISCRIMINATE PK-ING!
HEH.
HEH HEH.
AHA HA HA HA!
WH-WHAT'S SO FUNNY!?
KEE HEE HEE!
OH MY GOSH, THAT WAS SO FUNNY! YOU'RE SO INSISTENT THAT YOU'RE HER FRIEND...
...AND YET YOU HAVE NO IDEA WHAT SHE'S REALLY LIKE! ♪
WHAT DO YOU MEAN... REALLY LIKE?

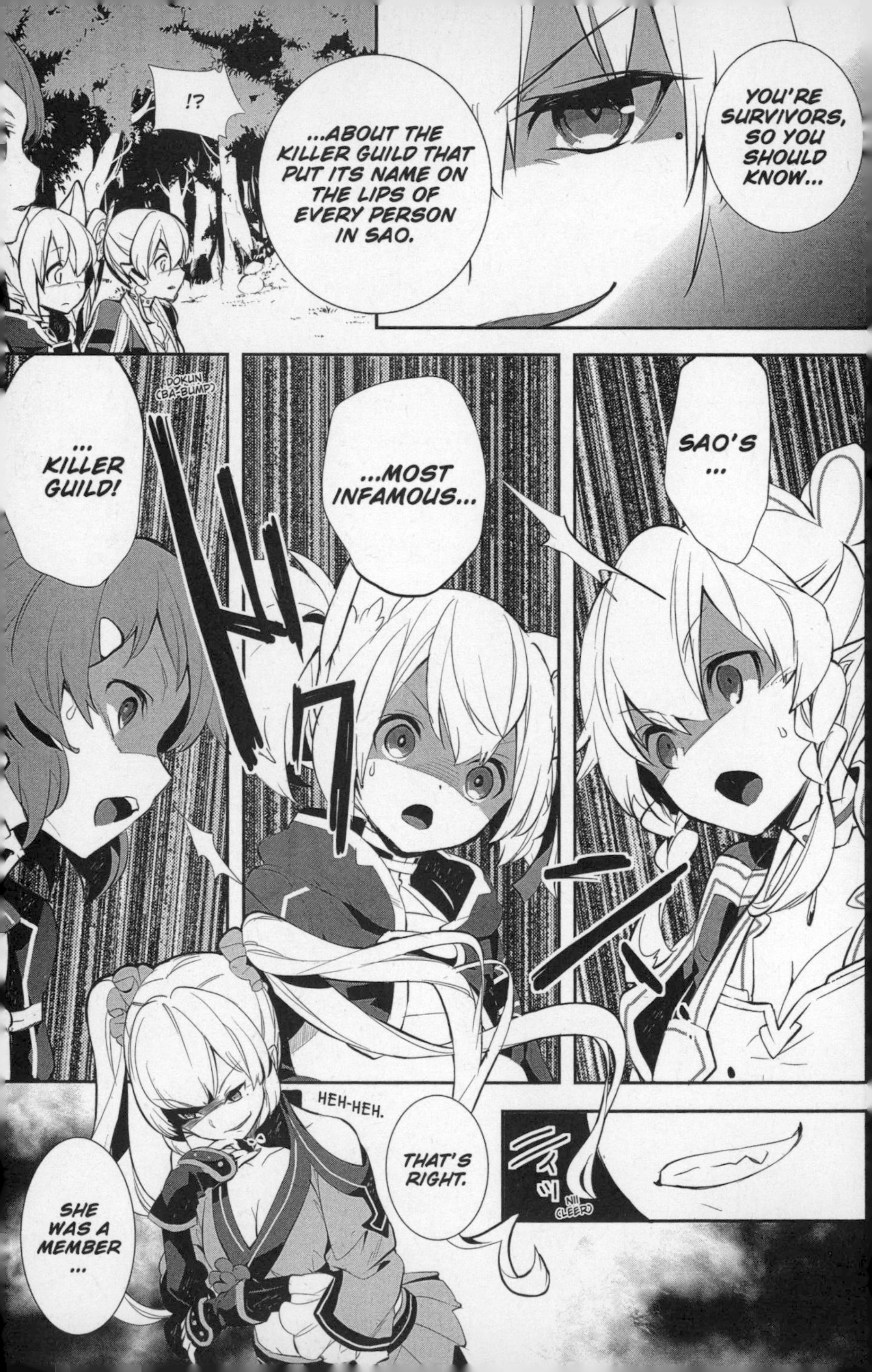
YOU'RE SURVIVORS, SO YOU SHOULD KNOW...
...ABOUT THE KILLER GUILD THAT PUT ITS NAME ON THE LIPS OF EVERY PERSON IN SAO.
!?
SAO'S ...
...MOST INFAMOUS...
DOKUN (BA-BUMP)
... KILLER GUILD!
NII (LEER)
HEH-HEH.
THAT'S RIGHT.
SHE WAS A MEMBER ...

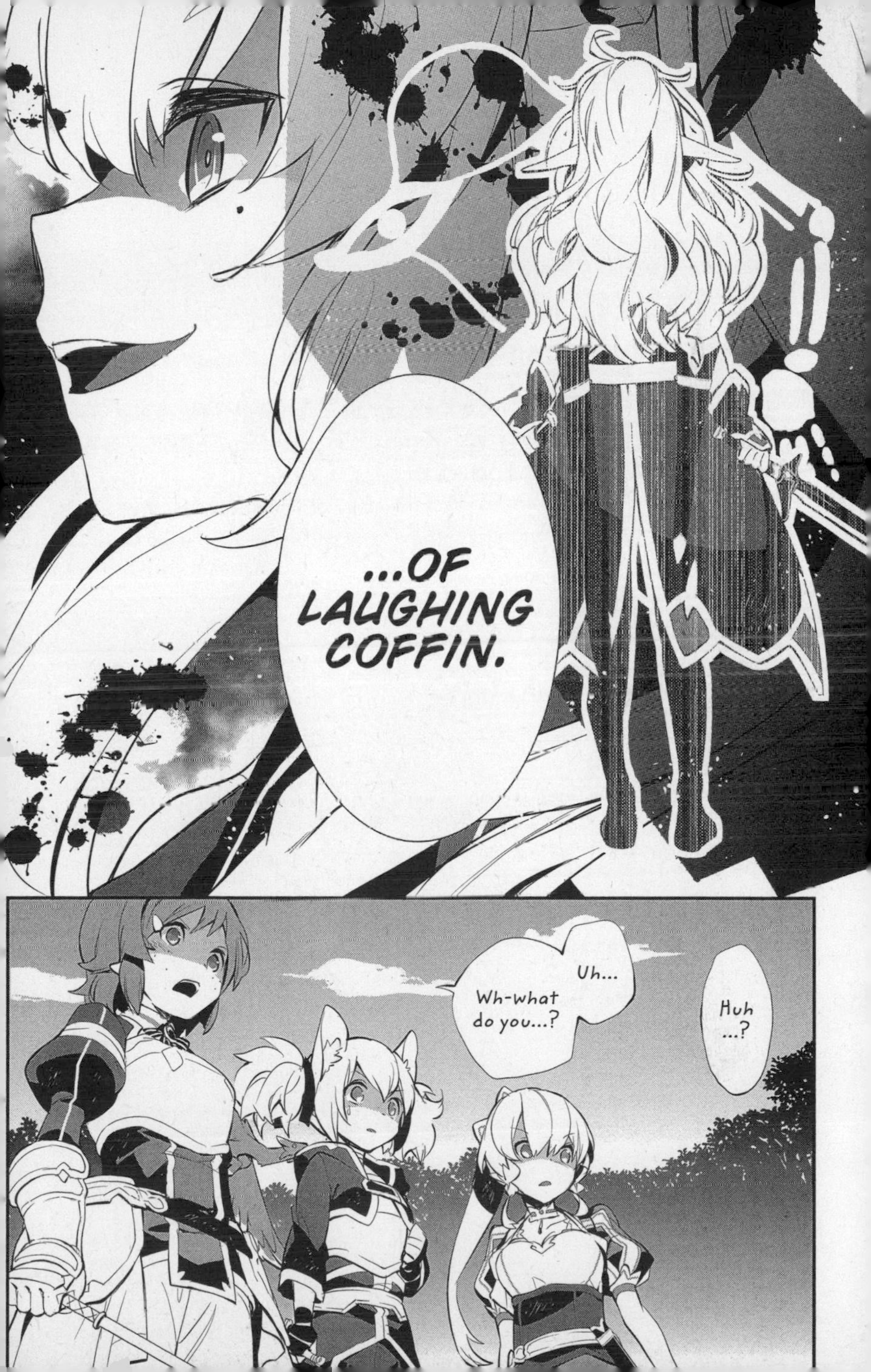
...OF LAUGHING COFFIN.
Huh ...?
Uh... Wh-what do you...?

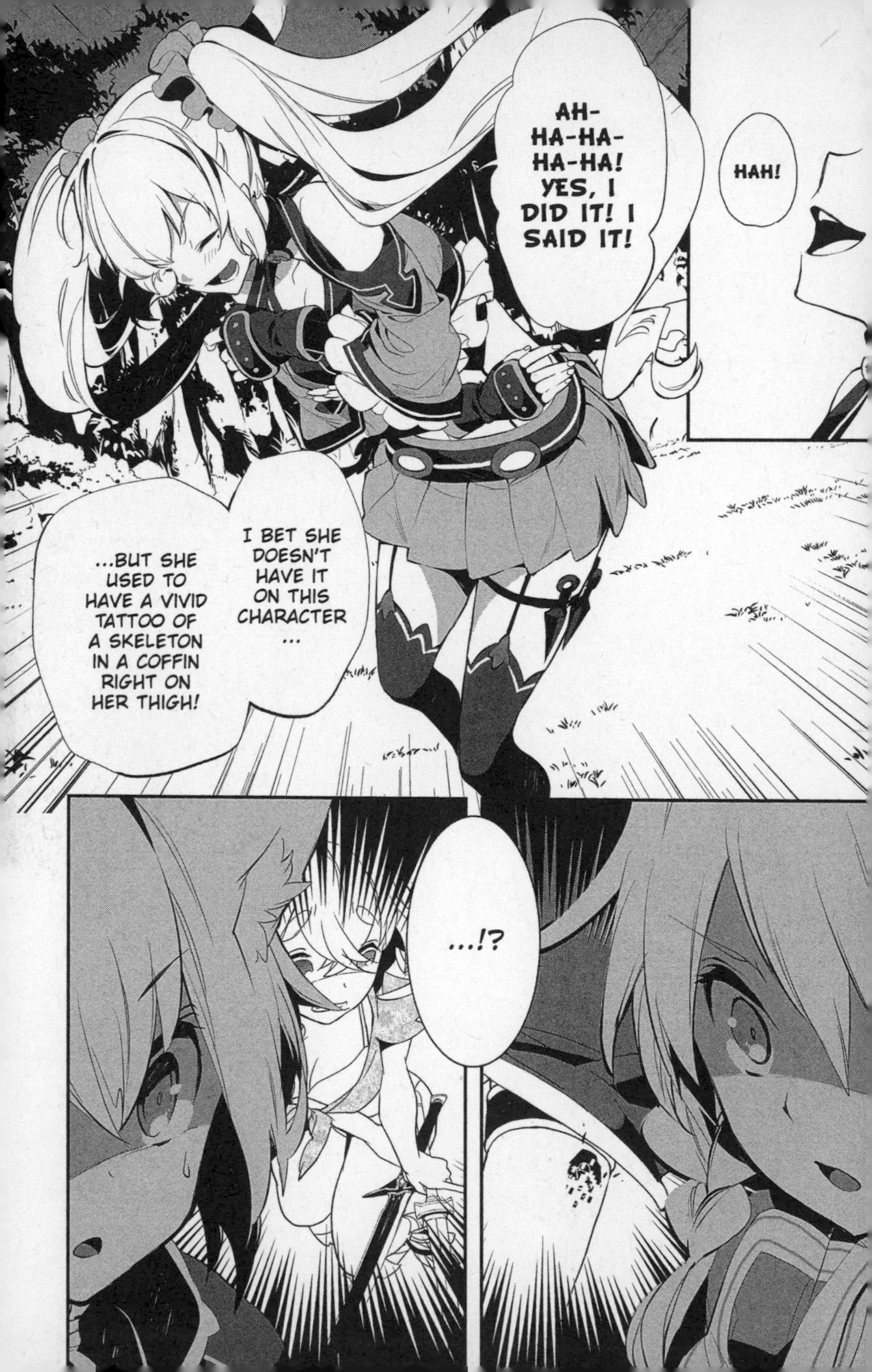
HAH!
AH-HA-HA-HA-HA! YES, I DID IT! I SAID IT!
I BET SHE DOESN'T HAVE IT ON THIS CHARACTER...
...BUT SHE USED TO HAVE A VIVID TATTOO OF A SKELETON IN A COFFIN RIGHT ON HER THIGH!
...!?

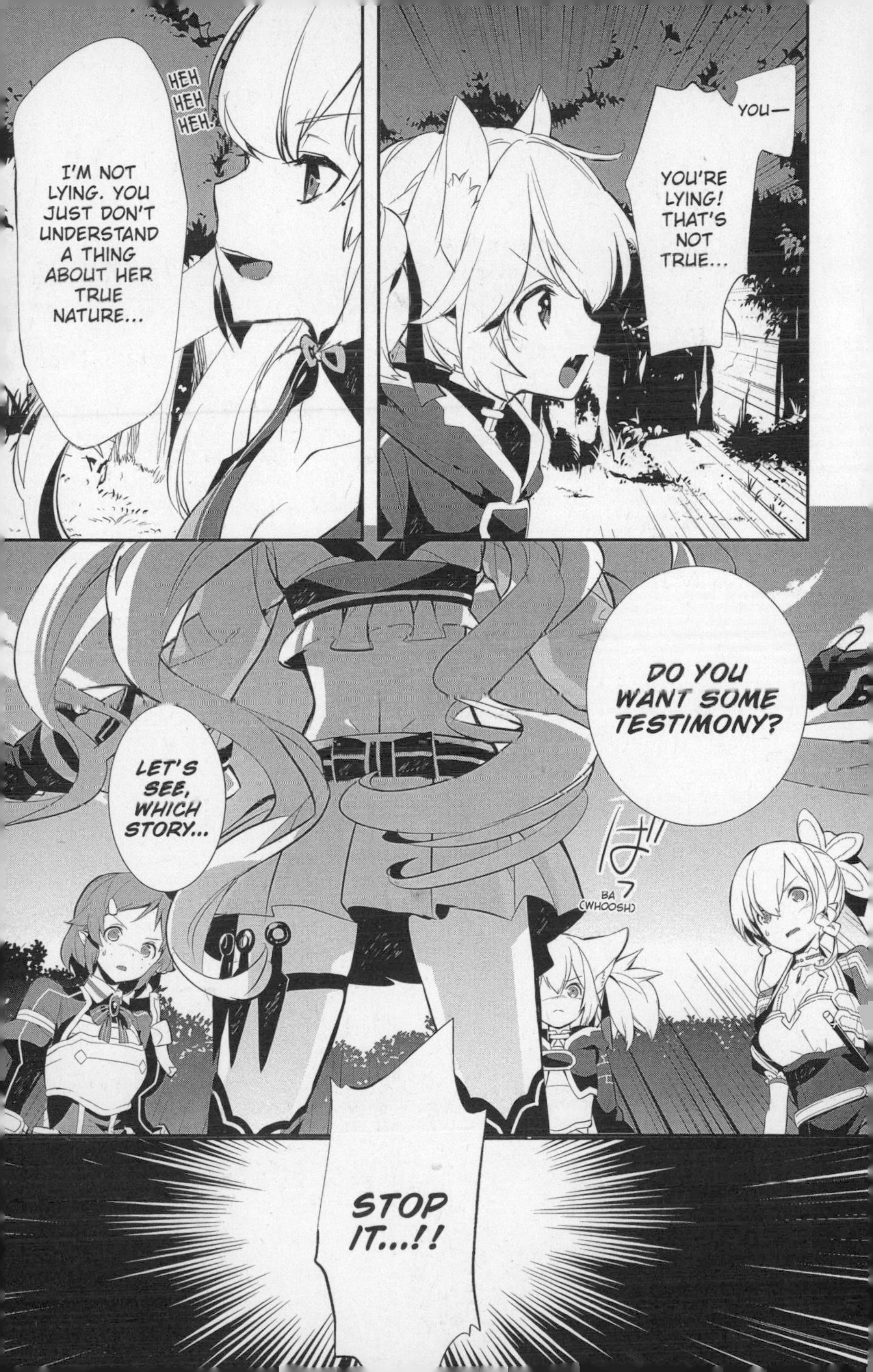
YOU—
YOU'RE LYING! THAT'S NOT TRUE...
HEH HEH HEH.
I'M NOT LYING. YOU JUST DON'T UNDERSTAND A THING ABOUT HER TRUE NATURE...
DO YOU WANT SOME TESTIMONY?
LET'S SEE, WHICH STORY...
ばっ
BA (WHOOSH)
STOP IT...!!

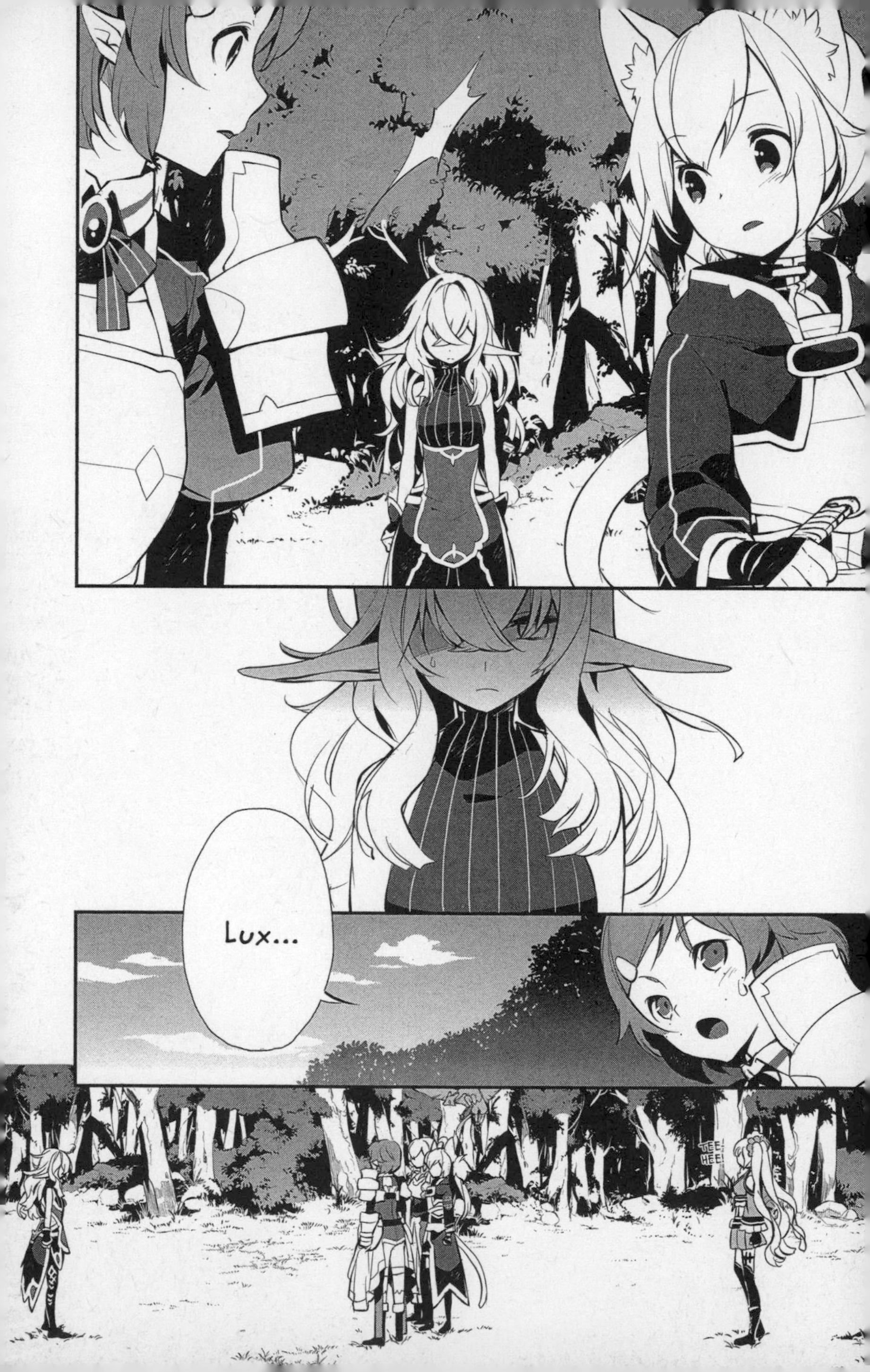
Lux...
TEE HEE!

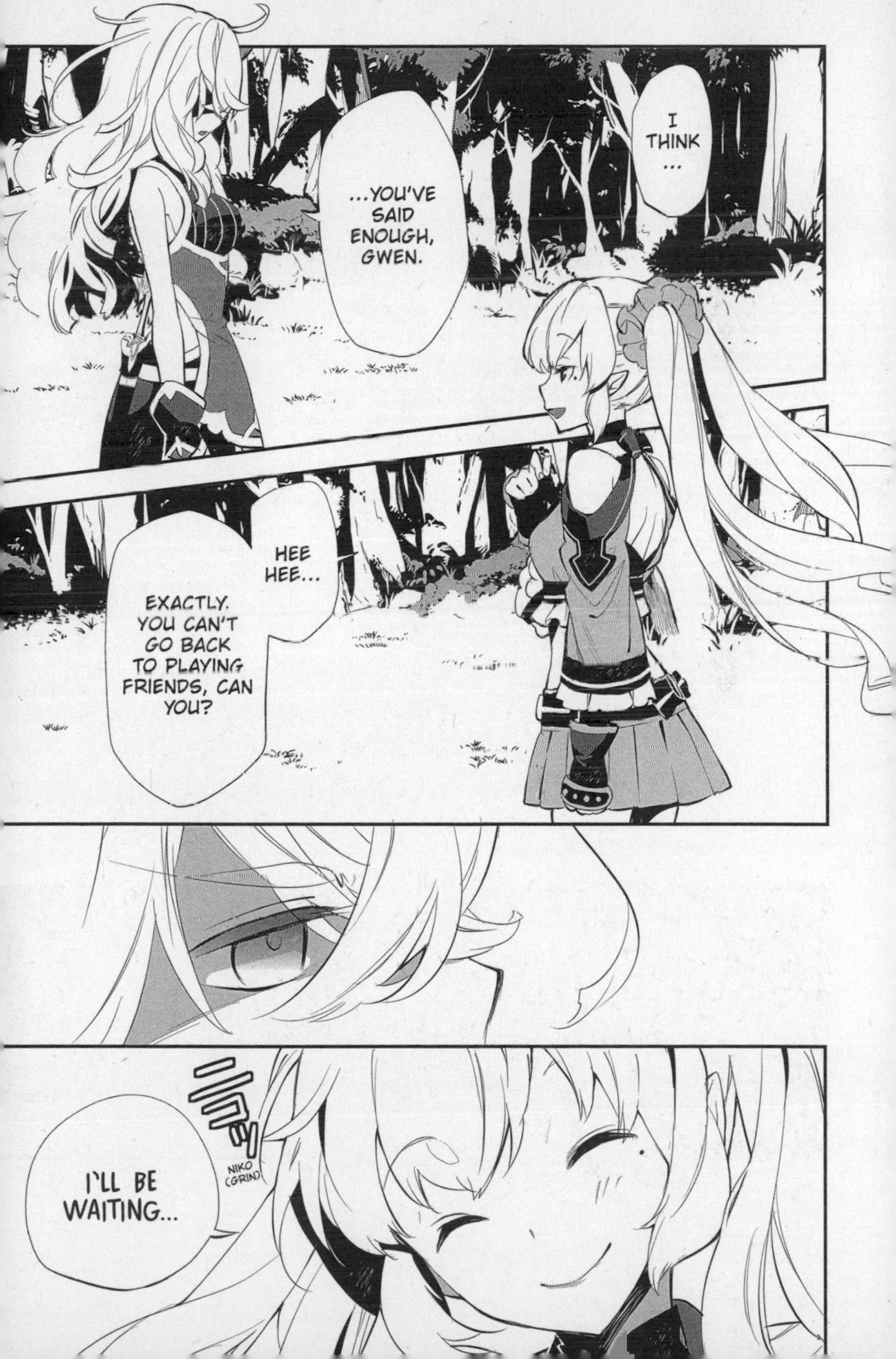
I THINK...
...YOU'VE SAID ENOUGH, GWEN.
HEE HEE...
EXACTLY. YOU CAN'T GO BACK TO PLAYING FRIENDS, CAN YOU?
NIKO (GRIN)
I'LL BE WAITING...

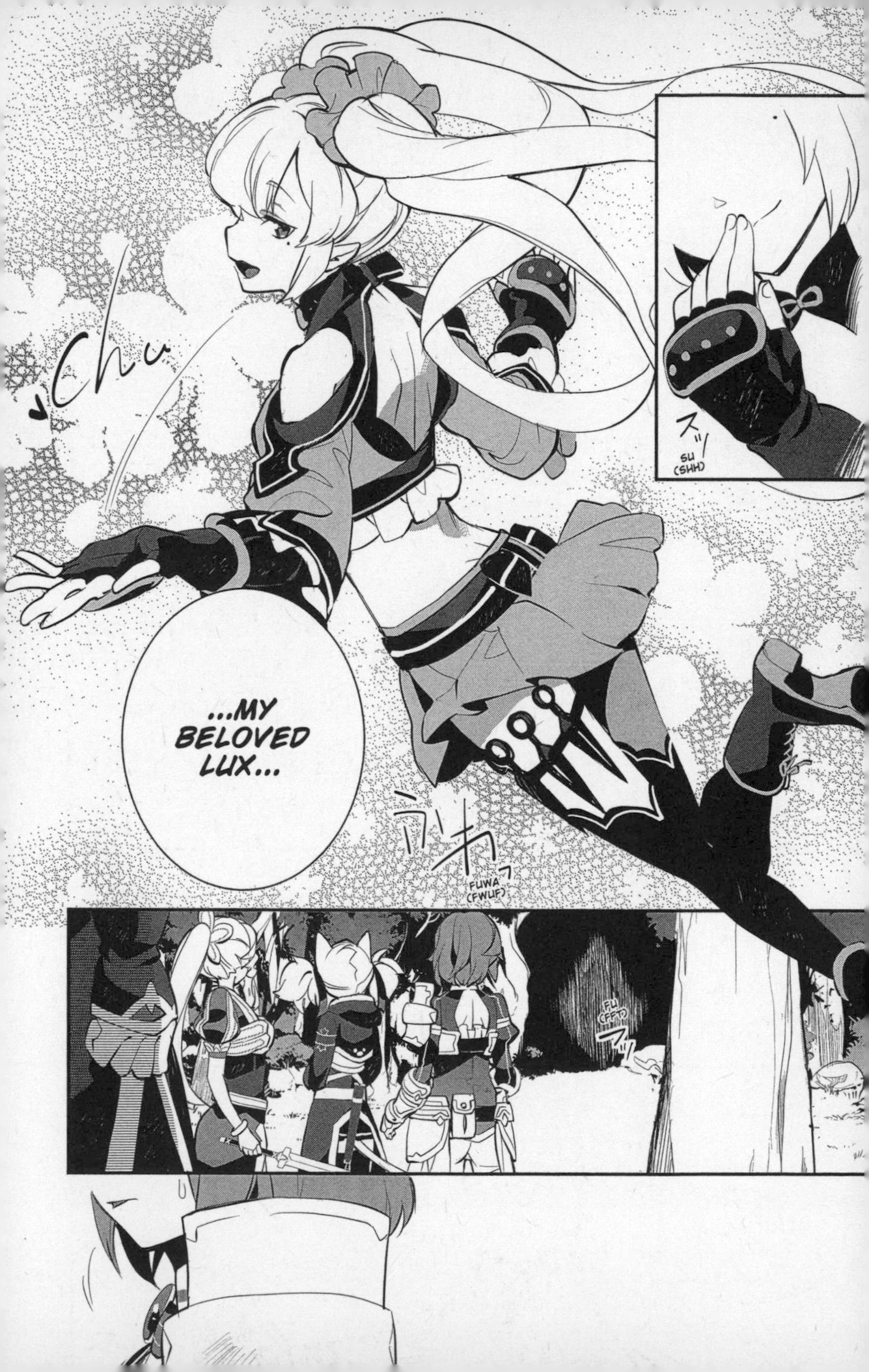
SU
(SHH)
Chu
...MY BELOVED LUX...
FUWA
(FWUF)
FU
(FFT)

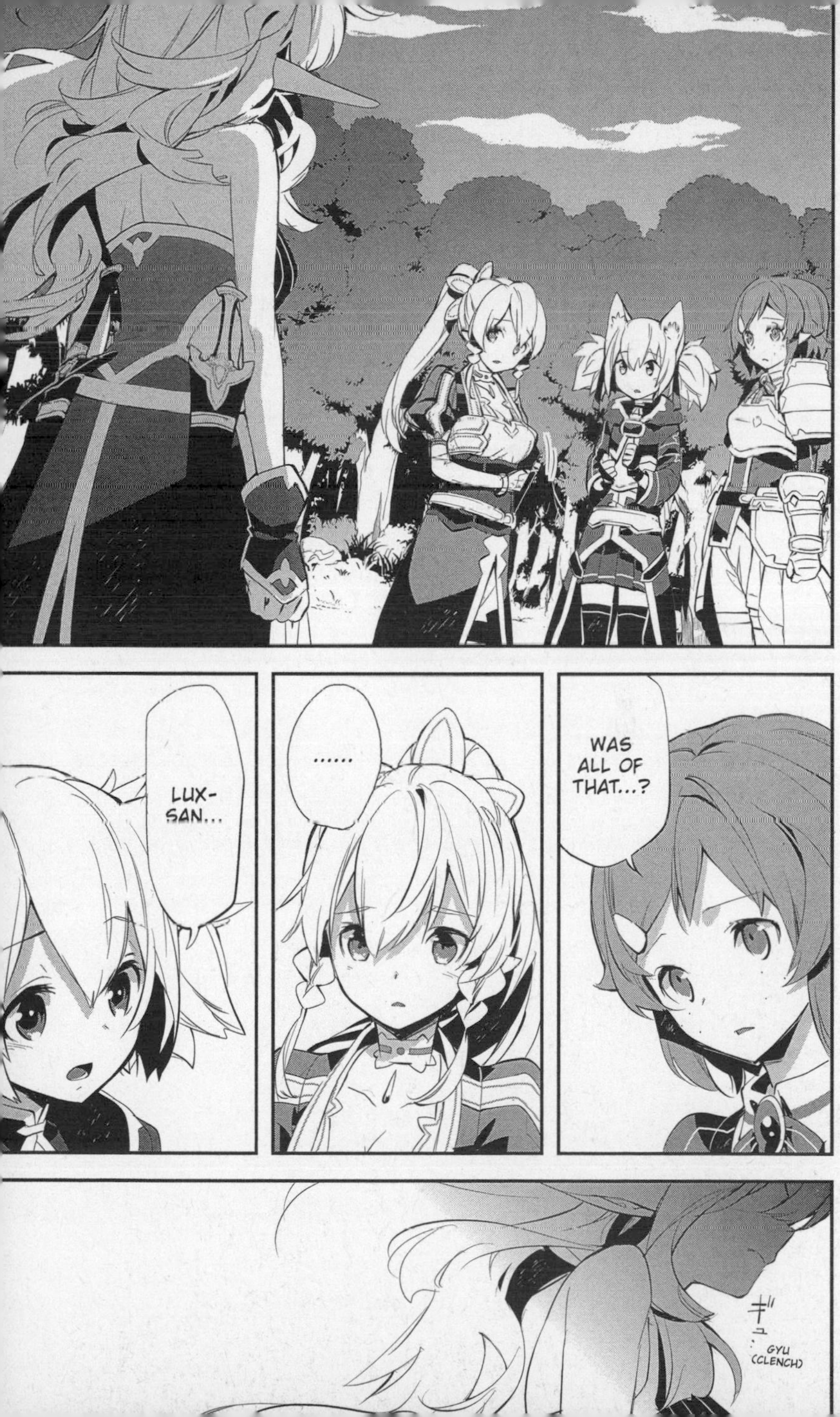
WAS ALL OF THAT...?
......
LUX-SAN...
ギュ
GYU (CLENCH)

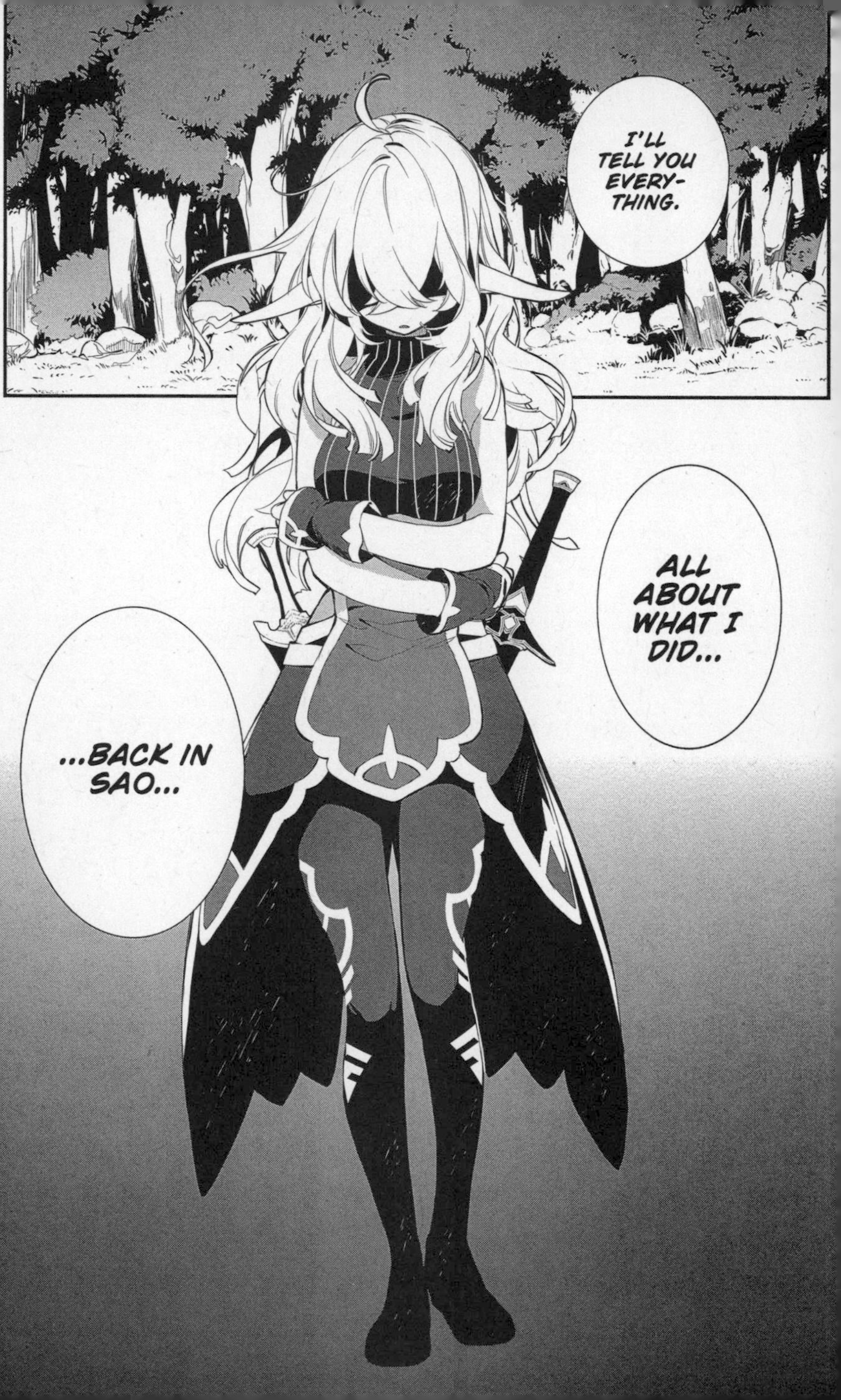
I'LL TELL YOU EVERY-THING.
ALL ABOUT WHAT I DID...
...BACK IN SAO...

SWORD ART ONLINE
GIRLS' OPS

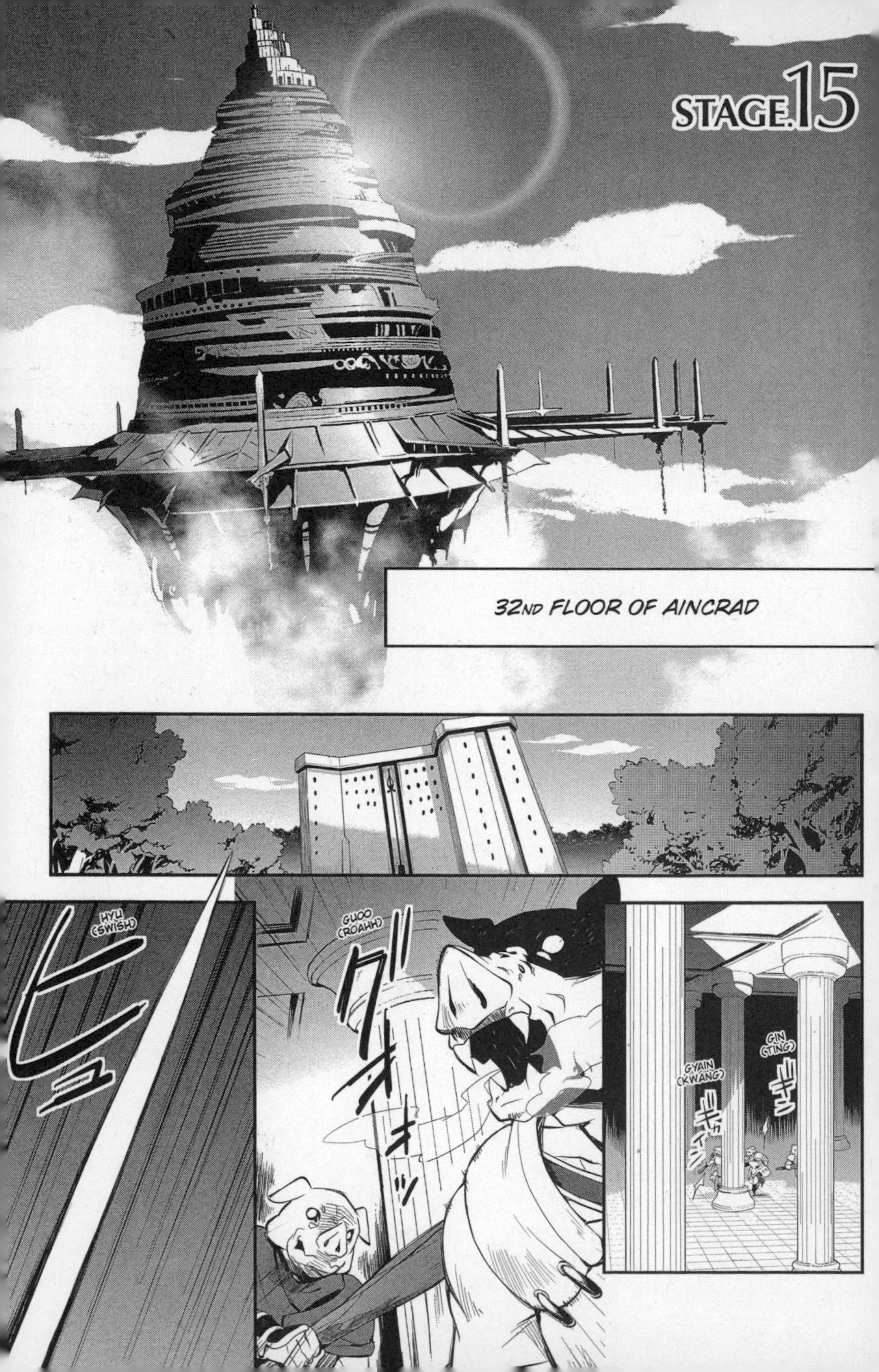

STAGE.15
32ND FLOOR OF AINCRAD
GIN (TING)
GYAIN (KWANG)
GUOO (ROAHH)
HYU (SWISH)

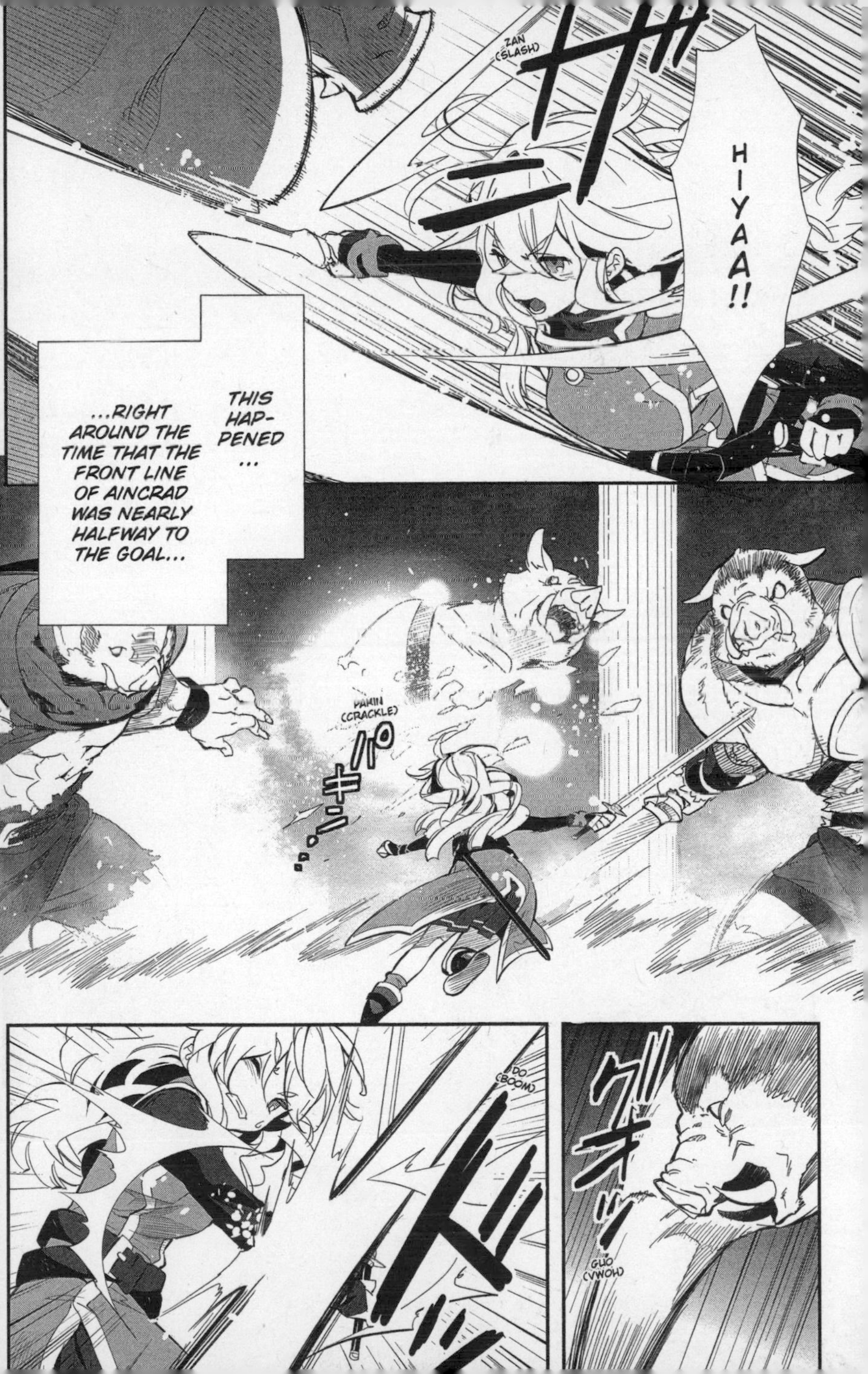
ZAN (SLASH)
HIYAAA!!
THIS HAP-PENED...
...RIGHT AROUND THE TIME THAT THE FRONT LINE OF AINCRAD WAS NEARLY HALFWAY TO THE GOAL...
PAKIN (CRACKLE)
GUO (VWOH)
DO (BOOM)

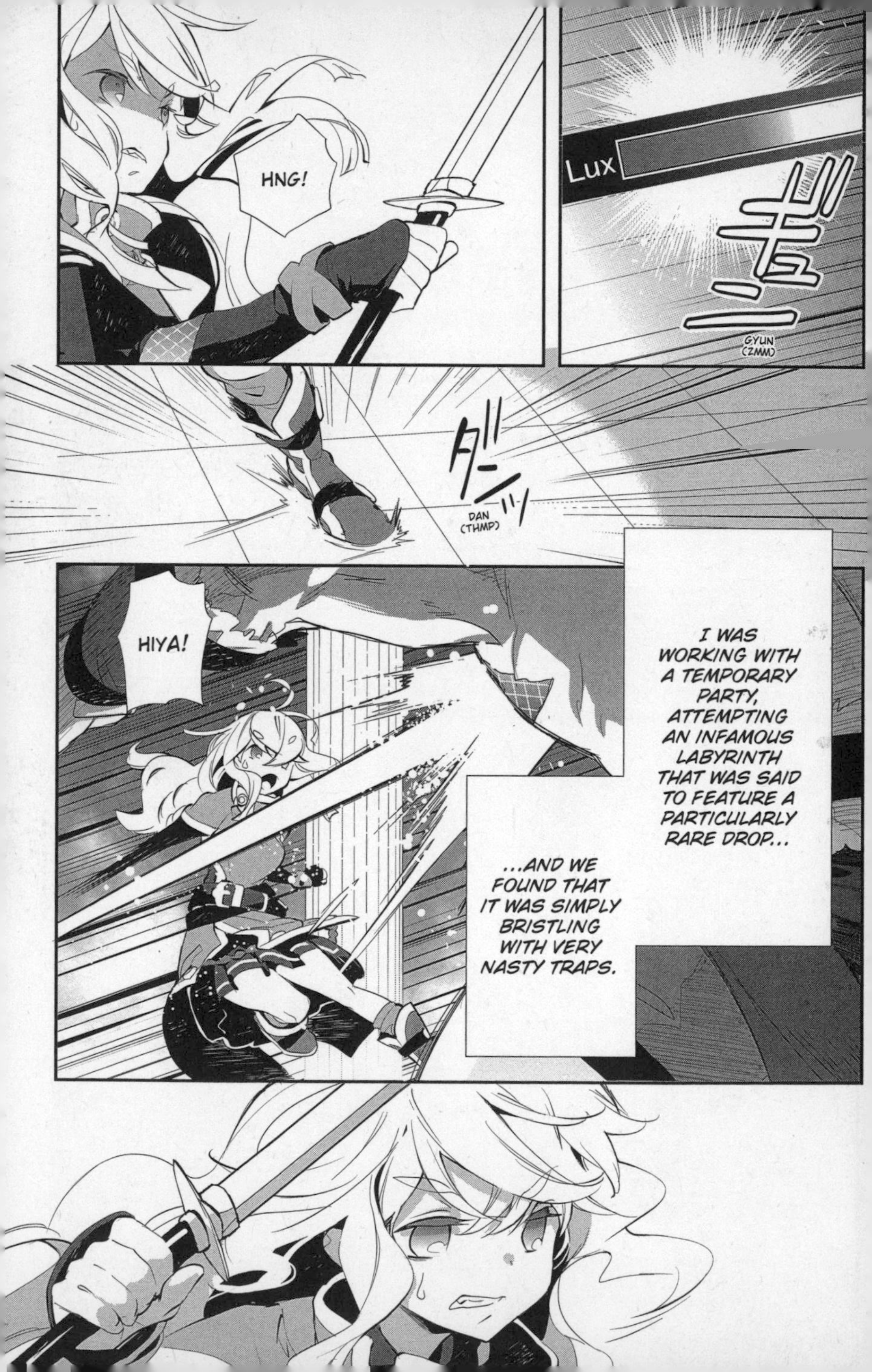
Lux
GYUN (ZMM)
HNG!
DAN (THMP)
I WAS WORKING WITH A TEMPORARY PARTY, ATTEMPTING AN INFAMOUS LABYRINTH THAT WAS SAID TO FEATURE A PARTICULARLY RARE DROP...
...AND WE FOUND THAT IT WAS SIMPLY BRISTLING WITH VERY NASTY TRAPS.
HIYA!

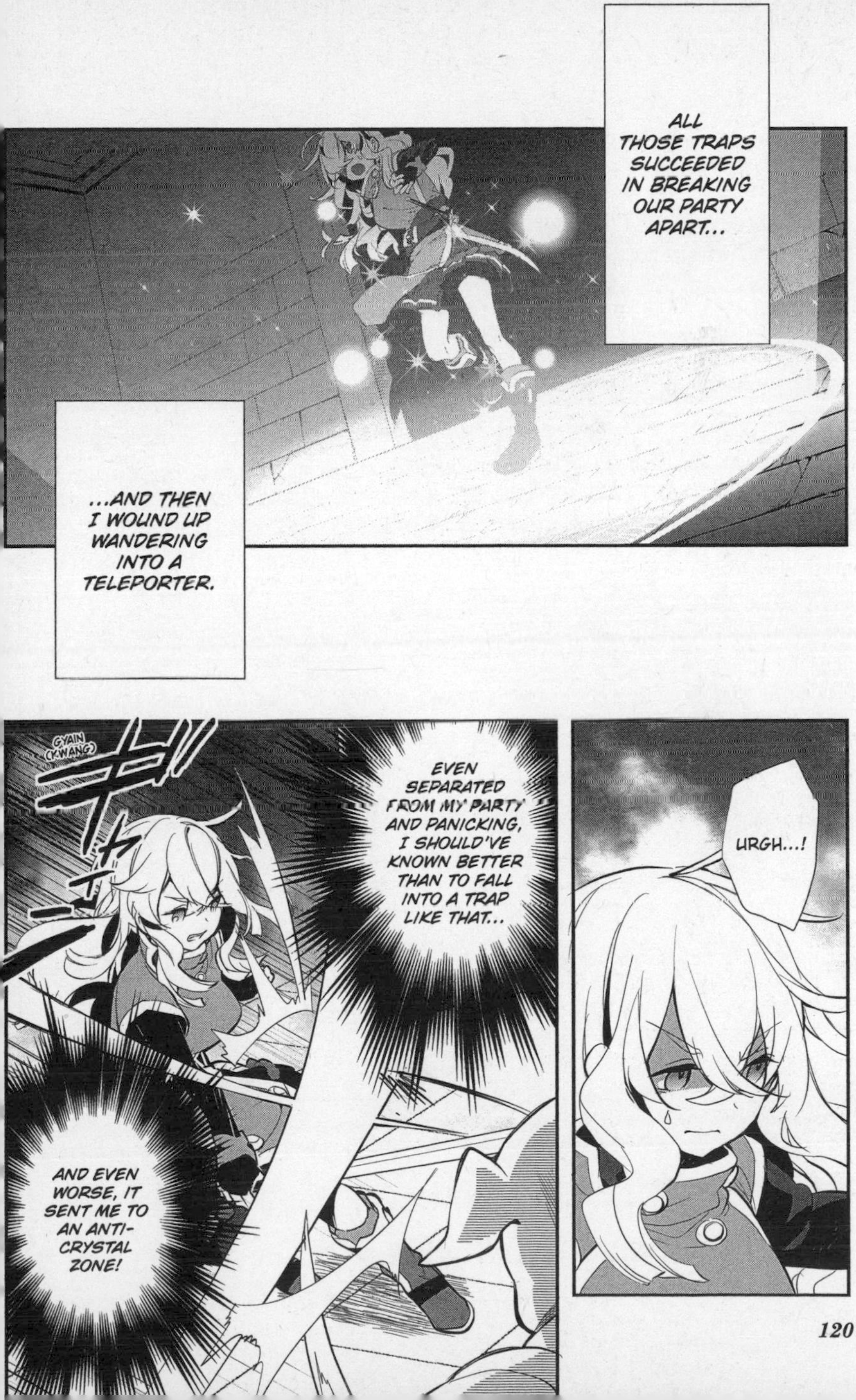
ALL THOSE TRAPS SUCCEEDED IN BREAKING OUR PARTY APART...
...AND THEN I WOUND UP WANDERING INTO A TELEPORTER.
URGH...!
EVEN SEPARATED FROM MY PARTY AND PANICKING, I SHOULD'VE KNOWN BETTER THAN TO FALL INTO A TRAP LIKE THAT...
GYAIN (KWANG)
AND EVEN WORSE, IT SENT ME TO AN ANTI-CRYSTAL ZONE!

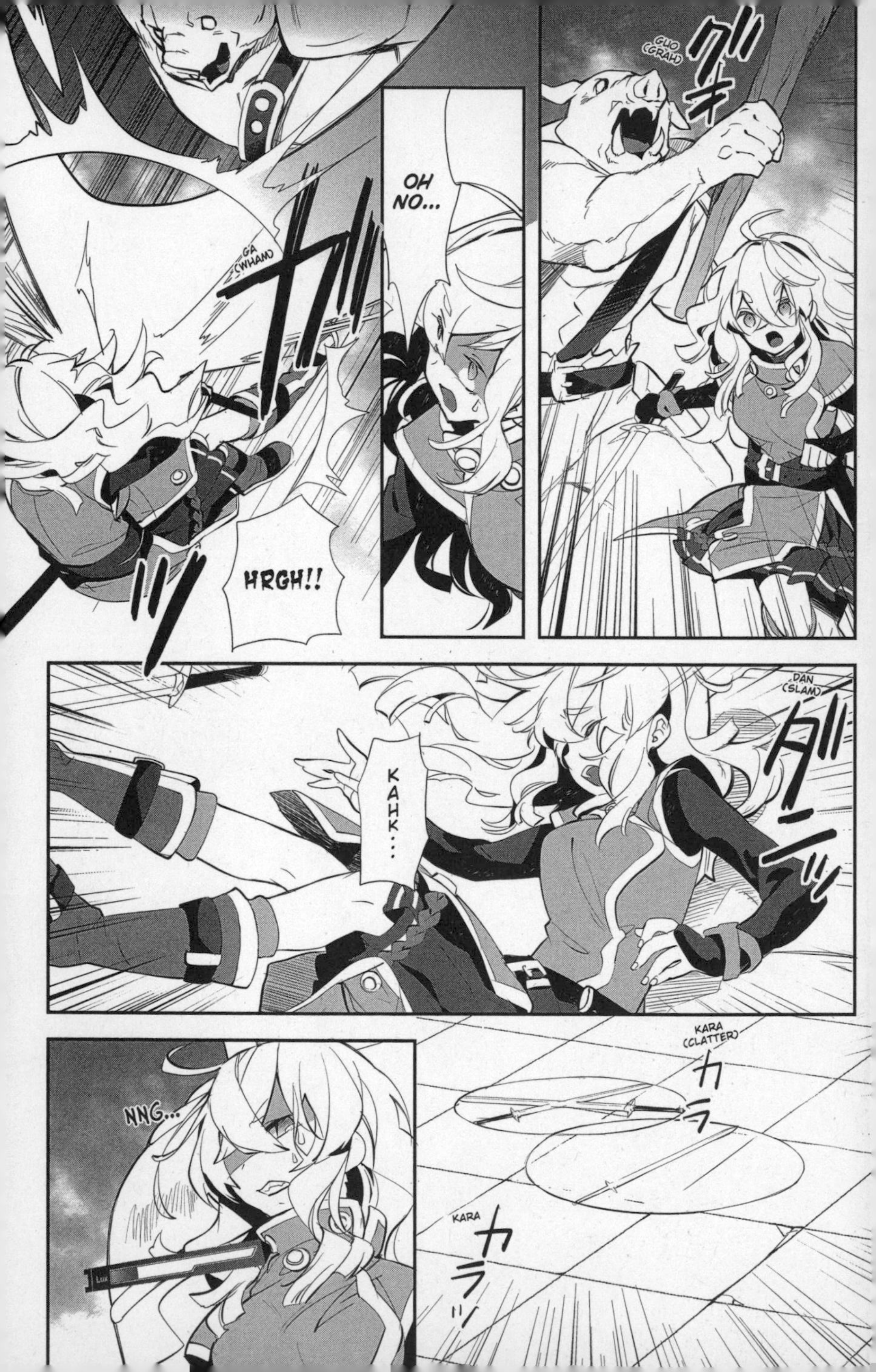
GUO (GRAH)
OH NO...
GA (WHAM)
HRGH!!
DAN (SLAM)
KAHK...
KARA (CLATTER)
KARA
NNG...

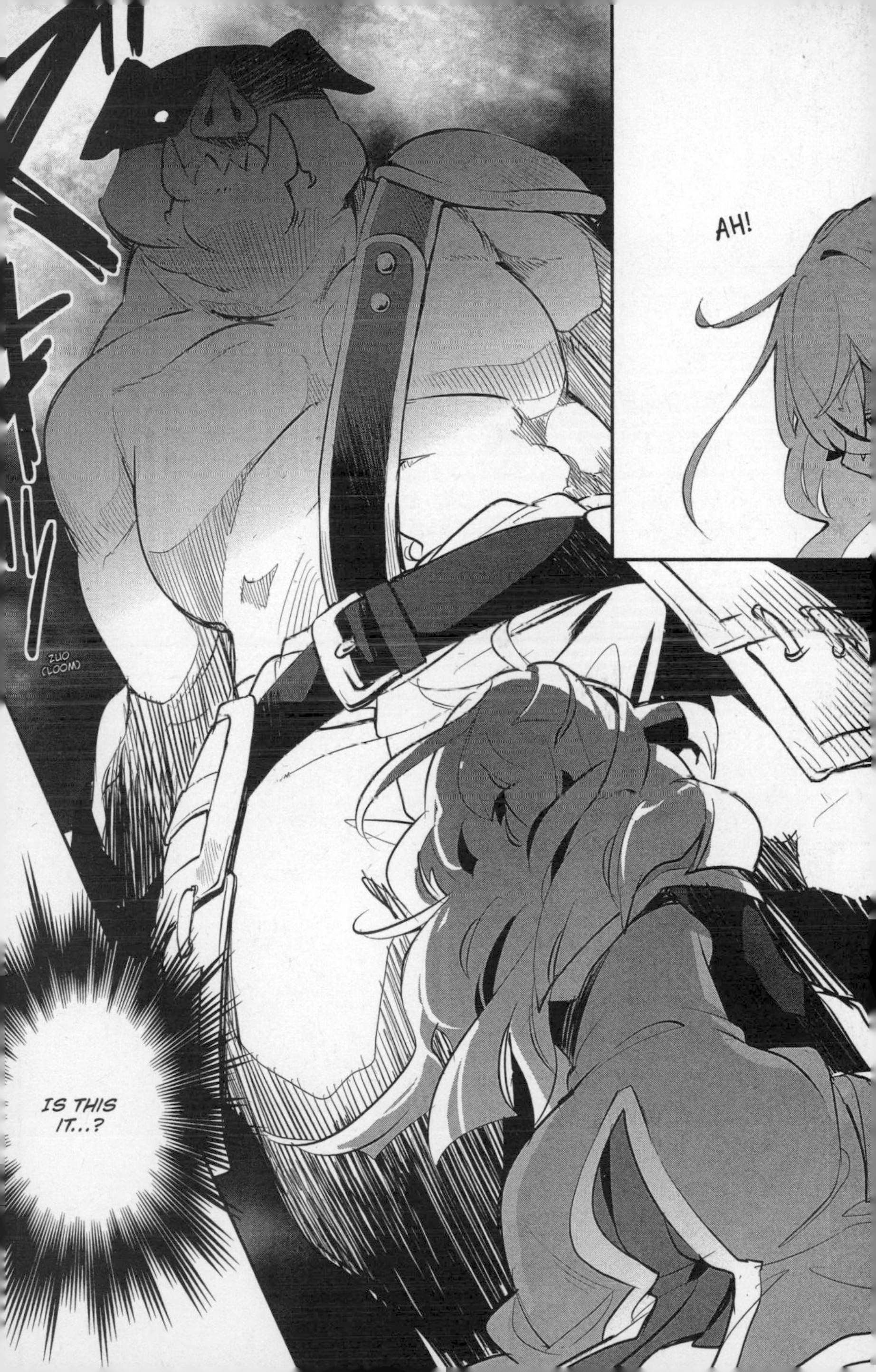
AH!
ZUO (LOOM)
IS THIS IT...?

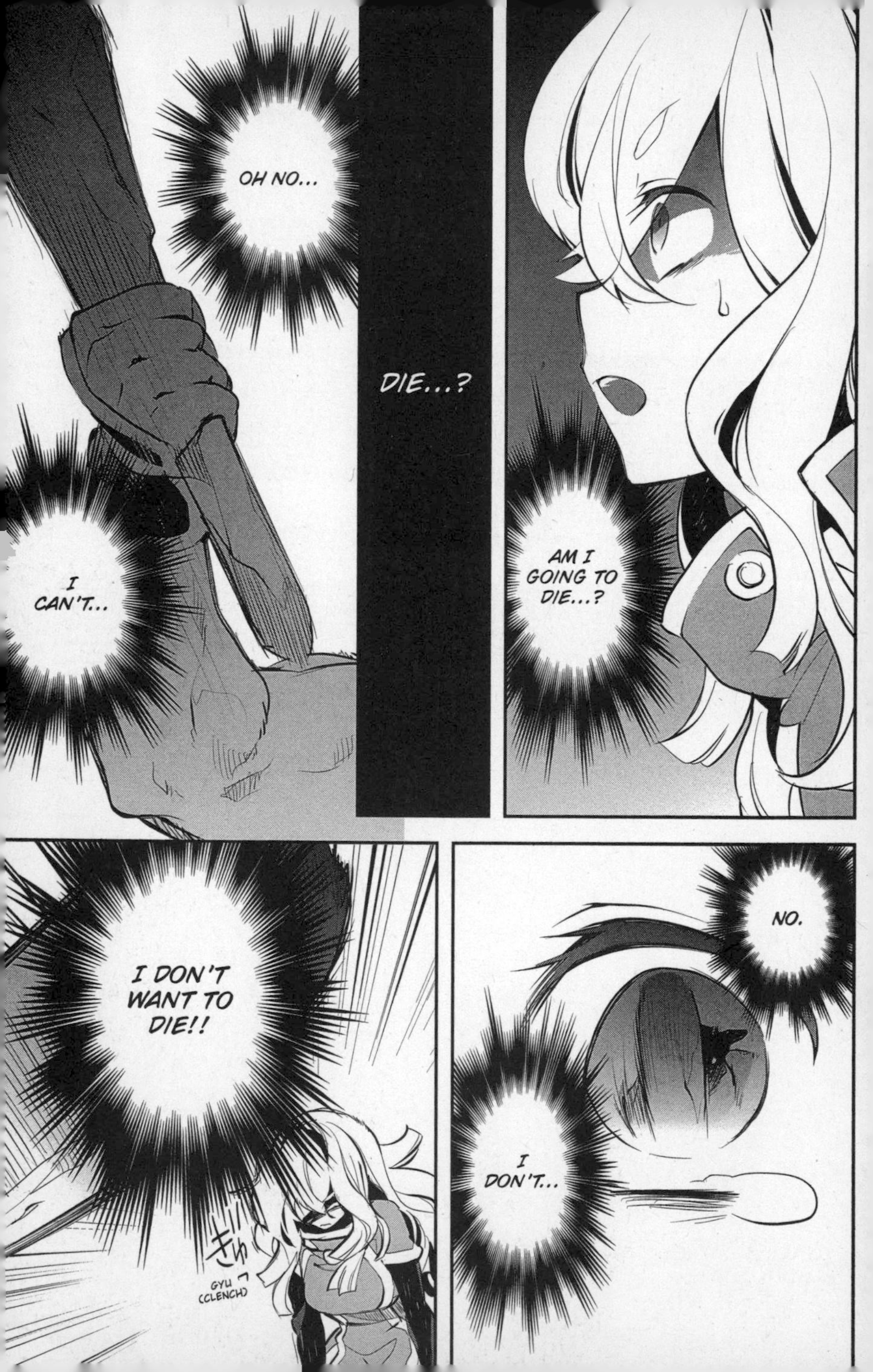
AM I GOING TO DIE...?
DIE...?
OH NO...
I CAN'T...
NO.
I DON'T...
I DON'T WANT TO DIE!!
きゅ
GYU (CLENCH)

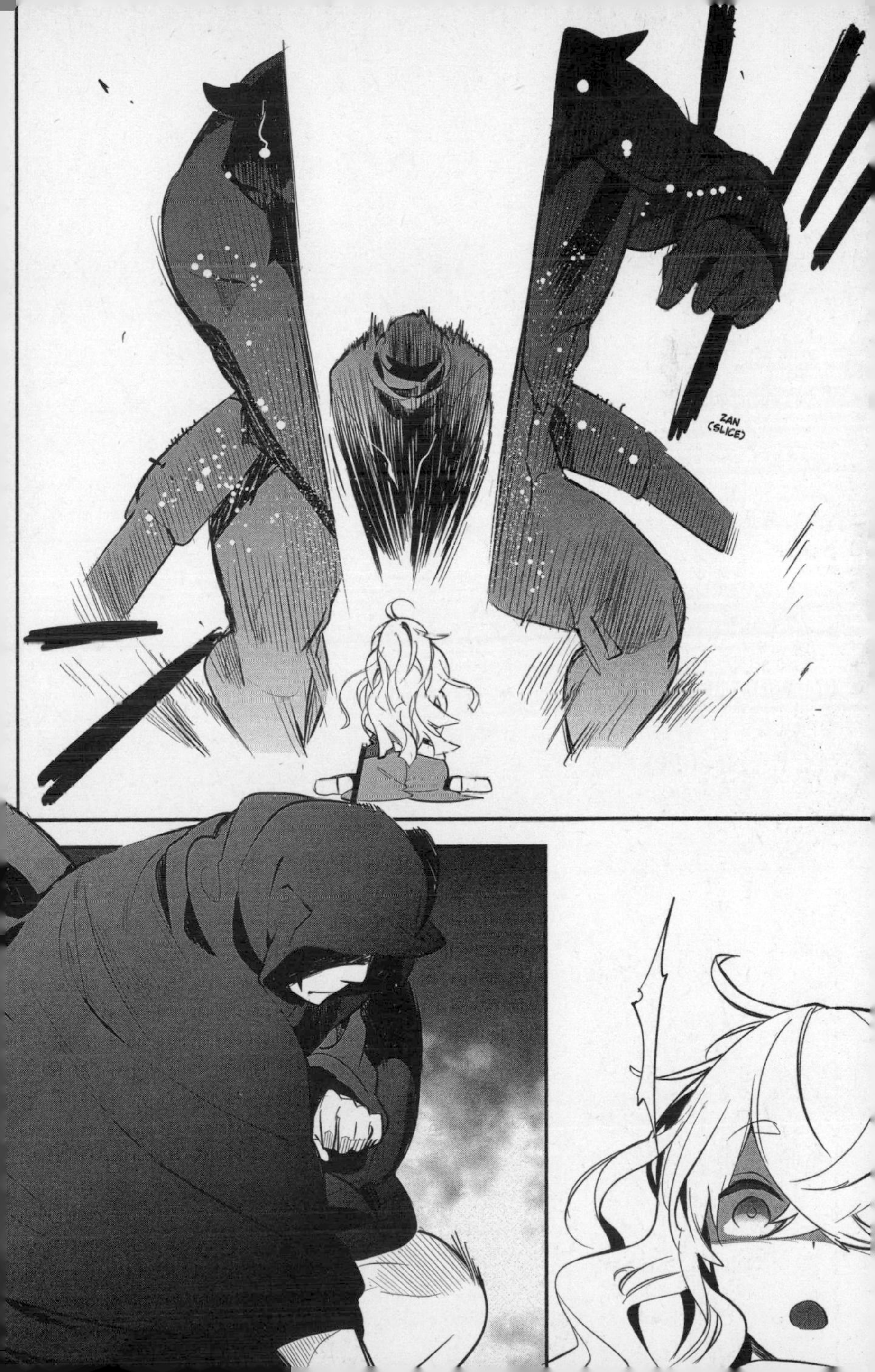
ZAN
(SLICE)

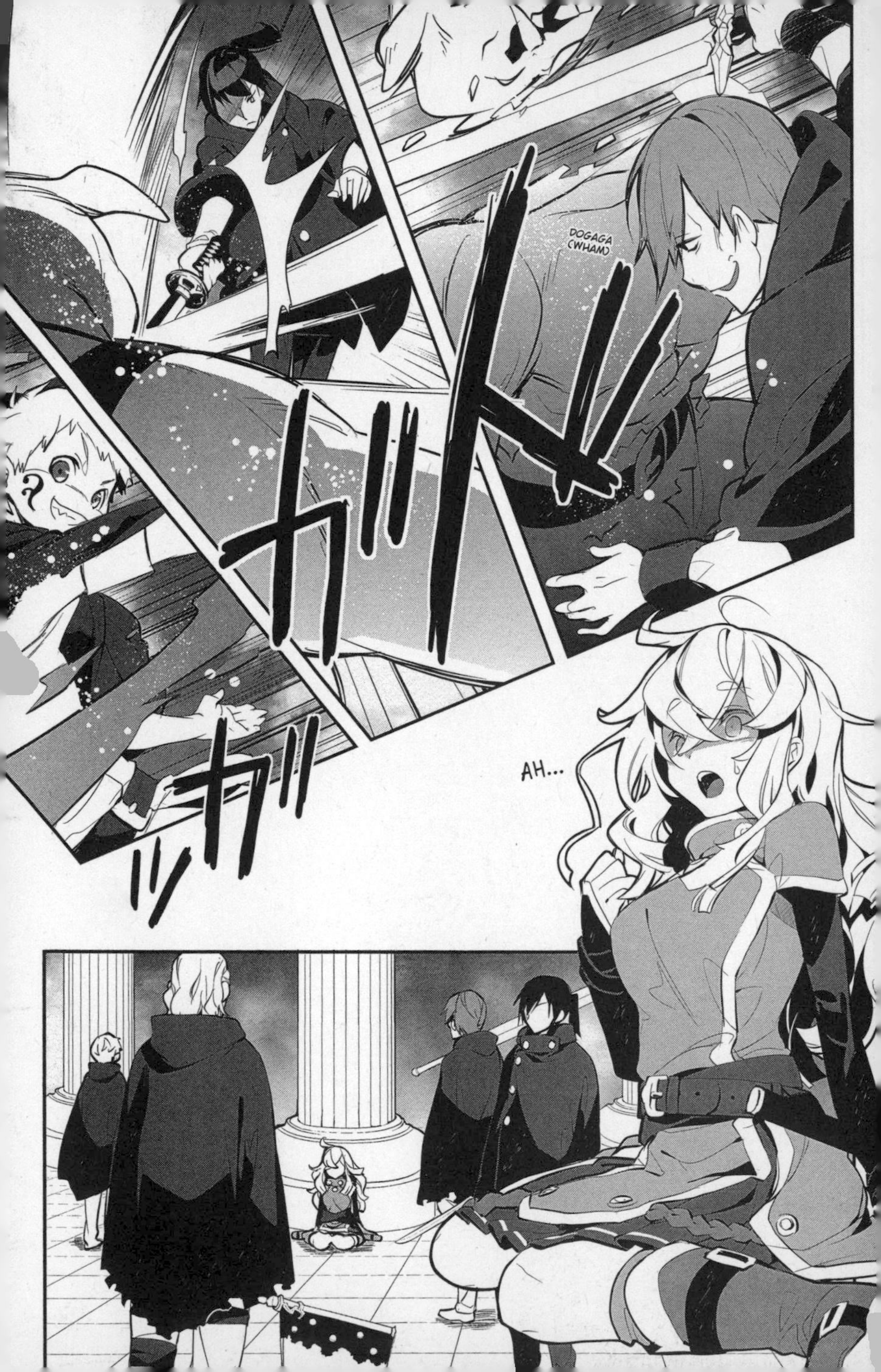
DOGAGA
(WHAM)
AH...

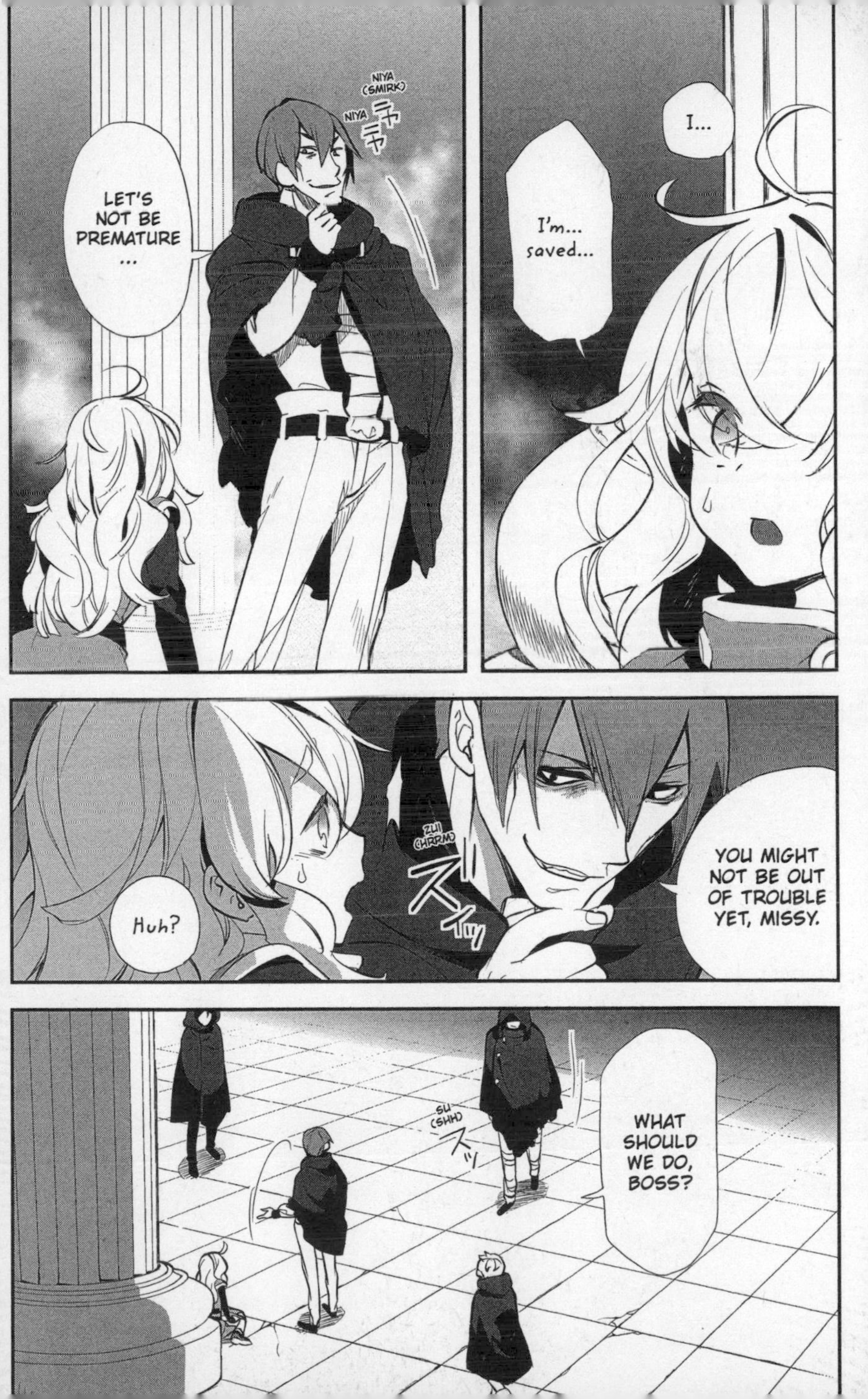
I...
I'm... saved...
NIYA (SMIRK) NIYA
ニヤニヤ
LET'S NOT BE PREMATURE ...
YOU MIGHT NOT BE OUT OF TROUBLE YET, MISSY.
ZUI (HRRM)
ズイッ
Huh?
WHAT SHOULD WE DO, BOSS?
SU (SHH)
スッ

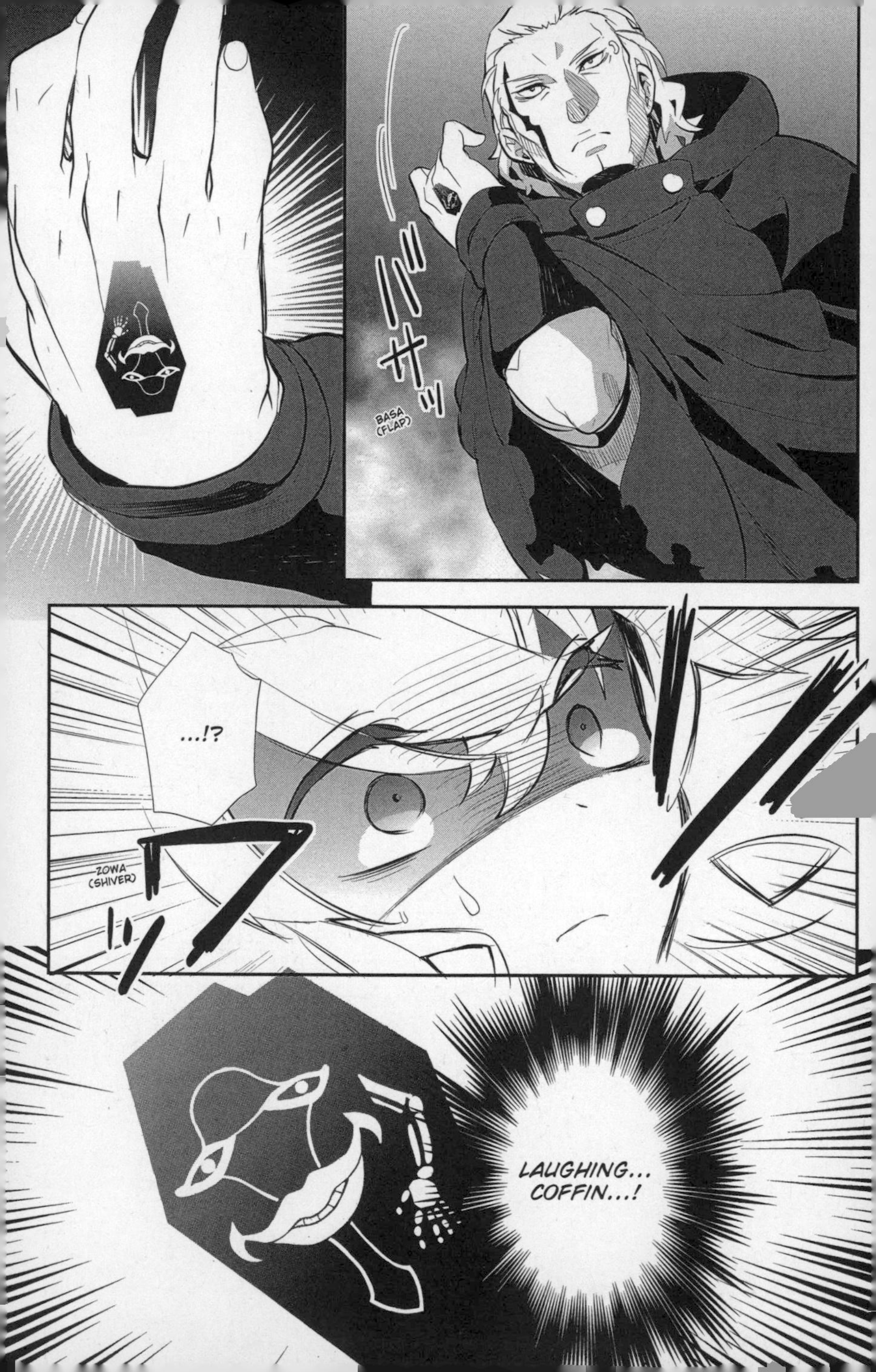
BASA
(FLAP)
...!?
ZOWA
(SHIVER)
LAUGHING...
COFFIN...!

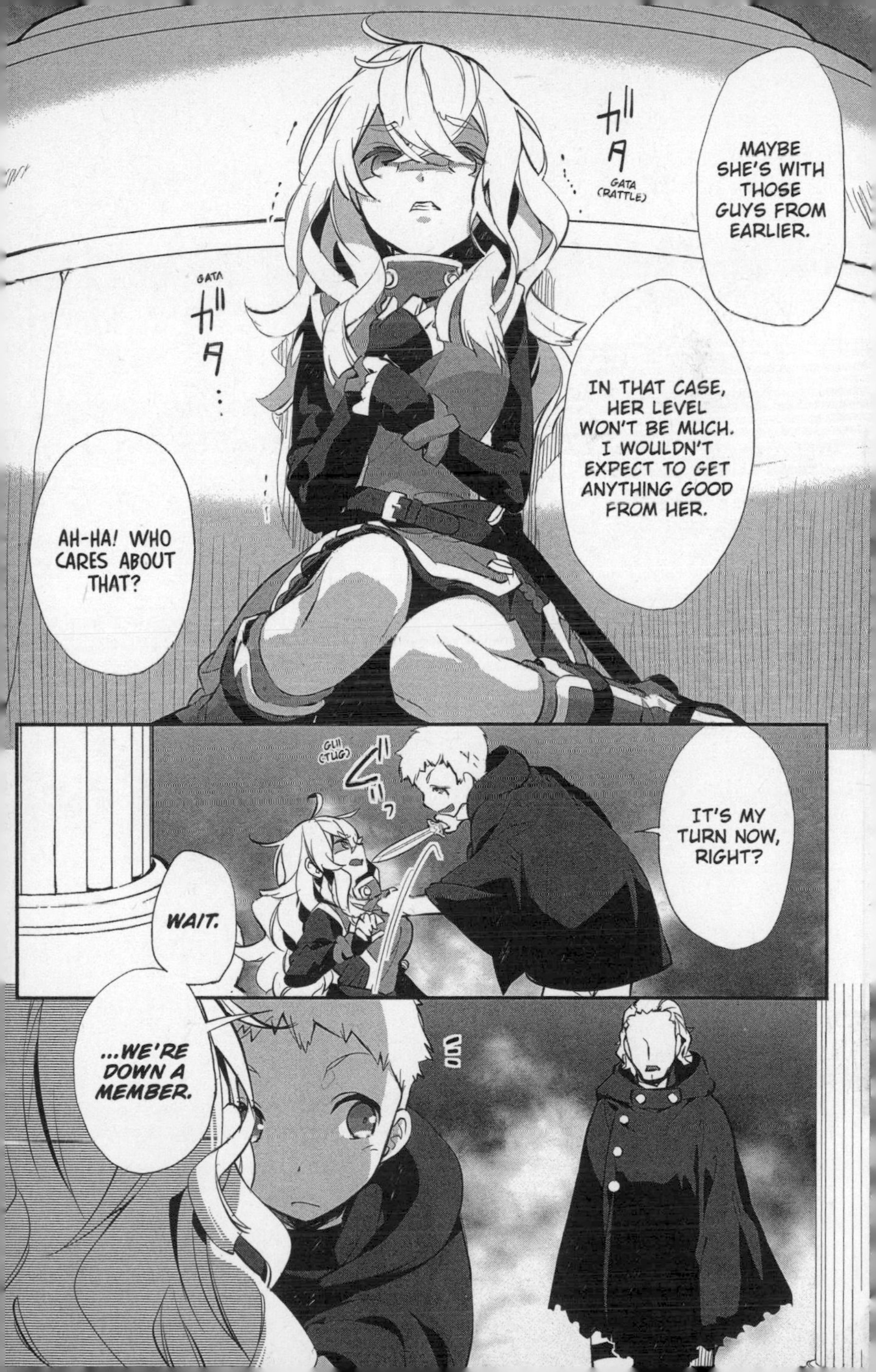
MAYBE SHE'S WITH THOSE GUYS FROM EARLIER.
ガタ
GATA (RATTLE)
IN THAT CASE, HER LEVEL WON'T BE MUCH. I WOULDN'T EXPECT TO GET ANYTHING GOOD FROM HER.
GATA
ガタ
AH-HA! WHO CARES ABOUT THAT?
GUI (TUG)
IT'S MY TURN NOW, RIGHT?
WAIT.
...WE'RE DOWN A MEMBER.

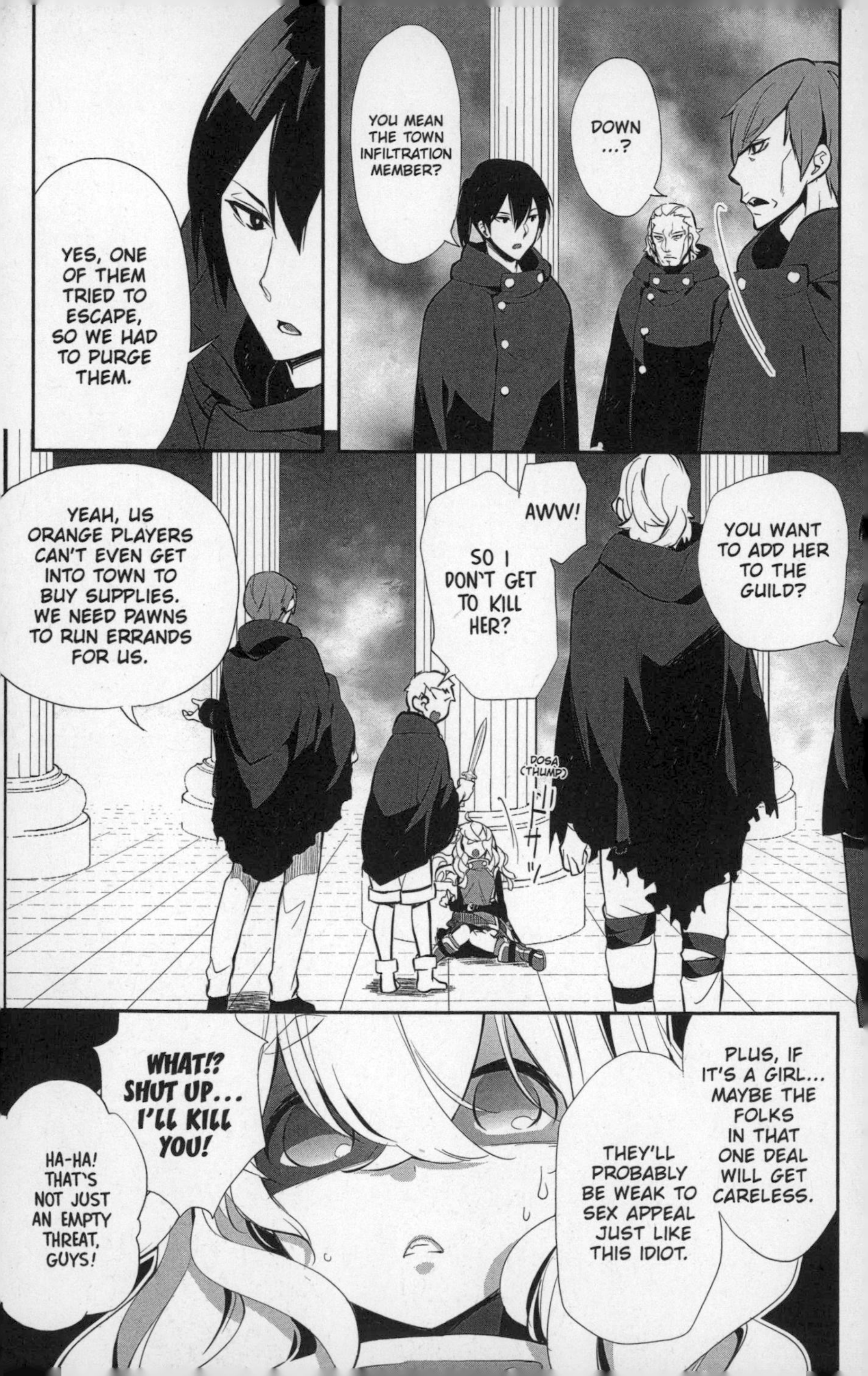
DOWN ...?
YOU MEAN THE TOWN INFILTRATION MEMBER?
YES, ONE OF THEM TRIED TO ESCAPE, SO WE HAD TO PURGE THEM.
YOU WANT TO ADD HER TO THE GUILD?
AWW!
SO I DON'T GET TO KILL HER?
DOSA (THUMP)
YEAH, US ORANGE PLAYERS CAN'T EVEN GET INTO TOWN TO BUY SUPPLIES. WE NEED PAWNS TO RUN ERRANDS FOR US.
PLUS, IF IT'S A GIRL... MAYBE THE FOLKS IN THAT ONE DEAL WILL GET CARELESS.
THEY'LL PROBABLY BE WEAK TO SEX APPEAL JUST LIKE THIS IDIOT.
WHAT!? SHUT UP... I'LL KILL YOU!
HA-HA! THAT'S NOT JUST AN EMPTY THREAT, GUYS!

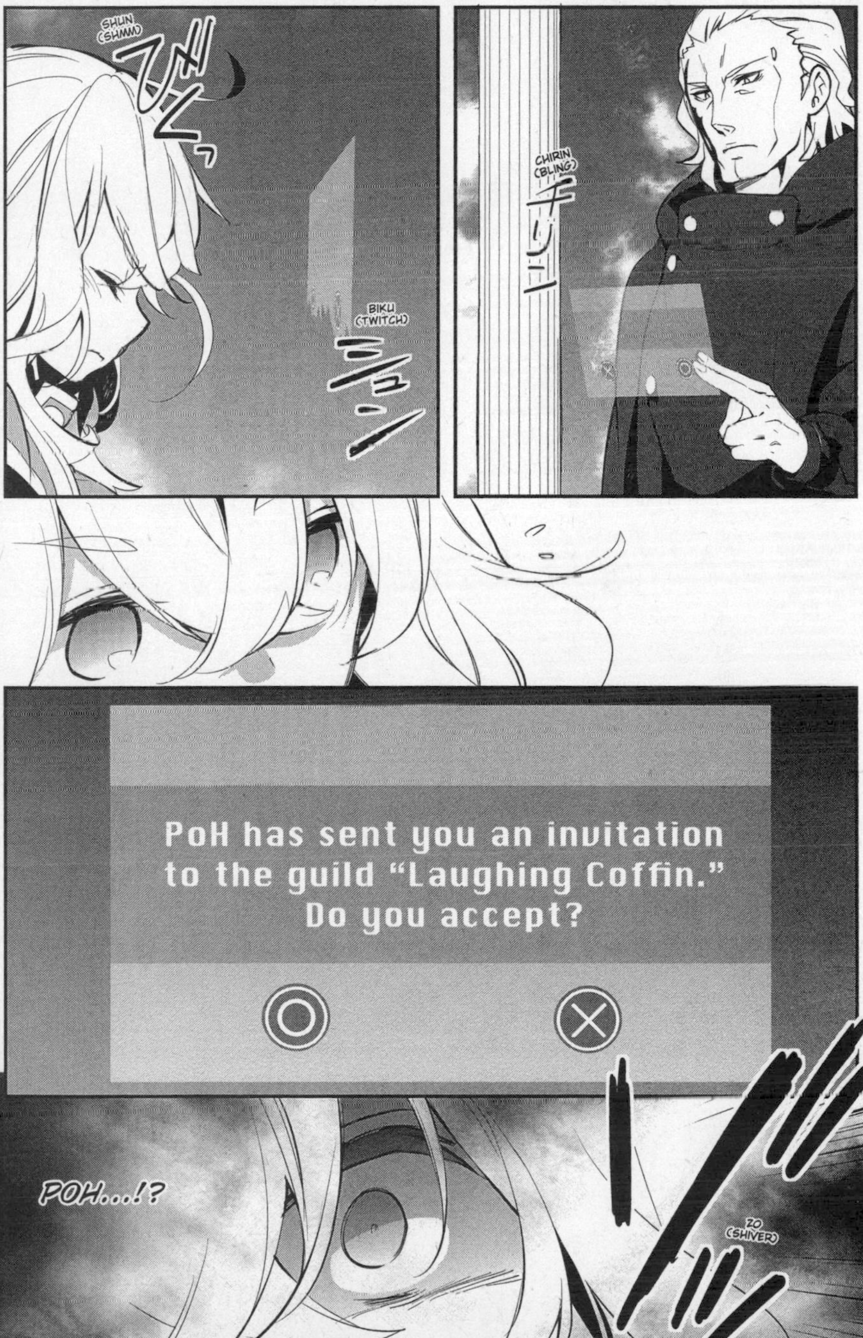
CHIRIN (BLING)
SHUN (SHWM)
BIKU (TWITCH)
PoH has sent you an invitation to the guild "Laughing Coffin." Do you accept?
POH...!?
ZO (SHIVER)

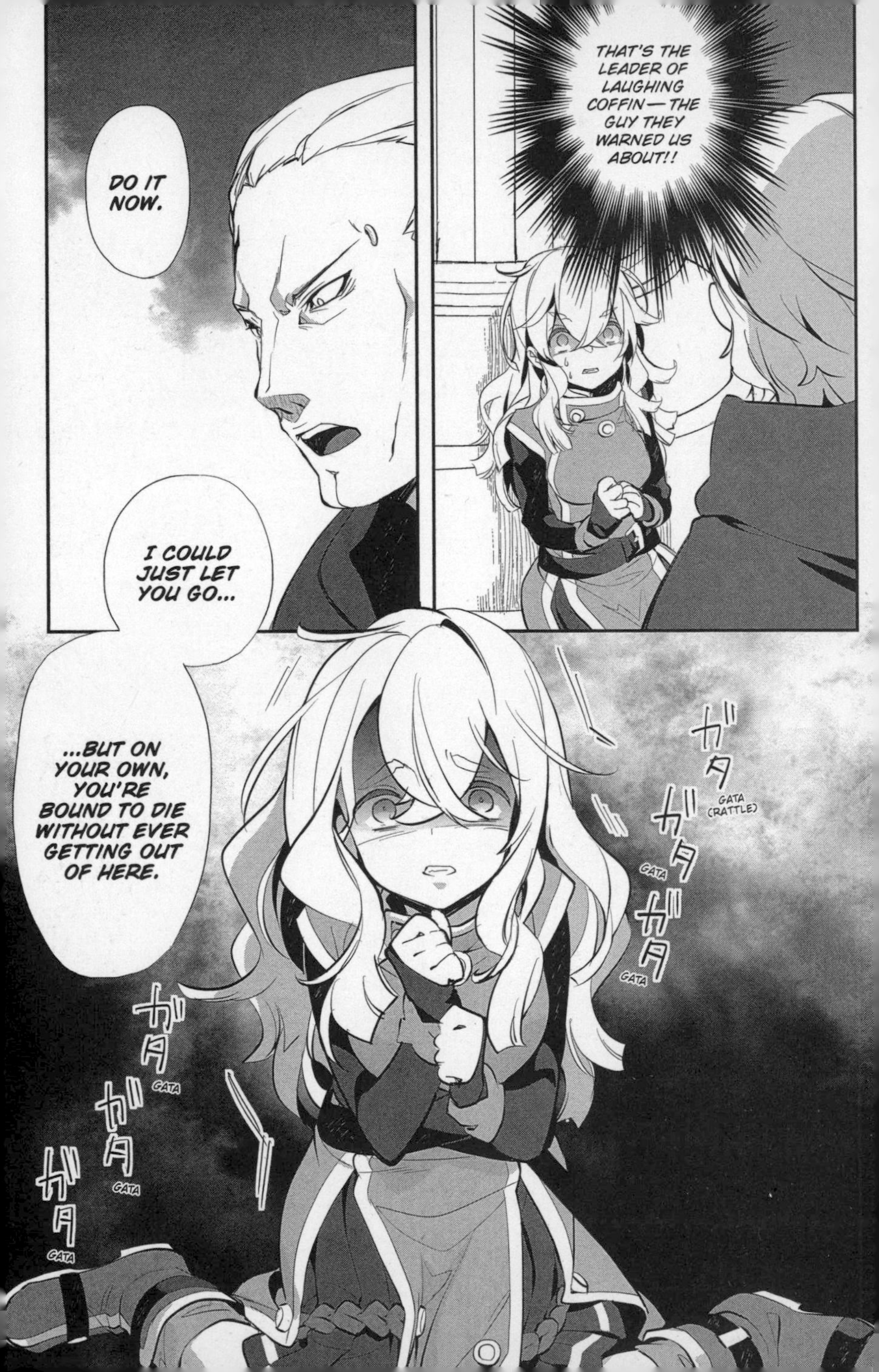
THAT'S THE LEADER OF LAUGHING COFFIN—THE GUY THEY WARNED US ABOUT!!
DO IT NOW.
I COULD JUST LET YOU GO...
...BUT ON YOUR OWN, YOU'RE BOUND TO DIE WITHOUT EVER GETTING OUT OF HERE.
ガタ
GATA (RATTLE)
ガタ
GATA
ガタ
GATA
ガタ
GATA
ガタ
GATA
ガタ
GATA

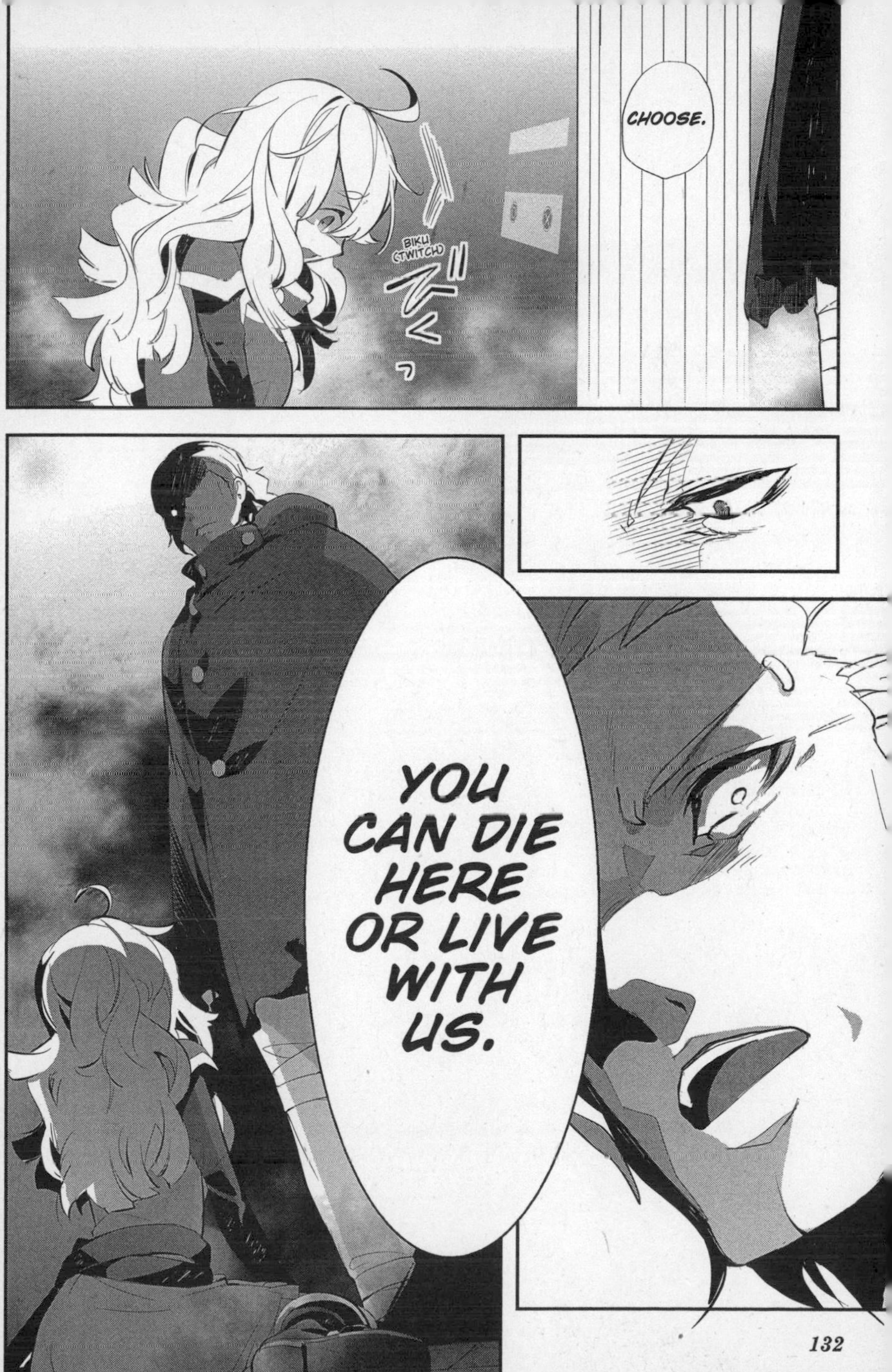
CHOOSE.
BIKU (TWITCH)
YOU CAN DIE HERE OR LIVE WITH US.

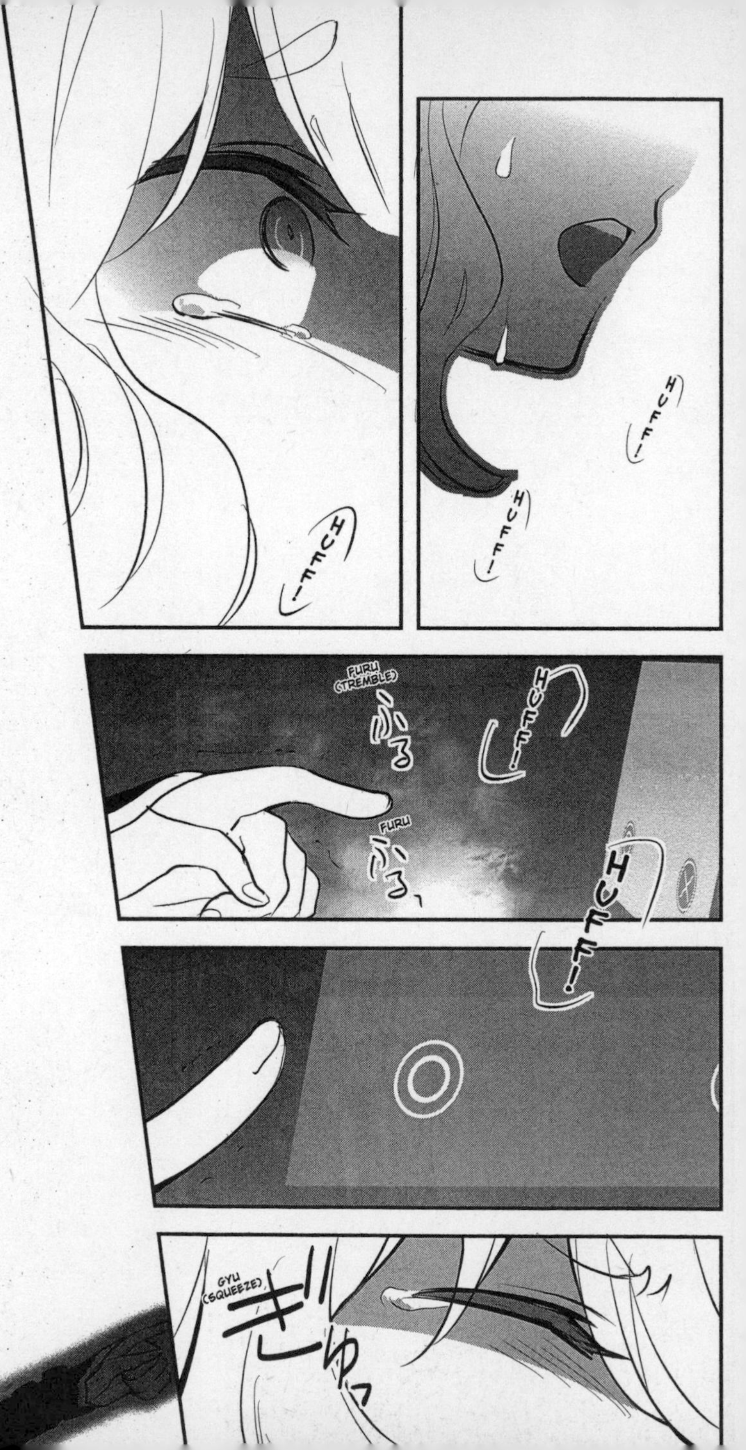
HUFF!
HUFF!
HUFF!
HUFF!
FURU (TREMBLE)
ふる
FURU
ふる
HUFF!
GYU (SQUEEZE)
ぎゅっ

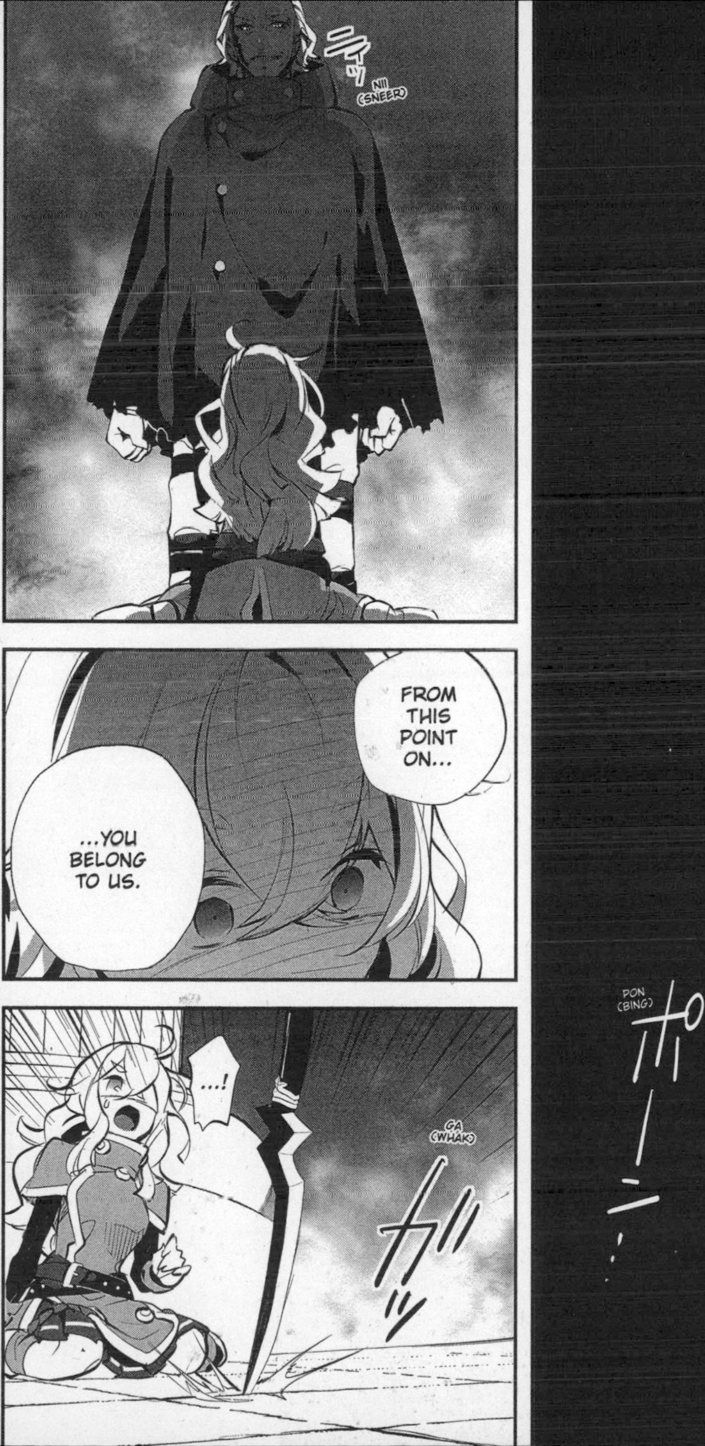
NII (SNEER)
FROM THIS POINT ON...
...YOU BELONG TO US.
PON (BING)
GA (WHAK)
...!

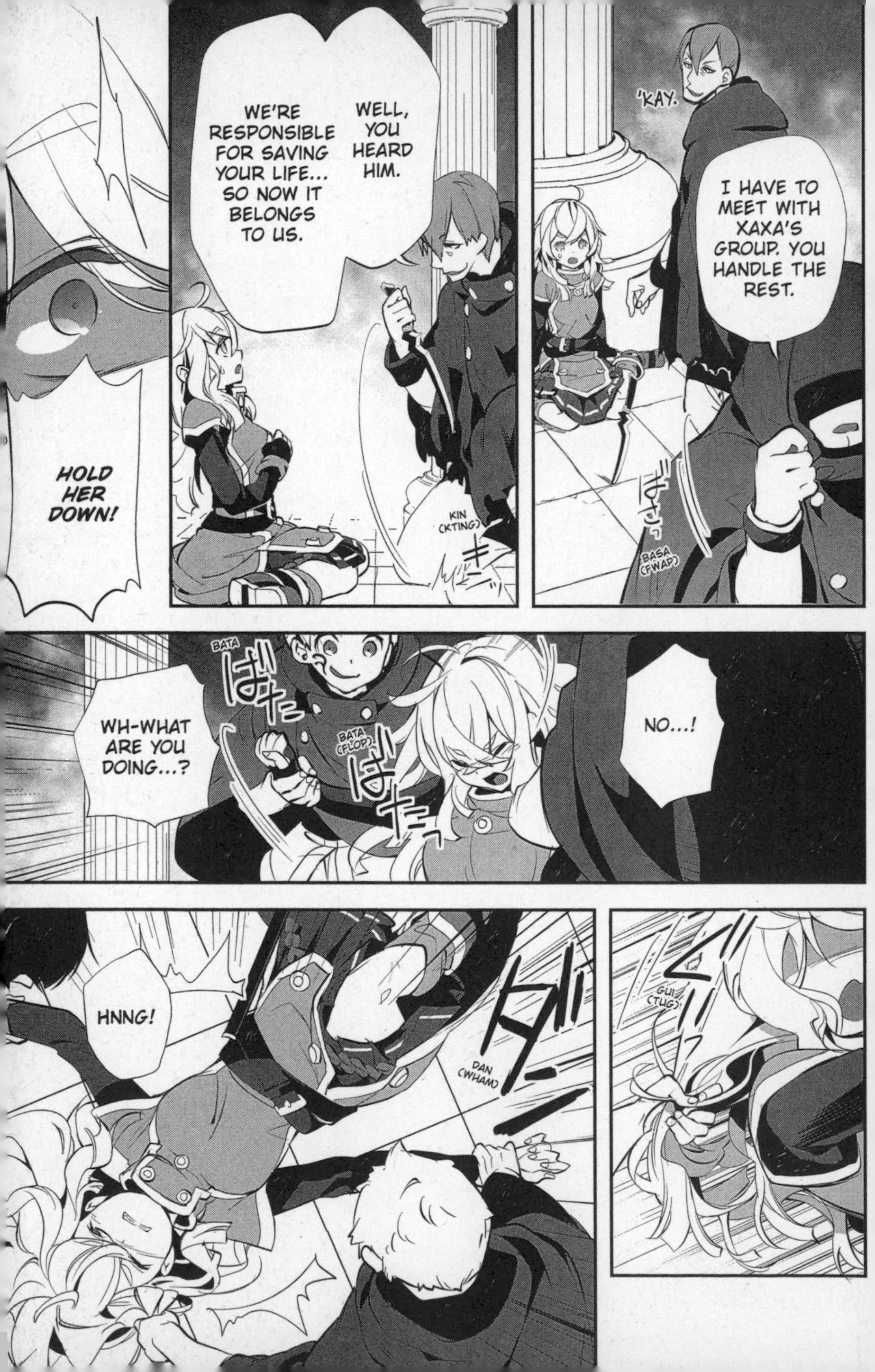

I HAVE TO MEET WITH XAXA'S GROUP. YOU HANDLE THE REST.
'KAY.
BASA (FWAP)
WELL, YOU HEARD HIM.
WE'RE RESPONSIBLE FOR SAVING YOUR LIFE... SO NOW IT BELONGS TO US.
KIN (KTING)
HOLD HER DOWN!
NO...!
BATA
BATA (FLOP)
WH-WHAT ARE YOU DOING...?
GUI (TUG)
DAN (WHAM)
HNNG!

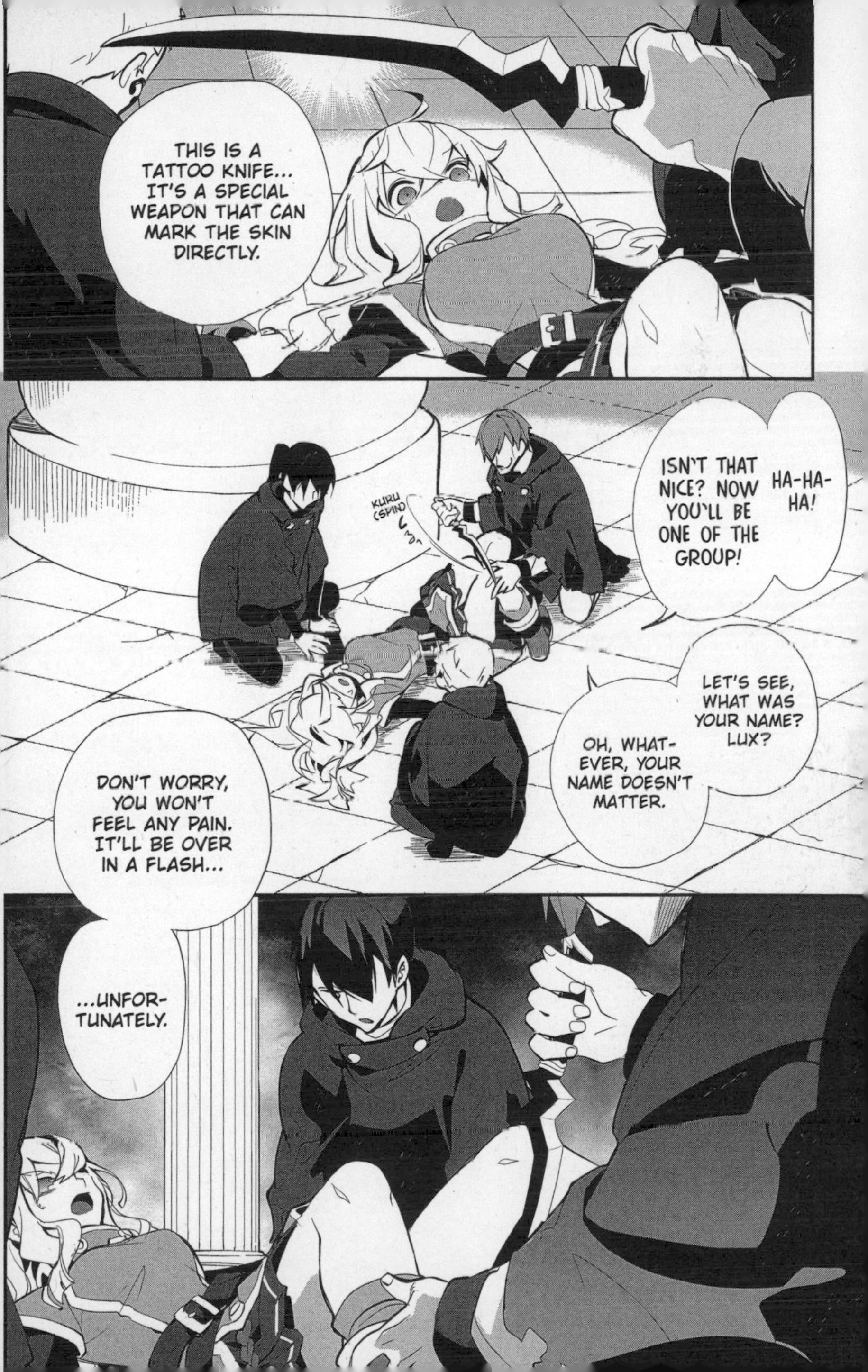
THIS IS A TATTOO KNIFE... IT'S A SPECIAL WEAPON THAT CAN MARK THE SKIN DIRECTLY.
HA-HA-HA!
ISN'T THAT NICE? NOW YOU'LL BE ONE OF THE GROUP!
KURU (SPIN)
LET'S SEE, WHAT WAS YOUR NAME? LUX?
OH, WHAT-EVER, YOUR NAME DOESN'T MATTER.
DON'T WORRY, YOU WON'T FEEL ANY PAIN. IT'LL BE OVER IN A FLASH...
...UNFOR-TUNATELY.

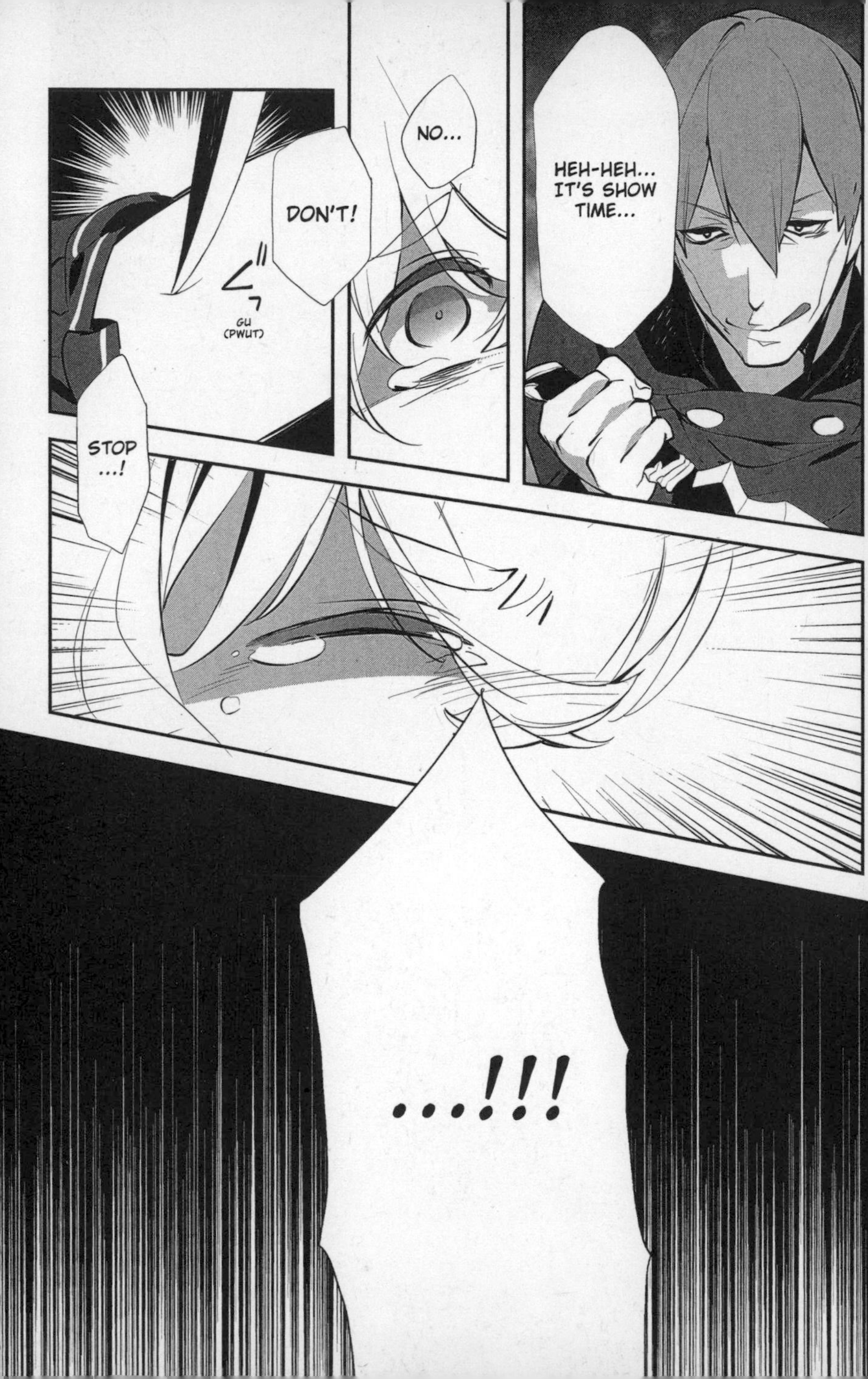
HEH-HEH... IT'S SHOW TIME...
NO...
DON'T!
GU (PWUT)
STOP ...!
...!!!

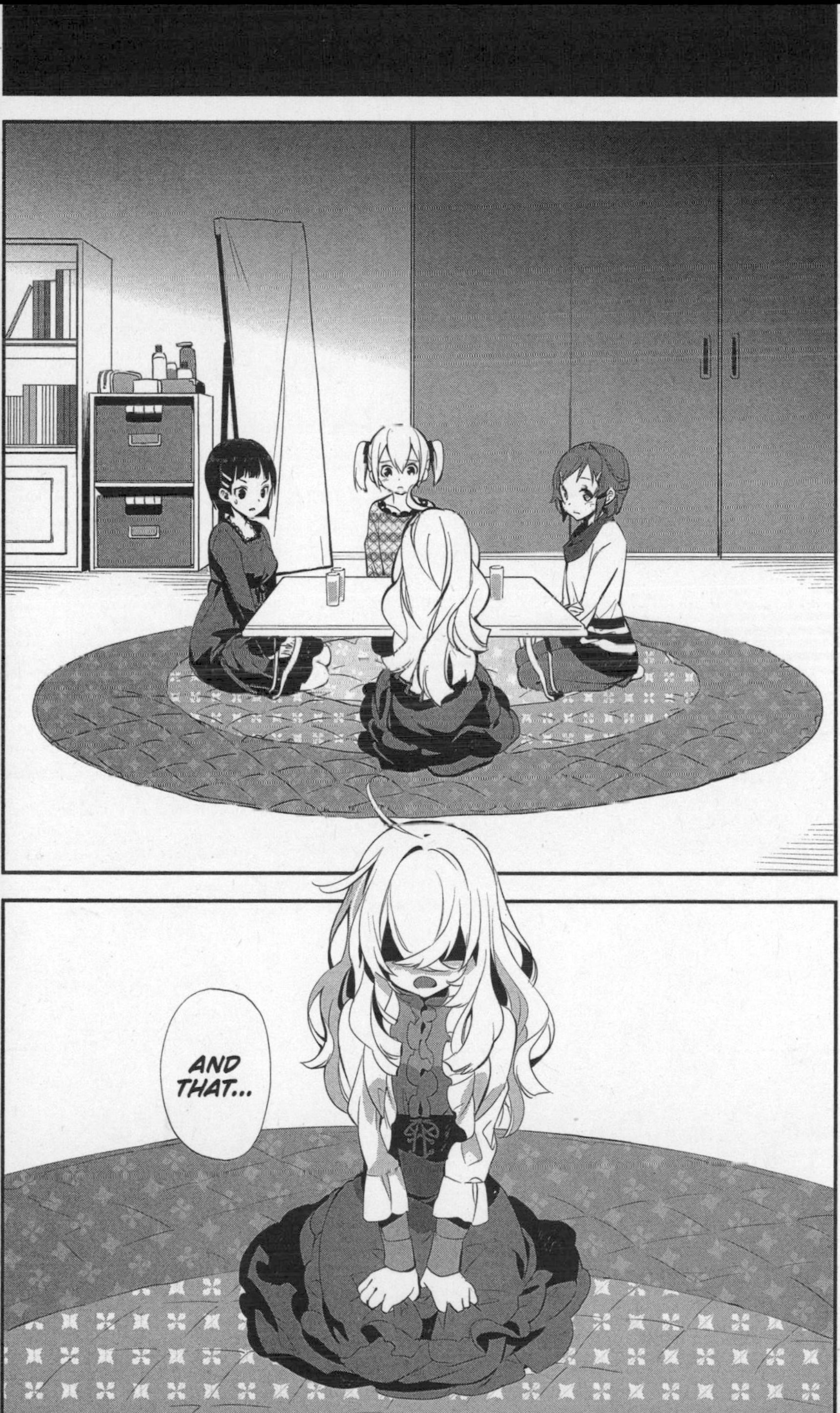
AND THAT...

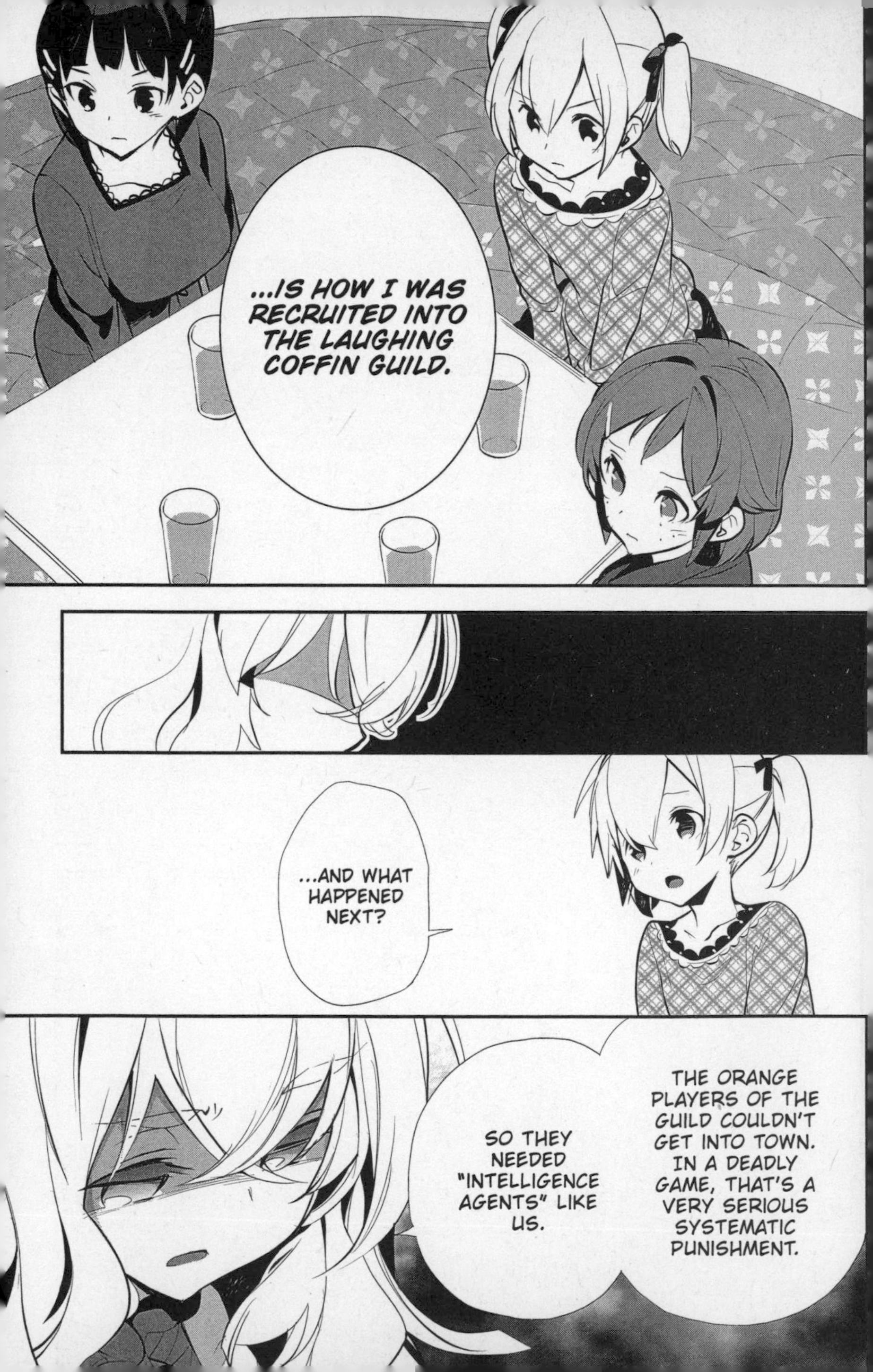
...IS HOW I WAS RECRUITED INTO THE LAUGHING COFFIN GUILD.
...AND WHAT HAPPENED NEXT?
THE ORANGE PLAYERS OF THE GUILD COULDN'T GET INTO TOWN. IN A DEADLY GAME, THAT'S A VERY SERIOUS SYSTEMATIC PUNISHMENT.
SO THEY NEEDED "INTELLIGENCE AGENTS" LIKE US.

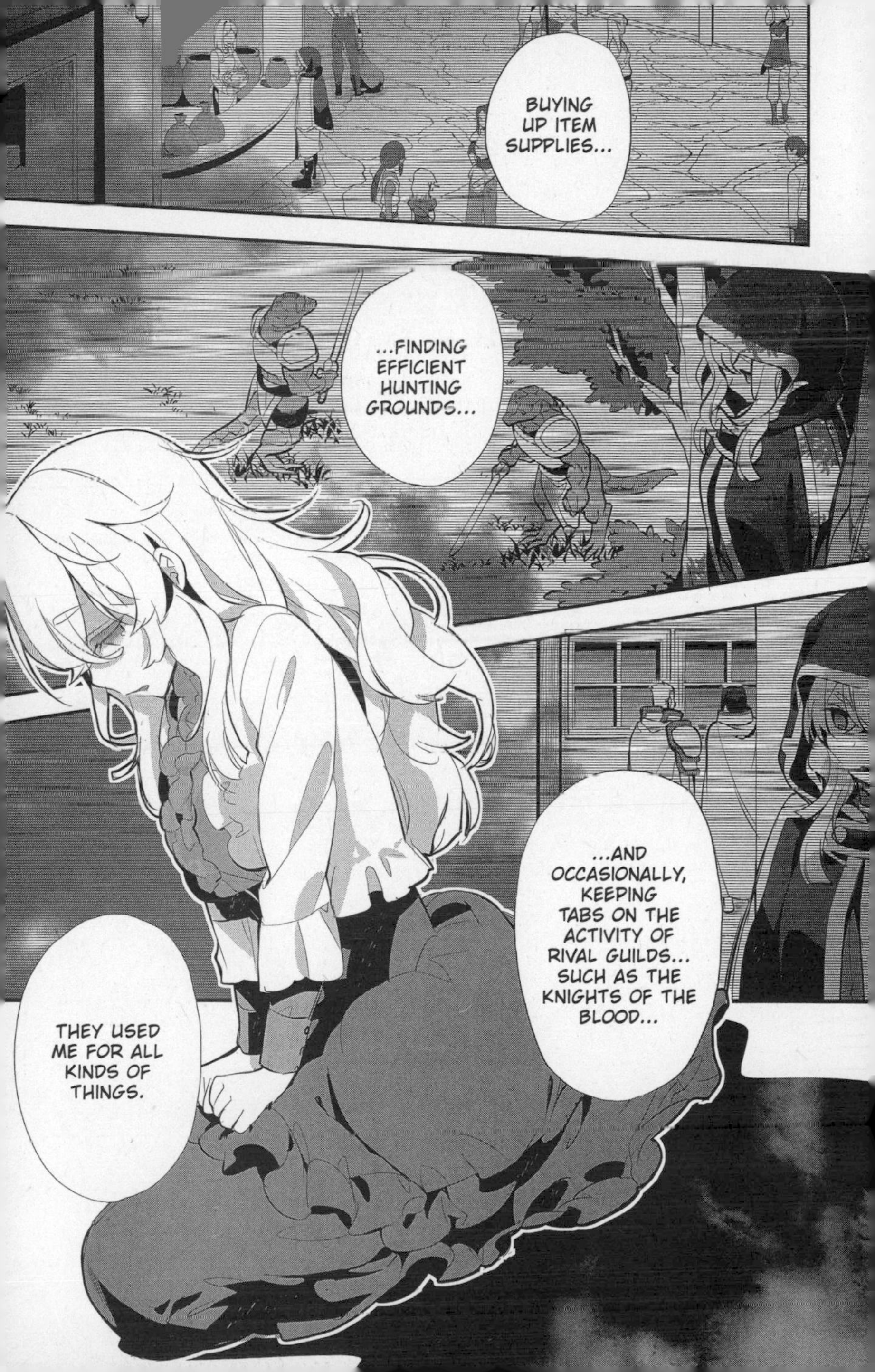
BUYING UP ITEM SUPPLIES...
...FINDING EFFICIENT HUNTING GROUNDS...
...AND OCCASIONALLY, KEEPING TABS ON THE ACTIVITY OF RIVAL GUILDS... SUCH AS THE KNIGHTS OF THE BLOOD...
THEY USED ME FOR ALL KINDS OF THINGS.

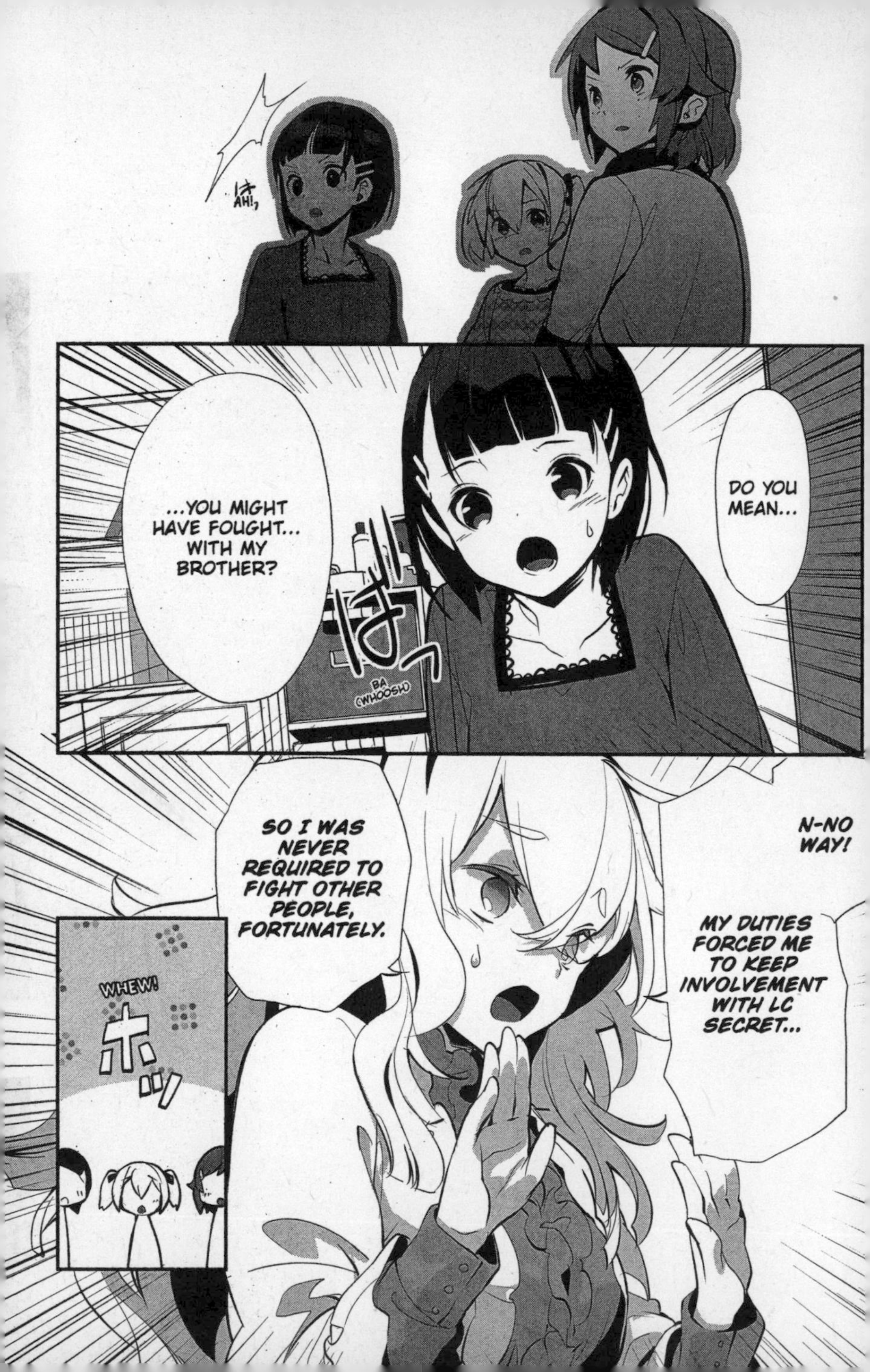
は
AH!
DO YOU MEAN...
...YOU MIGHT HAVE FOUGHT... WITH MY BROTHER?
ばっ
BA (WHOOSH)
N-NO WAY!
MY DUTIES FORCED ME TO KEEP INVOLVEMENT WITH LC SECRET...
SO I WAS NEVER REQUIRED TO FIGHT OTHER PEOPLE, FORTUNATELY.
WHEW!
ホッ

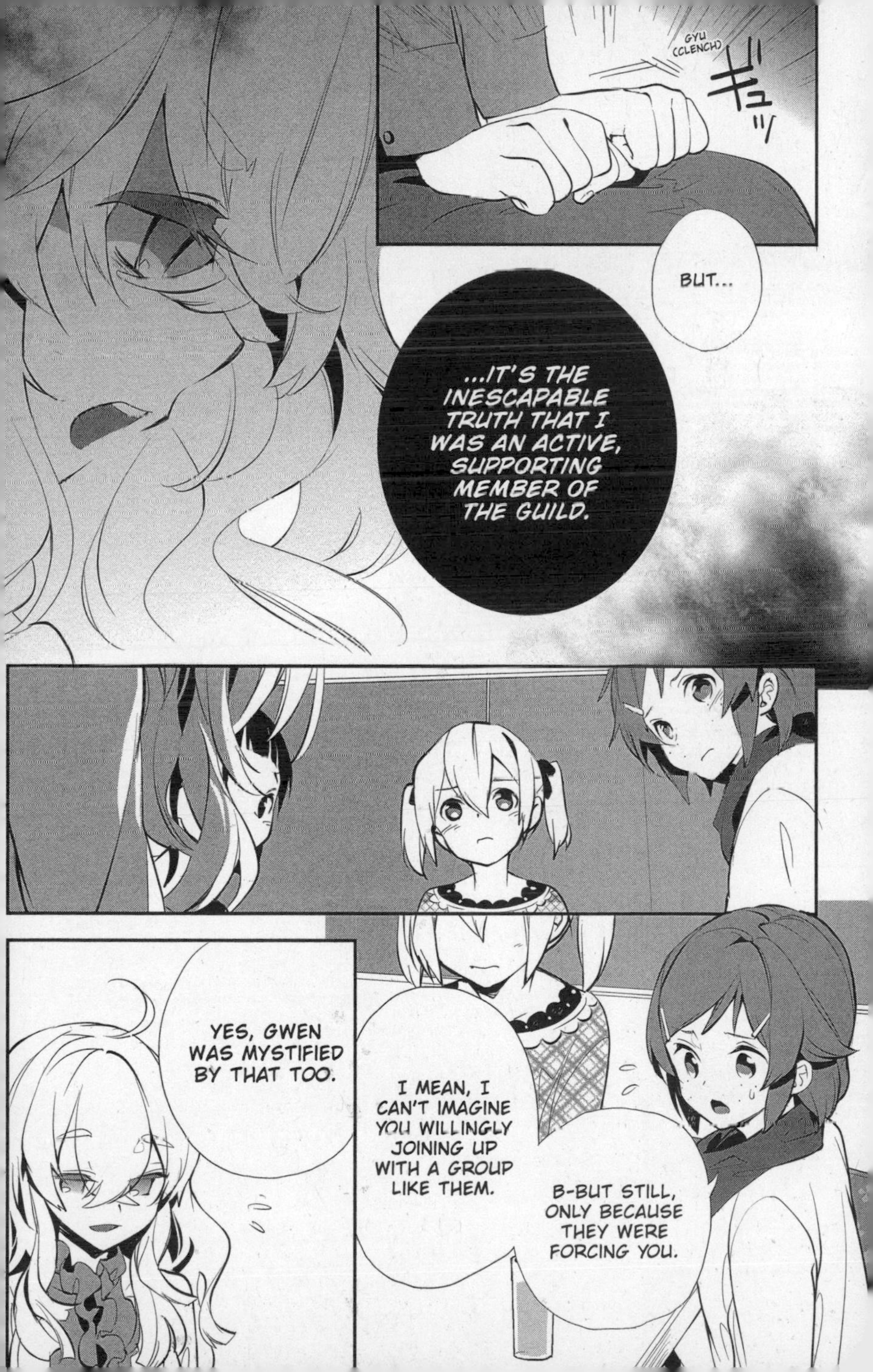
GYU (CLENCH)
ギュッ
BUT...
...IT'S THE INESCAPABLE TRUTH THAT I WAS AN ACTIVE, SUPPORTING MEMBER OF THE GUILD.
B-BUT STILL, ONLY BECAUSE THEY WERE FORCING YOU.
I MEAN, I CAN'T IMAGINE YOU WILLINGLY JOINING UP WITH A GROUP LIKE THEM.
YES, GWEN WAS MYSTIFIED BY THAT TOO.

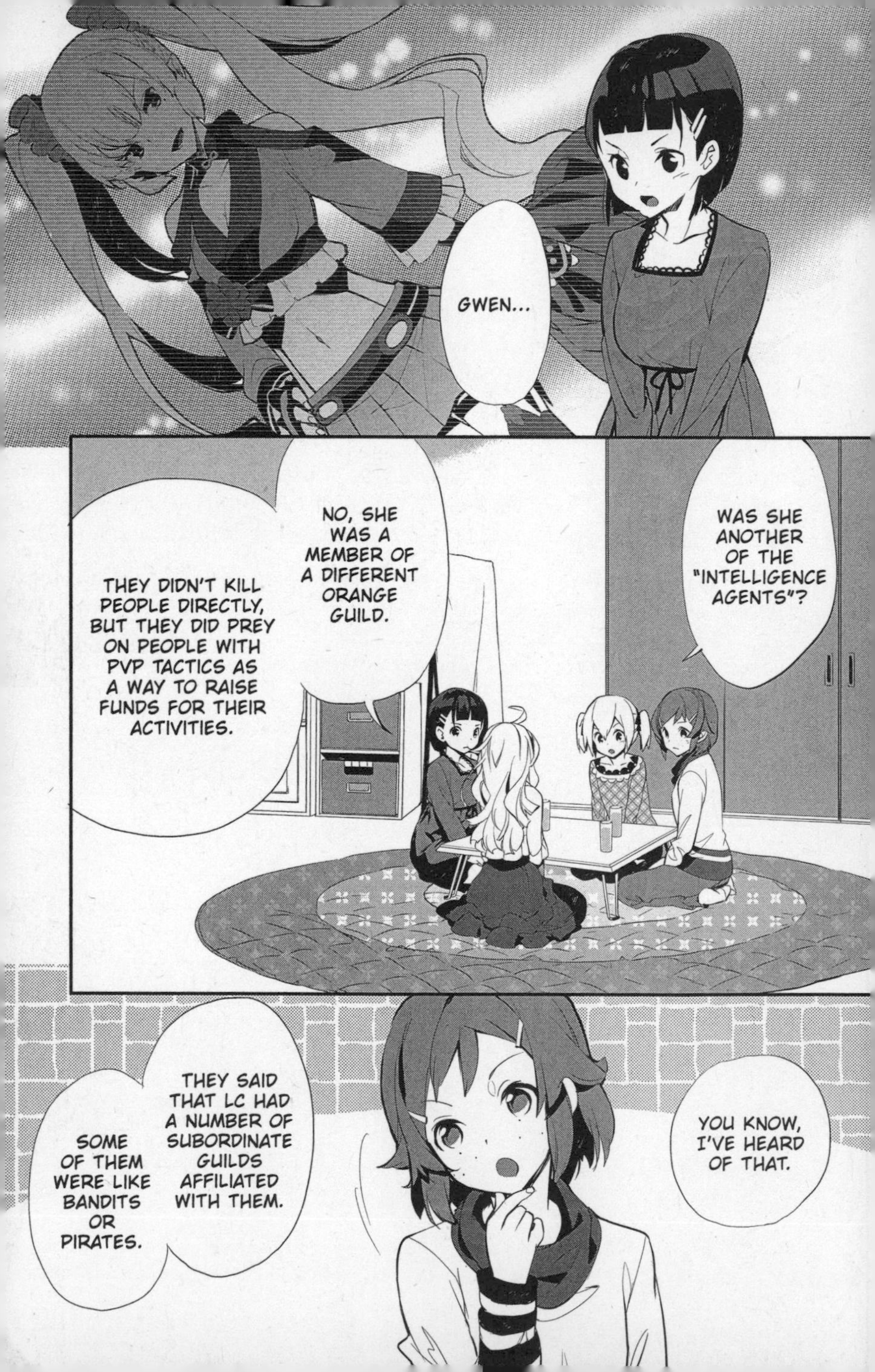
GWEN...
WAS SHE ANOTHER OF THE "INTELLIGENCE AGENTS"?
NO, SHE WAS A MEMBER OF A DIFFERENT ORANGE GUILD.
THEY DIDN'T KILL PEOPLE DIRECTLY, BUT THEY DID PREY ON PEOPLE WITH PVP TACTICS AS A WAY TO RAISE FUNDS FOR THEIR ACTIVITIES.
YOU KNOW, I'VE HEARD OF THAT.
THEY SAID THAT LC HAD A NUMBER OF SUBORDINATE GUILDS AFFILIATED WITH THEM.
SOME OF THEM WERE LIKE BANDITS OR PIRATES.

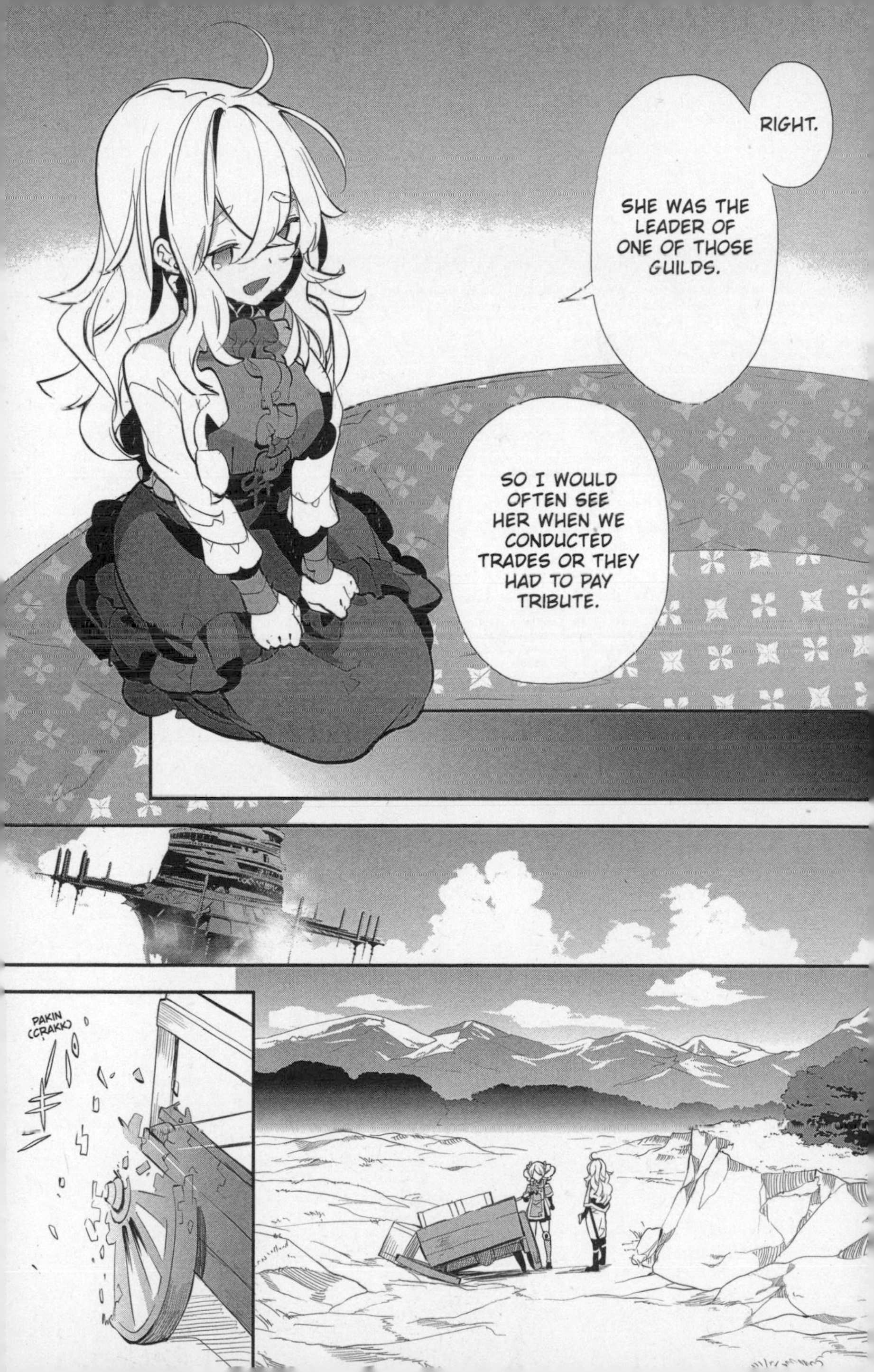
RIGHT.
SHE WAS THE LEADER OF ONE OF THOSE GUILDS.
SO I WOULD OFTEN SEE HER WHEN WE CONDUCTED TRADES OR THEY HAD TO PAY TRIBUTE.
PAKIN (CRAKK)

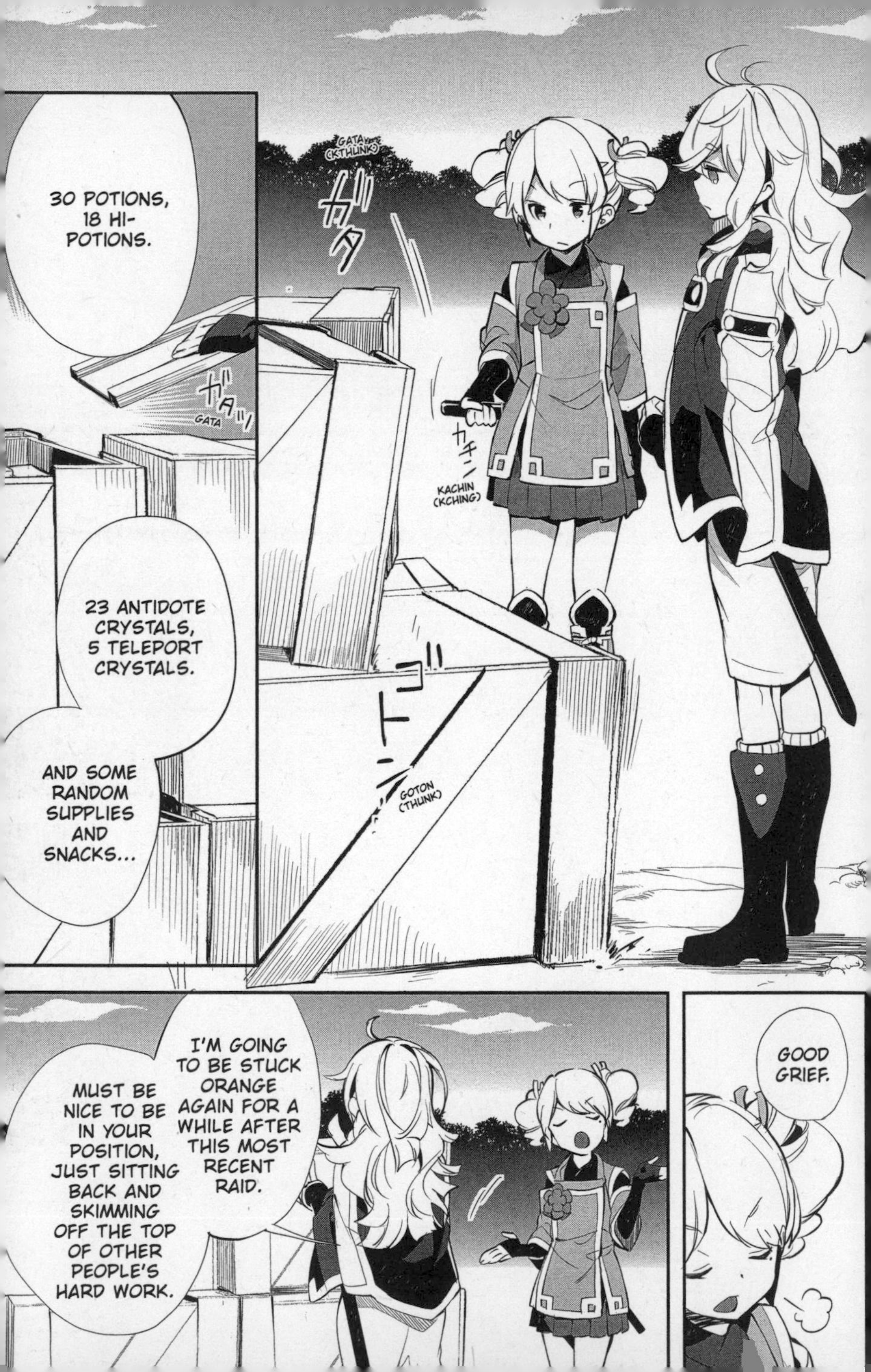
GATA (KTHUNK)
ガタ
30 POTIONS, 18 HI-POTIONS.
ガタッ
GATA
カチン
KACHIN (KCHING)
23 ANTIDOTE CRYSTALS, 5 TELEPORT CRYSTALS.
ゴトン
GOTON (THUNK)
AND SOME RANDOM SUPPLIES AND SNACKS...
GOOD GRIEF.
I'M GOING TO BE STUCK ORANGE AGAIN FOR A WHILE AFTER THIS MOST RECENT RAID.
MUST BE NICE TO BE IN YOUR POSITION, JUST SITTING BACK AND SKIMMING OFF THE TOP OF OTHER PEOPLE'S HARD WORK.

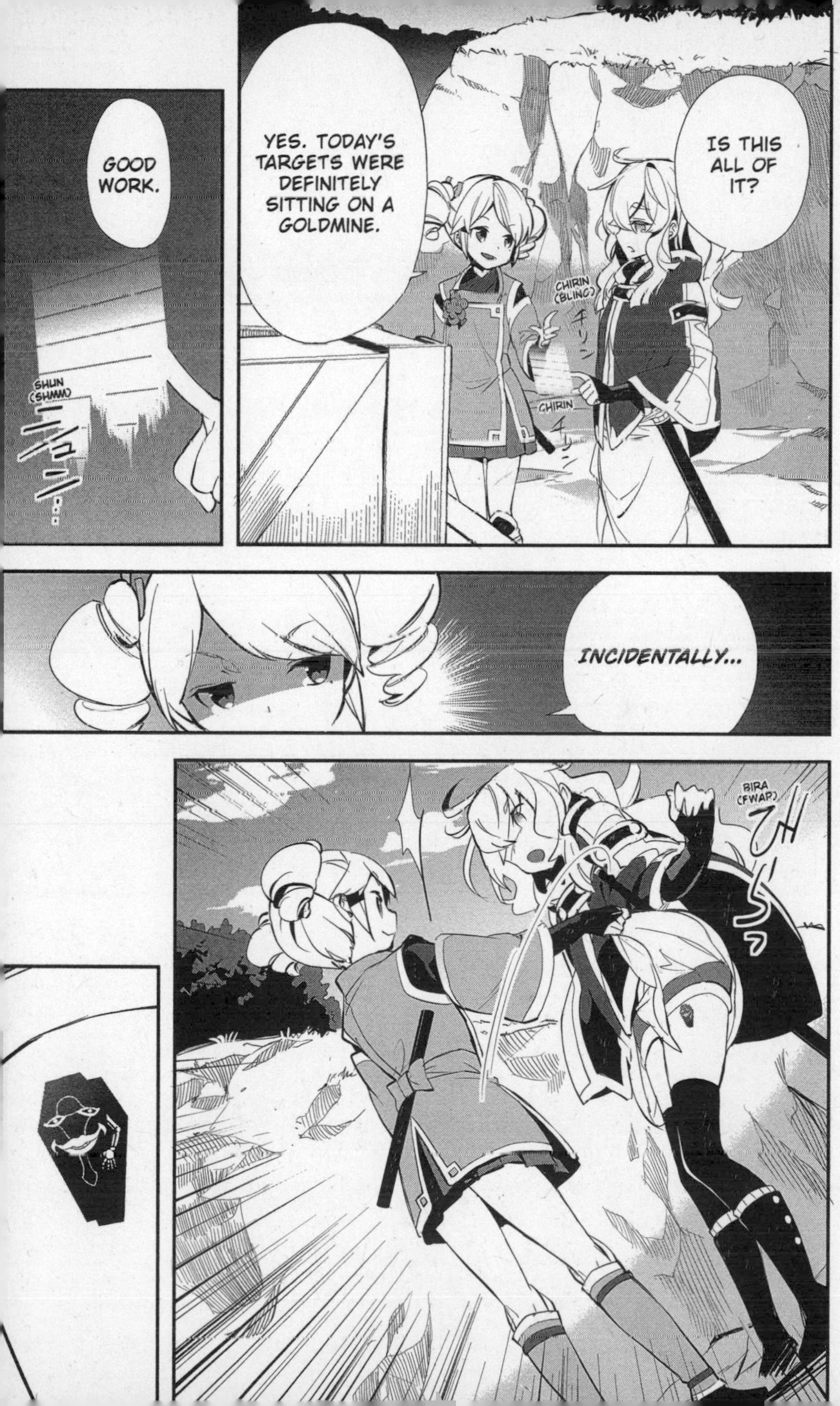
IS THIS ALL OF IT?
YES. TODAY'S TARGETS WERE DEFINITELY SITTING ON A GOLDMINE.
CHIRIN (BLING)
CHIRIN
GOOD WORK.
SHUN (SHMM)
INCIDENTALLY...
BIRA (FWAP)

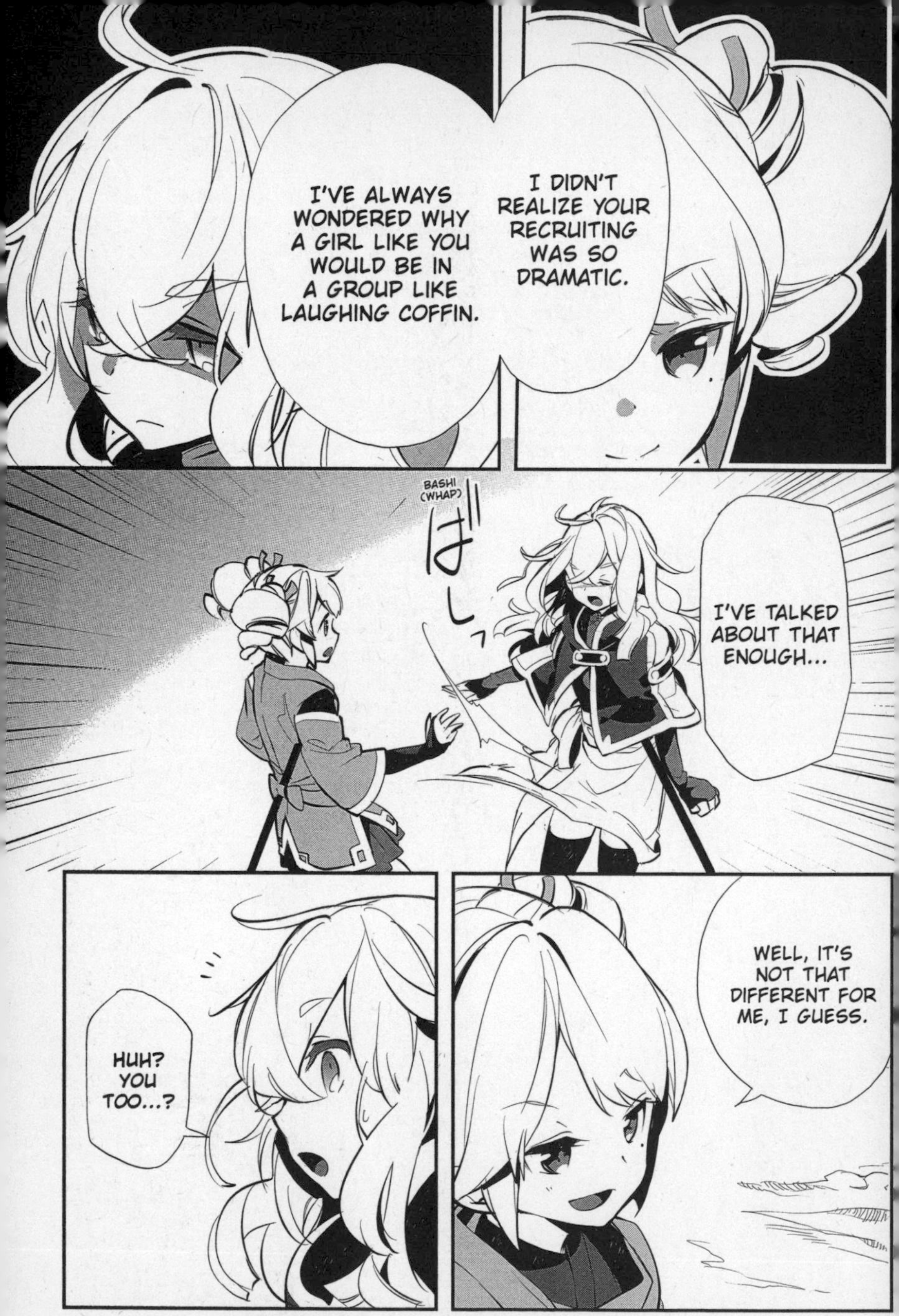
I DIDN'T REALIZE YOUR RECRUITING WAS SO DRAMATIC.
I'VE ALWAYS WONDERED WHY A GIRL LIKE YOU WOULD BE IN A GROUP LIKE LAUGHING COFFIN.
BASHI (WHAP)
ばしっ
I'VE TALKED ABOUT THAT ENOUGH...
WELL, IT'S NOT THAT DIFFERENT FOR ME, I GUESS.
HUH? YOU TOO...?

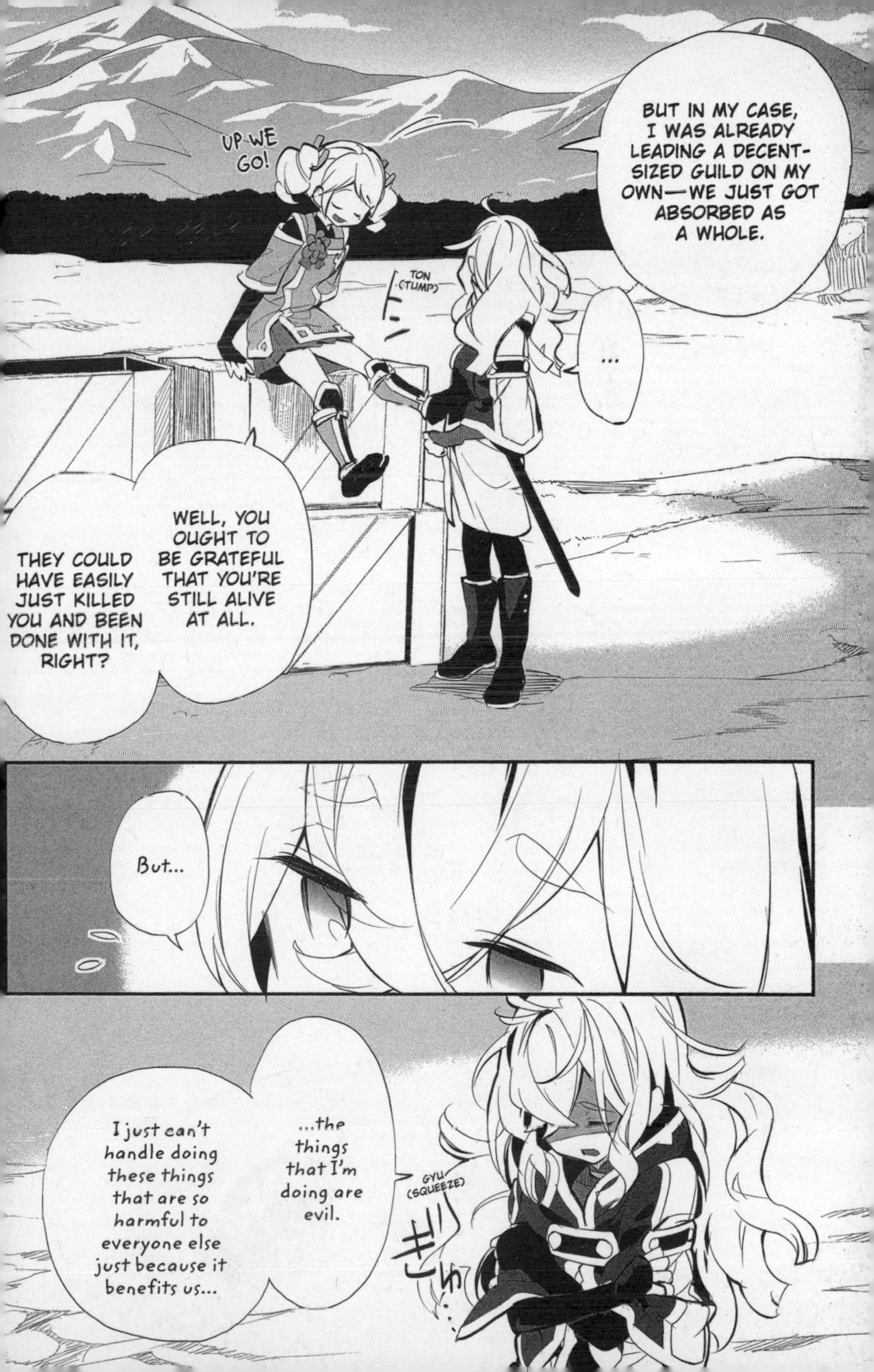

BUT IN MY CASE, I WAS ALREADY LEADING A DECENT-SIZED GUILD ON MY OWN—WE JUST GOT ABSORBED AS A WHOLE.
UP WE GO!
TON (TUMP)
...
WELL, YOU OUGHT TO BE GRATEFUL THAT YOU'RE STILL ALIVE AT ALL.
THEY COULD HAVE EASILY JUST KILLED YOU AND BEEN DONE WITH IT, RIGHT?
But...
I just can't handle doing these things that are so harmful to everyone else just because it benefits us...
...the things that I'm doing are evil.
GYU (SQUEEZE)

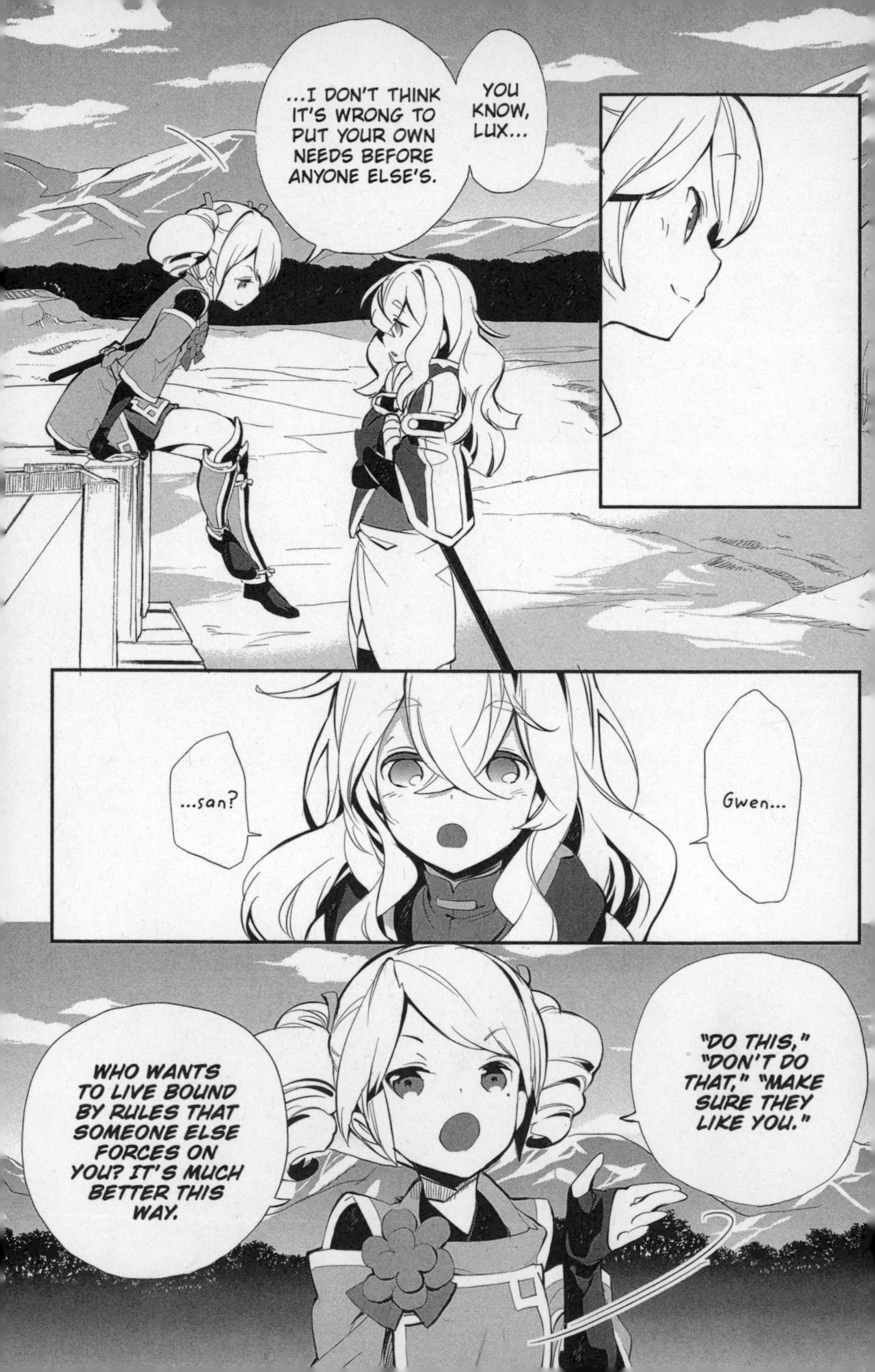
YOU KNOW, LUX...
...I DON'T THINK IT'S WRONG TO PUT YOUR OWN NEEDS BEFORE ANYONE ELSE'S.
Gwen...
...san?
"DO THIS," "DON'T DO THAT," "MAKE SURE THEY LIKE YOU."
WHO WANTS TO LIVE BOUND BY RULES THAT SOMEONE ELSE FORCES ON YOU? IT'S MUCH BETTER THIS WAY.

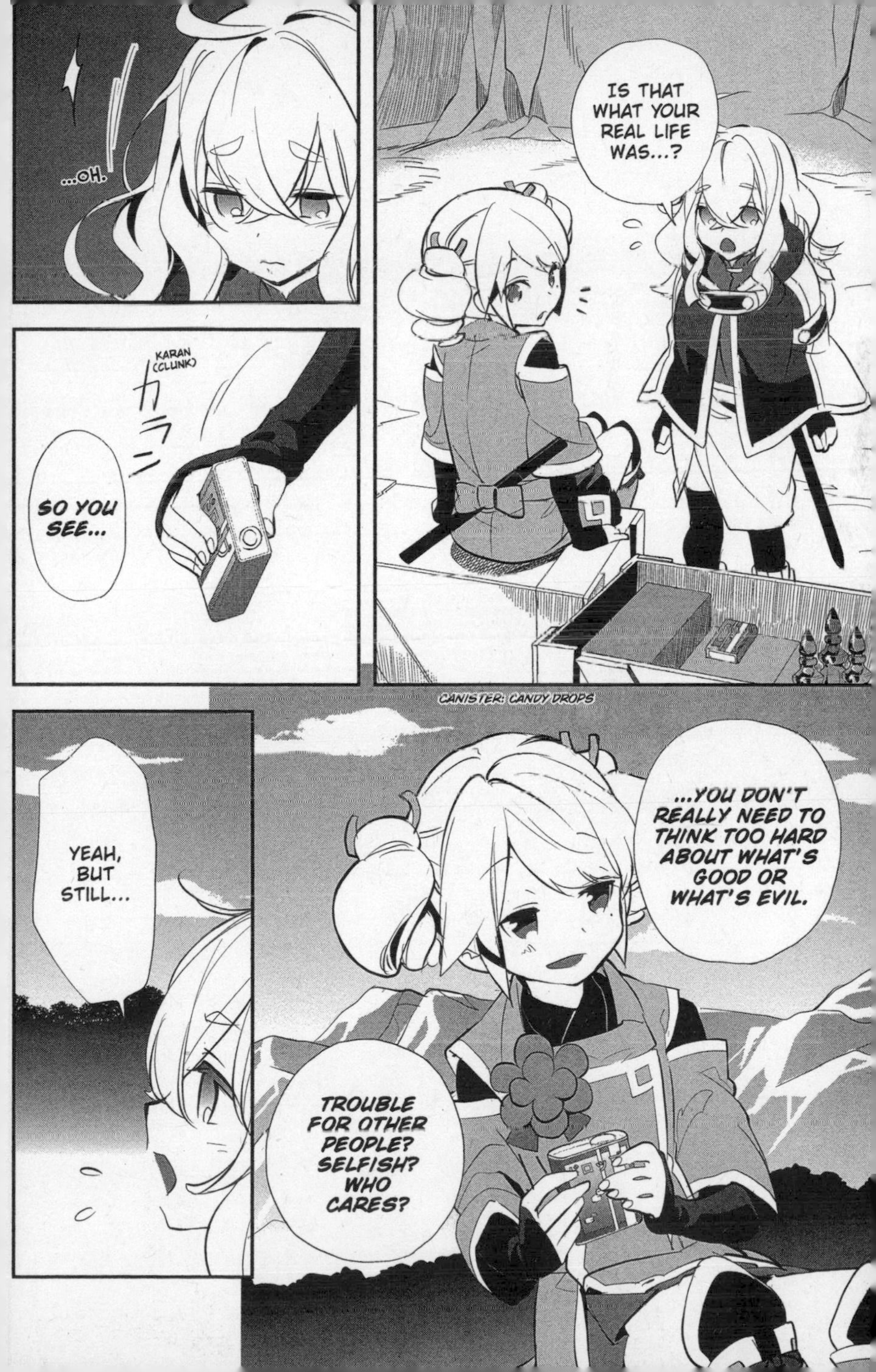
IS THAT WHAT YOUR REAL LIFE WAS...?
...OH.
KARAN (CLUNK)
SO YOU SEE...
CANISTER: CANDY DROPS
...YOU DON'T REALLY NEED TO THINK TOO HARD ABOUT WHAT'S GOOD OR WHAT'S EVIL.
YEAH, BUT STILL...
TROUBLE FOR OTHER PEOPLE? SELFISH? WHO CARES?

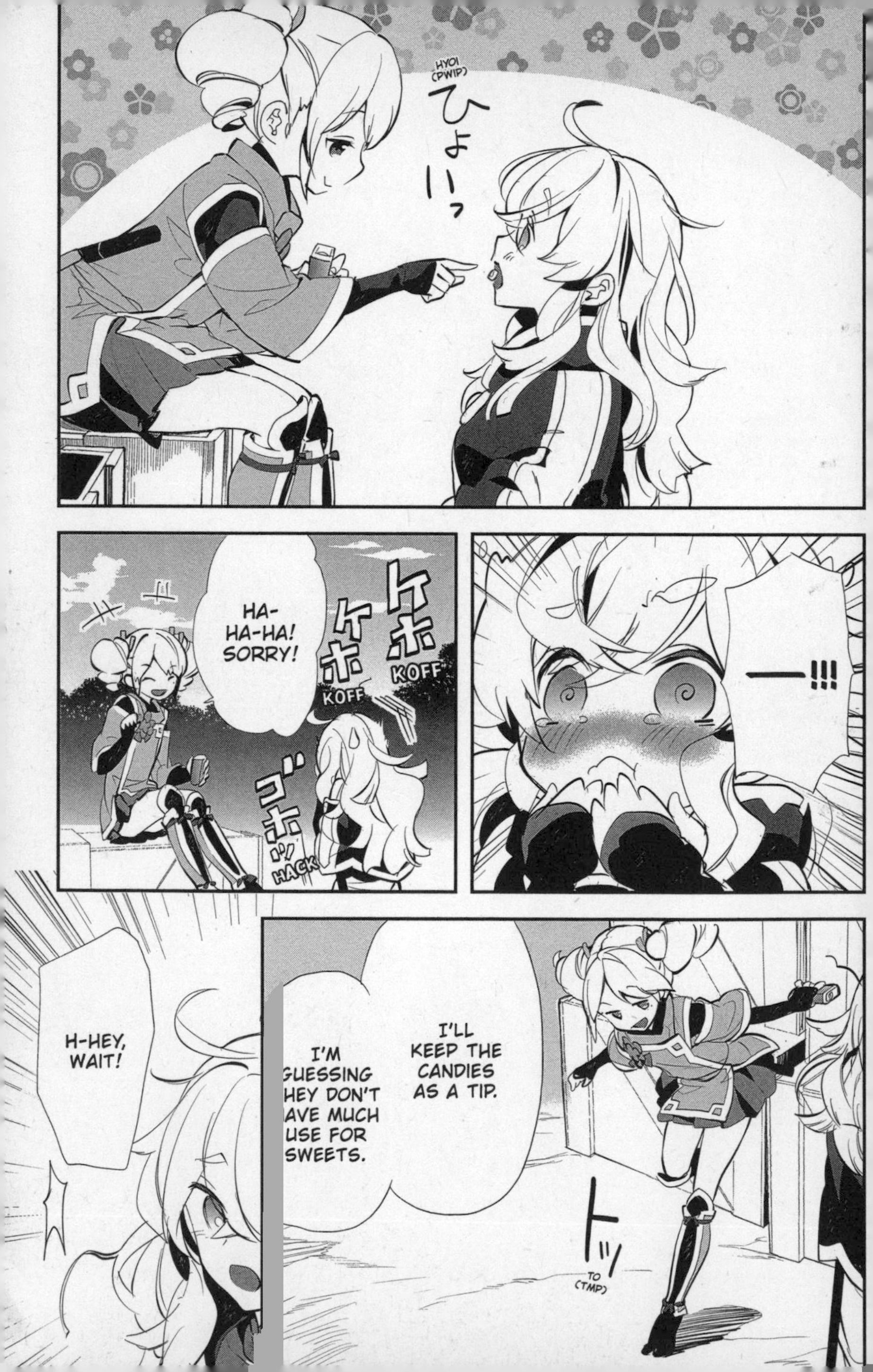
HYOI (PWIP)
ひょいっ
—!!!
HA-HA-HA! SORRY!
ケホ
KOFF
ケホ
KOFF
ゴホッ
HACK
I'LL KEEP THE CANDIES AS A TIP.
I'M GUESSING HEY DON'T AVE MUCH USE FOR SWEETS.
トッ
TO (TMP)
H-HEY, WAIT!

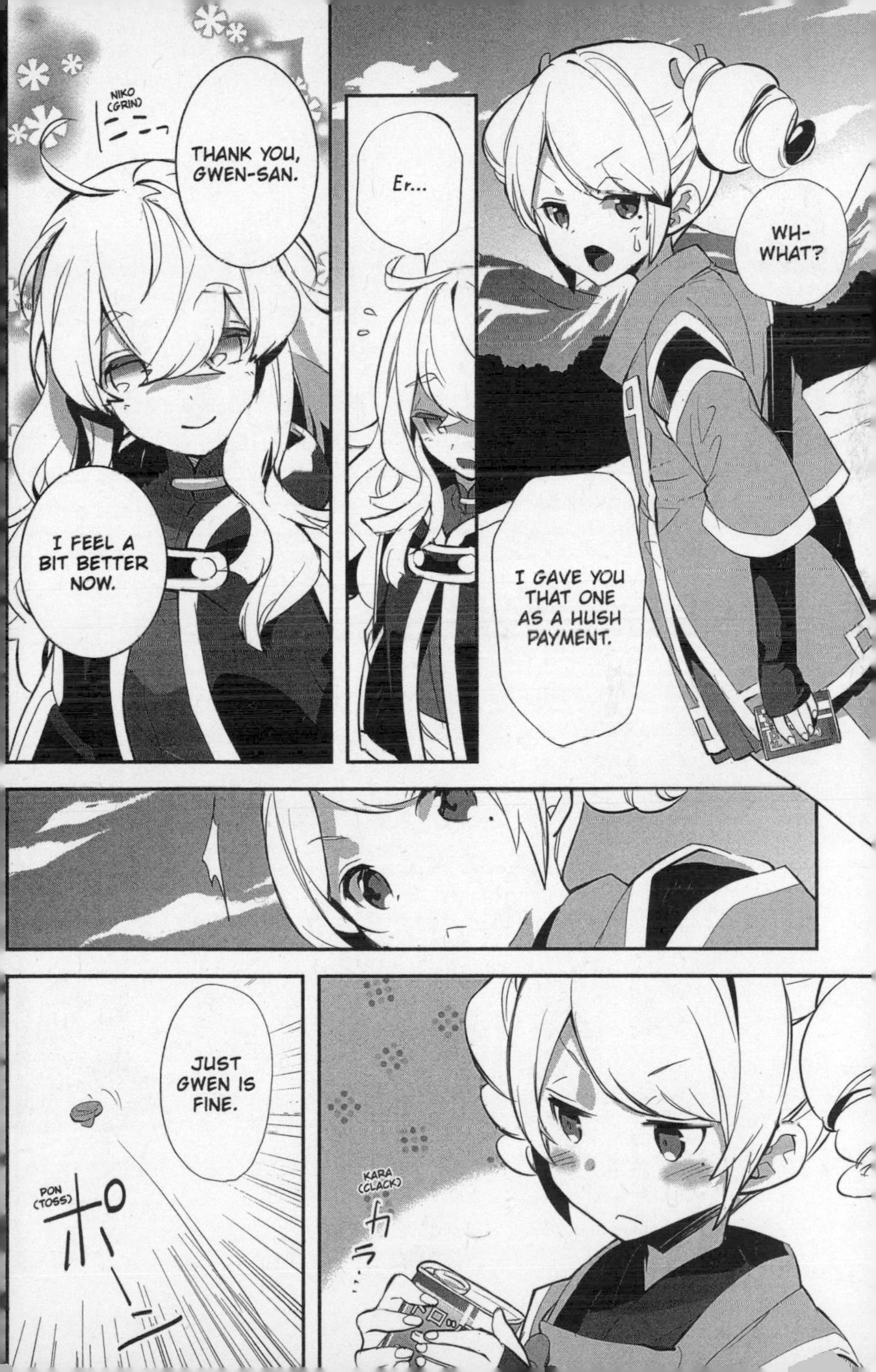
WH-
WHAT?
I GAVE YOU THAT ONE AS A HUSH PAYMENT.
Er...
NIKO (GRIN)
THANK YOU, GWEN-SAN.
I FEEL A BIT BETTER NOW.
KARA (CLACK)
JUST GWEN IS FINE.
PON (TOSS)

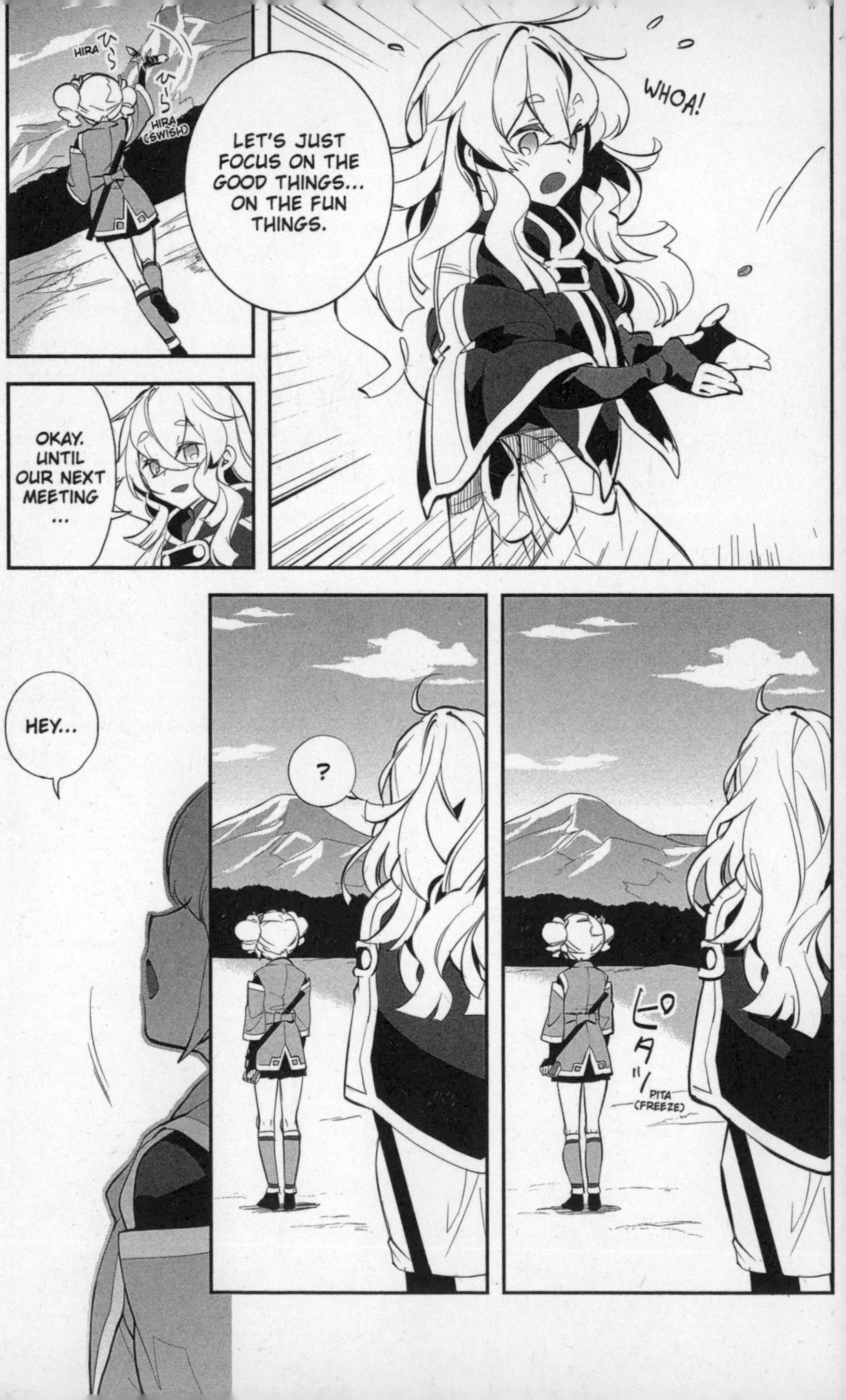
WHOA!
LET'S JUST FOCUS ON THE GOOD THINGS... ON THE FUN THINGS.
ひら HIRA
ひら HIRA (SWISH)
OKAY. UNTIL OUR NEXT MEETING...
ピタッ PITA (FREEZE)
?
HEY...

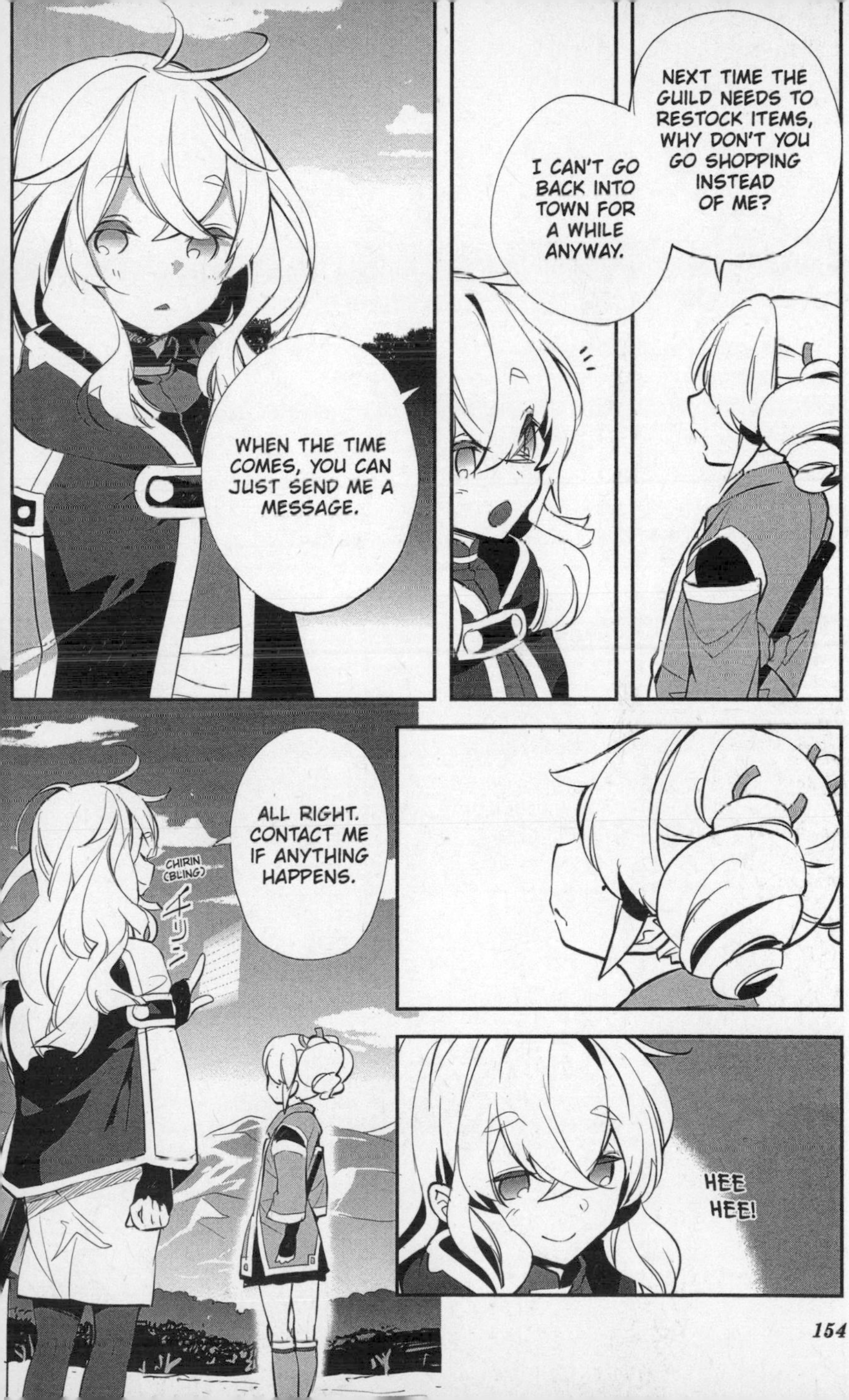
NEXT TIME THE GUILD NEEDS TO RESTOCK ITEMS, WHY DON'T YOU GO SHOPPING INSTEAD OF ME?
I CAN'T GO BACK INTO TOWN FOR A WHILE ANYWAY.
WHEN THE TIME COMES, YOU CAN JUST SEND ME A MESSAGE.
HEE HEE!
ALL RIGHT. CONTACT ME IF ANYTHING HAPPENS.
CHIRIN (BLING)

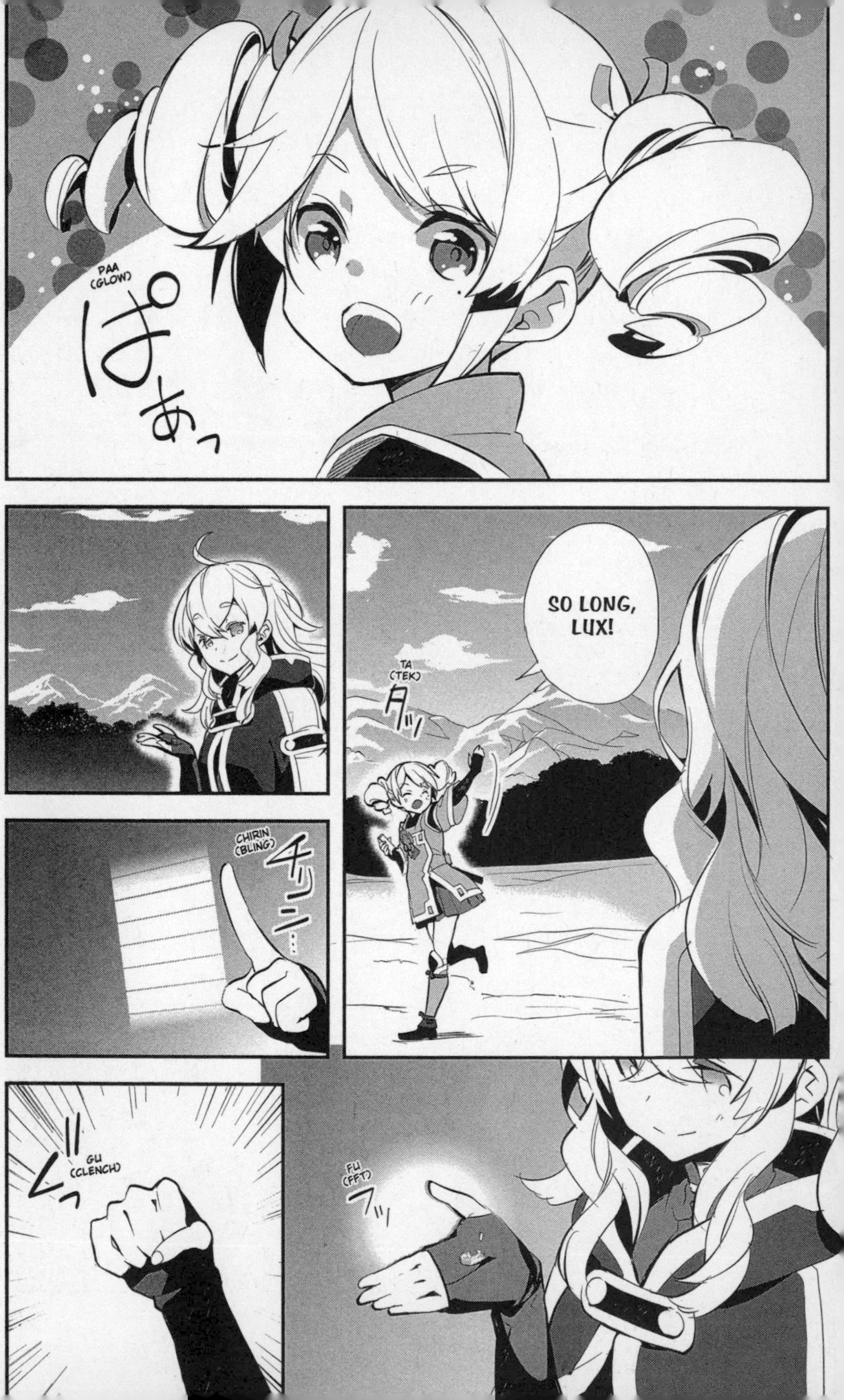
PAA (GLOW)
ぱあっ
SO LONG, LUX!
TA (TEK)
タッ
CHIRIN (BLING)
チリーン…
FU (FFT)
フッ
GU (CLENCH)
ぐっ

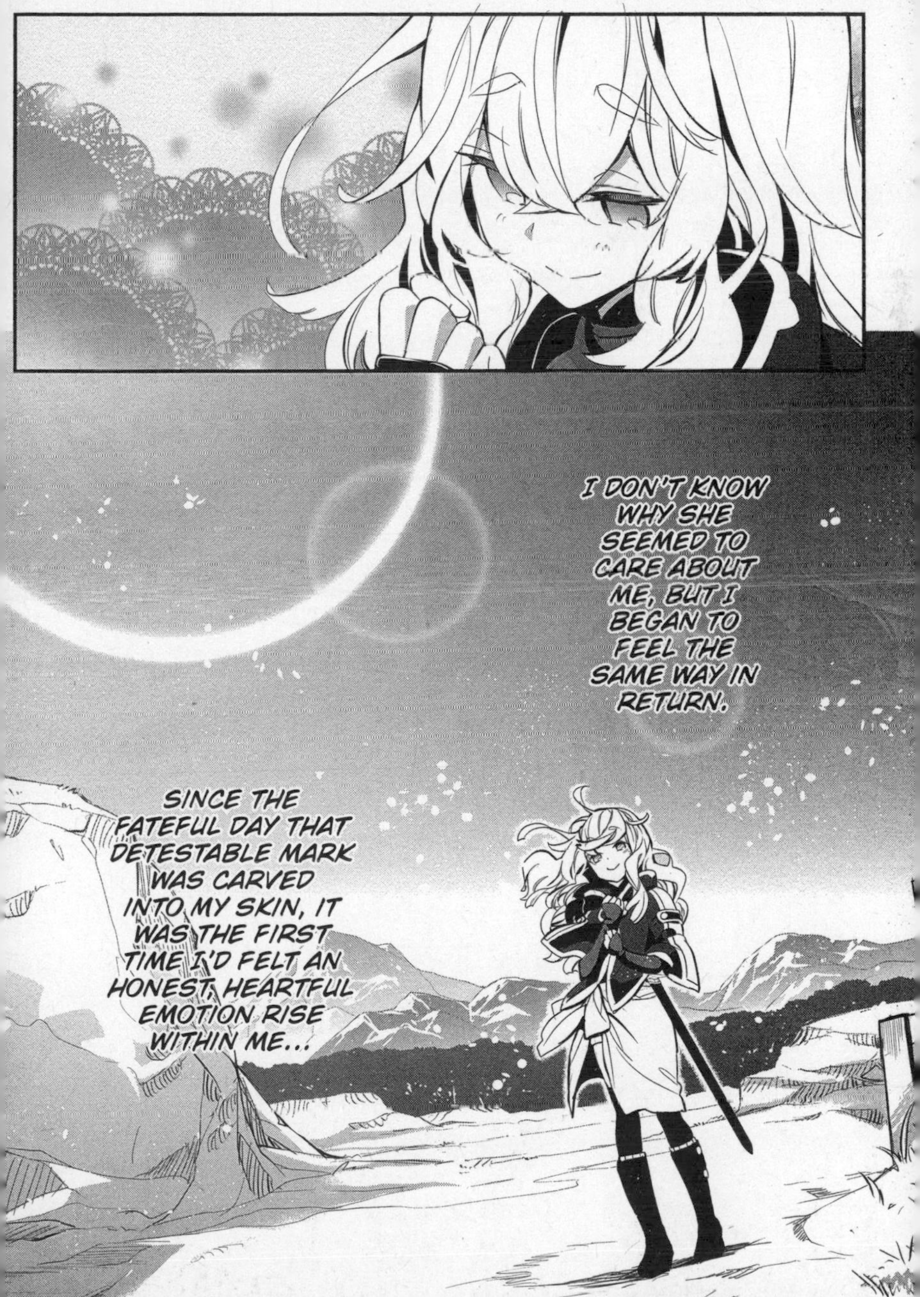
I DON'T KNOW WHY SHE SEEMED TO CARE ABOUT ME, BUT I BEGAN TO FEEL THE SAME WAY IN RETURN.
SINCE THE FATEFUL DAY THAT DETESTABLE MARK WAS CARVED INTO MY SKIN, IT WAS THE FIRST TIME I'D FELT AN HONEST, HEARTFUL EMOTION RISE WITHIN ME...

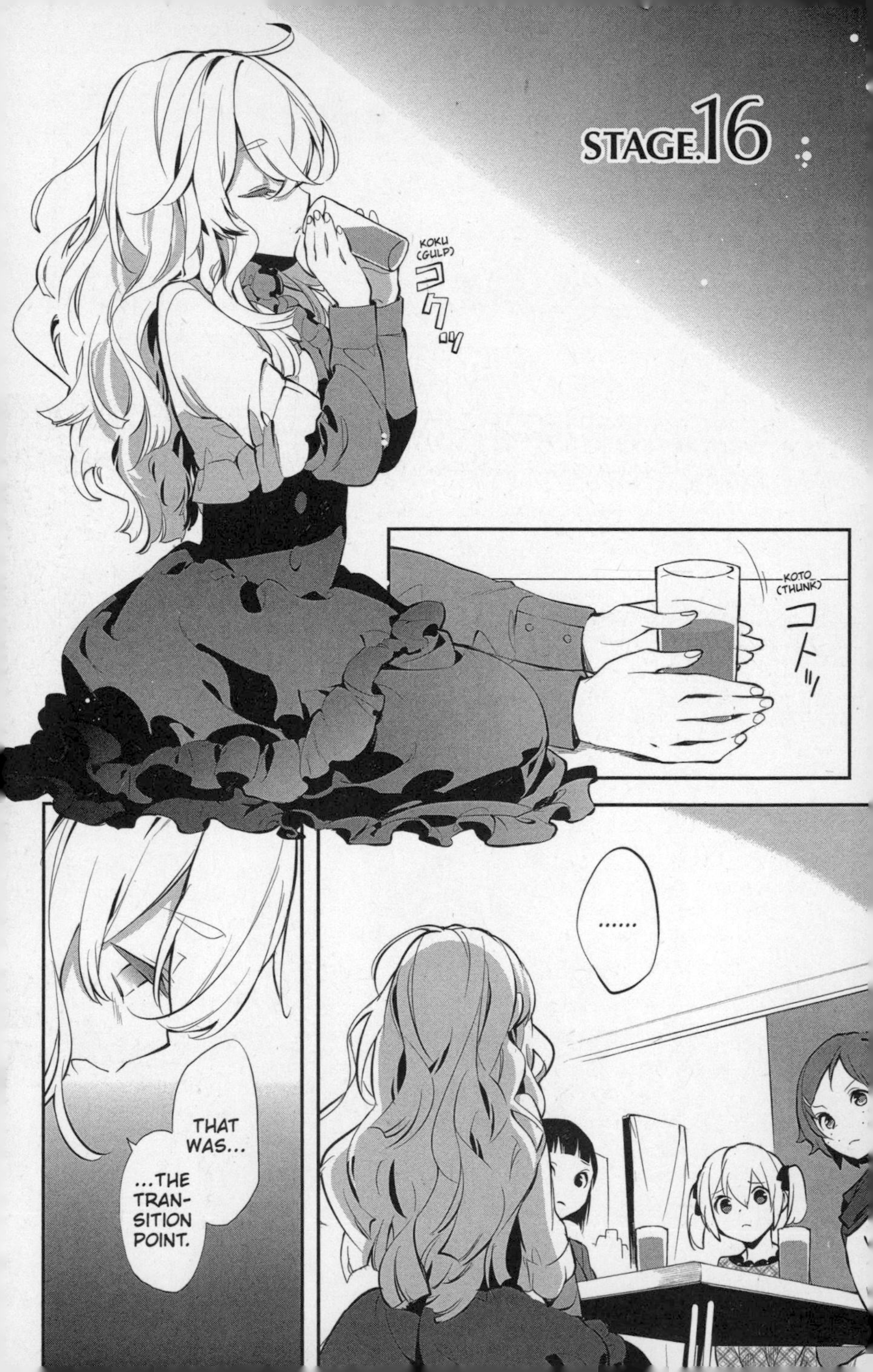
STAGE.16
KOKU (GULP)
コクッ
KOTO (THUNK)
コトッ
......
THAT WAS...
...THE TRAN-SITION POINT.

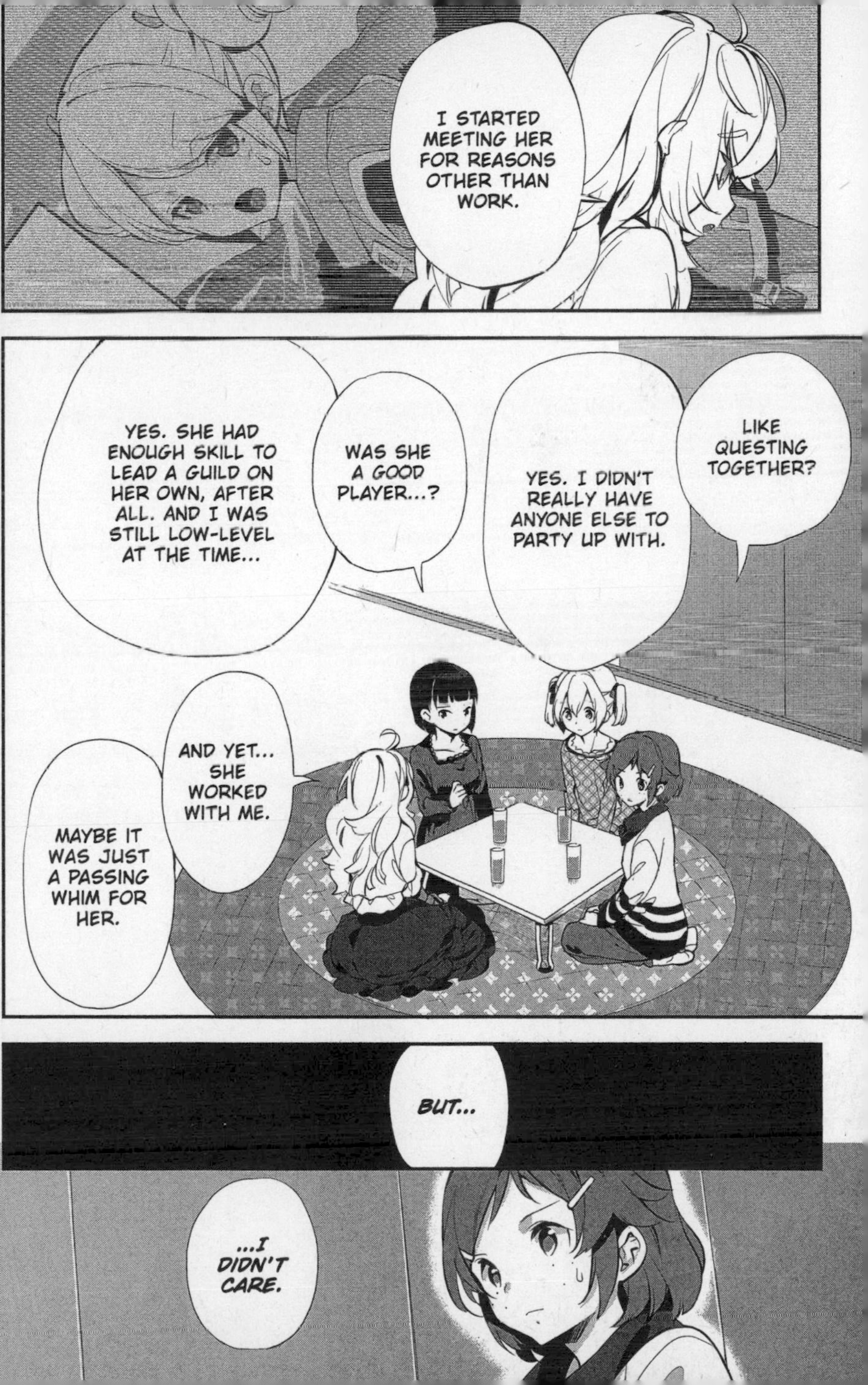
I STARTED MEETING HER FOR REASONS OTHER THAN WORK.
LIKE QUESTING TOGETHER?
YES. I DIDN'T REALLY HAVE ANYONE ELSE TO PARTY UP WITH.
WAS SHE A GOOD PLAYER...?
YES. SHE HAD ENOUGH SKILL TO LEAD A GUILD ON HER OWN, AFTER ALL. AND I WAS STILL LOW-LEVEL AT THE TIME...
AND YET... SHE WORKED WITH ME.
MAYBE IT WAS JUST A PASSING WHIM FOR HER.
BUT...
...I DIDN'T CARE.

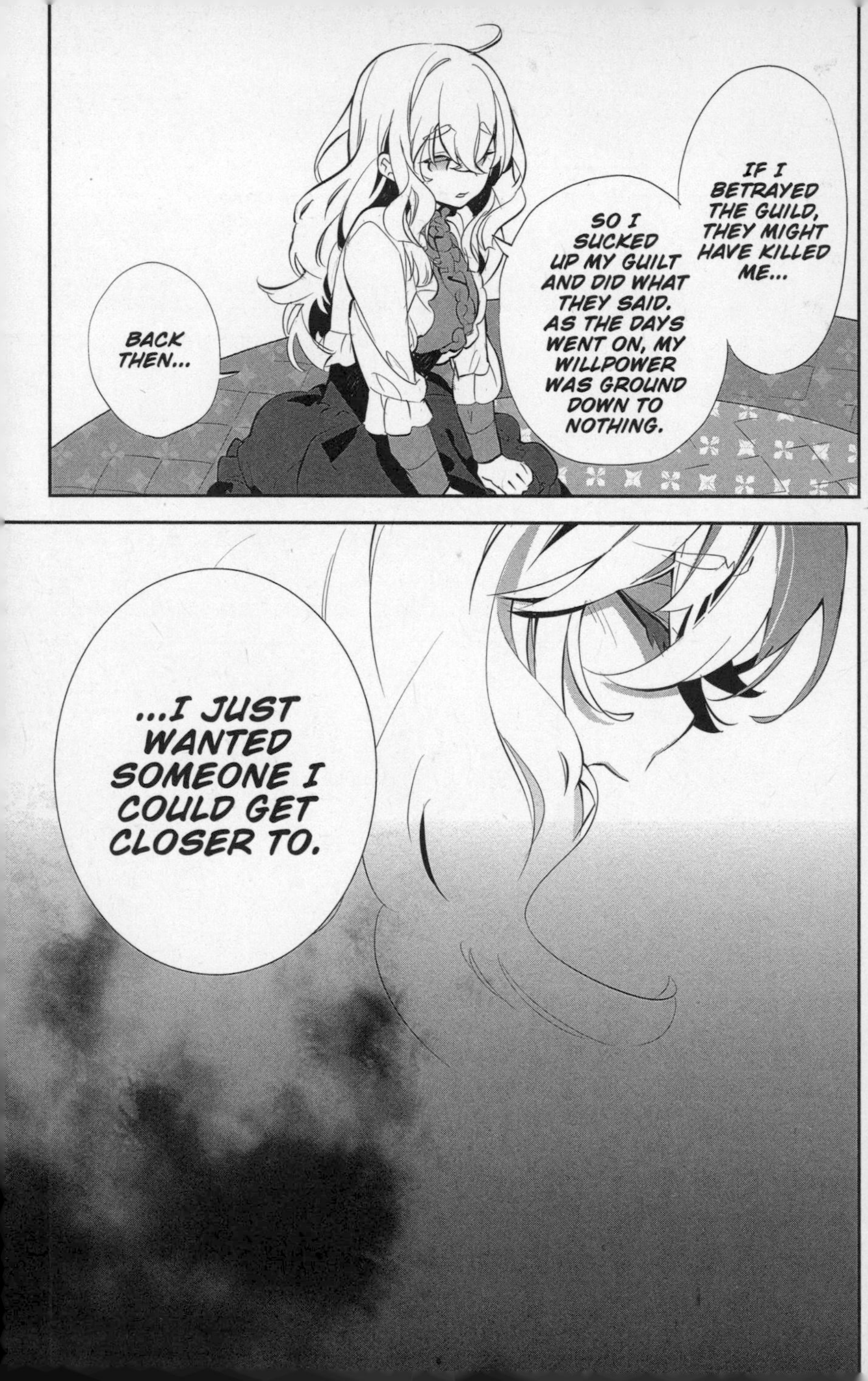
IF I BETRAYED THE GUILD, THEY MIGHT HAVE KILLED ME...
SO I SUCKED UP MY GUILT AND DID WHAT THEY SAID. AS THE DAYS WENT ON, MY WILLPOWER WAS GROUND DOWN TO NOTHING.
BACK THEN...
...I JUST WANTED SOMEONE I COULD GET CLOSER TO.

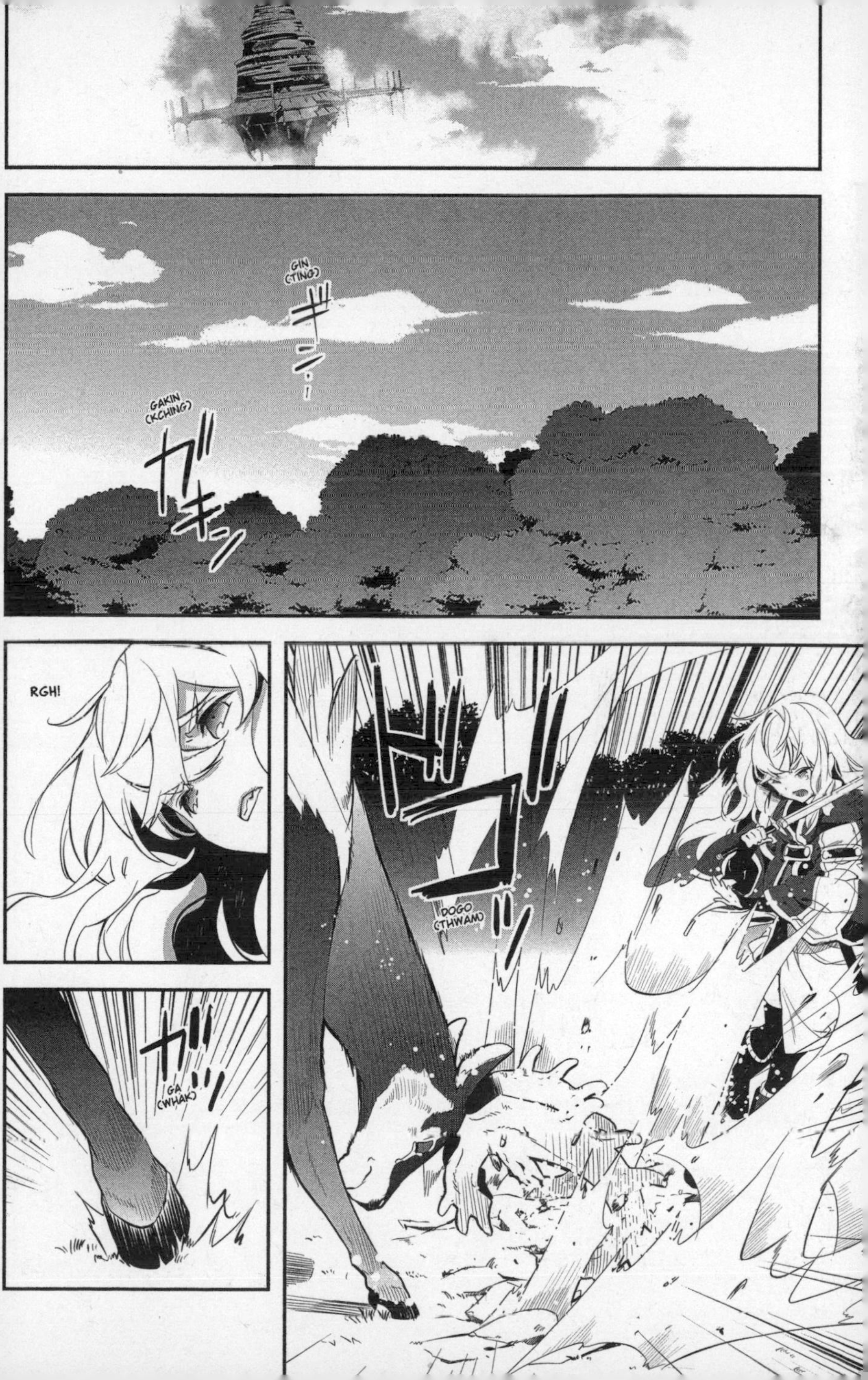
GIN (TING)
GAKIN (KCHING)
DOGO (THWAM)
RGH!
GA (WHAK)

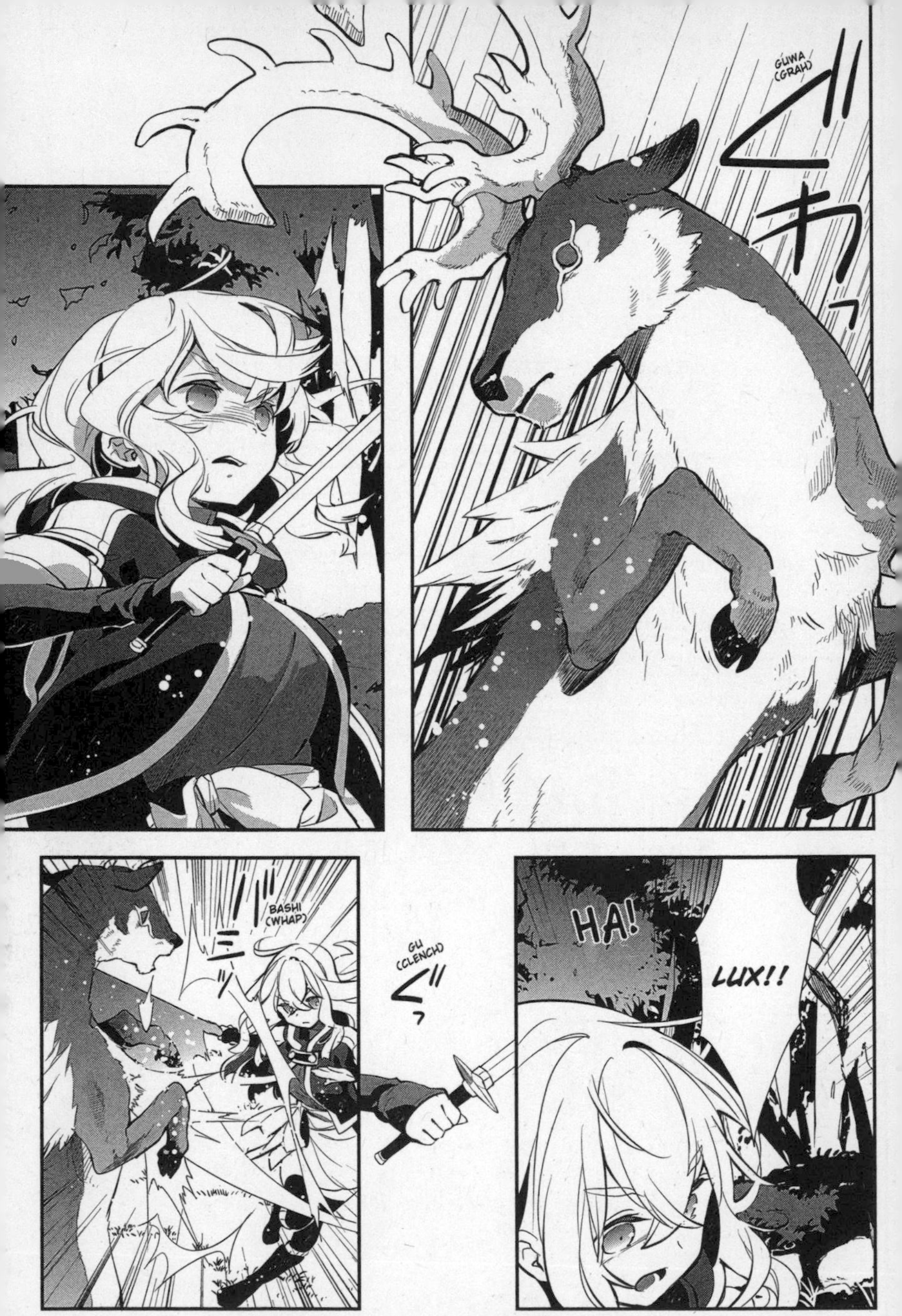
GUWA (GRAH)
HA!
LUX!!
BASHI (WHAP)
GU (CLENCH)

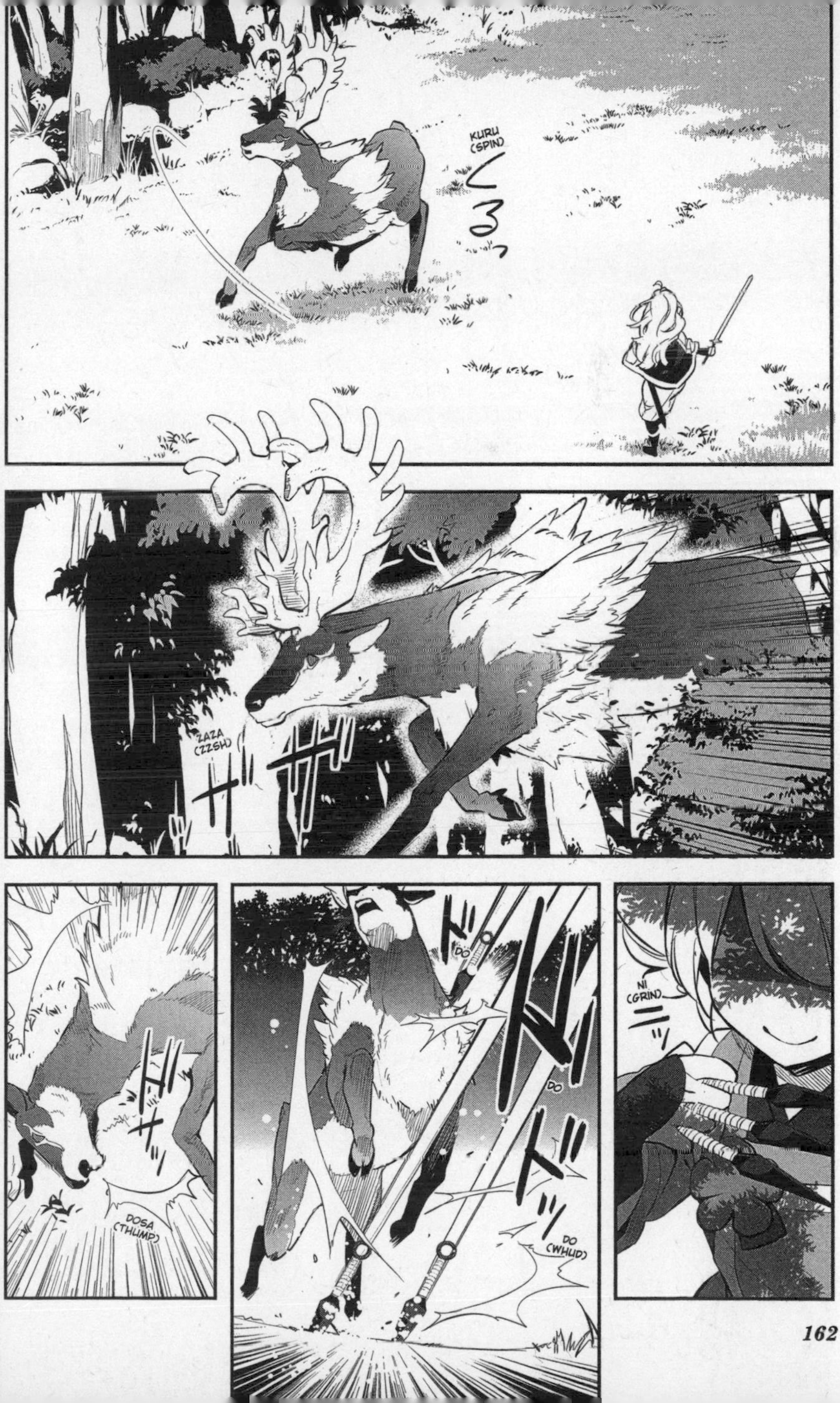
KURU (SPIN)
くるっ
ZAZA (ZZSH)
NI (GRIN)
DO
DO
DO (WHUD)
DOSA (THUMP)

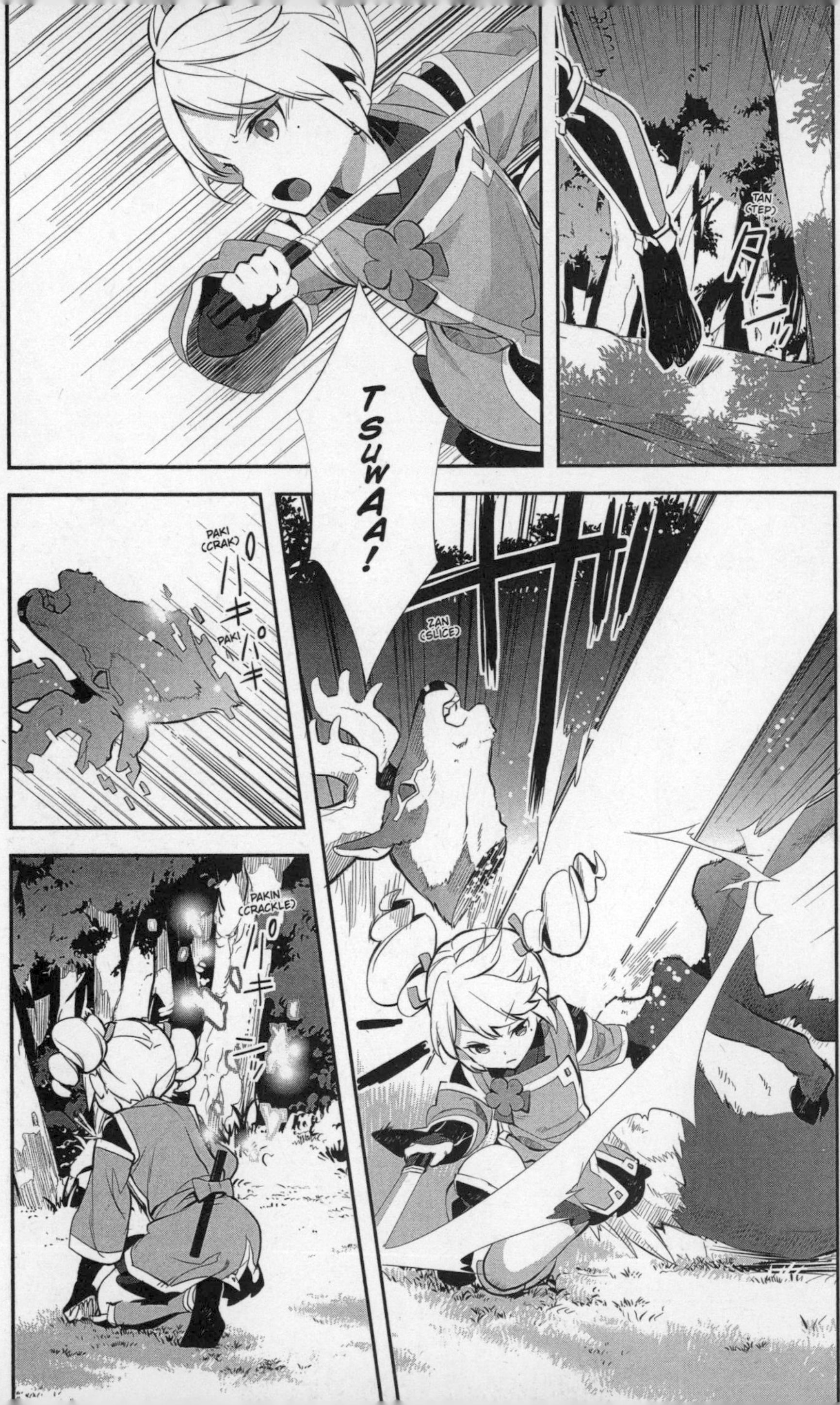
TAN (TEP)
TSUWAA!
ZAN (SLICE)
PAKI (CRAK)
PAKI
PAKIN (CRACKLE)

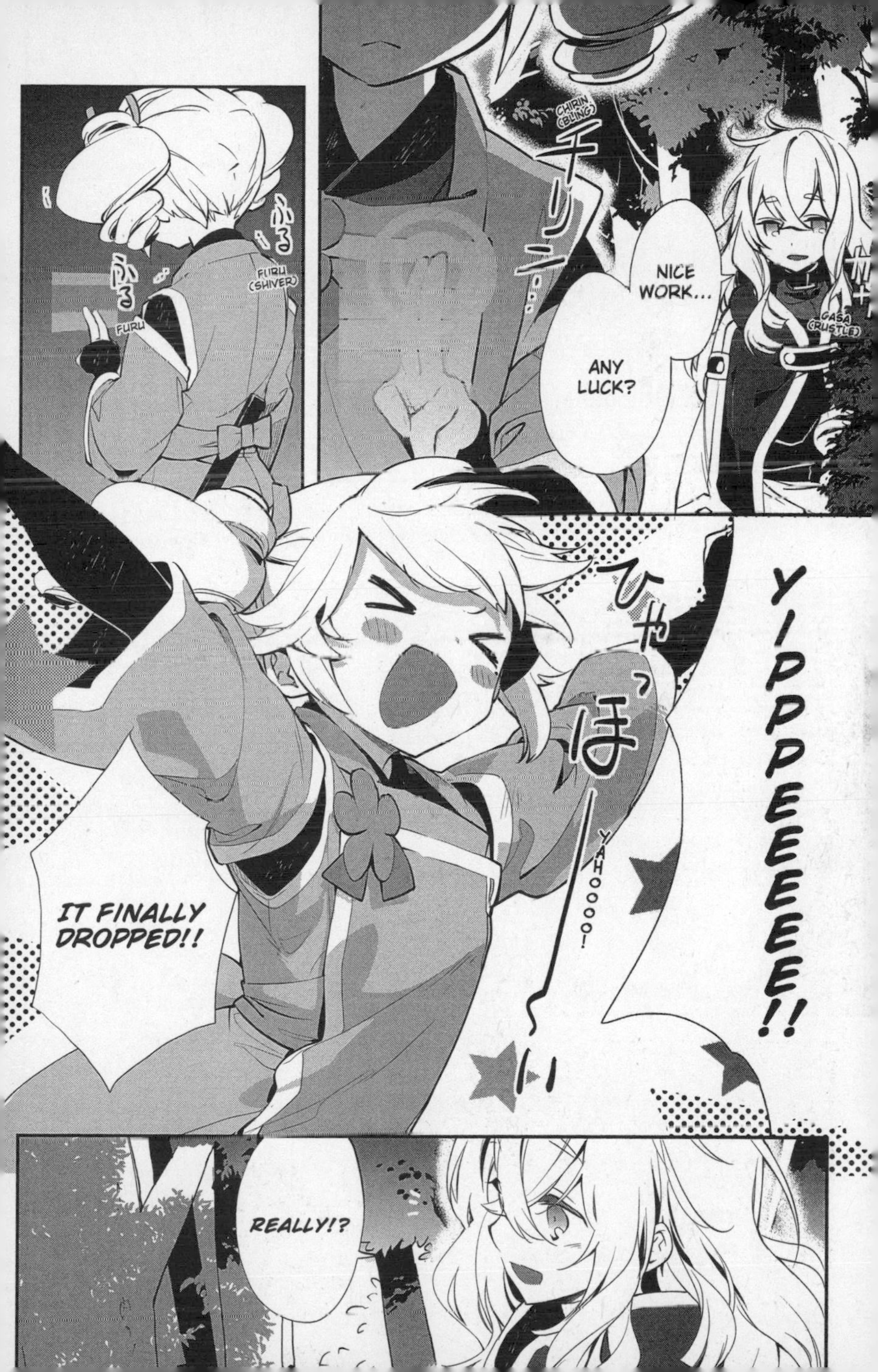
GASA (RUSTLE)
NICE WORK...
ANY LUCK?
チリーン…
CHIRIN (BLING)
ふる
ふる
FURU (SHIVER)
FURU
YIPPEEEEEE!!
ひゃっほー
YAHOOOOO!
IT FINALLY DROPPED!!
REALLY!?

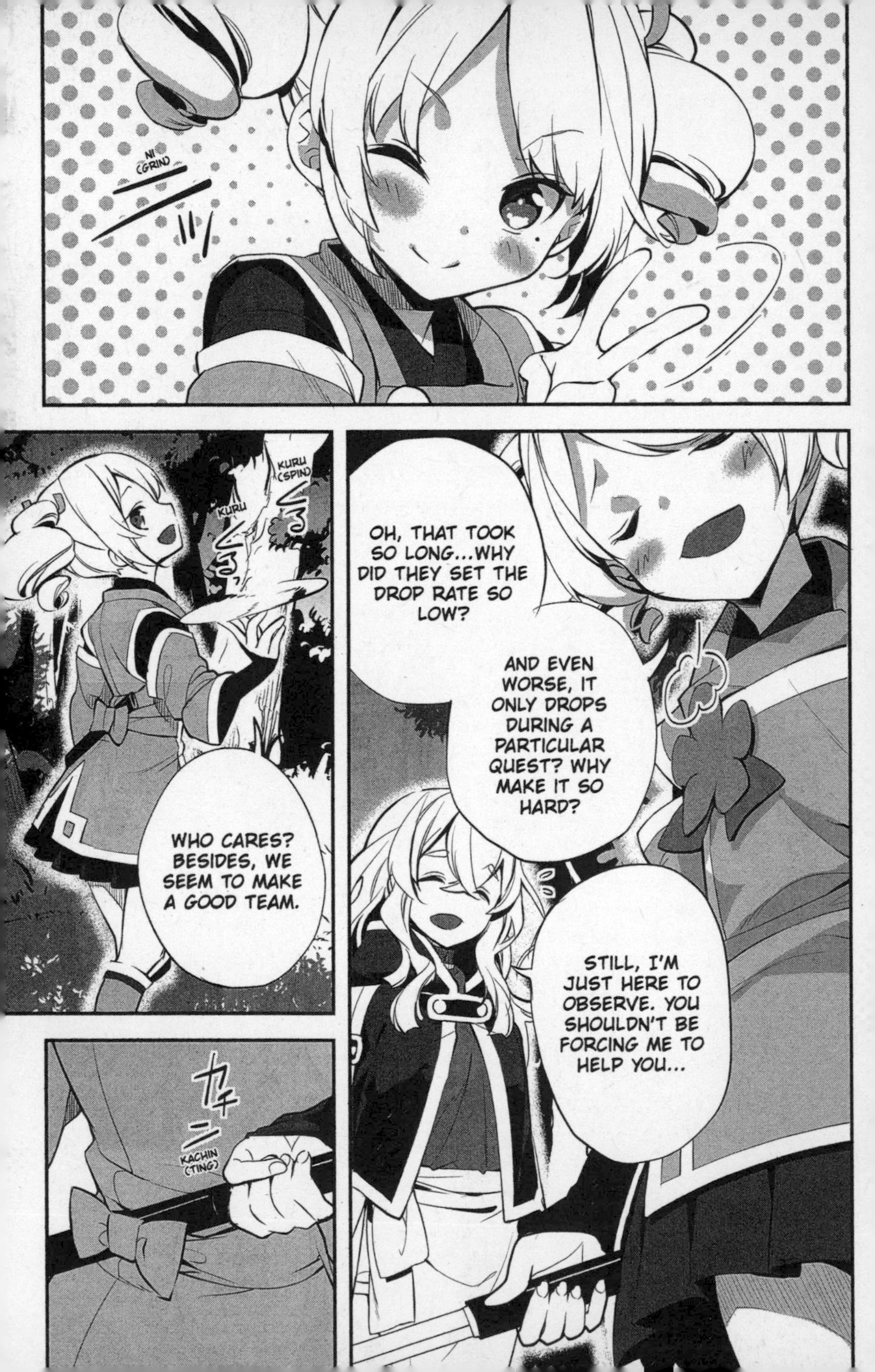
NI (GRIND)
OH, THAT TOOK SO LONG...WHY DID THEY SET THE DROP RATE SO LOW?
AND EVEN WORSE, IT ONLY DROPS DURING A PARTICULAR QUEST? WHY MAKE IT SO HARD?
STILL, I'M JUST HERE TO OBSERVE. YOU SHOULDN'T BE FORCING ME TO HELP YOU...
KURU (SPIN)
KURU
WHO CARES? BESIDES, WE SEEM TO MAKE A GOOD TEAM.
KACHIN (TING)

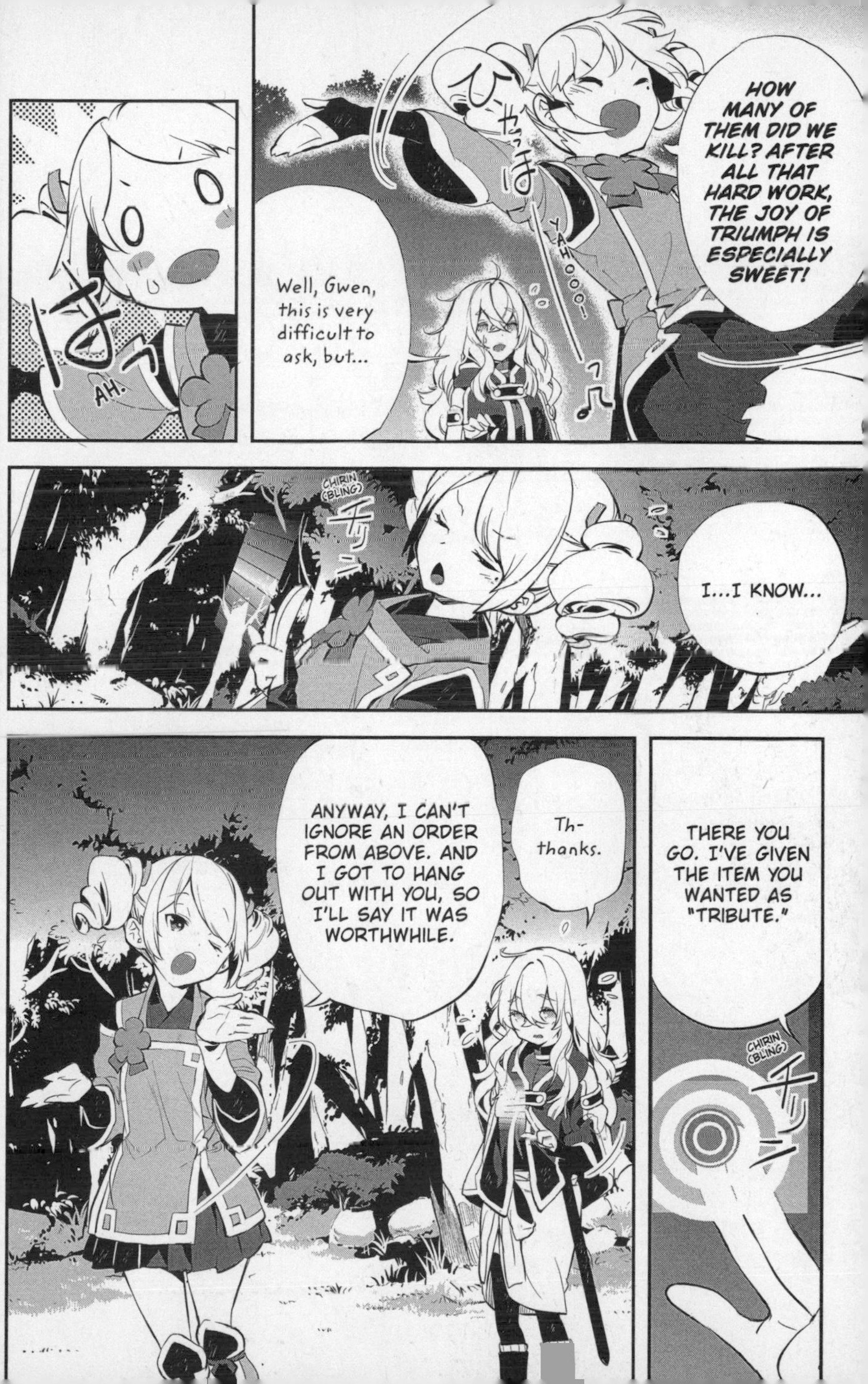
HOW MANY OF THEM DID WE KILL? AFTER ALL THAT HARD WORK, THE JOY OF TRIUMPH IS ESPECIALLY SWEET!
YAHOOOO!
Well, Gwen, this is very difficult to ask, but...
AH.
CHIRIN (BLING)
I...I KNOW...
THERE YOU GO. I'VE GIVEN THE ITEM YOU WANTED AS "TRIBUTE."
CHIRIN (BLING)
ANYWAY, I CAN'T IGNORE AN ORDER FROM ABOVE. AND I GOT TO HANG OUT WITH YOU, SO I'LL SAY IT WAS WORTHWHILE.
Th-thanks.

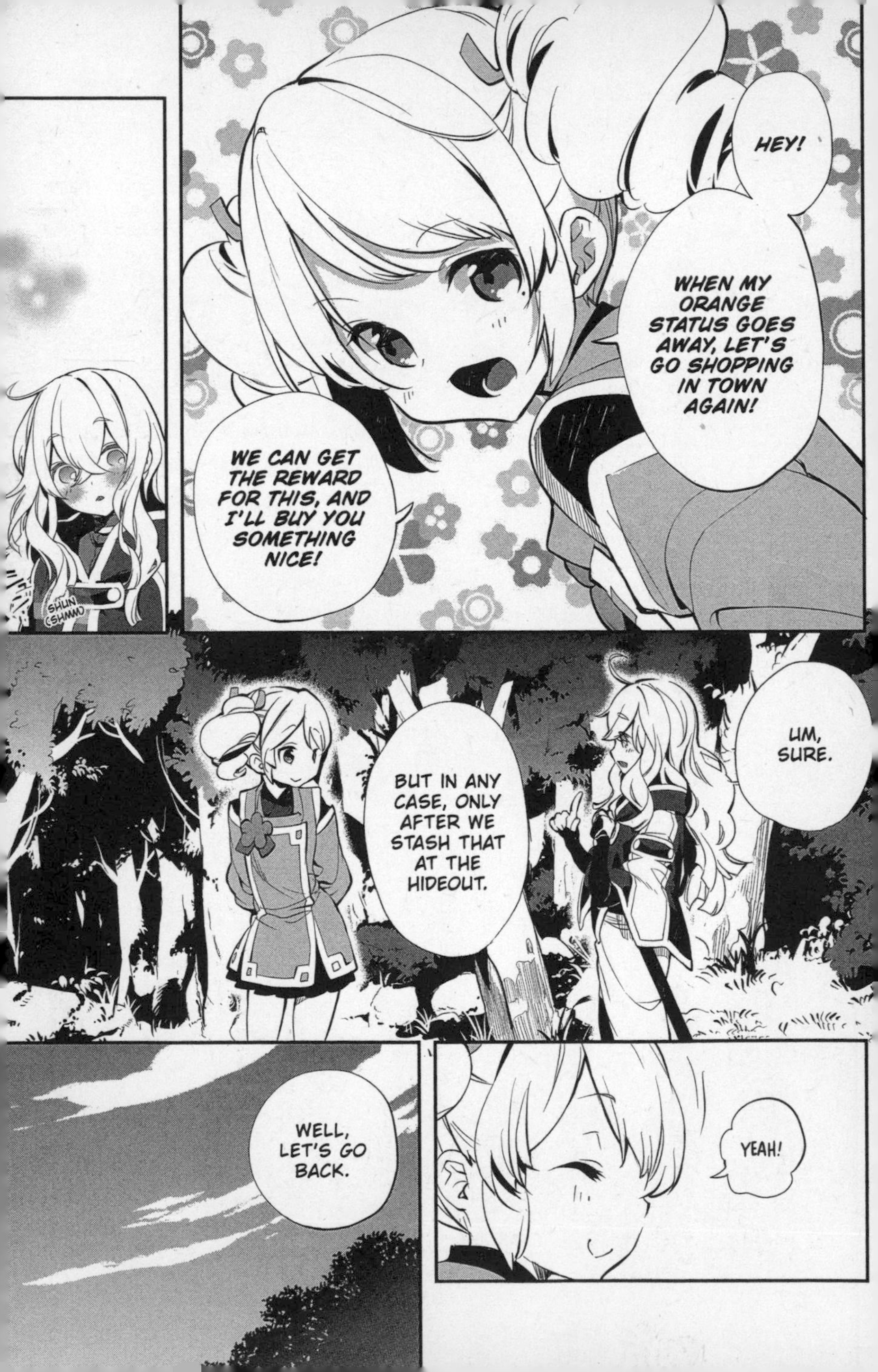
HEY!
WHEN MY ORANGE STATUS GOES AWAY, LET'S GO SHOPPING IN TOWN AGAIN!
WE CAN GET THE REWARD FOR THIS, AND I'LL BUY YOU SOMETHING NICE!
SHUN (SHMM)
UM, SURE.
BUT IN ANY CASE, ONLY AFTER WE STASH THAT AT THE HIDEOUT.
YEAH!
WELL, LET'S GO BACK.

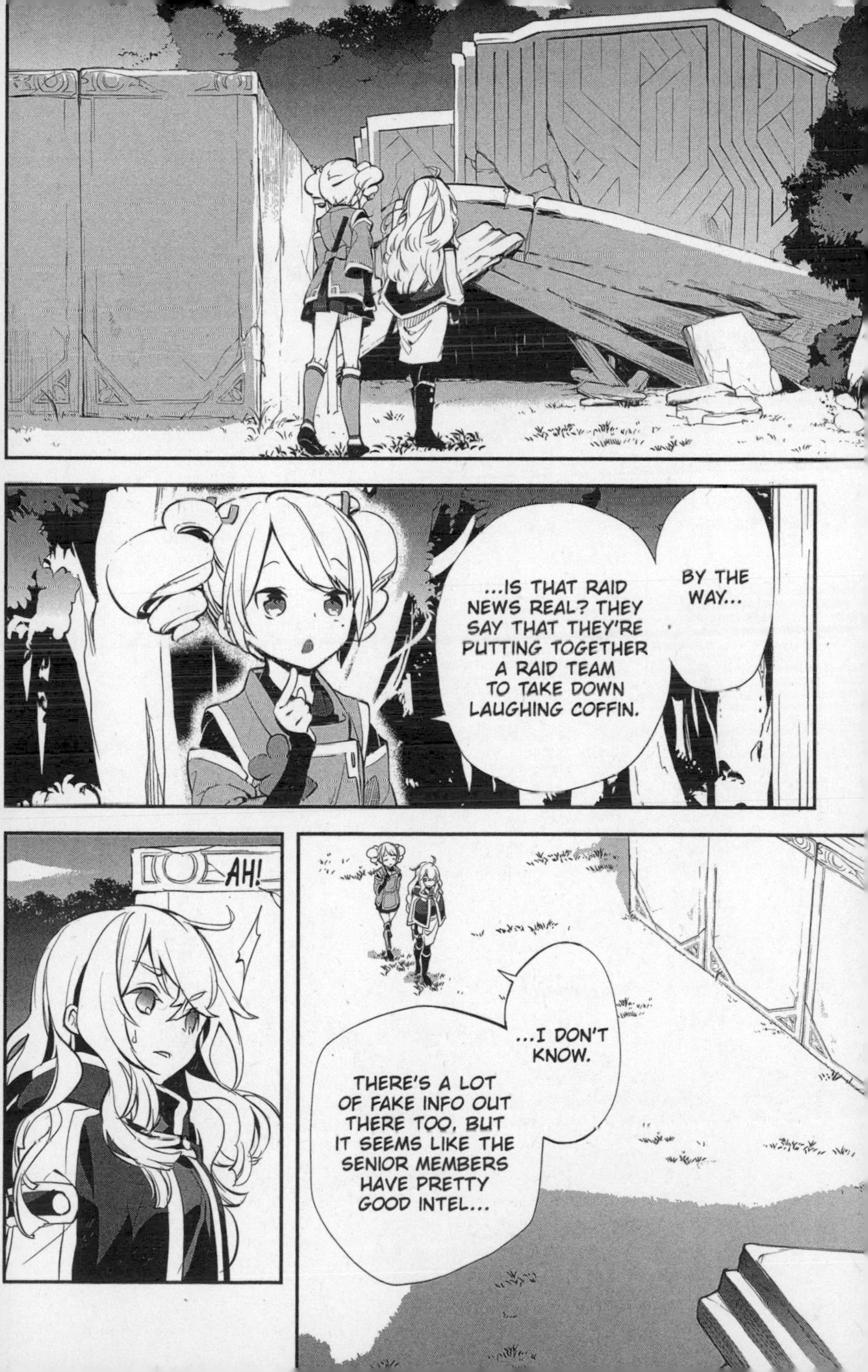
BY THE WAY...
...IS THAT RAID NEWS REAL? THEY SAY THAT THEY'RE PUTTING TOGETHER A RAID TEAM TO TAKE DOWN LAUGHING COFFIN.
...I DON'T KNOW.
THERE'S A LOT OF FAKE INFO OUT THERE TOO, BUT IT SEEMS LIKE THE SENIOR MEMBERS HAVE PRETTY GOOD INTEL...
AH!

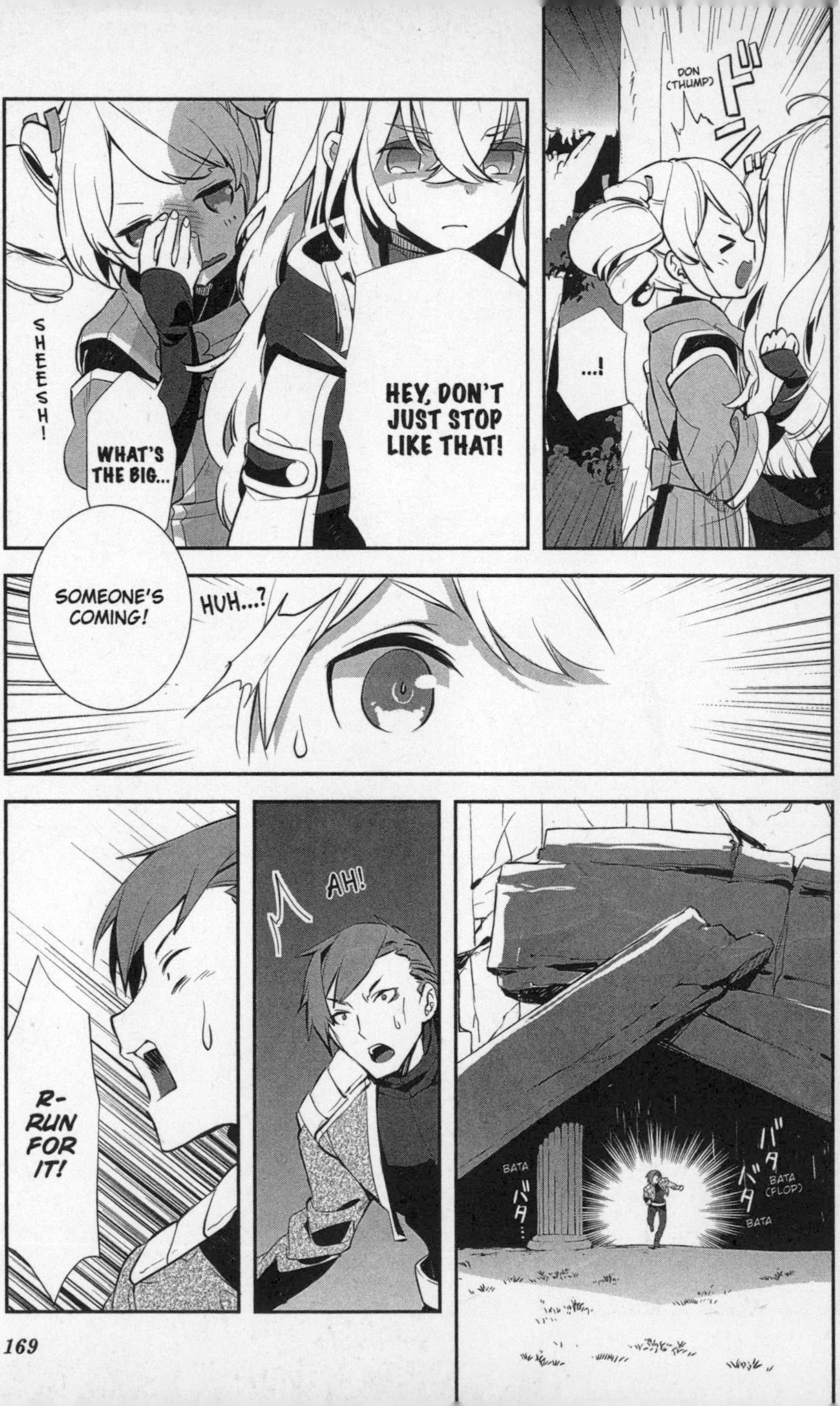
ドン
DON (THUMP)
...!
HEY, DON'T JUST STOP LIKE THAT!
WHAT'S THE BIG...
SHEESH!
HUH...?
SOMEONE'S COMING!
バタバタ
BATA
BATA (FLOP)
BATA
BATA
バタ...
AH!
R-RUN FOR IT!

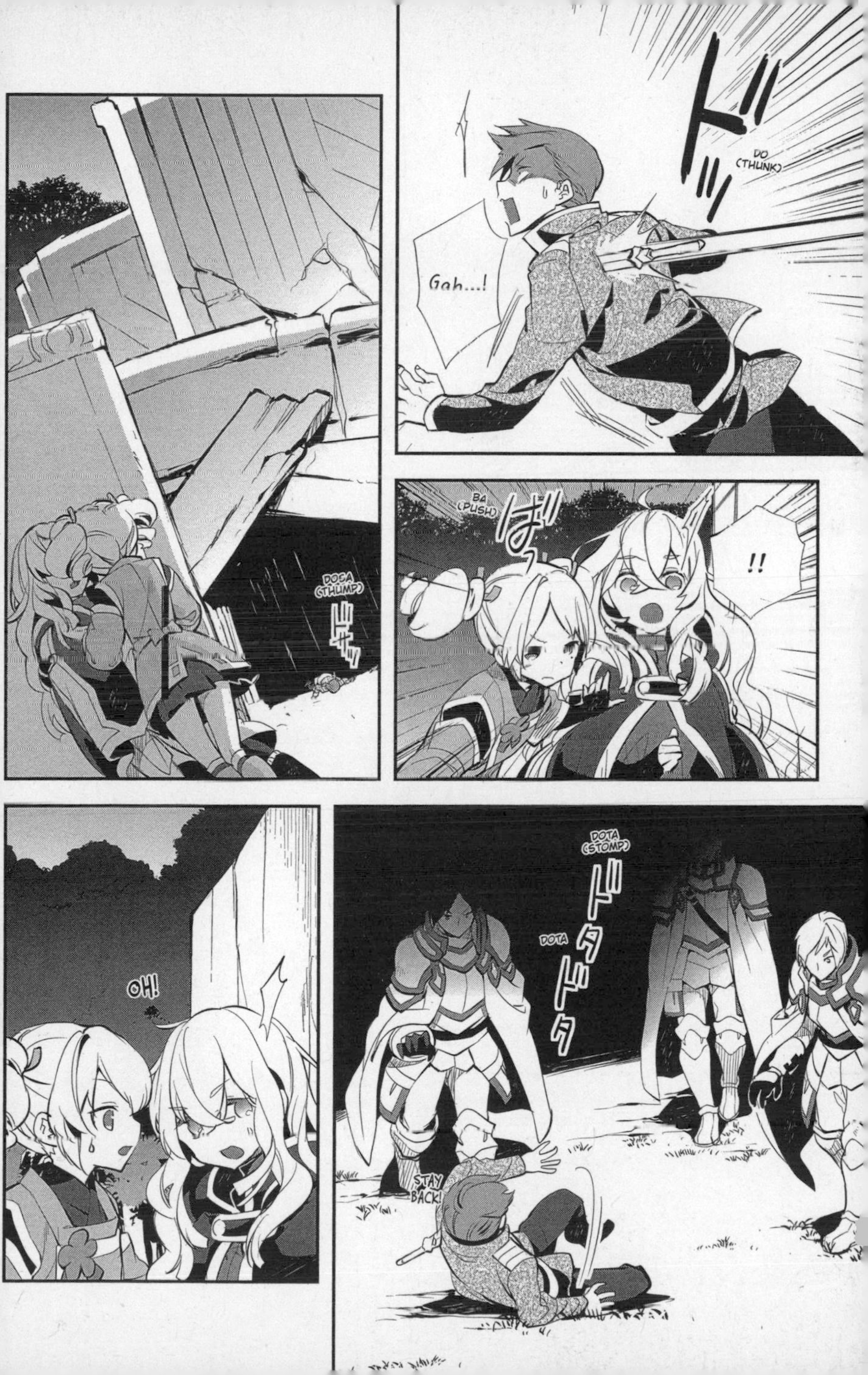
ドッ
DO (THUNK)
Gah...!
ばっ
BA (PUSH)
!!
DOGA (THUMP)
DOTA (STOMP)
ドタドタ
DOTA
STAY BACK!
OH!

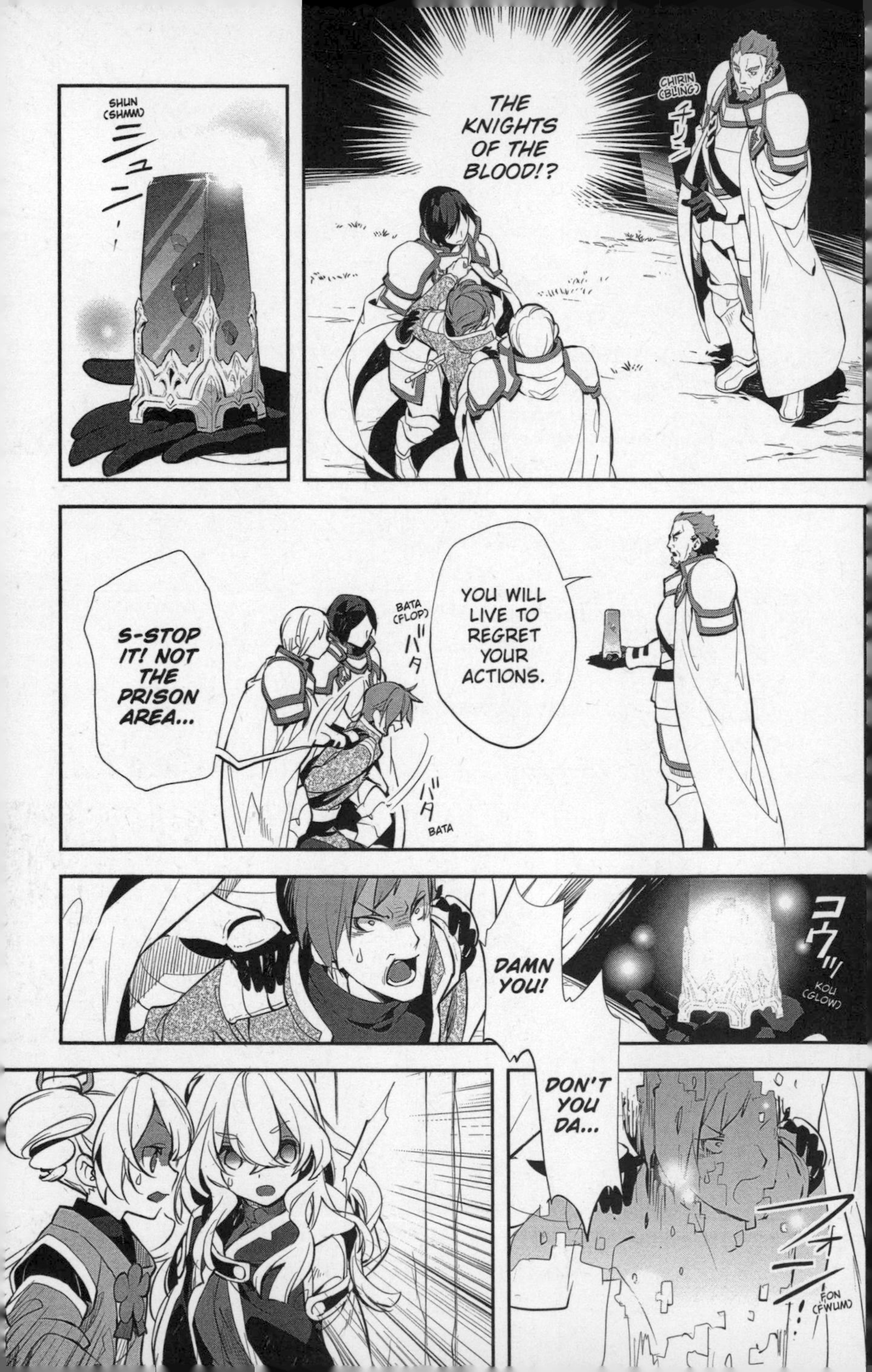
CHIRIN (BLING)
THE KNIGHTS OF THE BLOOD!?
SHUN (SHMM)
YOU WILL LIVE TO REGRET YOUR ACTIONS.
BATA (FLOP)
BATA
S-STOP IT! NOT THE PRISON AREA...
KOU (GLOW)
DAMN YOU!
DON'T YOU DA...
FON (FWUM)

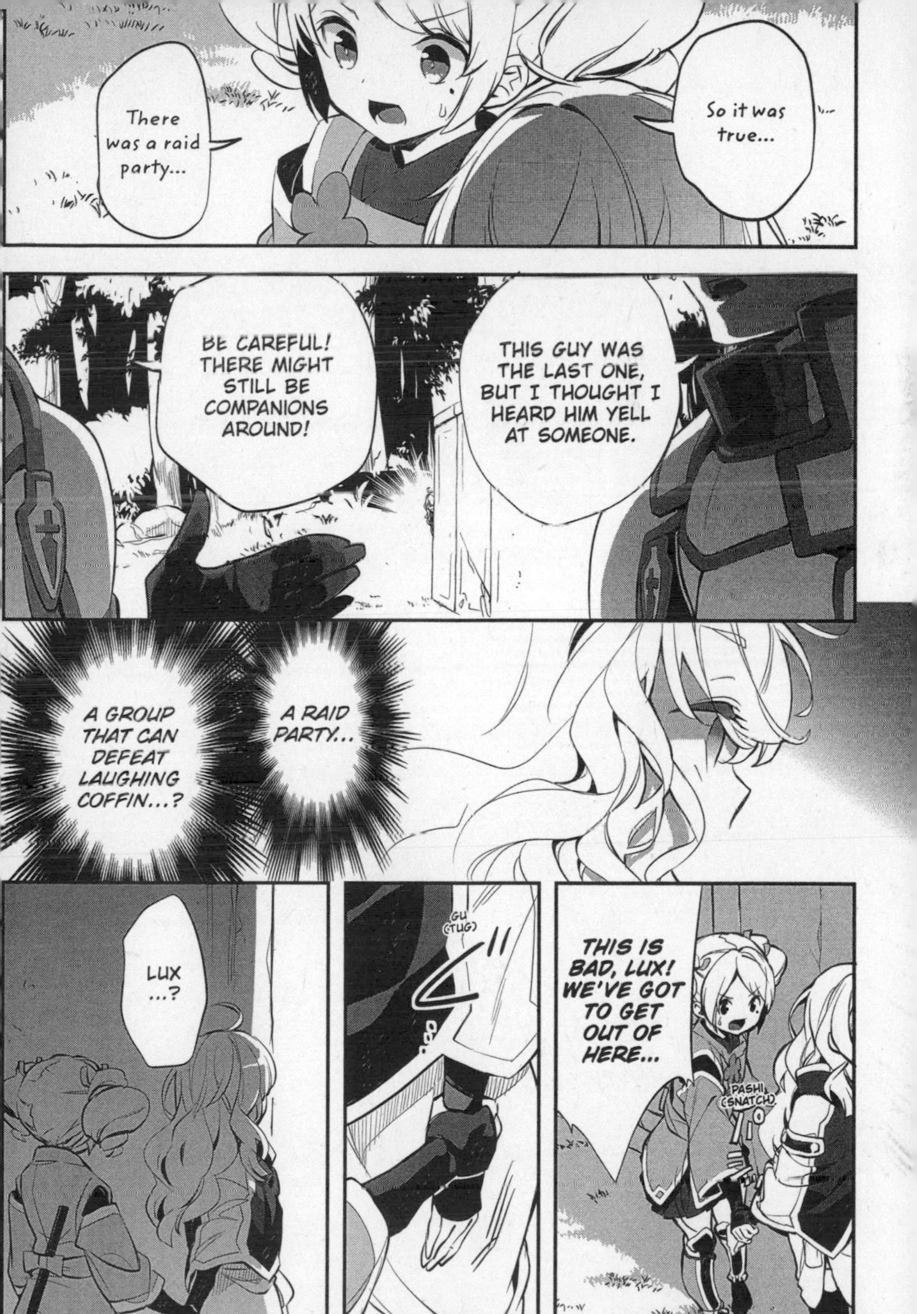
So it was true...
There was a raid party...
THIS GUY WAS THE LAST ONE, BUT I THOUGHT I HEARD HIM YELL AT SOMEONE.
BE CAREFUL! THERE MIGHT STILL BE COMPANIONS AROUND!
A RAID PARTY...
A GROUP THAT CAN DEFEAT LAUGHING COFFIN...?
THIS IS BAD, LUX! WE'VE GOT TO GET OUT OF HERE...
PASHI (SNATCH)
GU (TUG)
LUX ...?

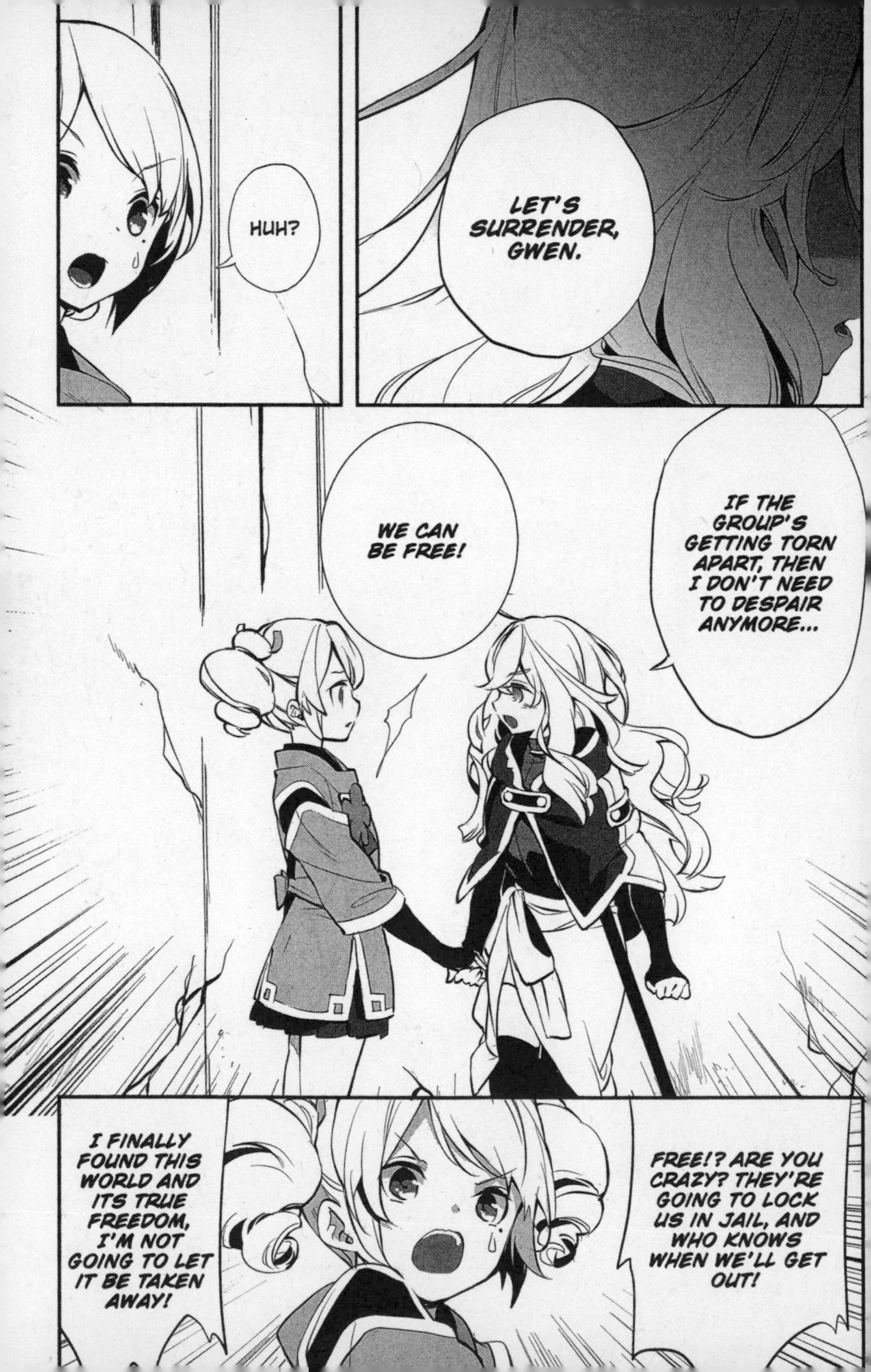
LET'S SURRENDER, GWEN.
HUH?
IF THE GROUP'S GETTING TORN APART, THEN I DON'T NEED TO DESPAIR ANYMORE...
WE CAN BE FREE!
FREE!? ARE YOU CRAZY? THEY'RE GOING TO LOCK US IN JAIL, AND WHO KNOWS WHEN WE'LL GET OUT!
I FINALLY FOUND THIS WORLD AND ITS TRUE FREEDOM, I'M NOT GOING TO LET IT BE TAKEN AWAY!

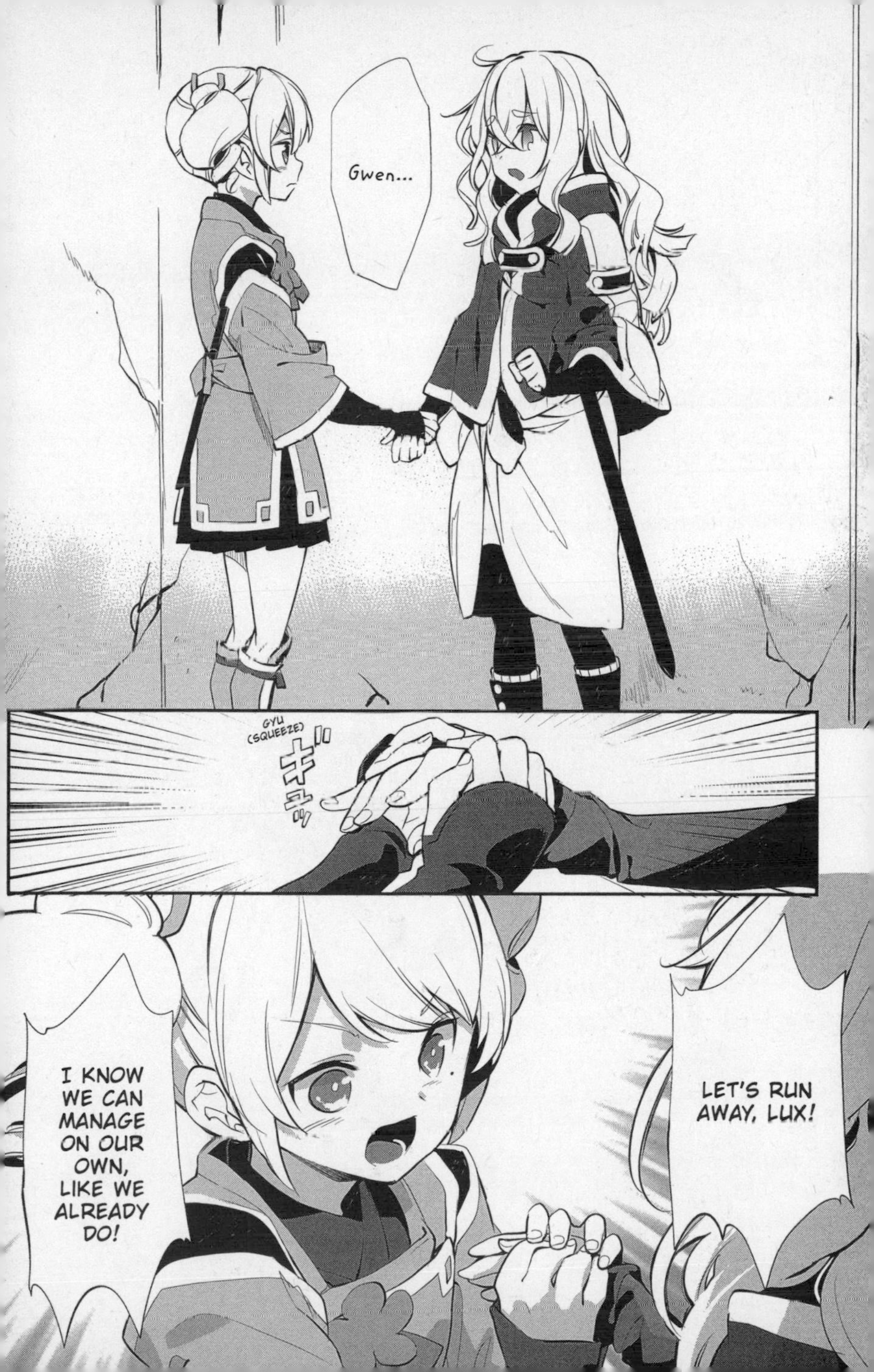
Gwen...
GYU (SQUEEZE)
LET'S RUN AWAY, LUX!
I KNOW WE CAN MANAGE ON OUR OWN, LIKE WE ALREADY DO!

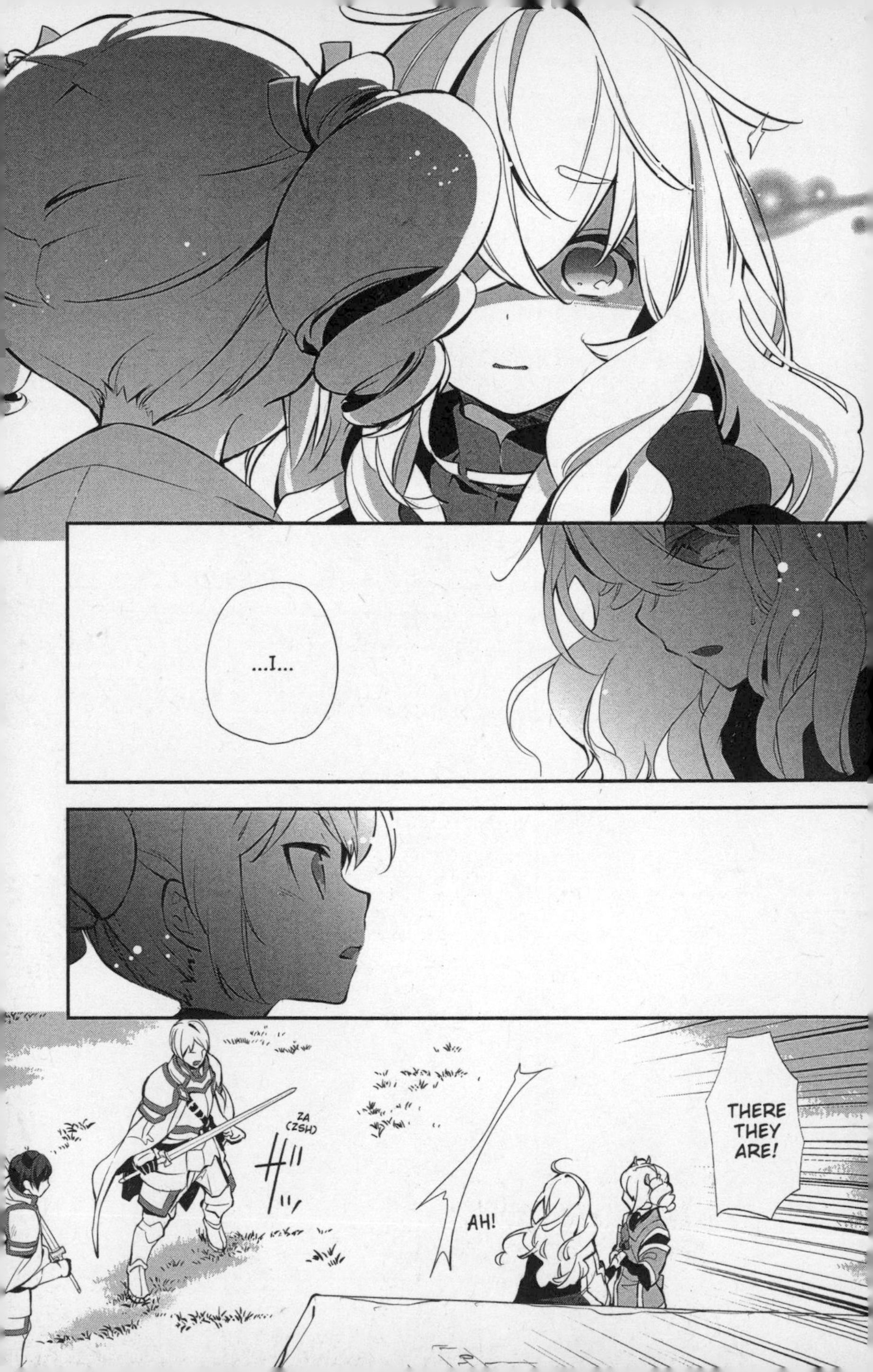
...I...
THERE THEY ARE!
AH!
ZA (ZSH)

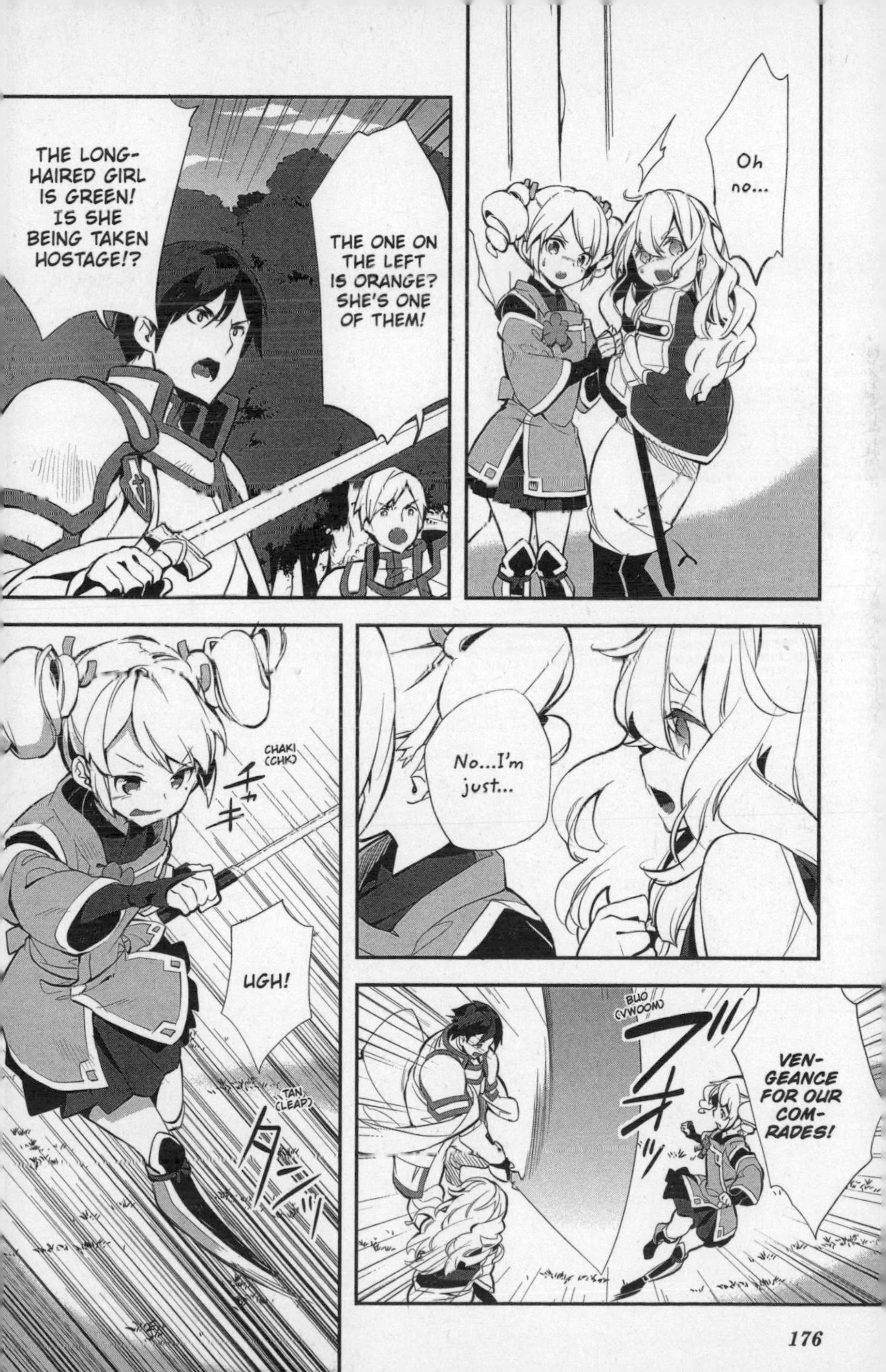
Oh no...
THE ONE ON THE LEFT IS ORANGE? SHE'S ONE OF THEM!
THE LONG-HAIRED GIRL IS GREEN! IS SHE BEING TAKEN HOSTAGE!?
No...I'm just...
BUO (VWOOM)
VENGEANCE FOR OUR COMRADES!
CHAKI (CHK)
UGH!
TAN (LEAP)

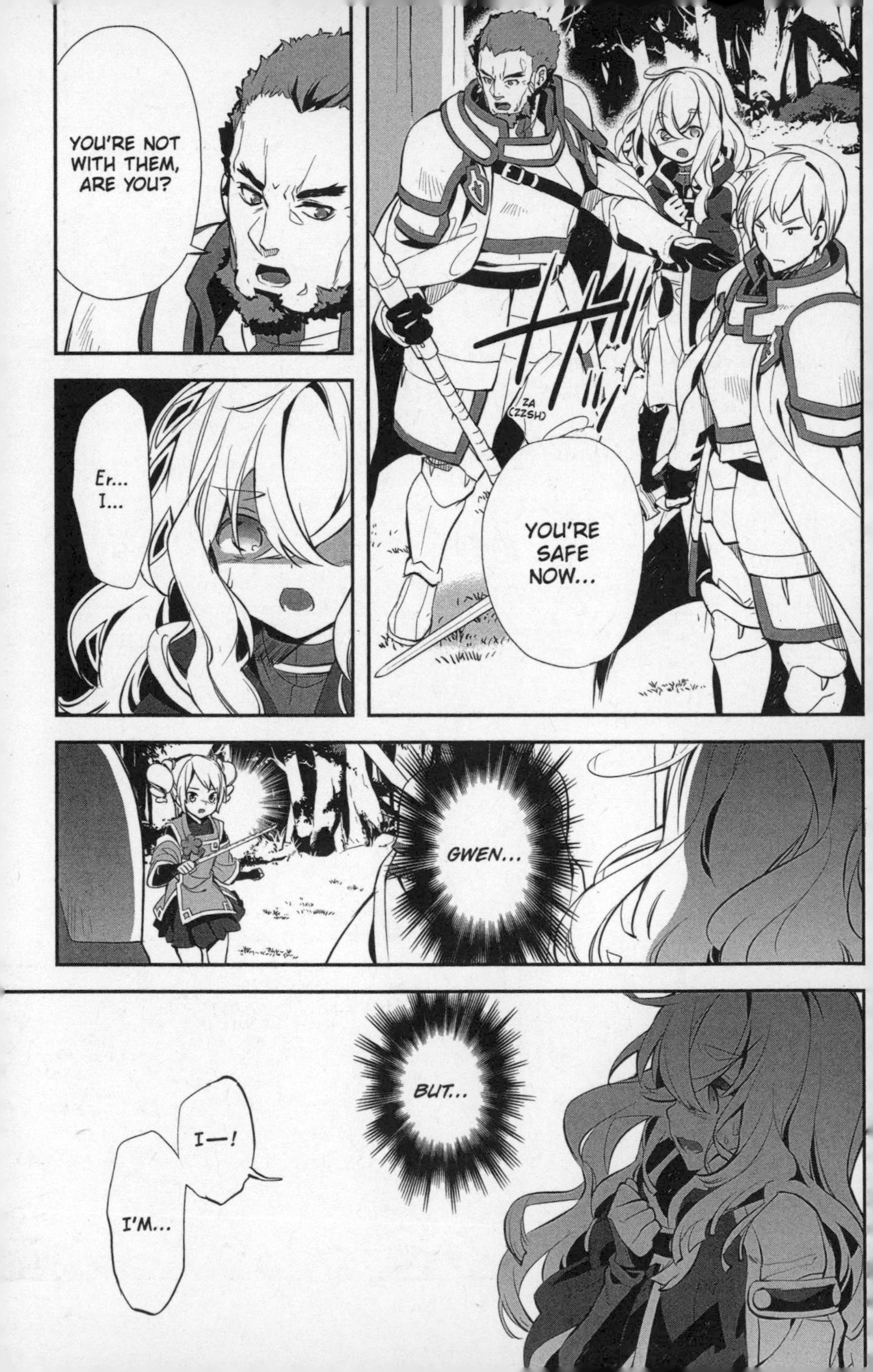
ZA (ZZSH)
YOU'RE SAFE NOW...
YOU'RE NOT WITH THEM, ARE YOU?
Er... I...
GWEN...
BUT...
I—!
I'M...

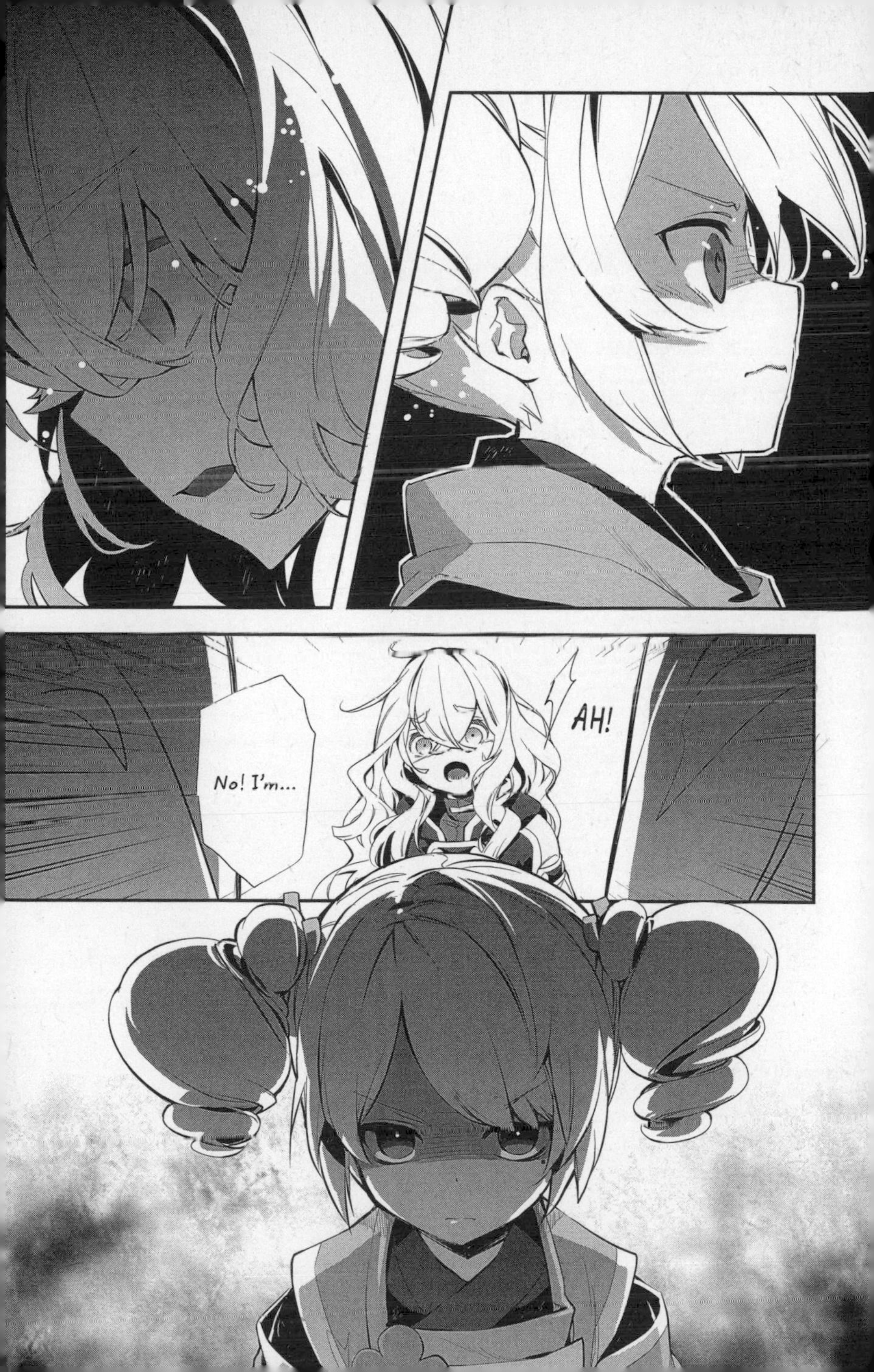
AH!
No! I'm...

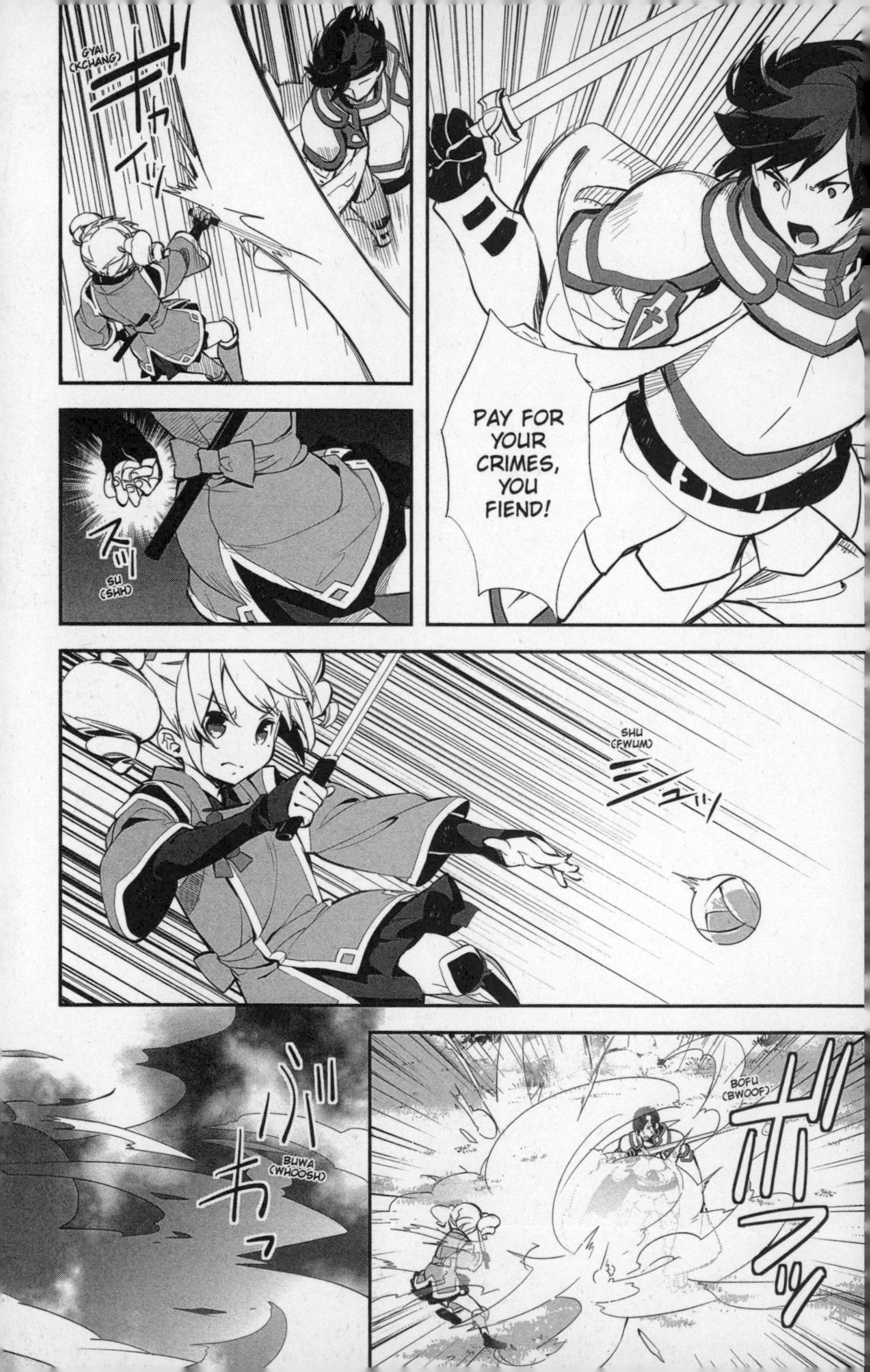
PAY FOR YOUR CRIMES, YOU FIEND!
GYAI (KCHANG)
SU (SHH)
SHU (FWUM)
BOFU (BWOOF)
BUWA (WHOOSH)

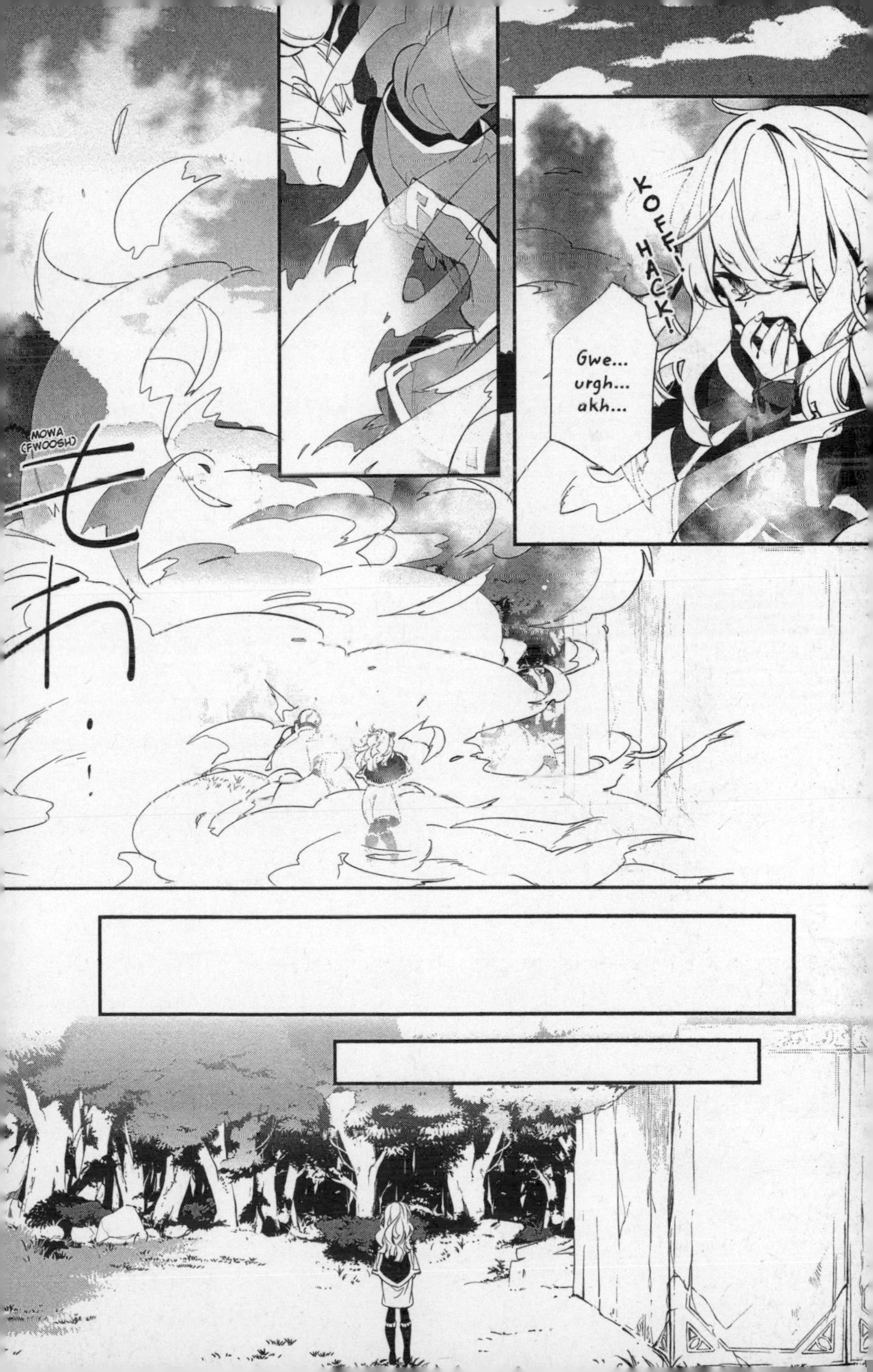
KOFF! HACK!
Gwe... urgh... akh...
MOWA (FWOOSH)
もわ…!

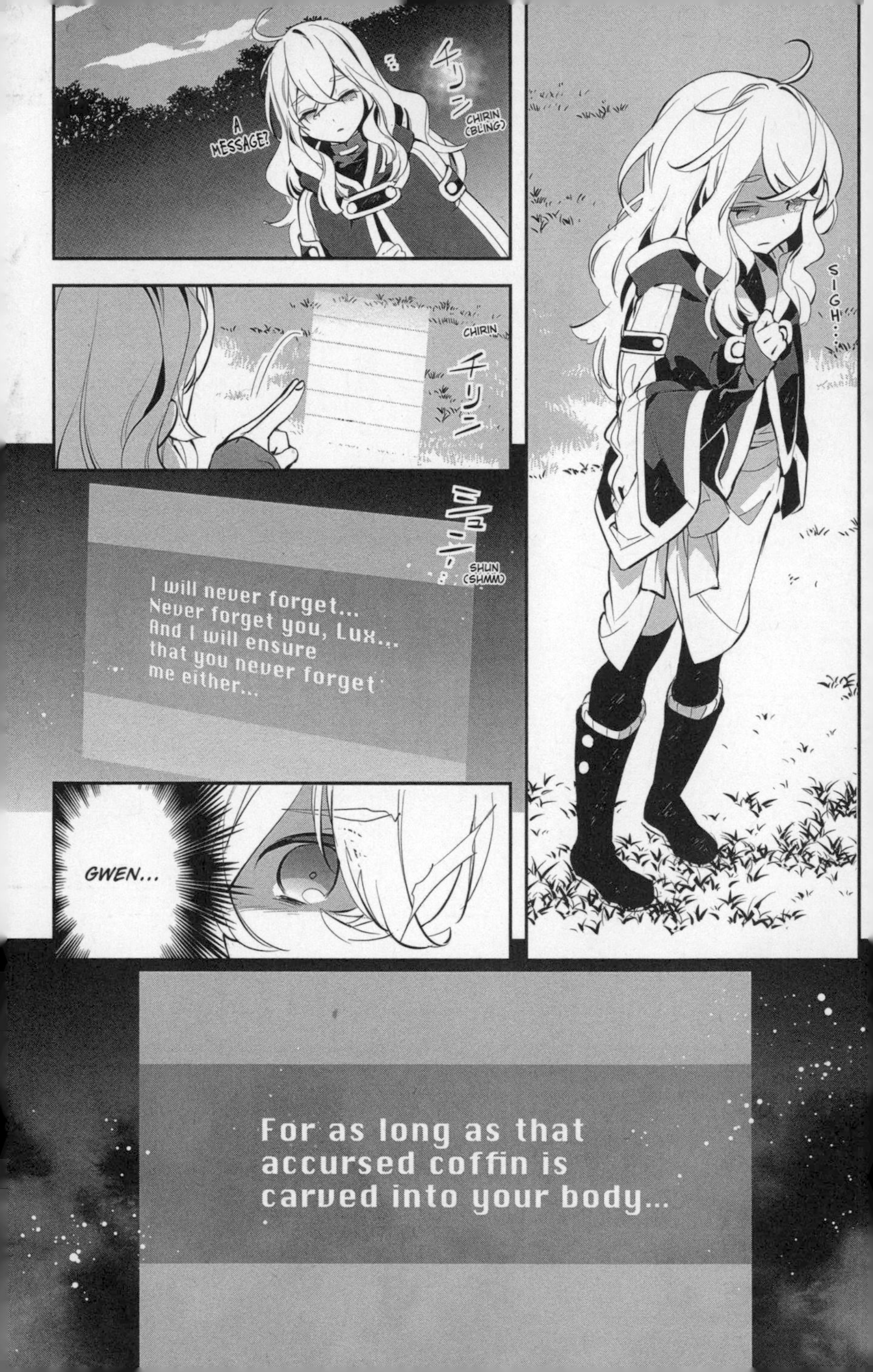
SIGH...
A MESSAGE?
チリン
CHIRIN (BLING)
CHIRIN
チリン
シュン
SHUN (SHMM)
I will never forget...
Never forget you, Lux...
And I will ensure
that you never forget
me either...
GWEN...
For as long as that
accursed coffin is
carved into your body...

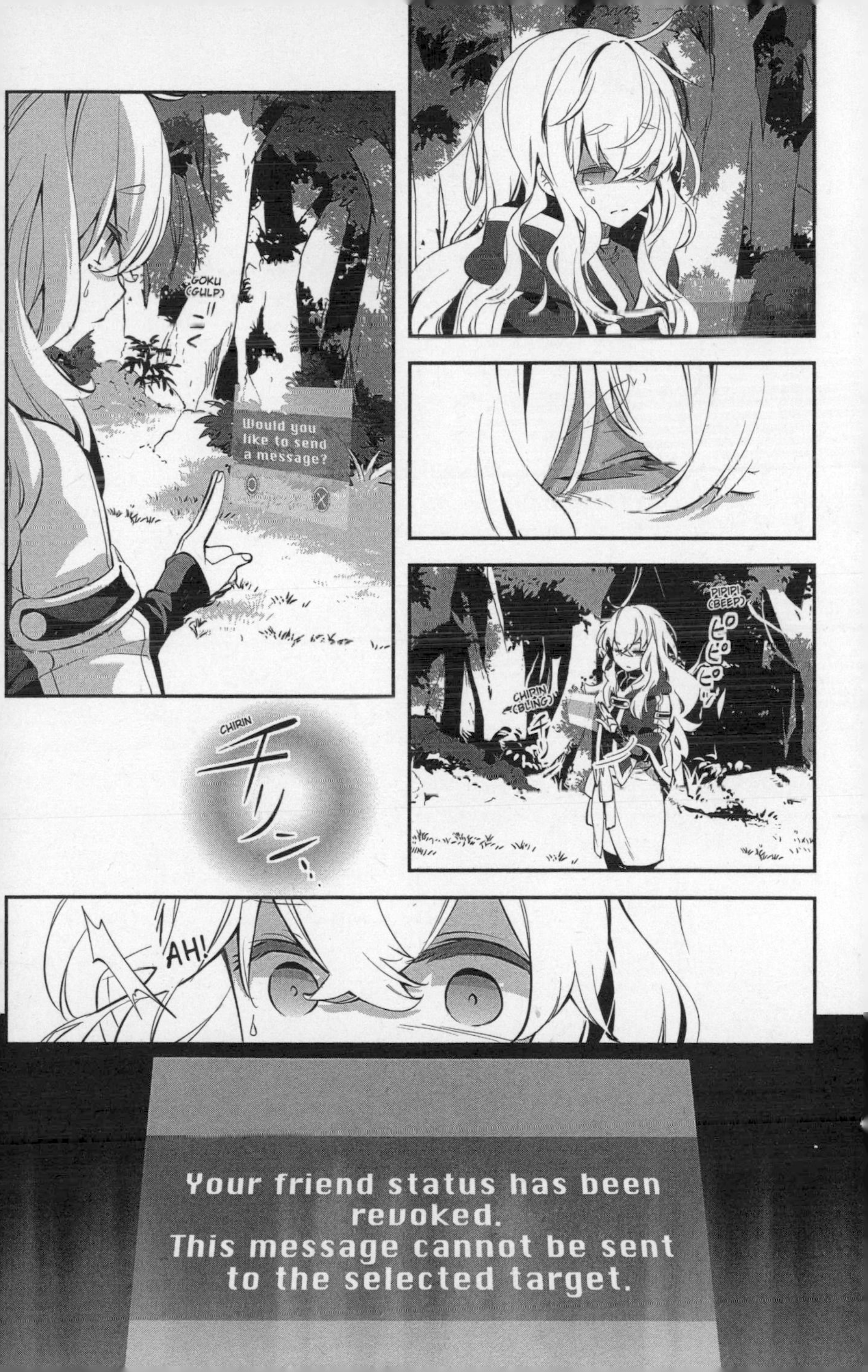
PIPIPI (BEEP)
CHIRIN (BLING)
GOKU (GULP)
Would you like to send a message?
CHIRIN
AH!
Your friend status has been revoked.
This message cannot be sent to the selected target.

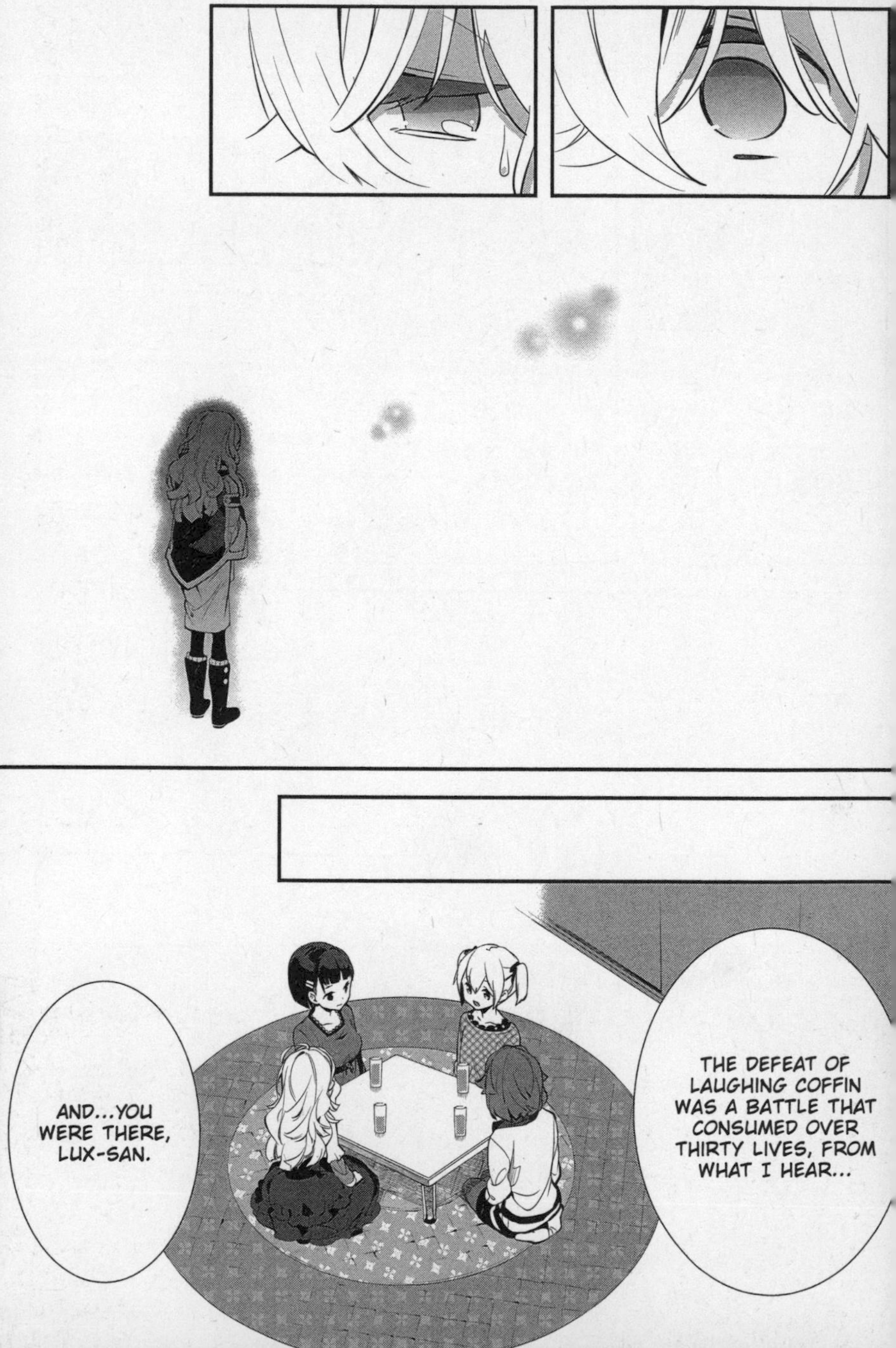
THE DEFEAT OF LAUGHING COFFIN WAS A BATTLE THAT CONSUMED OVER THIRTY LIVES, FROM WHAT I HEAR...
AND...YOU WERE THERE, LUX-SAN.

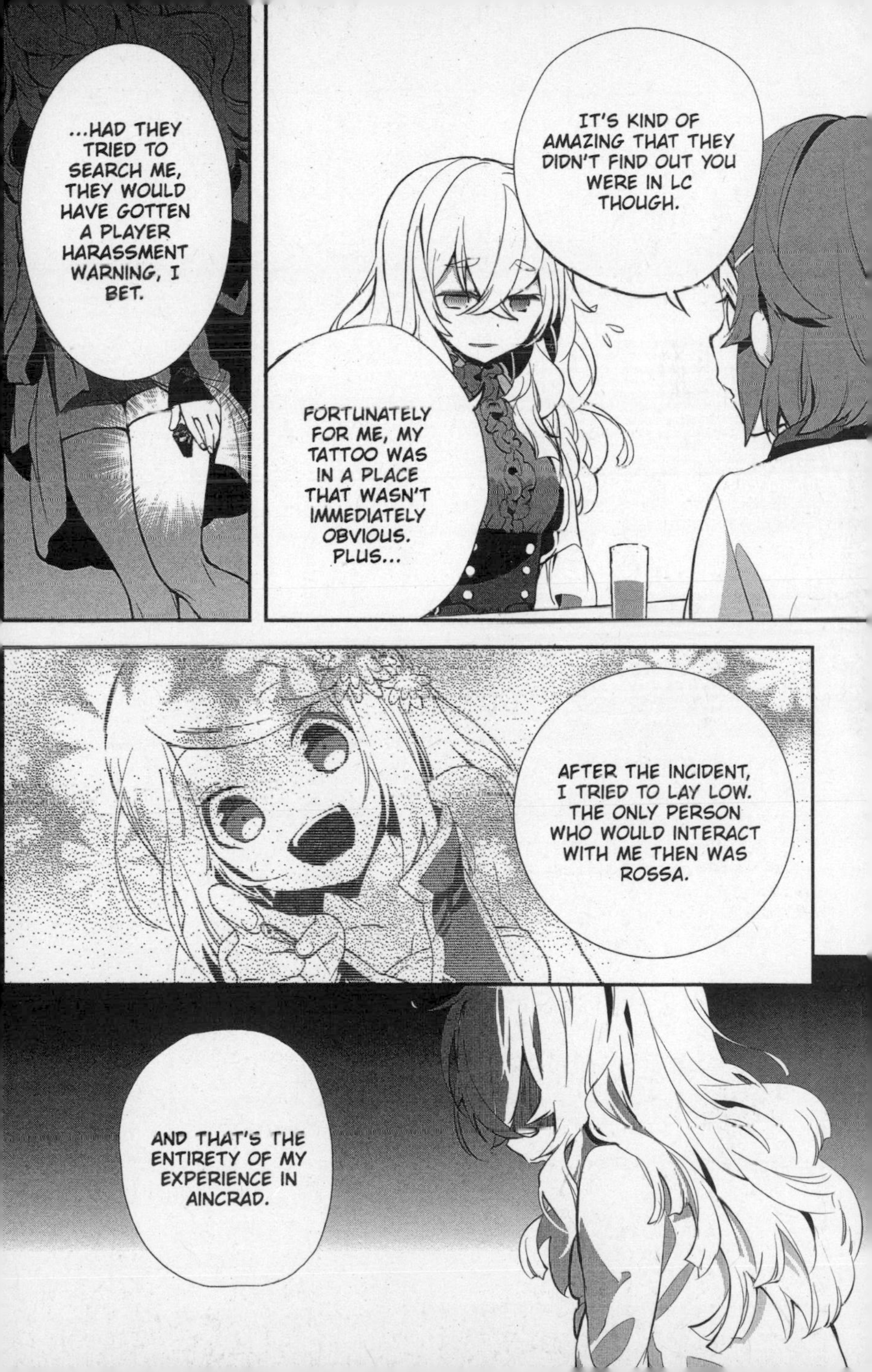
IT'S KIND OF AMAZING THAT THEY DIDN'T FIND OUT YOU WERE IN LC THOUGH.
FORTUNATELY FOR ME, MY TATTOO WAS IN A PLACE THAT WASN'T IMMEDIATELY OBVIOUS. PLUS...
...HAD THEY TRIED TO SEARCH ME, THEY WOULD HAVE GOTTEN A PLAYER HARASSMENT WARNING, I BET.
AFTER THE INCIDENT, I TRIED TO LAY LOW. THE ONLY PERSON WHO WOULD INTERACT WITH ME THEN WAS ROSSA.
AND THAT'S THE ENTIRETY OF MY EXPERIENCE IN AINCRAD.

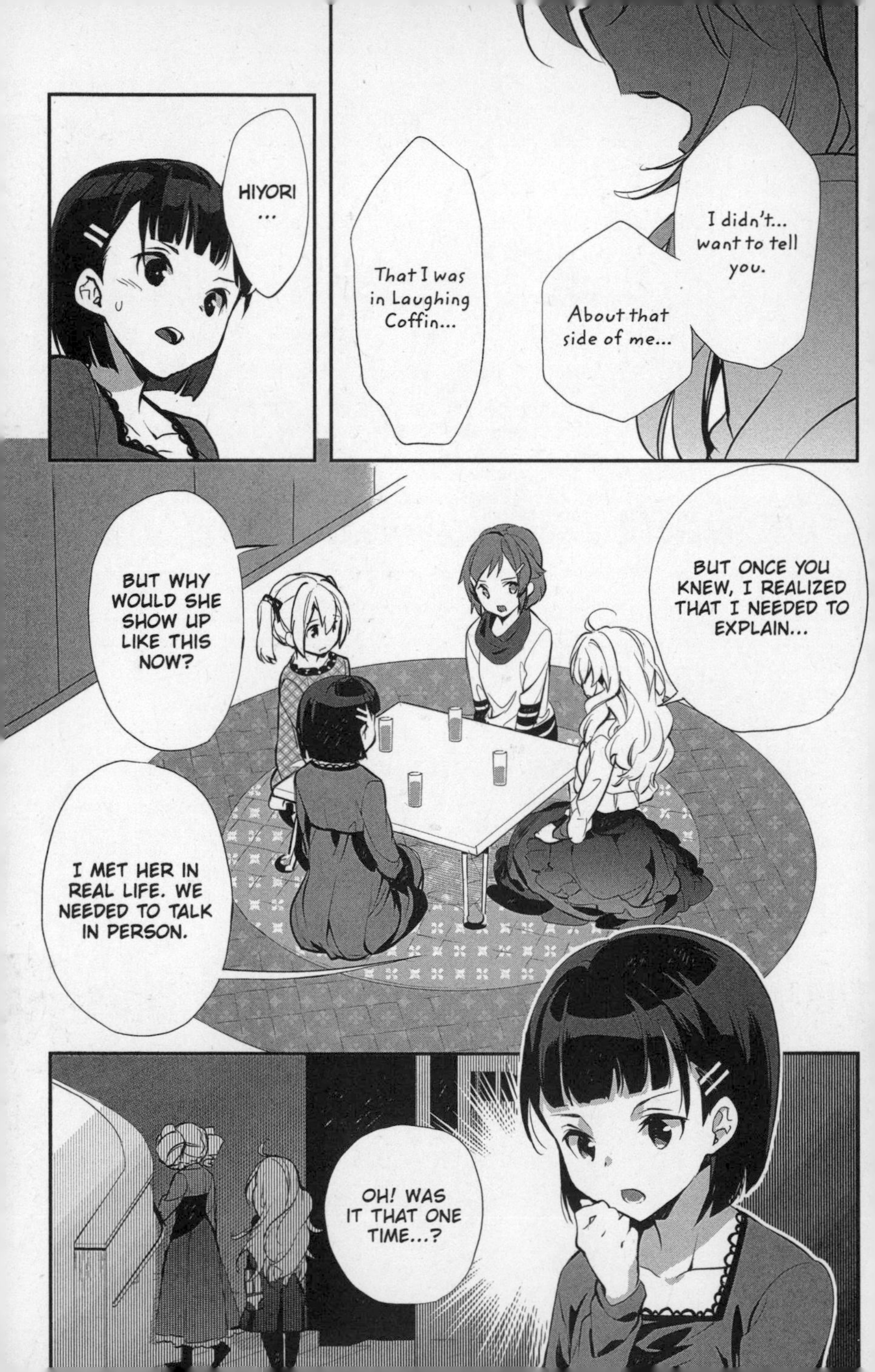
I didn't... want to tell you.
About that side of me...
That I was in Laughing Coffin...
HIYORI ...
BUT ONCE YOU KNEW, I REALIZED THAT I NEEDED TO EXPLAIN...
BUT WHY WOULD SHE SHOW UP LIKE THIS NOW?
I MET HER IN REAL LIFE. WE NEEDED TO TALK IN PERSON.
OH! WAS IT THAT ONE TIME...?

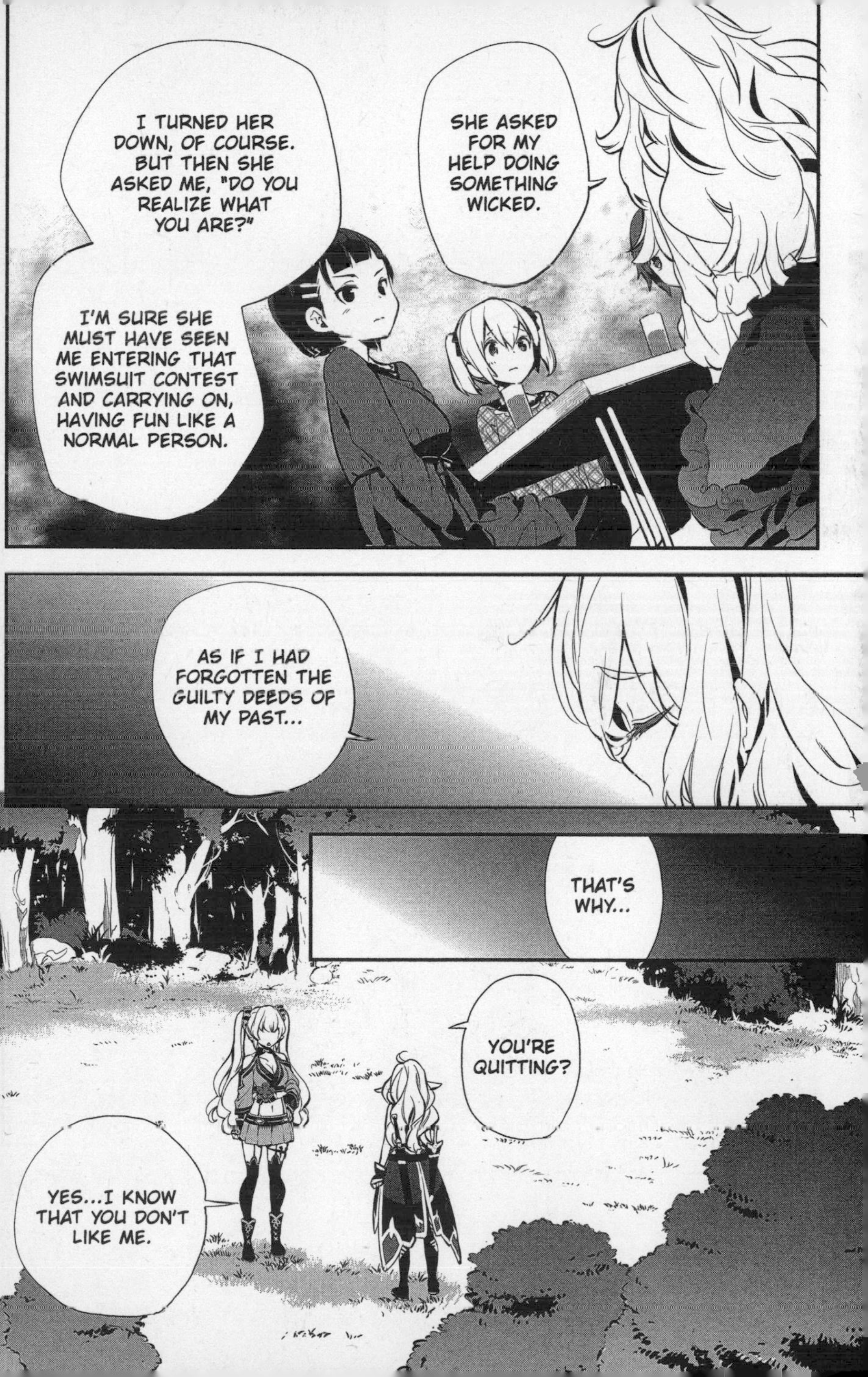
SHE ASKED FOR MY HELP DOING SOMETHING WICKED.
I TURNED HER DOWN, OF COURSE. BUT THEN SHE ASKED ME, "DO YOU REALIZE WHAT YOU ARE?"
I'M SURE SHE MUST HAVE SEEN ME ENTERING THAT SWIMSUIT CONTEST AND CARRYING ON, HAVING FUN LIKE A NORMAL PERSON.
AS IF I HAD FORGOTTEN THE GUILTY DEEDS OF MY PAST...
THAT'S WHY...
YOU'RE QUITTING?
YES...I KNOW THAT YOU DON'T LIKE ME.

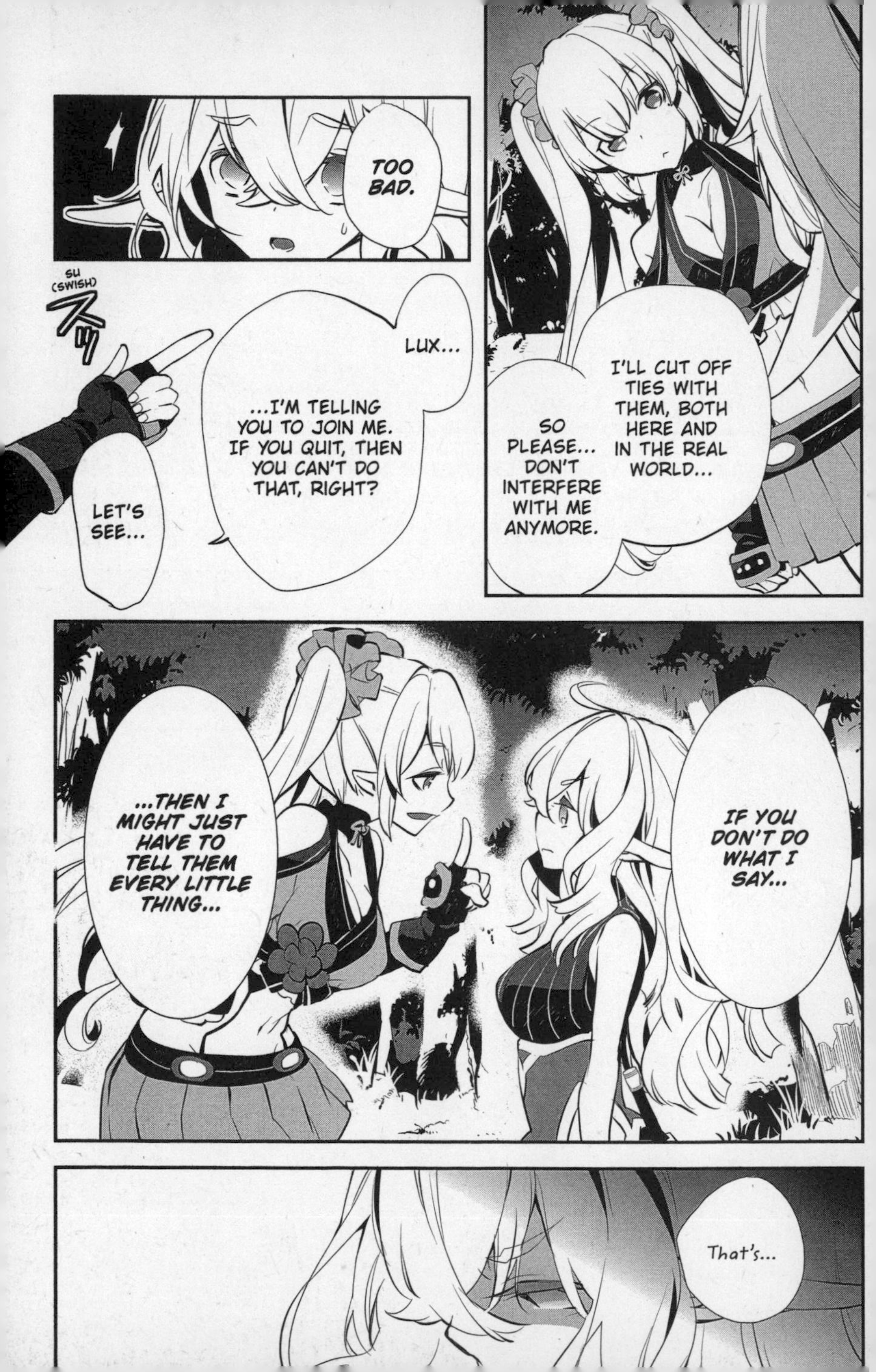
I'LL CUT OFF TIES WITH THEM, BOTH HERE AND IN THE REAL WORLD...
SO PLEASE... DON'T INTERFERE WITH ME ANYMORE.
TOO BAD.
SU (SWISH)
LUX...
...I'M TELLING YOU TO JOIN ME. IF YOU QUIT, THEN YOU CAN'T DO THAT, RIGHT?
LET'S SEE...
IF YOU DON'T DO WHAT I SAY...
...THEN I MIGHT JUST HAVE TO TELL THEM EVERY LITTLE THING...
That's...

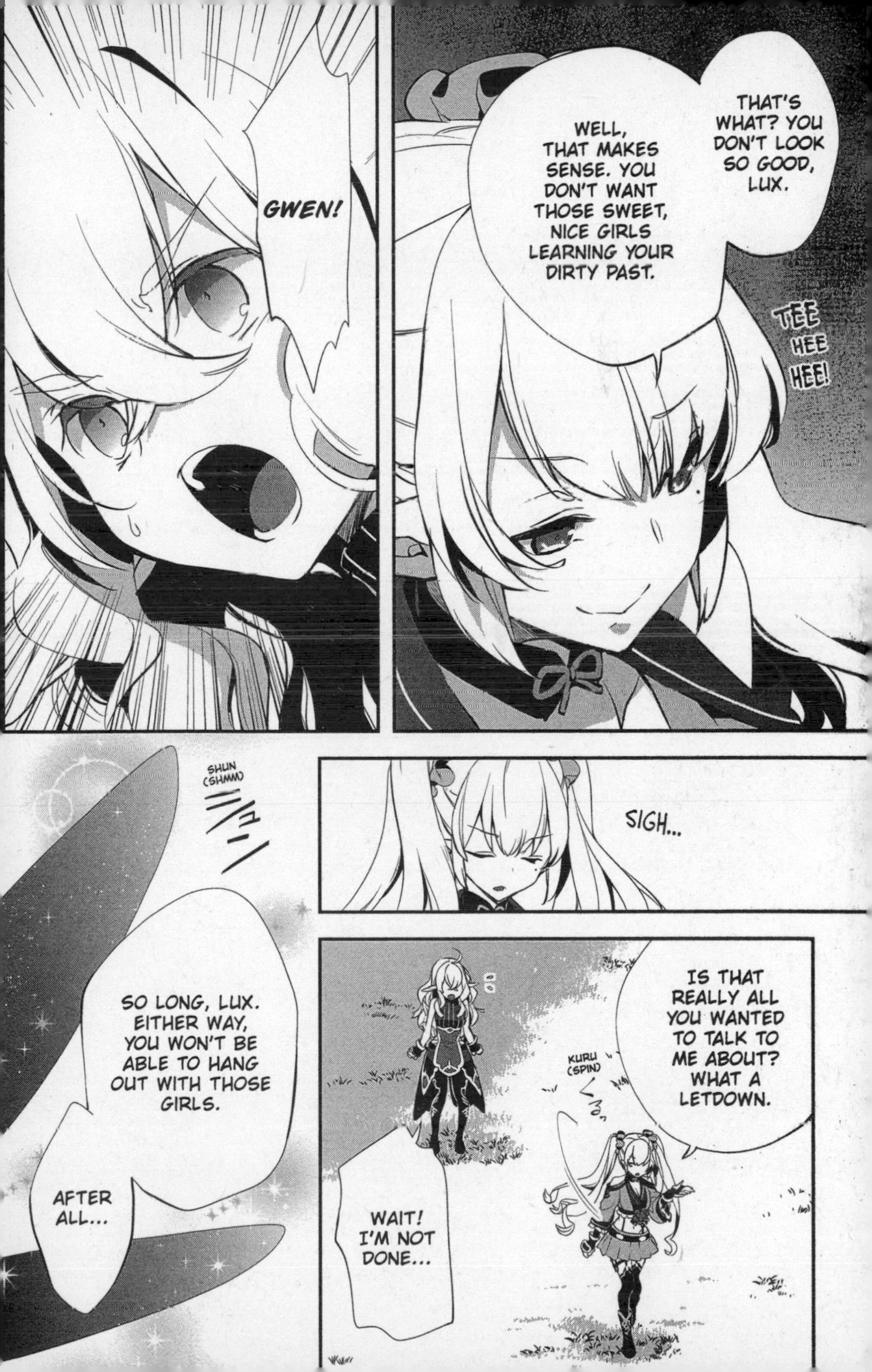
THAT'S WHAT? YOU DON'T LOOK SO GOOD, LUX.
WELL, THAT MAKES SENSE. YOU DON'T WANT THOSE SWEET, NICE GIRLS LEARNING YOUR DIRTY PAST.
TEE HEE HEE!
GWEN!
SIGH...
IS THAT REALLY ALL YOU WANTED TO TALK TO ME ABOUT? WHAT A LETDOWN.
KURU (SPIN)
WAIT! I'M NOT DONE...
SHUN (SHMM)
SO LONG, LUX. EITHER WAY, YOU WON'T BE ABLE TO HANG OUT WITH THOSE GIRLS.
AFTER ALL...

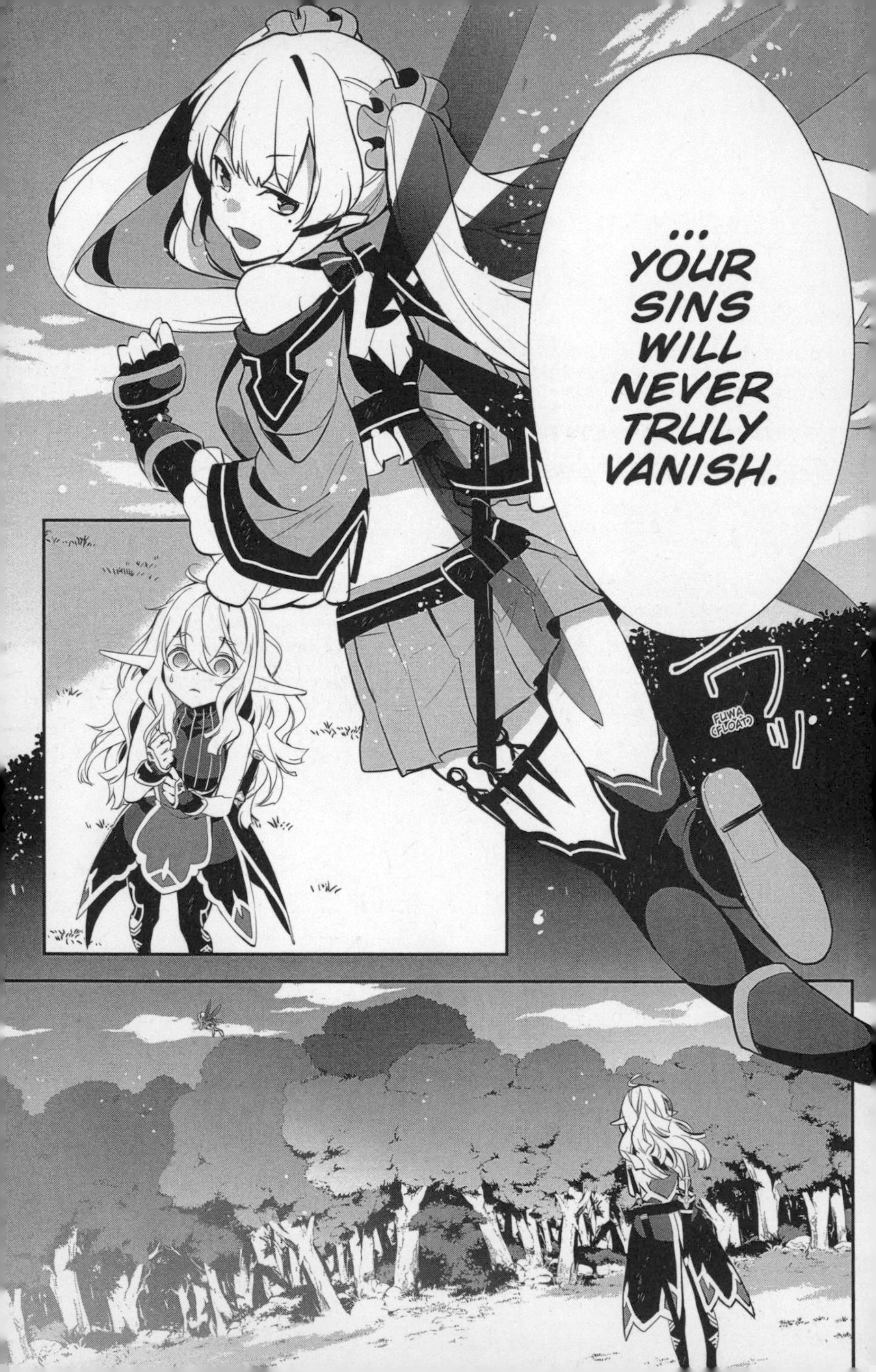
...YOUR SINS WILL NEVER TRULY VANISH.
FUWA (FLOAT)

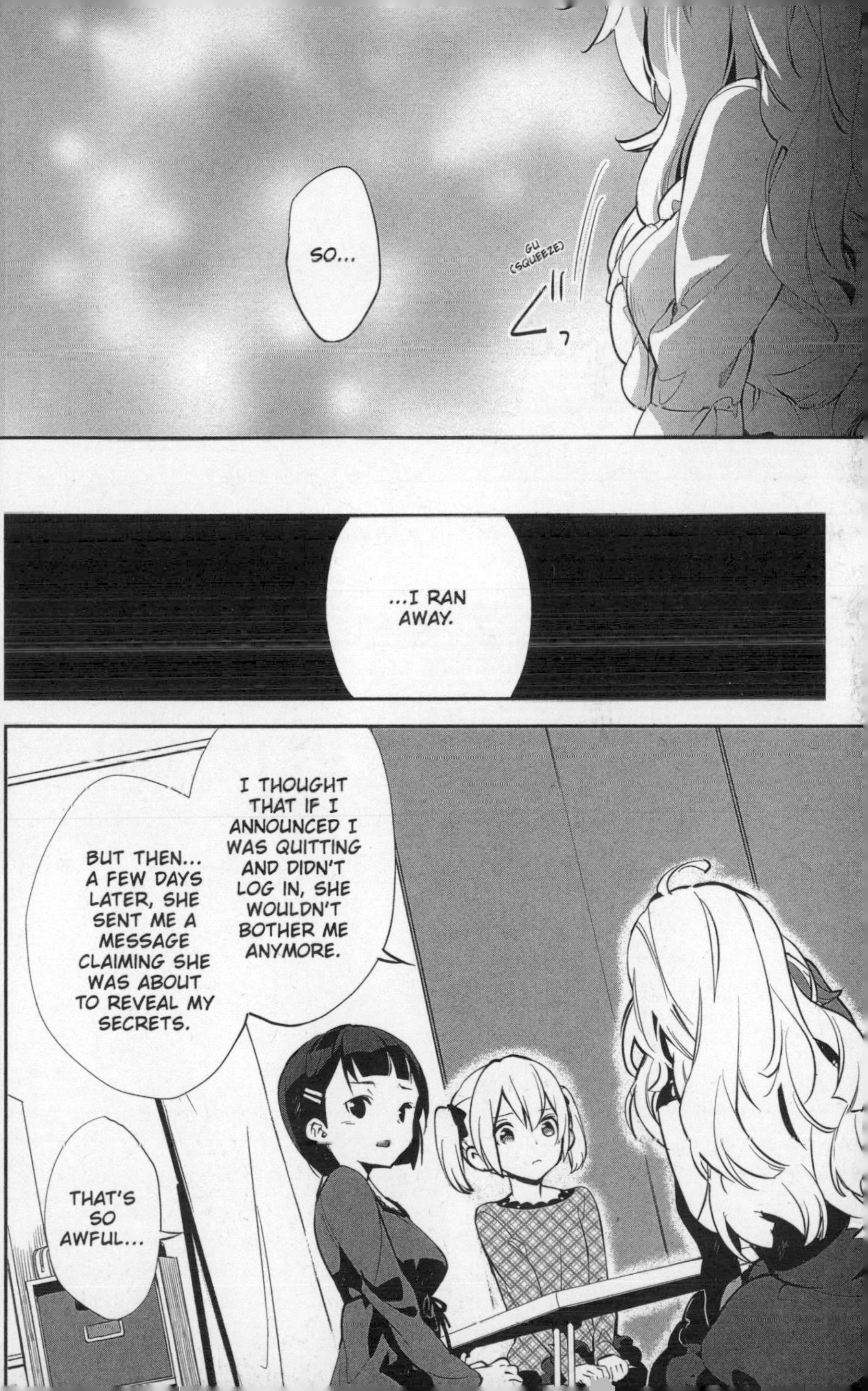
GU (SQUEEZE)
SO...
...I RAN AWAY.
I THOUGHT THAT IF I ANNOUNCED I WAS QUITTING AND DIDN'T LOG IN, SHE WOULDN'T BOTHER ME ANYMORE.
BUT THEN... A FEW DAYS LATER, SHE SENT ME A MESSAGE CLAIMING SHE WAS ABOUT TO REVEAL MY SECRETS.
THAT'S SO AWFUL...

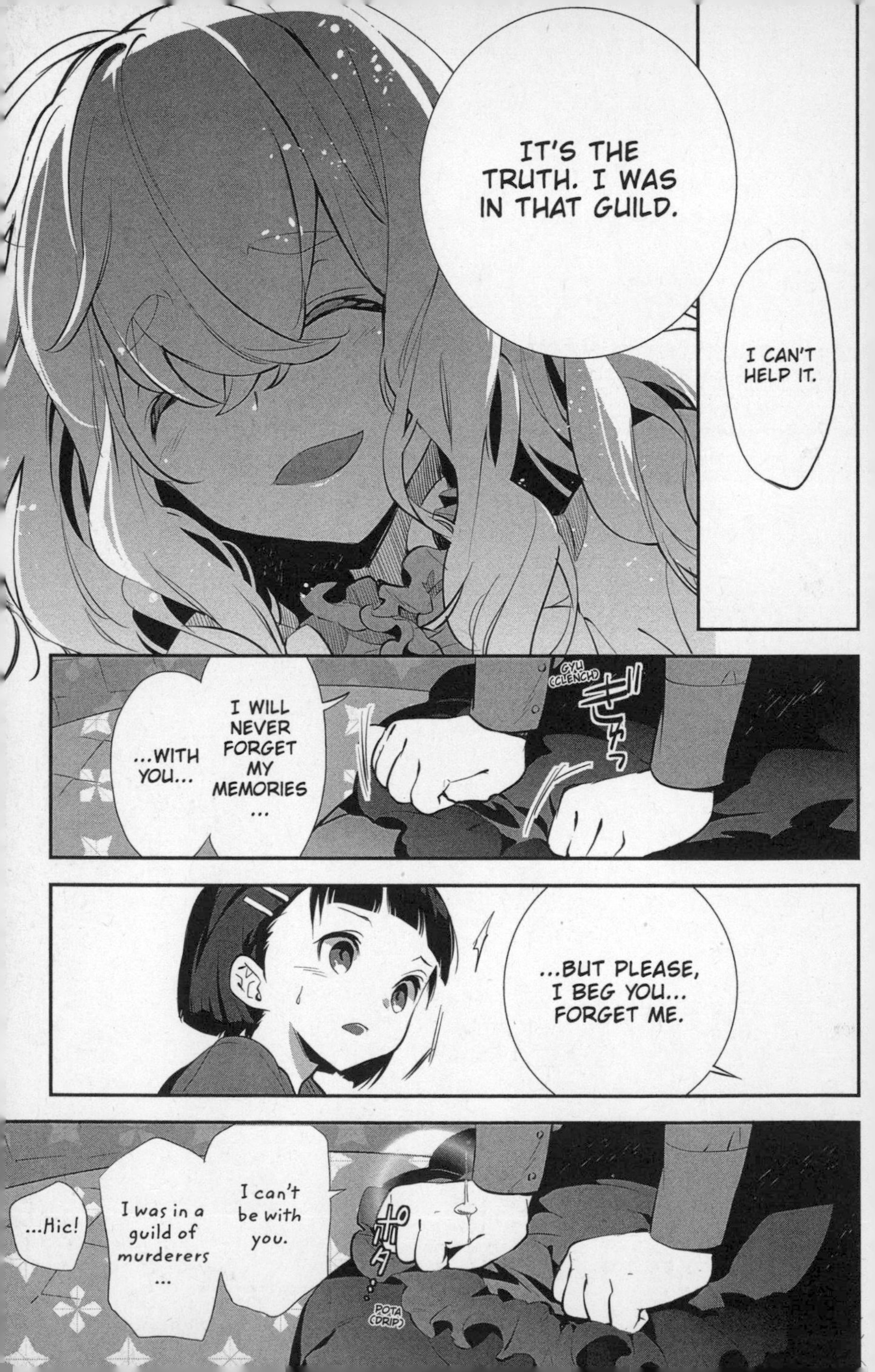
I CAN'T HELP IT.
IT'S THE TRUTH. I WAS IN THAT GUILD.
GYU (CLENCH)
I WILL NEVER FORGET MY MEMORIES...
...WITH YOU...
...BUT PLEASE, I BEG YOU... FORGET ME.
I can't be with you.
I was in a guild of murderers...
...Hic!
POTA (DRIP)

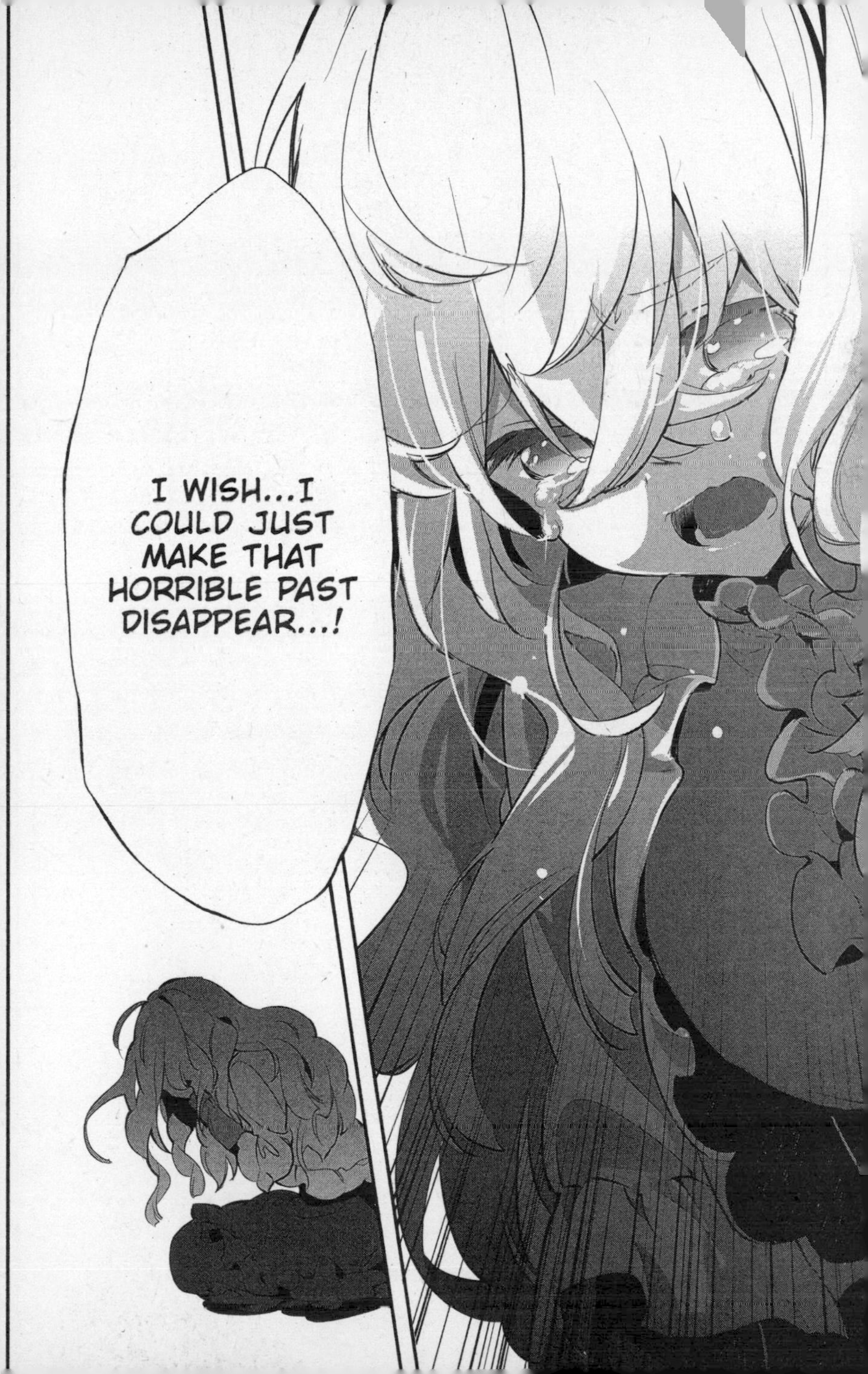
I WISH...I COULD JUST MAKE THAT HORRIBLE PAST DISAPPEAR...!

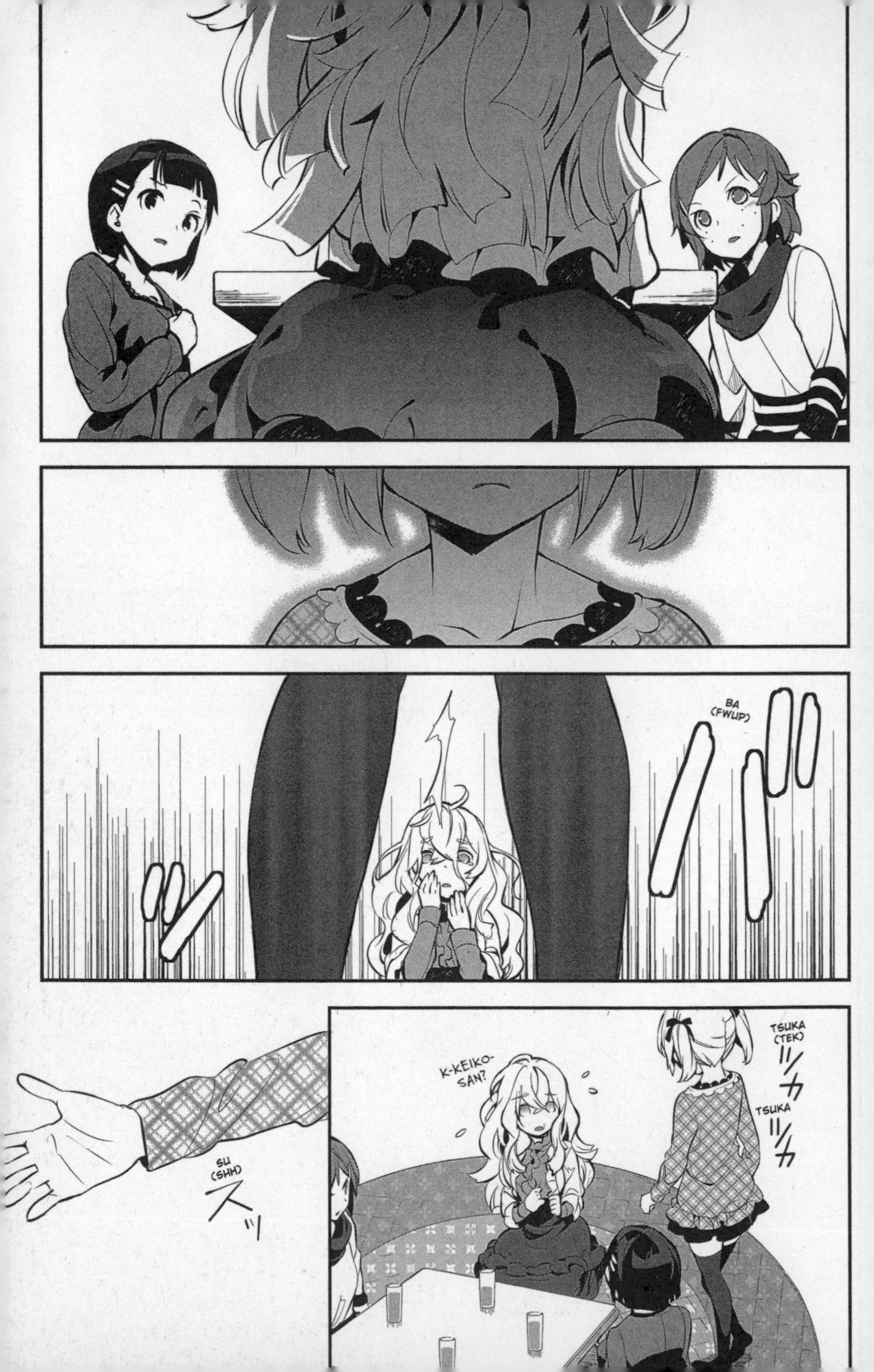
BA (FWUP)
TSUKA (TEK)
TSUKA
K-KEIKO-SAN?
SU (SHH)

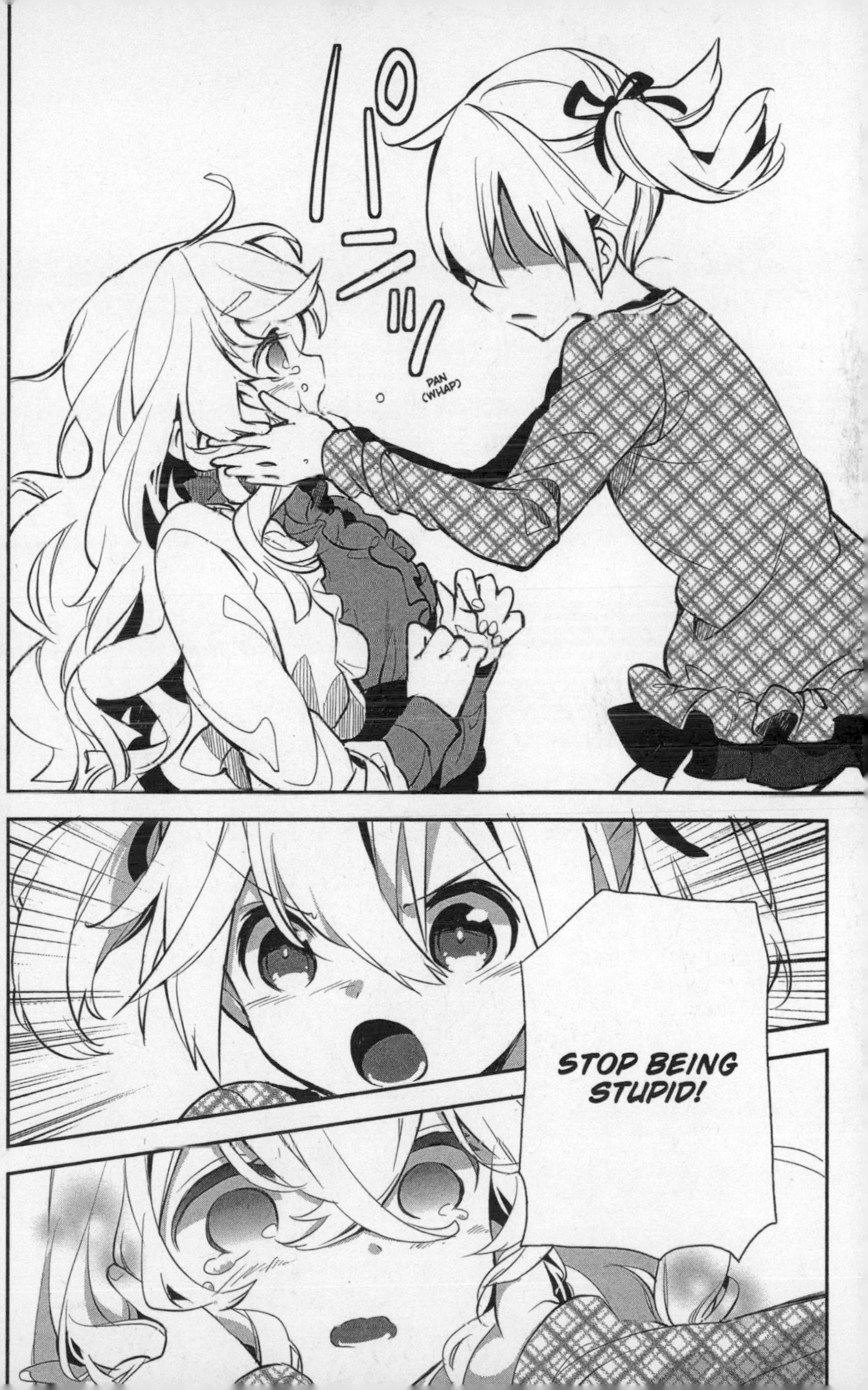
PAN
(WHAP)
STOP BEING STUPID!

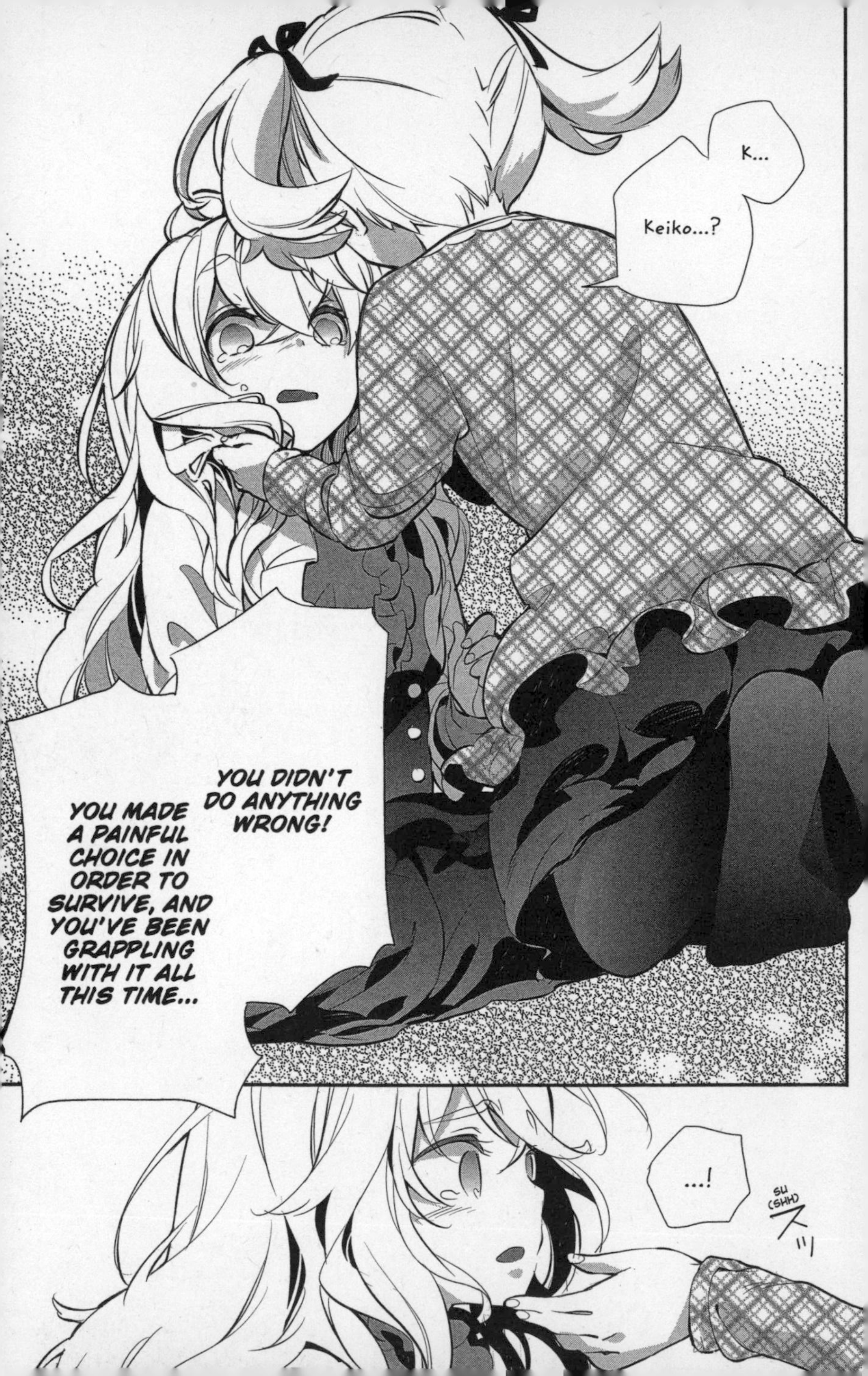
K...
Keiko...?
YOU DIDN'T DO ANYTHING WRONG!
YOU MADE A PAINFUL CHOICE IN ORDER TO SURVIVE, AND YOU'VE BEEN GRAPPLING WITH IT ALL THIS TIME...
...!
SU (SHH)

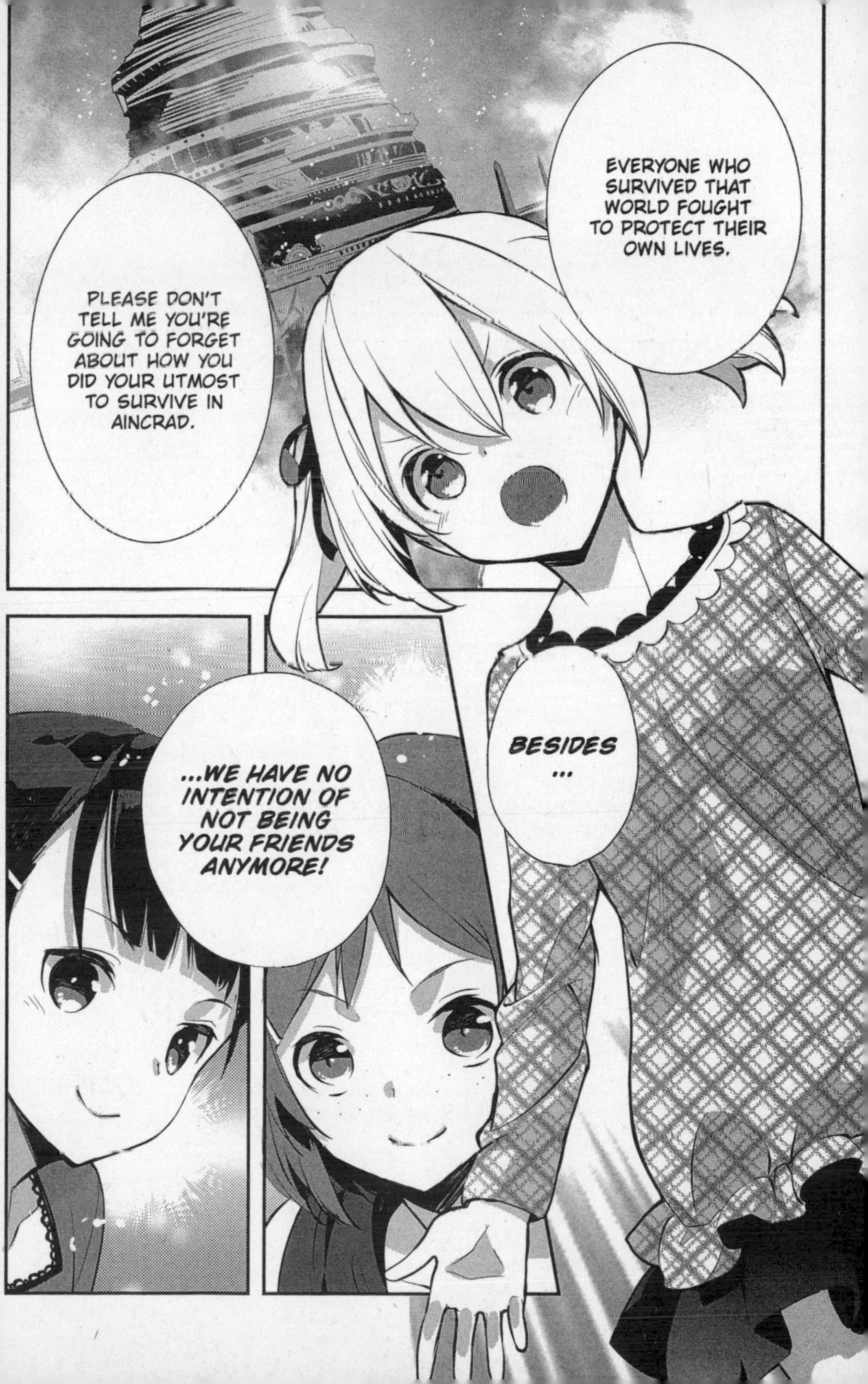
EVERYONE WHO SURVIVED THAT WORLD FOUGHT TO PROTECT THEIR OWN LIVES.
PLEASE DON'T TELL ME YOU'RE GOING TO FORGET ABOUT HOW YOU DID YOUR UTMOST TO SURVIVE IN AINCRAD.
BESIDES ...
...WE HAVE NO INTENTION OF NOT BEING YOUR FRIENDS ANYMORE!

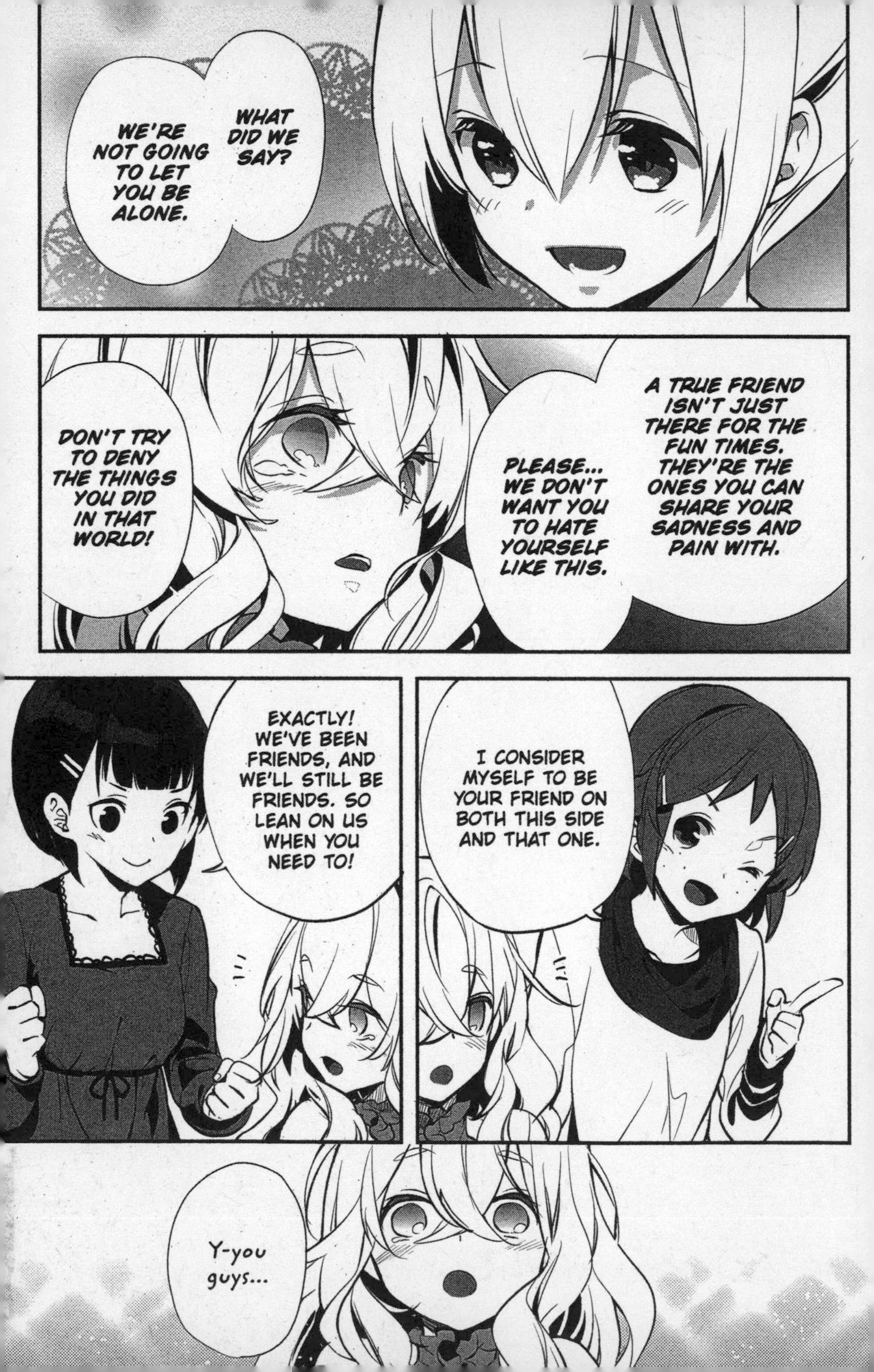
WHAT DID WE SAY?
WE'RE NOT GOING TO LET YOU BE ALONE.
A TRUE FRIEND ISN'T JUST THERE FOR THE FUN TIMES. THEY'RE THE ONES YOU CAN SHARE YOUR SADNESS AND PAIN WITH.
PLEASE... WE DON'T WANT YOU TO HATE YOURSELF LIKE THIS.
DON'T TRY TO DENY THE THINGS YOU DID IN THAT WORLD!
I CONSIDER MYSELF TO BE YOUR FRIEND ON BOTH THIS SIDE AND THAT ONE.
EXACTLY! WE'VE BEEN FRIENDS, AND WE'LL STILL BE FRIENDS. SO LEAN ON US WHEN YOU NEED TO!
Y-you guys...

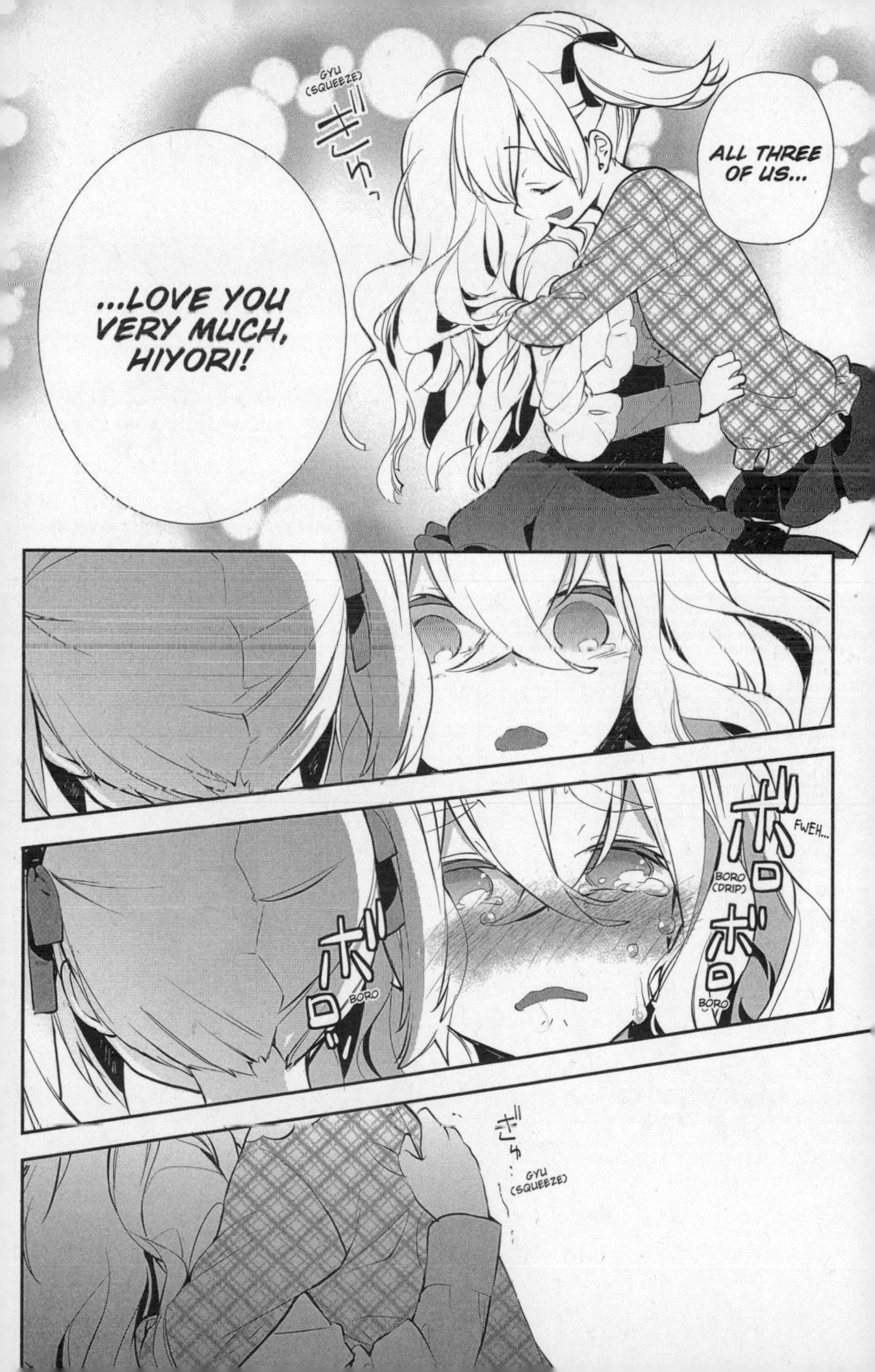
ALL THREE OF US...
ぎゅっ
GYU (SQUEEZE)
...LOVE YOU VERY MUCH, HIYORI!
FWEH...
ボロ
BORO (DRIP)
ボロ
BORO
ボロ
BORO
ぎゅ
GYU (SQUEEZE)

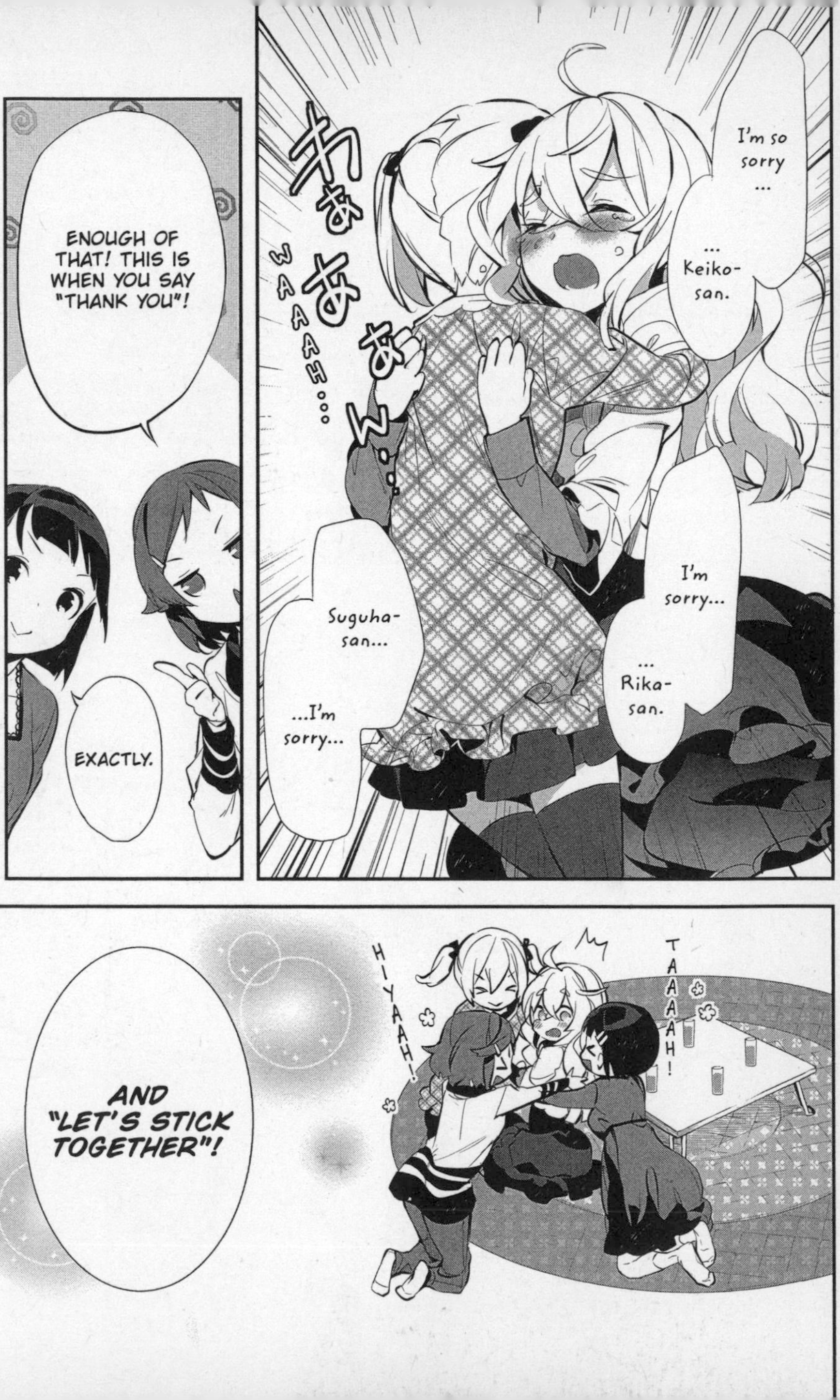
I'm so sorry ... ... Keiko-san.
WAAAAH...
I'm sorry... ... Rika-san.
Suguha-san... ...I'm sorry...
ENOUGH OF THAT! THIS IS WHEN YOU SAY "THANK YOU"!
EXACTLY.
TAAAAAH!
HIYAAH!
AND "LET'S STICK TOGETHER"!

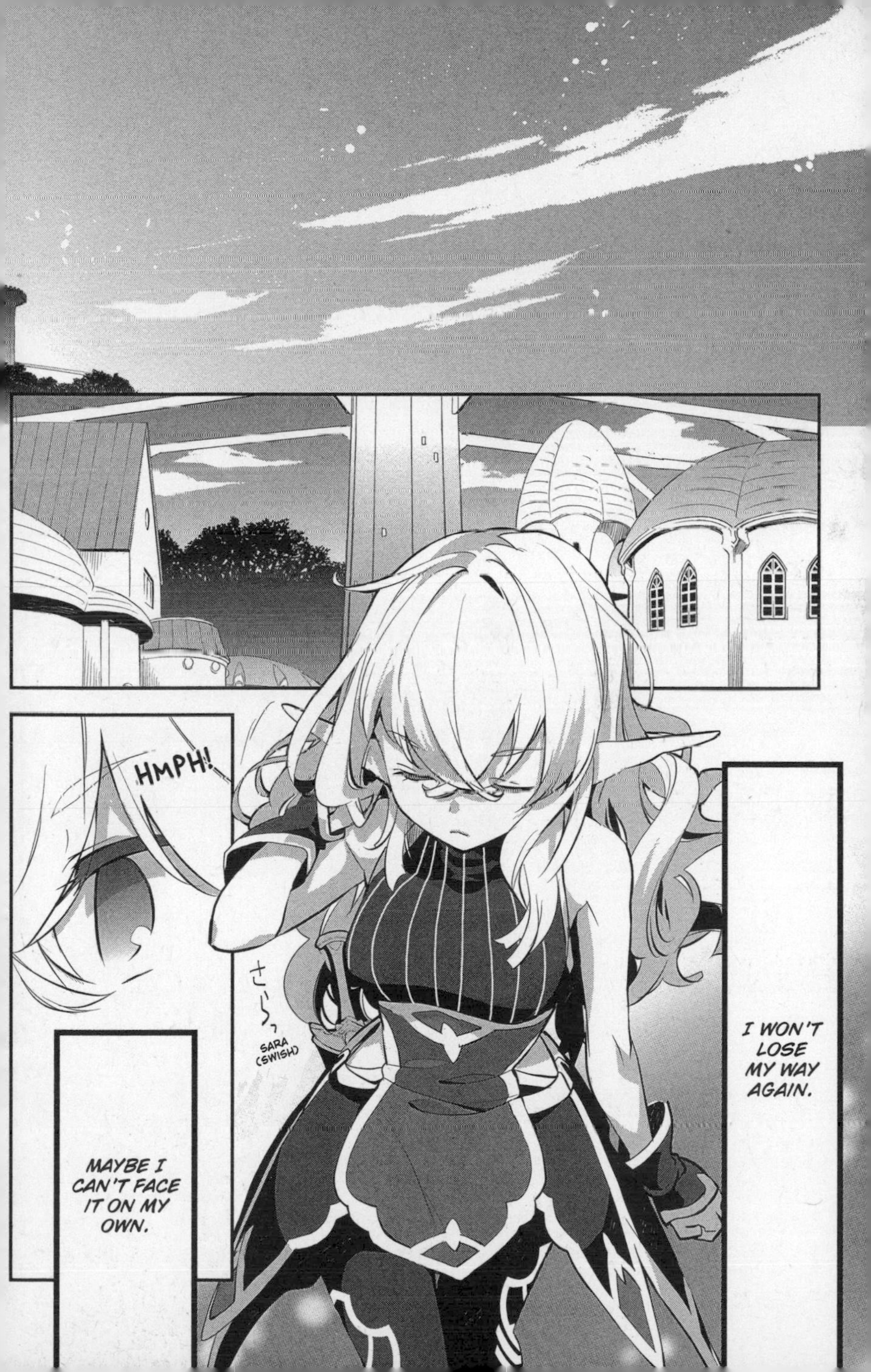
I WON'T LOSE MY WAY AGAIN.
HMPH!
さらっ
SARA (SWISH)
MAYBE I CAN'T FACE IT ON MY OWN.

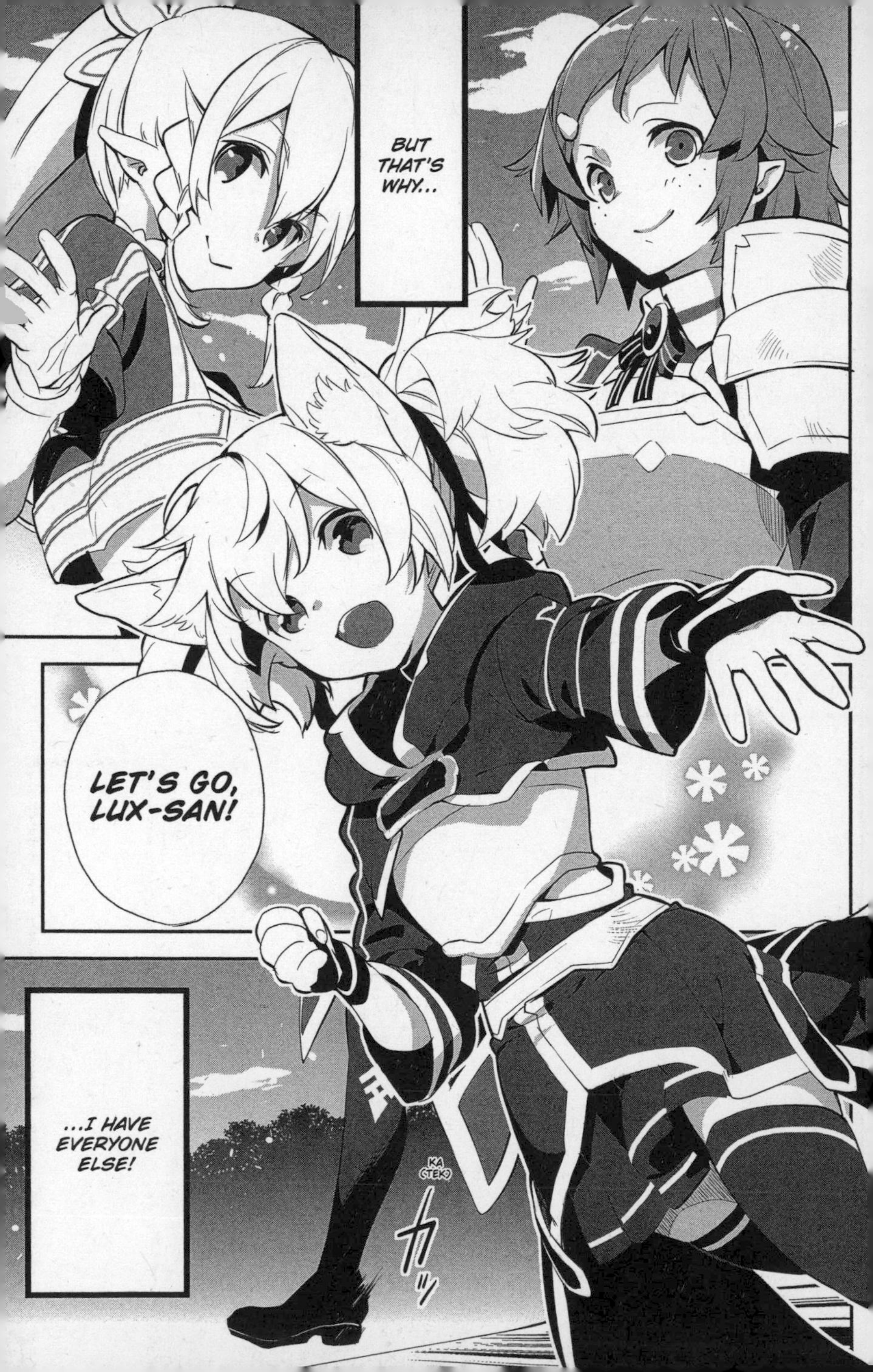
BUT THAT'S WHY...
LET'S GO, LUX-SAN!
...I HAVE EVERYONE ELSE!
KA (TEK)

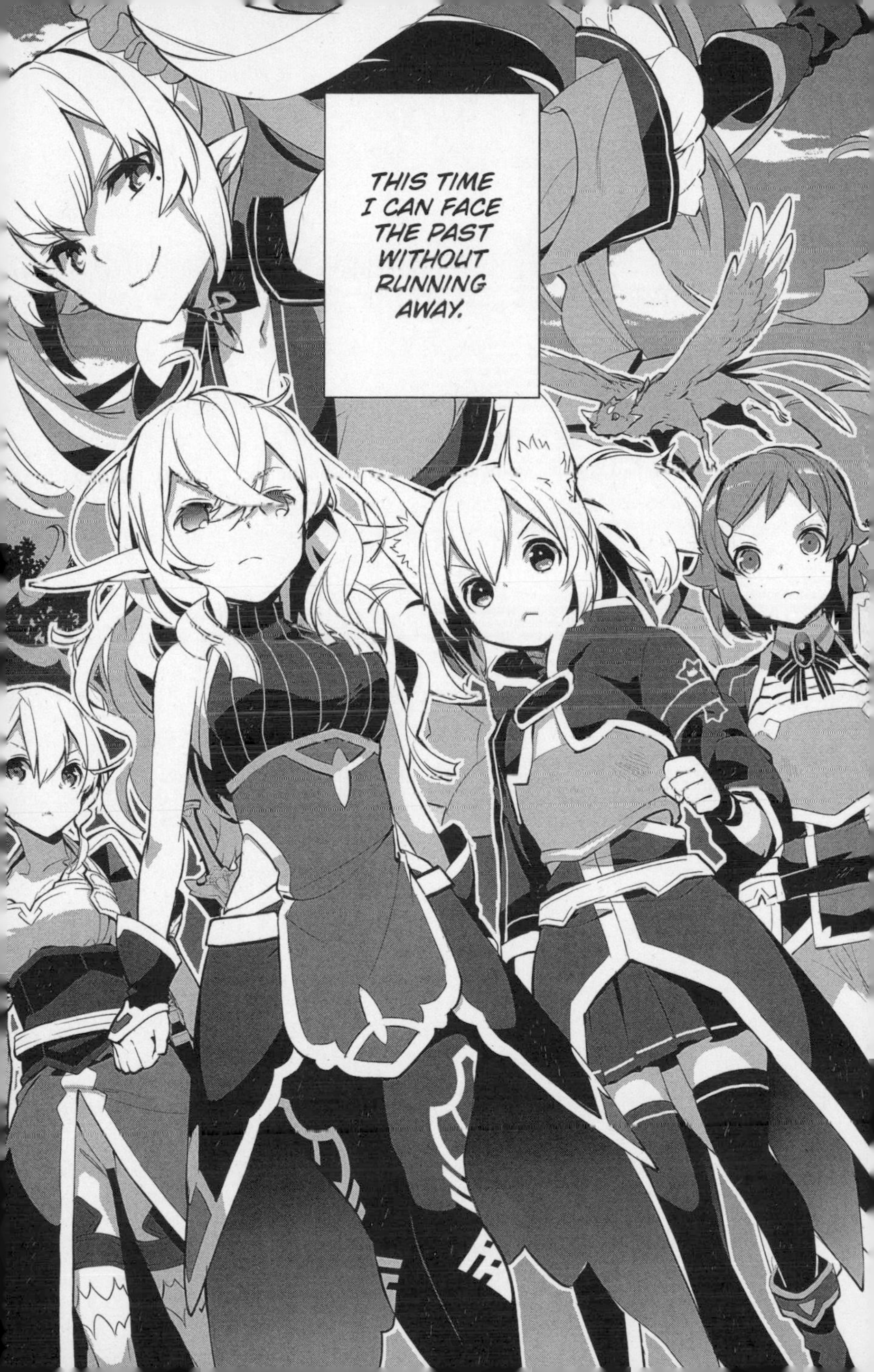
THIS TIME I CAN FACE THE PAST WITHOUT RUNNING AWAY.

SWORD ART ONLINE
GIRLS' OPS

SWORD ART ONLINE
GIRLS' OPERATIONS

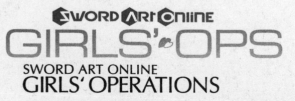

To be continued in the next volume!

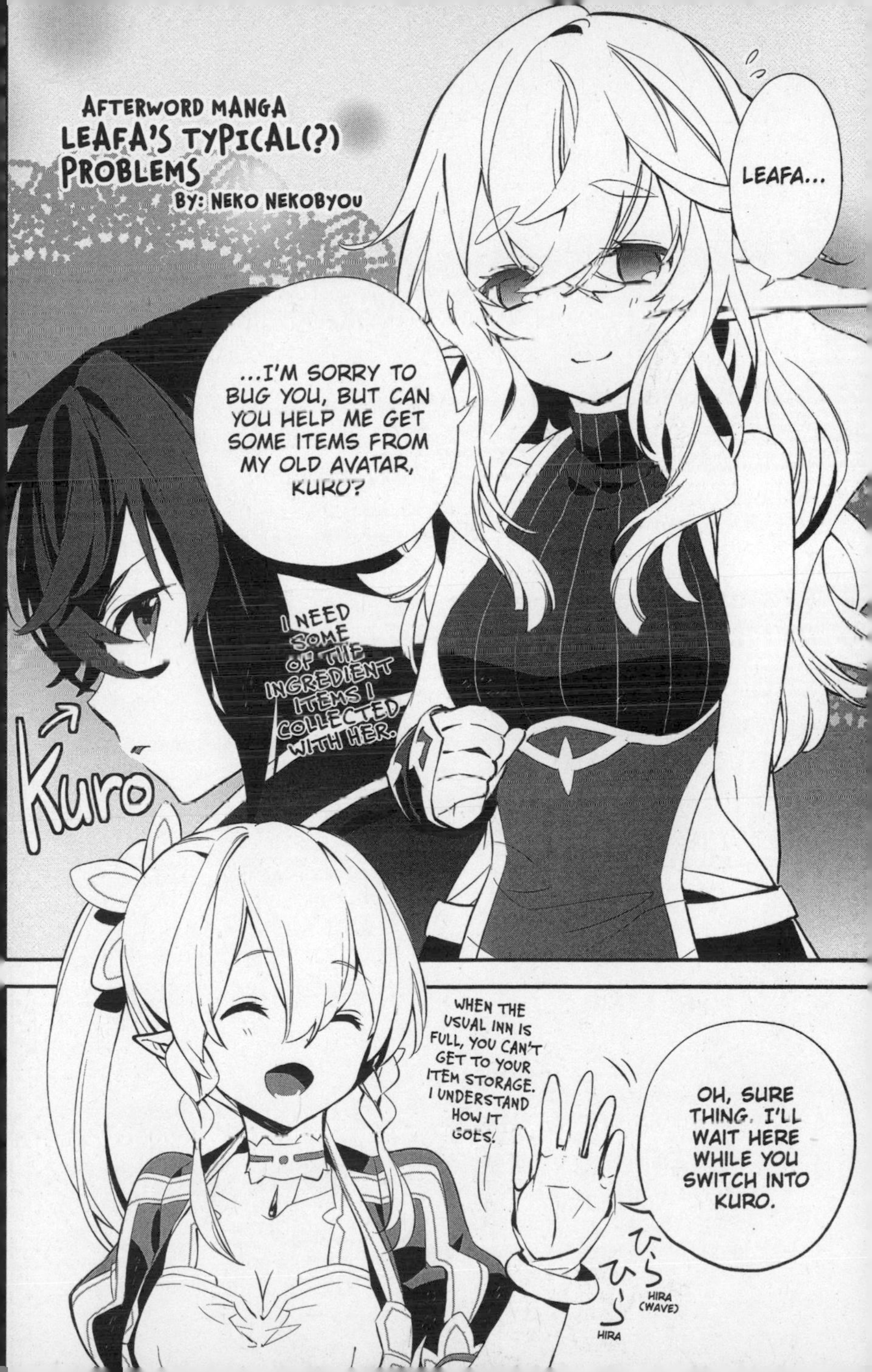
Afterword Manga
Leafa's Typical(?) Problems
By: Neko Nekobyou
Leafa...
...I'm sorry to bug you, but can you help me get some items from my old avatar, Kuro?
I need some of the ingredient items I collected with her.
Kuro
Oh, sure thing. I'll wait here while you switch into Kuro.
When the usual inn is full, you can't get to your item storage. I understand how it goes.
Hira (wave)
Hira

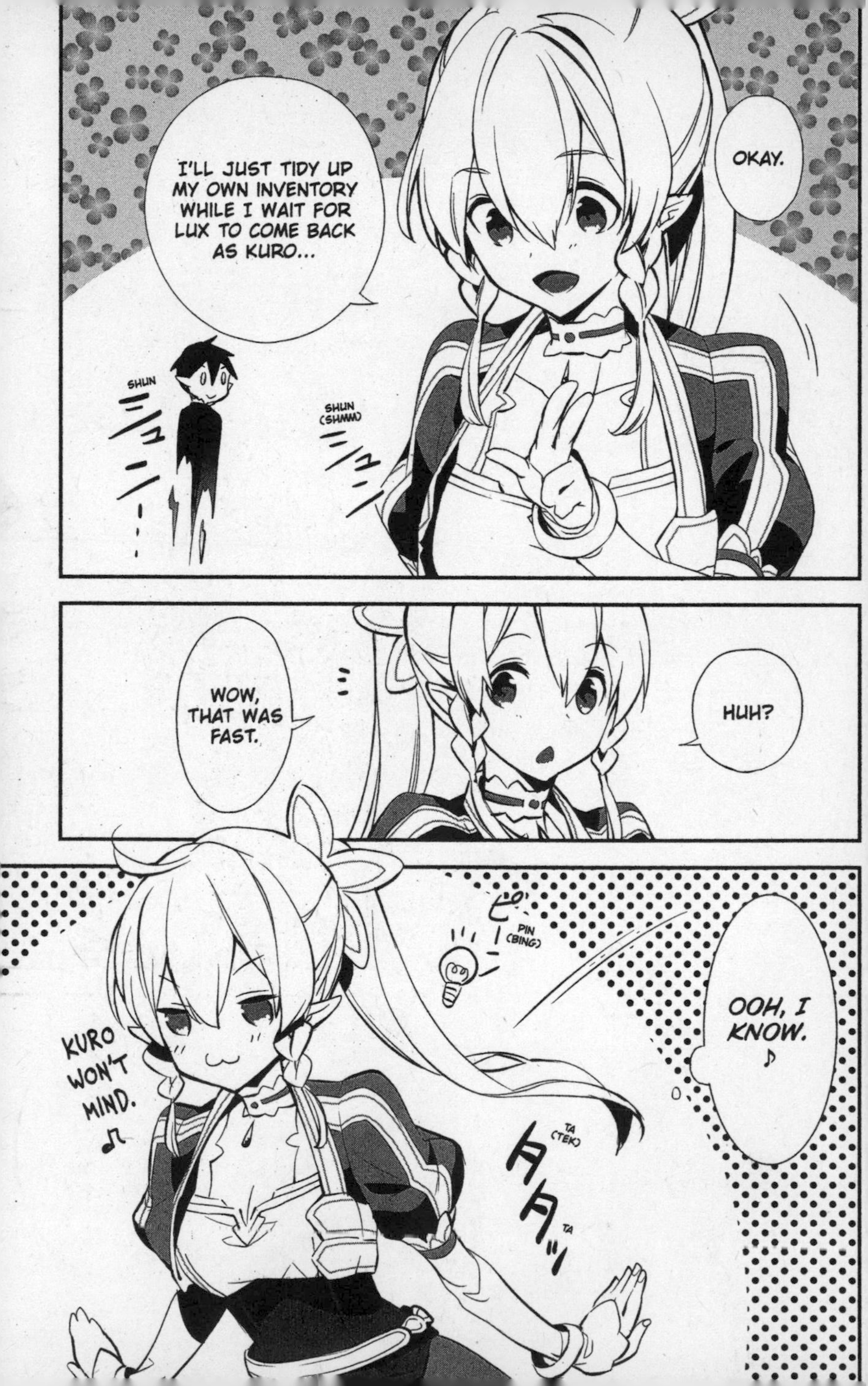
OKAY.
I'LL JUST TIDY UP MY OWN INVENTORY WHILE I WAIT FOR LUX TO COME BACK AS KURO...
SHUN (SHMM)
SHUN
HUH?
WOW, THAT WAS FAST.
PIN (BING)
OOH, I KNOW. ♪
TA (TEK)
TA
KURO WON'T MIND. ♫

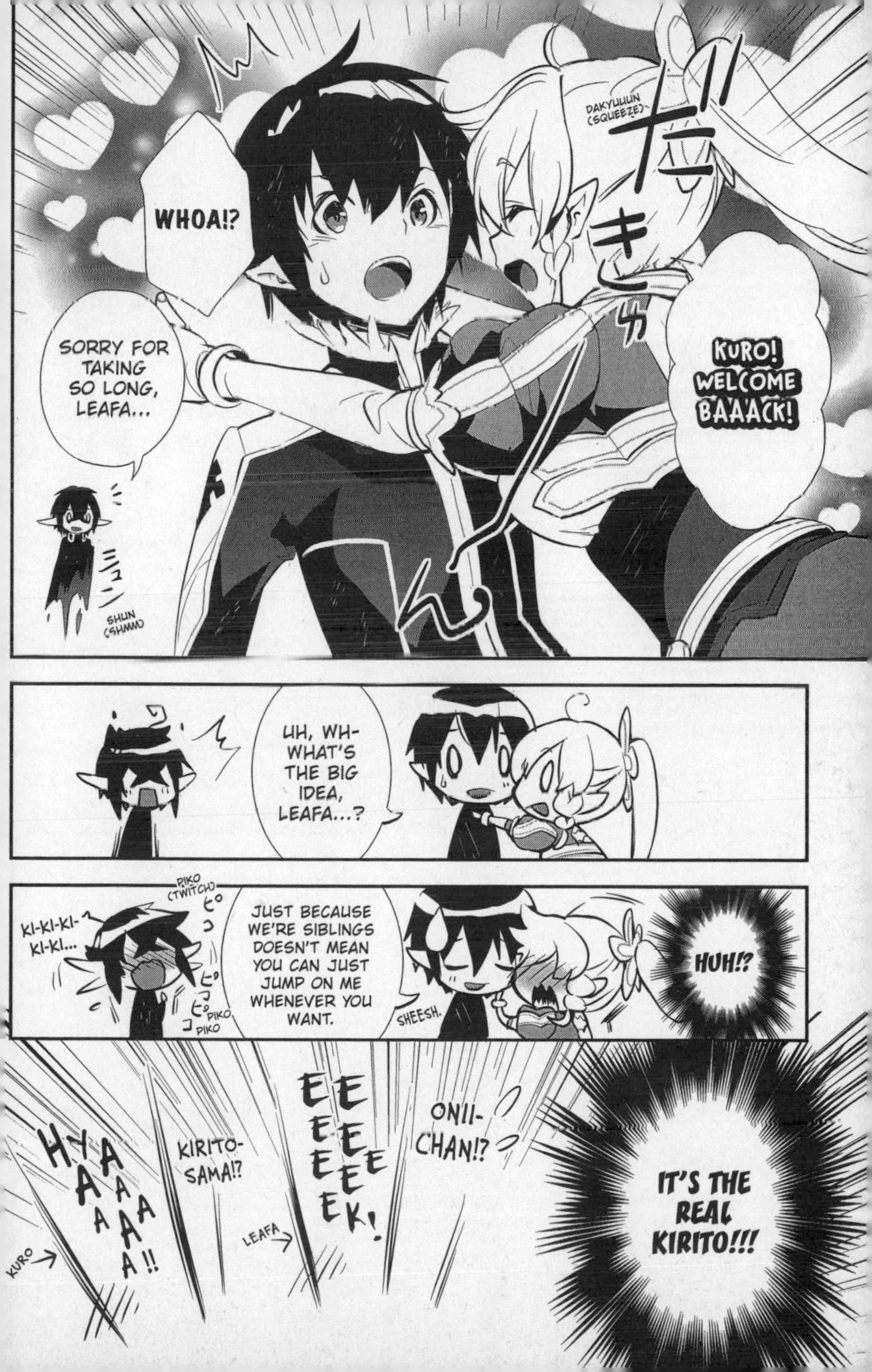
DAKYUUUN (SQUEEZE)
KURO! WELCOME BAAACK!
WHOA!?
SORRY FOR TAKING SO LONG, LEAFA...
SHUN (SHMM)
UH, WH-WHAT'S THE BIG IDEA, LEAFA...?
HUH!?
SHEESH.
JUST BECAUSE WE'RE SIBLINGS DOESN'T MEAN YOU CAN JUST JUMP ON ME WHENEVER YOU WANT.
PIKO (TWITCH)
PIKO PIKO
KI-KI-KI-KI-KI...
IT'S THE REAL KIRITO!!!
ONII-CHAN!?
EEEEEEEEEEK!
LEAFA
KIRITO-SAMA!?
HYAAAAAAAA!!
KURO

Special Thanks!!

YAJI

REKI KAWAHARA-SENSEI

ABEC-SENSEI

SHINGO NAGAI-SENSEI

KAZUMI MIKI-SAMA

TOMOYUKI TSUCHIYA-SAMA

EVERYONE WHO READ THIS BOOK!

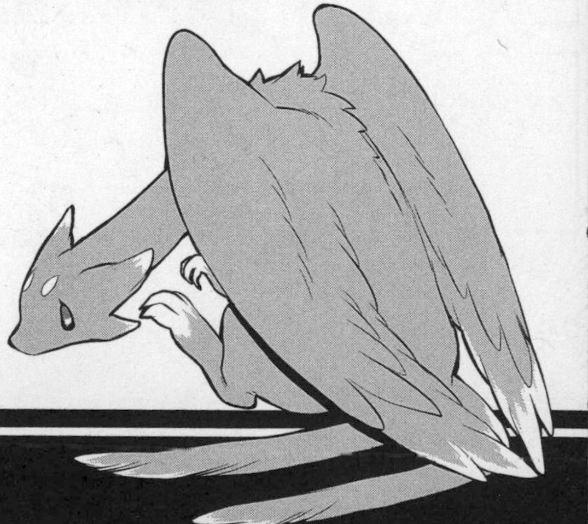

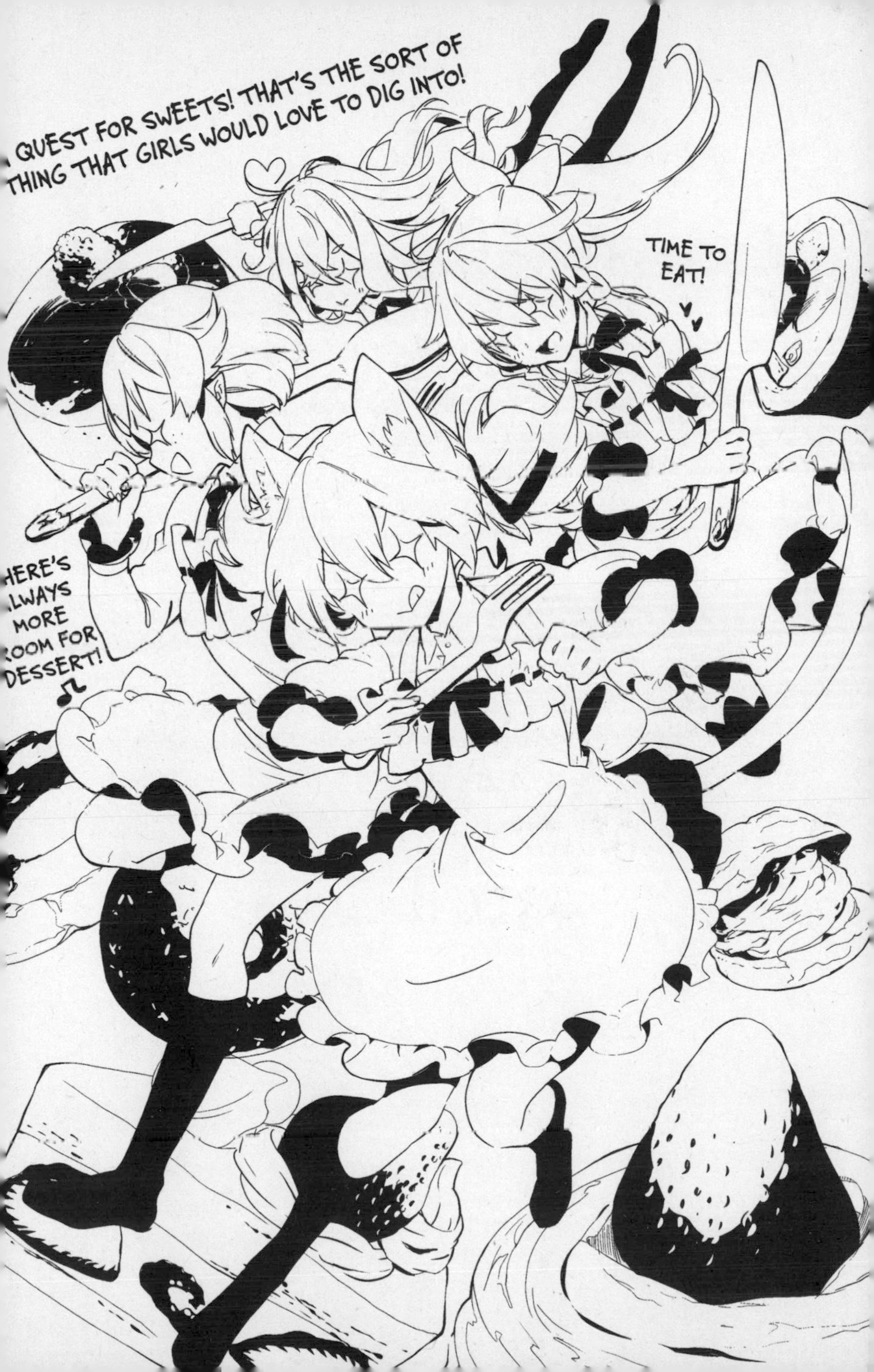
QUEST FOR SWEETS! THAT'S THE SORT OF
THING THAT GIRLS WOULD LOVE TO DIG INTO!
TIME TO EAT!
HERE'S LWAYS MORE ROOM FOR DESSERT! ♫

REEEEED LIGHT...

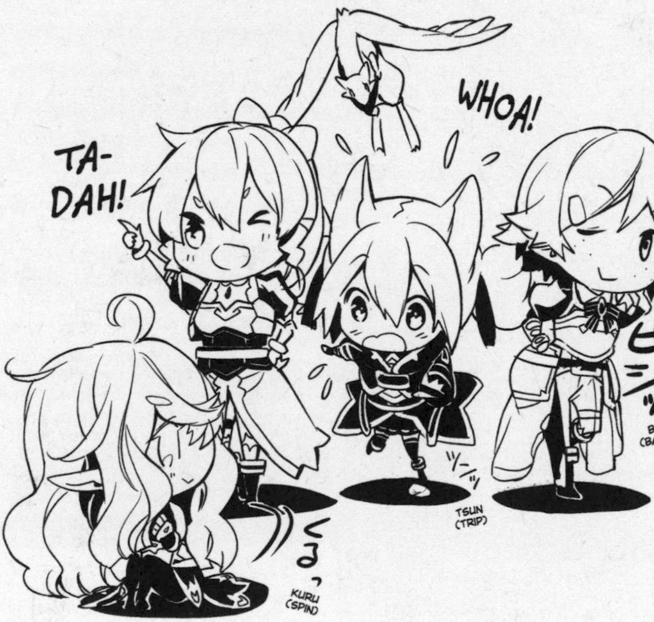
WHOA!
ビシッ
BISHI (BAZING)
TA-DAH!
TSUN (TRIP)
KURU (SPIN)

GREEN LIGHT!

SWORD ART ONLINE: GIRLS' OPS 3

ART: NEKO NEKOBYOU
ORIGINAL STORY: REKI KAWAHARA
CHARACTER DESIGN: abec

Translation: Stephen Paul
Lettering: Brndn Blakeslee

SWORD ART ONLINE: GIRLS' OPS
© REKI KAWAHARA/NEKO NEKOBYOU 2016
All rights reserved.
Edited by ASCII MEDIA WORKS
First published in Japan in 2016 by KADOKAWA CORPORATION, Tokyo.
English translation rights arranged with KADOKAWA CORPORATION, Tokyo, through Tuttle-Mori Agency, Inc., Tokyo.

English translation © 2016 by Yen Press, LLC

Yen Press
1290 Avenue of the Americas
New York, NY 10104

Visit us at yenpress.com
facebook.com/yenpress
twitter.com/yenpress
yenpress.tumblr.com
instagram.com/yenpress

First Yen Press Edition: November 2016

Yen Press is an imprint of Yen Press, LLC.
The Yen Press name and logo are trademarks of Yen Press, LLC.

The publisher is not responsible for websites (or their content) that are not owned by the publisher.

Library of Congress Control Number: 2015952509

ISBNs: 978-0-316-55267-7 (paperback)
        978-0-316-50624-3 (ebook)

10 9 8 7 6 5 4 3 2 1

BVG

Printed in the United States of America